PRAISE FOR TINA WAINSCOTT AND

Unforgivable

"UNFORGIVABLE is unforgettable, a rich, dark tapestry of good and evil—and the threads that bind them together. Excellent suspense; it literally kept me up all night reading."   —Kay Hooper, author of *Touching Evil*

"UNFORGIVABLE is a truly great read! Wainscott creates finely honed tension in a first-rate thriller where no one is who they seem and everyone is someone to fear. Don't miss it!"

—Lisa Gardner, author of *The Next Accident*

A Trick of the Light

"Tina Wainscott is back and in a big way. A TRICK OF THE LIGHT is suspenseful, poignant and gripping. A great read."   —*Romantic Times*

"Wainscott delivers an unusual and satisfying romance with a supernatural twist."   —*Publishers Weekly*

more . . .

1/2002

D1304489

"A five-star reading experience to savor . . . unforgettable!"   —*The Belles and Beaux of Romance*

"Ms. Wainscott has done a great job and has written one for your keeper shelf."   —*Old Book Barn Gazette*

"Fans of paranormal romances will feel they are on the way to heaven reading Tina Wainscott's latest winner . . . Wainscott makes the unbelievable feel real and right in such an exciting manner that her audience will want her next novel to be published tomorrow." —*Affaire de Coeur*

"Quintessential romantic suspense. Wainscott, an award-winning author, knows how to keep her story moving and the sexual tension flowing . . . a book that will speak to both the primary fear of all parents and the hearts of all readers."   —*Once A Warrior Review*

"Remarkable . . . one of the most touching love stories I've read in awhile . . . this is truly a 5-star!"
          —*ADC's Five Star Reads*

In a Heartbeat

"Contemporary romance with an intriguing twist. A pleasure for fans of romantic suspense."

—Deb Smith, *New York Times* best-selling author

"Wainscott . . . makes the impossible possible."

—Harriet Klausner

"Tina Wainscott has her finger firmly on the pulse of the romance genre, and with IN A HEARTBEAT she catapults to the top of her peers . . . run, don't walk, to the nearest bookstore to buy this novel, which could possibly be the best contemporary of the year."

—*Under the Covers*

Second Time Around

"Ms. Wainscott has a talent for making unusual situations believable . . . bravo!"   —*Rendezvous*

"A fabulous romantic suspense drama that melts readers' hearts . . . SECOND TIME AROUND is worth reading the first time around, the second time around, and the nth time around."   —*Affaire de Coeur*

"A must-read . . . well-written, romantic, feel-good story."

—*Gothic Journal*

*St. Martin's Paperbacks Titles
by Tina Wainscott*

BACK IN BABY'S ARMS
A TRICK OF THE LIGHT
IN A HEARTBEAT
SECOND TIME AROUND
DREAMS OF YOU
SHADES OF HEAVEN
ON THE WAY TO HEAVEN

Unforgivable

Tina Wainscott

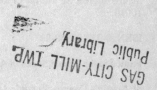

GAS CITY-MILL TWP.
Public Library

St. Martin's Paperbacks

NOTE: If you purchased this book without a cover you should be aware that this book is stolen property. It was reported as "unsold and destroyed" to the publisher, and neither the author nor the publisher has received any payment for this "stripped book."

UNFORGIVABLE

Copyright © 2001 by Tina Wainscott.

All rights reserved. No part of this book may be used or reproduced in any manner whatsoever without written permission except in the case of brief quotations embodied in critical articles or reviews. For information address St. Martin's Press, 175 Fifth Avenue, New York, N.Y. 10010.

ISBN: 0-312-97908-8

Printed in the United States of America

St. Martin's Paperbacks edition / November 2001

St. Martin's Paperbacks are published by St. Martin's Press, 175 Fifth Avenue, New York, N.Y. 10010.

10 9 8 7 6 5 4 3 2 1

To Dave, my friend, soulmate, husband . . . for being there always.

∼ ACKNOWLEDGMENTS

I wish to thank my resident medical expert, Jackie Bielowicz, for her continued and generous assistance with things medical.

I am very grateful for Frank Martorana's help with the veterinarian research. I'm sure he must have rolled his eyes more than once when he saw yet another e-mail from me. Frank, I wish you all the luck in the world to make your dreams come true.

Thank you, Lisa Pulitzer, for your inside information on being a crime writer, and for some great reads as well!

Any errors, however, are solely the author's.

~~~ CHAPTER I

FOR THE THIRD day in a row, Katie Malloy made the long walk from Possum Holler into town carrying the cardboard box. This time only one of the kittens was left inside . . . her favorite, Gus. Mama said not to name them, 'cause that would only make it harder to give them away. Katie didn't want to give them away, at least not Gus. How much could one little ole kitten cost, anyway? Porch Kitty having those kittens was the most excitement she'd had in her whole nine years, and what else could a kid do in their stinking, dusty Georgia town except fall in love with kittens?

She especially hadn't wanted to leave the house after she'd seen that dead bird in their yard. It was a bad omen, especially since it was a black bird. But Mama had insisted, like waiting one more day would have hurt anything.

The road stretched on forever, giving off waves of invisible flames. There was nothing around for the longest time other than the gravel driveway that disappeared into the woods to the creepy Koole house, and another driveway leading to reclusive old lady Babbage's house. Then she'd pass the abandoned convenience store, cross the old bypass, and go past the ancient cemetery. The town itself was to the left, another twenty minutes before she'd reach the Piggly Wiggly grocery store.

Orange dust coated her feet and ground between her toes. Mama said it was no use buying a new pair of shoes for the summer when she'd just grow out of 'em by the time school started.

Gary Savino's shiny new bike was parked outside the old store. He was fourteen and his daddy was the DA, which people said like it was important. Gary always had the best clothes, the best toys, even the best looks. She'd had a tiny crush on him when she was younger, but Mama had set her straight about that. "Don't you go near Gary or his family. I mean it. Stay away from the whole lot of them. We don't belong with the likes of them."

Now that she'd grown up, she knew Mama was right. But her heart still kinda thrummed whenever she saw him.

"Hey, Katie," he said, coming around from the back of the old store zipping up his pants. He always said her name funny, drawing it out. She didn't know whether he was making fun or just liked her name.

"Hey," she said, clutching the box tighter. Gus meowed, slowly blinking his green eyes. That was his way of saying he loved her.

Gary had dark hair and brown eyes, and he was tall for a boy of his age. "What'cha got there?" he asked, leaning over the box.

"This is Gus. I'm trying to find him a home."

"I'll take it." Without even waiting for her to say okay, he picked the kitten out of the box and held him up.

"Really?"

She should have been thrilled that Gary Savino was going to take her kitten, give him a nice, rich home. But she wasn't. "You want the box to take him in?"

He was already walking toward his bike. "Nah. Won't need it."

And then he threw the kitten against the plate-glass window.

She felt her insides drop out of her as Gus fell to the walkway. Her voice sounded shrill when she screamed, *"Why'd you do that?"* She was already running toward Gary.

"Stop polluting the world with unwanted cats," he said, climbing on his bike.

She could hardly breathe. She wanted to run to Gus, but instead kept her focus on the vicious animal on the bike. She threw herself at him.

His blasé expression changed to irritation. "What the—"

"You creep!" She scratched at his face and kneed him in the nuts. She wanted to hurt him bad, she wanted him to never forget what he'd done. "You hurt him! For no reason, you hurt him!" she screamed, horrified to hear tears slipping into her voice.

"Get off me, you little twit!"

He might be bigger, but he was no match for a furious girl. His face was scratched and bleeding, his shirt was ripped, and his body was contorted to protect himself from her thrusting knees. When he put his mind to it, though, he finally pushed her off him. She skidded across the concrete, but her scratches were nothing compared to the screaming pain inside her. When she started to run at him again, the gleam in his eyes halted her.

"Don't mess with me, little girl."

"I'm going to tell the sheriff," she said, backing away toward Gus.

That always worked to scare the troublemakers in her neighborhood, but it didn't faze Gary at all. "Yeah, you go tell him. You think they'll believe some piece of white trash that Sam Savino's boy hurt some dumb ole cat." He narrowed his eyes. "Don't peddle your bastard kittens again, you hear?"

He didn't wait for an answer, just started riding away fast. He didn't look back once.

She stumbled to the kitten. "Gus," she whimpered, letting the tears come now. She could see the smudge on the dusty window, and it caved in her heart even more. His head was bleeding where he'd hit the glass. But . . . he was alive! He was breathing and his mouth quivered. His eyes were all wobbly. He tried to get up, but he swayed and rolled on his side again. What really broke her heart were his mewling sounds.

He'd trusted her, and she'd let him down.

She started back to the trailer park hunched over the box to protect Gus from the sun. Halfway back she had a better idea.

After making sure Gary wasn't watching, she tucked Gus in the shade of a maple tree and ran home.

Mama wasn't surprised, and that surprised Katie. "I know his father, honey. I cleaned for his family after school years ago. Meanness runs in the family, though they keep it hidden well. That's why we pray for their victims every night, victims of mean people."

"This isn't meanness," Katie said, hardly finding the breath to speak. "This is . . . evil! I'm gonna tell the sheriff. But first we gotta help Gus."

"Honey, don't do that. The sheriff ain't gonna believe a word of it. And if he does, he ain't gonna care anyway."

"How do you know?"

Her face shadowed. "I just know. 'Sides, we can't afford to take him to the vet. You know that."

"I'm taking him to Dr. Sewell," Katie said. "And I'm going to talk him into fixing Gus for free."

"I don't want you going to the vet. 'Member, it's not Dr. Sewell anymore. It's that young man that took his place. We don't even know him."

"I don't care. I'm going to see him anyway."

But first she had to get to the vet's office. They didn't have a car, not since the tranny had gone on the old Ford. Katie ran to some of the other mobile homes in their area. If they weren't drunk from the night before, they were either carless or at work. She'd walk to town if she had to. It was better than sitting there watching her kitty die.

Once she retrieved Gus from his hiding place, the mid-morning heat pressed down on her like an iron. Not many people drove this far out of town, not much chance of a ride.

She neared the long driveway that disappeared back into the woods. Silas Koole lived there with his dad. Silas was older than her by at least five years. People said his dad hit him sometimes, but Silas never said a word about it. The kids called him Spooky Silas. Whenever she'd seen him in town, he seemed nice enough. Kids said she was strange too because she had a purple birthmark on her neck, but she couldn't see anything wrong with Silas.

A breeze toyed with the leaves of the trees flanking the driveway, giving an eerie feeling to the dark place beyond. Gus needed her to be brave, so she whispered, "Wish me luck," and started down the shady driveway.

Country music blared as she neared the home. Silas and his daddy were rich by her standards, living in a house with four huge columns along the front porch that went all the way up to the second floor. But the house was run-down, and the yard was sprinkled with weeds. Hope washed through her when she saw two long, jean-clad legs sticking out from beneath the old truck. Something metallic clanked, and he swore.

"Please"—she cleared her throat—"please help me."

Silas slid from beneath the truck, his eyes wide with surprise. He was tall and thin, with dark hair, smoky blue eyes, and a lean face. There was something dangerous about him, like a wild animal you couldn't trust. Like a wolf, she realized, even the way he moved. Mama would kill her if she knew she was here, but Silas might be her last hope to save Gus. He was wearing a gold cross on a chain; that had to count for something.

Silas rubbed his hands down his grease-smudged jeans and walked up to her. "Is he all right?" he asked as he peered into the box.

She tried to be cool about it, but the concern in his eyes melted her strength. "Gary threw him against the store window, and he's gonna die if I don't get him to the vet. Please . . . can you take us there?" She swiped at her tears.

"I've been trying to get the damn thing going. Hold on a minute." He slid back under the truck slick as a snake. He jerked on something, banged on something else. Three of the longest minutes of her life slid by, and then he pulled himself back out again. "Let's give it a try."

"Will your dad let you take the truck?" she asked.

He didn't even glance toward the house. "He won't say nothing about it."

She held her breath as the engine churned a couple of times, and finally started. She felt a hitch in her chest when Silas took the box from her and set it on the bench seat. Then he helped her up into the old truck and shut the door behind her. Gus was trying to sit up, with his paws wide for balance. His eyes were still wobbly, and he was crying again. Nothing really bad had ever happened to her before today. Now she was alone with Silas Koole. Spooky Silas Koole. She remembered the dead black bird in the yard. The bad omen had come true.

He didn't say a word as they stopped by the intersection that turned left into downtown where people didn't know about bad things happening to helpless kittens. A lone shopping strip plaza sat ahead of them, half of the store-fronts empty. People were busy shopping at the Dollar Store's sidewalk sale. They glanced up at her and Silas and the noisy truck, and then looked away just as fast. To the right was the ancient cemetery tucked away in the oaks. Past that was the veterinary hospital.

"I'll wait out here," he said once he'd parked.

The pinch she felt in her chest made her realize she'd hoped he'd come in with her. Not Silas, she thought, climbing down and taking the box he held out to her. He walked to school alone, returned alone, and never hung out with other kids. But he'd brought her here.

All-Animals Hospital was small, very white, and smelled like disinfectant. One woman sat in the waiting area with her cat in a carrier. The new doctor's name was Ben Ferguson, and he was writing on something at the desk when she held up the kitten and pleaded through her tears, "He's gonna die if you don't help him."

Mr. Ferguson was older, probably in his late twenties, and his eyes were compassionate as he listened to her story, then took the kitten into his office. She waited with the other woman, not missing the looks she gave her dirty feet and tear-stained face. Pity and disgust. She hated going into town, hated school, and at the moment, hated just about everybody.

Except Dr. Ferguson, who told her that Gus was going to live. "But it doesn't look good, Katie. His brain got hurt." He put his hand over her head. "The brain is a very complex organ, the most important one in the body. We've got to wait and see how bad and where his brain was hurt. I've given him some medication to reduce the swelling and bruising and something to keep him from going into shock."

She walked to the table where Gus looked so tiny. He was resting just like normal, only his eyes were closed. "Now what happens?"

"I'm going to put a catheter in him, right here." He pointed to his leg. "You've probably seen catheters on TV with the bag of fluid that drips into the person's vein. This will give Gus electrolytes. He's going to stay here where I can keep an eye on him, watch what he eats and drinks. That will tell me how he's doing. And you . . ." He smiled. "You can come visit him."

She lifted her chin. "I will, every day."

Dr. Ferguson followed her gaze back to the kitten. "Katie, you're a smart, tough girl. I'm going to be honest with you, because I know that's what you want. He's not going to be like normal kittens. Which means it's going to be real hard to find him a home."

She looked at the gray striped kitten on the table. "I'm gonna keep him," she said in a thick voice. "Nobody's ever gonna hurt him again." She couldn't look at Gus without crying, so she looked at the doctor. "We don't have a lot of money to pay the bills."

"Tell you what: you can work here to help pay the bill. We're going to make him better together, you and me."

"I can work good. I'm strong. I hoe the garden, climb up on the roof and fix the holes, mow the yard . . . my daddy left when I was little, so Mama and I do everything. Thank you for saving him, Dr. Ferguson."

He knelt down to her level. "You're looking at me like I'm some hero. I just did my job."

She shook her head. "You are a hero."

A change came over his face, as though her words touched him in some way. "I want to be your hero, Katie. That would make me very happy. And I want you to call me Ben."

She nodded, but moved back a few inches. Mama said not to get too close to men. "What about Gary? He did this to my kitten. Shouldn't he have to pay the bill?"

Ben looked down for a moment, then said, "Are you sure it was Gary who did this? What you said he did . . . it's a horrible thing. And you know, Gary's father is a pretty important person in town. Accusing him of this, well, it isn't going to be easy. Maybe it's better not to raise a stink."

He sounded like her mama. Anger and injustice balled up in her throat. "But he did it! I don't care who his daddy is!"

Ben's smile wasn't really a smile at all. It looked sad. "You may not, but a lot of people do. Believe me, I know how towns like this work. Gary is the DA's only child. Everybody's hoping he'll go to college and come back smart so he can bring commerce back into town. Nobody's going to believe he threw a kitten against a window."

She blinked back the tears. "But everybody's gotta pay. When I stole some of Mrs. Granson's strawberries, I had to weed her yard to pay for 'em."

Lordy, it looked like Ben was gonna cry, too, the way his eyes watered up for a second. He touched her cheek. "Sometimes life isn't fair, hon. But I'm going to make it fair for you. I'm going to be your hero, now and always."

When she walked outside, she wasn't sure Silas would still be out there. But he was, and that somehow touched her. That he seemed to really care about the kitten touched her more.

"How is he?" Silas asked as he helped her up into the truck. She only nodded. "It's okay to cry, Katie. I know you want to."

She'd been trying really hard not to cry in front of him or anybody. Her mouth was tight, her chin quivering. Talking made it worse, so she tried not to say anything. But his words released the dam, and she let the tears come.

He started to reach for her, halted, then touched her hand instead. "You're just mad. I know how it feels to be helpless, powerless."

She rubbed her shirt over her running nose and looked at him. How did he know what she was feeling? Is that why the kids called him Spooky Silas? But she didn't want to ask, because then he'd take away his hand, and his hand felt so good on hers. He'd go back to being silent like he was when the kids teased him.

"I wanna tell the sheriff on him. I want him to pay for what he did. Ben said they wouldn't believe me."

"He's probably right."

"He said I shouldn't raise a stink."

"What do you want to do?"

"Raise a stink."

Silas removed his hand and started the truck. There was a ghost of a smile on his mouth. He drove to the sheriff's office. And he walked inside with her.

"Little girl, surely you're mistaken," Sheriff Tate said when she'd related her story in the waiting area. He was older than Ben, but not by much. All the dark wood on the walls and floors made the area look warm, but it didn't feel warm. The sunlight pouring in through the front windows was almost blinding. "Gary might raise a ruckus now and again, but he's no cat killer." He looked at Silas, who stood behind her. "You see this happen?"

Silas paused, as though he were considering saying he did. But he shook his head. "She isn't lying."

At that moment, she knew that even if no one believed her, if Gary never paid for his crime, that Silas's standing up for her would help the pain.

The sheriff turned back to her. "Are you sure you didn't drop the kitten and are looking for someone else to blame?"

"I didn't drop him! I love . . ." She gulped down the sob that threatened to tear out. "I love him," she finished on a thick whisper.

The sheriff looked at the receptionist. "Call Sam over."

Gary's dad. Surely now Silas would back down, tell her she didn't have a chance. But he didn't. He was as silent and thin as a wooden post, and just as sturdy. Sheriff Tate squinted out the front window where the battered truck was parked. Then he looked at Silas. "You old enough to drive that thing?"

"I got my learner's permit. My dad wasn't around, and we had to get the kitten to the hospital."

Uh-oh. Now she'd gotten Silas into trouble.

"Seen you driving into town by yourself before. Does your old man know it's illegal for a fifteen-year-old to drive by himself?"

Silas's face went a shade paler, though his body didn't give away an ounce of discomfort. "He's been laid up with a broken ankle, can't manage the shifter. Soon as he's able, he'll be driving again."

"Maybe I'll have me a talk with him."

"He's gone a lot, selling his statues."

"With a broken ankle?"

Silas shrugged. "I drive him."

Once in a while Katie would see Silas and his dad at their makeshift stand by the crossroads selling pieces of wood carved into the shapes of horses and wolves.

"What the hell is going on?" Sam boomed in a loud voice as he walked inside. He was Italian, her mama had said, and reminded her of Marlon Brando. He was in the middle of swabbing his forehead when he saw Katie and went dead still. "What's *she* doing here?"

"Says Gary threw her kitten against a glass window, hurt it bad."

"And what does she want with me?" He hadn't even looked at her since the first glance.

She didn't like being ignored. "I want him to be punished for what he did."

Sam didn't look the least bit surprised or shamed by what his son had done. He hardened his brown eyes at her. "You got proof of that, little girl?"

"I saw him do it! That's proof!"

Sam picked up the phone at the reception desk and asked for his son. "You throw a kitten against a window?" he barked into the phone without greeting. Then he hung up. "He said he didn't. Looks like it's his word against yours."

"She ain't lying," Silas said.

Sam took in Silas's tall, rangy frame. "I don't have time for this crap. Sheriff, you going to book my son?"

Tate was leaning against the desk, his arms crossed. "Nope."

"I'm outta here."

Without another glance at Katie or Silas, he walked out. A burst of hot air from outside washed over her cheeks. She looked at the sheriff, but he was already walking to his office. The woman behind the desk quickly grabbed her coffee mug and scooted to the back. With his hands on her shoulders, Silas steered her out into the hot afternoon.

"How can they do that?" she said as they walked to the truck. "How?"

Silas leaned against the door for a moment, giving her a soft look. "That's how the world works. Bad things happen and nobody pays for it."

He was thinking about his father, maybe. She'd seen him wearing a black eye once. He'd tried to cover it up with makeup. "Like your dad hitting you?"

He blinked in surprise, but gave away no other emotion. "Yeah."

"Did you tell anyone?"

"When we lived in Monticello, north of here. I was younger than you. They didn't want to believe me because they didn't want to deal with my dad's temper." He helped her into the truck and closed the door.

"Does he still hit you?" she asked as soon as he got in.

"Not anymore."

Silas started the truck and headed down the dusty road that led out of town. All her life she'd been something of an outcast. There were only three other kids who lived in Possum Holler. Most of the kids in her school lived in nice neighborhoods where the homes weren't made of metal. Silas was an outcast, too, though he didn't even try to fit in. For the first time, she felt a bond with someone other than her mother. She liked it.

"I'll take you in to see your kitten tomorrow if you want," he said as he pulled into her trailer park.

"You'd do that?"

"Sure."

Her mama wasn't going to like this, not one bit. But she said, "Okay, thanks," anyway. "I can meet you out by the road here at one if that's okay."

"Sure."

He pulled right up to her mobile home.

"How'd you know where I live? That's right, Mama said you were here when she had me." Silas had only been a boy then, but her mama had said he'd been a big help until the midwife had arrived. And he'd held Katie with a tenderness her mama had never seen in a boy so young.

He nodded. "See you tomorrow."

She started to get out of the truck, and then paused. "Are you going to get into trouble driving to town again? Will the sheriff talk to your dad about it?"

"I hope not."

For two weeks, Katie's world revolved around riding with Silas to visit Gus and helping Ben groom the dogs and cats. Gus wasn't normal, as Ben had warned. His eyes were crossed, and he wasn't the bright cat he'd been before Gary threw him. But he was surviving, and she gave him lots of love to make up for his losses. Her innocence, shattered by Gary's assault, was starting to rebuild itself piece by piece.

Her mama wasn't happy about her hanging around with either Ben or Silas. It was inappropriate for a young girl to associate with a teenager and a grown man. Ben had even spoken to her mama to assure her that his intentions were nothing but honorable. Luckily, her mama was busy working during the day when Katie went to see Gus. Even more luckily, Gus was going to go home with her in a few days, and she would only have to help at the vet's hospital one day a week to pay for Gus's shots.

Even though there wasn't a dead bird in her yard that day, her luck evaporated. The sheriff was waiting to talk to Silas at the hospital. Ben tried to usher Katie inside, but she stayed next to Silas.

"We're going to have to bring you in and ask you some questions about your father's death." The sheriff's eyes hardened. "Why didn't you report his disappearance? You knew he was dead, didn't you? You knew his body was up in those woods rotting for six months, didn't you?"

She saw the nearly imperceptible tightening of Silas's mouth, but his eyes gave nothing away. His expression was resigned and hard and blank. "I knew."

The sheriff's voice went lower when he asked, "Were you with him when he died?"

"No. I never went hunting with him when he went during a school week. I went looking for him when he didn't come back by Saturday."

"And you found him?"

"Yes, I found him."

"And left him there."

"Yes, I left him there."

Despite her protests, the sheriff took Silas away, and Ben herded her into the hospital. When he took her home a few hours later, her mother was washing the windows. She threw the sponge in the bucket and stalked over, and Katie knew it wasn't going to be pretty. She jumped out of the truck before Mama got close, but she tapped on Ben's window.

"We'll pay you whatever it is we owe you for the kitten's care, but I don't want Katie over there anymore."

"Mrs. Malloy, let's talk about this. I think it's good for her to take on responsibility, and she's great with the animals."

Katie had never seen her mama look so hard and mean before. "If you see her again, I'll ask the sheriff to look into the matter for me. Go find someone your own age to hang around."

Ben spun dirt and gravel as he left the trailer park, and Mama stood her ground until he was out of sight. Then she turned to Katie. "Go into the house. You're grounded until you're sixteen."

Katie knew better than to argue; she turned and went inside. Now wouldn't be a good time to ask Mama to do something for Silas, either, she supposed. But she already knew Mama wouldn't do anything. She didn't fight for anything but Katie. She kicked at the wall in her bedroom, and Mama yelled at her to calm down. She hated feeling helpless. She was going to teach her a lesson and sneak out to Rebecca's for the night. When Mama found her missing, she'd be worried and maybe she'd rethink the hospital situation.

But Mama didn't come looking for her the next morning. In fact, from what Katie could see from Rebecca's window, there wasn't anything going on at home. Maybe Mama was sleeping in for a change, and Katie could sneak in and pretend she'd never left. It'd be just like normal.

But it wasn't normal. Mama was lying on the linoleum. She didn't answer Katie's calls, and she was cold and stiff. Katie dropped to her knees and shook her. She smelled chlorine and saw blue crystals spilled across the linoleum and her mama's nightdress. An open jar of Blue Devil drain opener lay on the floor. Bloody sores dribbled down the sides of her mama's mouth and nostrils. Her eyes were wide in terror, but they looked at nothing. As though she had been about to scream, and then had frozen.

Katie screamed for her.

~~~ CHAPTER 2

EIGHTEEN YEARS LATER . . .

THE HAPLESS BLACK bug flew into the spider's web in the light outside the kitchen window. It knew immediately that the gleaming strands of silk were the clutches of death. At first just its legs were stuck, and it strained its wings to fly away. It vibrated and twisted. The brown spider crept closer. With a burst of panic, the bug tried again to fly free. But the web had ensnared its wings now. The spider came in for the kill, skirting along the silvery thread and spinning its deadly cocoon around the bug. Still it fought, twisting and churning, but it was too late now.

Katie Ferguson could hardly see it now beneath the milky shroud. The macabre theater mesmerized her as she could feel the pull of the strands that trapped her in a tight hold, the sense of suffocation. Her hands squeezed the sponge in the sink full of warm, soapy water. *Enough! She's already caught, trapped forever, she can't get away now.* The spider kept spinning the bug around and around, until it disappeared completely. Now it would suck the life-blood from the bug.

"Honey, the Smiths called and need a hand with a foaling mare."

She started as Ben came up behind her and slid his arms around her waist. She twisted around, perhaps a little abruptly, and moved out of his hold.

"You startled me," she offered as an excuse.

He adjusted his glasses, his shoulders slumping. "Sorry,

honey. I thought you heard me come in. I saw you at the sink and couldn't resist giving you a hug."

She forced a smile that she hated having to force. "I'm sorry, I'm just . . . edgy lately. I'm sorry," she added again, and his hurt look changed to a smile.

"I told you, you're just being superstitious."

She dried her hands on the lacy kitchen towel. "I know it doesn't make sense, I know it's superstitious. But I can't help feeling it."

After another glance at the spider's web, she forced her gaze back to Ben. Her mother died at twenty-seven. *Not just died; took her own life.* Katie had just turned twenty-seven. Her birthdays were tainted by a mother who wasn't there to give her a silly gift or send her off on a treasure hunt to find trinkets. But this birthday had been different. She'd looked in the mirror and seen her mortality.

He put his arms around her again. "You're not going to die."

She laughed at the absurdity of the statement. "I know."

At forty-two, Ben was starting to soften around the edges. His silvery-brown hair shimmered in the light, and his gray eyes crinkled in a smile behind his glasses. He was a loving husband who didn't deserve a wife who felt as trapped as a bug in a web.

"Don't I make you happy?" he asked, tilting his head as he waited for her answer.

"Yes, of course you do." In many ways. In the ways that counted, she reminded herself. Security. A home. Working with the animals at the hospital.

"Am I still your hero, Katie?"

She remembered the months after her mother's suicide, such an ugly word, the way Ben helped convince the Emersons to keep Katie indefinitely. They had a farm in the outlying area of Flatlands, and six children. Ben had become part of their family, too, helping them out with the cost of treating their animals to help offset Katie's financial burden. Not that she didn't earn her keep. The Emerson children worked hard on the farm, from sunup to sundown, except for the hours they were home-schooled. But Ben had always been there. He'd helped her through her realization that the only reason the Emersons had taken her in was for the extra workhand. He'd been there for her since the day Gus had been hurt.

"Yes, you're still my hero," she whispered, feeling grateful and selfish and guilty all at once. He was the best thing that had ever happened to her. He was perfect in all the ways that mattered. He loved her and she loved him. She thought that would be enough.

It hurt like hell that it wasn't.

She felt the tears rise inside her and pushed them down. It had been like this all month, since her birthday. Bertrice, the high school girl who helped part-time at the hospital, teased her about being pregnant. Katie knew she wasn't pregnant. She was spiraling down a dark hole of irrational fear and depression.

"Don't I give you a nice life, Katie?"

"Yes, you have. You've . . . given me everything." She swallowed hard. "Maybe it would help if I got out more. Do you realize I have no friends?"

He looked surprised. "Of course you do. You have me. And Bertrice."

"Bertrice is a teenager. And you're my husband."

He took her face in his hands and said in earnest, "I'm your friend, too, Katie. Don't forget that."

She shook her head. "I meant female friends. I was thinking about volunteering at the County Fair."

"But then I wouldn't be able to spend the day with you. You'd be busy selling cupcakes or something silly like that. I'd have to wander around all by myself."

She opened her mouth to argue, but closed it with a sigh. Even volunteering was a selfish act. "I guess you're right."

"Don't be mad because I want to spend time with my wife. A man's entitled, you know."

"All right. What about helping at the playhouse? They're always looking for people to help with sets and sell tickets."

He put on his fatherly face. "Katie, I hate to remind you

of this, but you hardly have time to do your household chores as it is." He glanced around the kitchen, which was in need of spring-cleaning. It was already midsummer. The plain white cabinets were in need of a washing, maybe even a coat of paint. The wooden floor needed refinishing.

"I try to keep up with everything. It just gets away from me." Since Ben was busy with his veterinary outreach, it was her duty to run the house. That seemed fair enough, but between the yard and household maintenance, and the fact that she hated the latter, it seemed too much at times. Not that she'd complain.

Ben squeezed her hands. "Are you going to be all right? I'm only going to be gone for a couple of hours. Remember, they had trouble foaling with this horse before. They want me around just in case."

She gave him a hug. "You're a good person. I hope our customers appreciate that."

They seemed to. They were always thanking him for the free services he provided to those in need. For the strays he helped at no charge. Everybody loved him.

He squeezed her back. "I love you, Katie. Don't ever forget how much I love you. How much I need you."

"I won't."

He kissed her forehead. "Don't go wandering around outside. You know how it worries me."

She nodded instead of reminding him that they could move to one of the neighborhoods in town rather than living out in the woods not far from Possum Holler. But it was an old argument she wouldn't win. The house was nice enough, the Victorian-style cottage lived in by old lady Babbage until she died the year before Katie and Ben married.

She stood at the door and watched their custom van's headlights disappear down the dark driveway. Their van doubled for a "Bowie," the official veterinary mobile unit. How lucky she was to be married to a warm, compassionate man.

She walked back through a living room that resembled a Victorian dollhouse. He'd decorated the house just for her right before they'd gotten married. The flowery pink velvet and gold wallpaper closed in the front room with its heavy detail. Two couches imprinted in a pink flower pattern faced off against each other across a prissy coffee table. Even the fireplace was fussy with its frills etched into the marble.

"A place a woman will feel right at home," he'd announced when he'd brought her here on their wedding night. He'd been so proud, she couldn't bear to tell him she liked simpler lines and much more light.

So he'd added to it over the years, elegant draperies, intricate light fixtures, and a flowery carpet he didn't realize clashed with the couches and wallpaper.

All for her.

The sink full of lukewarm sudsy water looked like a greasy miasma. Ben would have bought her a dishwasher years ago, but the tiny kitchen didn't have room for one. He would do anything for her. Lucky, lucky woman.

Selfish, ungrateful woman.

She tossed the sponge in the water and walked to the back door. The lights mounted outside the kitchen window cast a glow that quickly dissipated into the murky night. To the west, the sky was shadowy blue with a hint of a glow: the day's last gasp. The yard was a neat square cut into the thick of the woods surrounding them. The simple white gazebo Ben had built was tucked into the far corner, lost in the shadows.

Lost in the shadows.

That's how she felt, lost in Ben's shadow and his identity. Maybe she was supposed to be happy with just him and their nice little life. That's how it was with her and her mama. Just the two of them, closer than Siamese twins. Mama didn't trust people, but she was adventurous in her own ways. They walked in the woods at night, went skinny-dipping in the tiny creek trailing deep in the woods. Katie had been fearless then. Adventurous, waiting impatiently to grow up so she could explore the world. She'd never left Flatlands except for one trip to Atlanta with Ben. And her mama had been swallowed up by a darkness darker than the woods behind their mobile home, darker than any monster.

She pushed open the door and walked outside. The evening air felt like the breath of God, warm and slightly humid, scented by the earth. A bright sliver of moon frosted everything in translucent silver. Twigs creaked in the distance, and something scurried across the layer of decaying leaves. Two feet beyond the far edge of the gazebo lay the black unknown. The forest that bordered her yard was a mix of maples, poplars and oaks, a lush menagerie during the day, a place of mystery at night.

There was nothing to fear out here; everything to fear was inside her. She settled onto the gazebo bench and ventured to the edge of that fear.

If she didn't deserve Ben, then he certainly didn't deserve her. What did she offer him? Maybe the unselfish thing to do would be to let him go.

And go where, without any money, friends, or prospects? Certainly she couldn't keep her job at the hospital if she left him. She'd have nothing, she'd hurt Ben, and . . .

You left your mama for one night, and look what happened to her. If you leave Ben . . .

A whining sound in the distance pulled her from her smothering thoughts. She tilted her head, trying to discern where it came from. It faded, then started up again a minute later. It sounded like a saw cutting through wood, a sound that always set her teeth on edge. Katie jolted to her feet. No one should be sawing out there. No one should be out there at all. The sound was coming from the direction of Silas Koole's old place a half-mile to the west, she was sure of it. Nobody had lived there in all the years since he'd been taken away.

She went inside to call Ben, but her finger halted on the final number. She would have to admit she was outside, because the sound was too faint to hear from inside the house. He'd give her that disappointed look, what a selfish wife he had, thoughtless of her hardworking husband, calling him away from a benevolent task.

Whoever was sawing wasn't exactly lurking in the dark. She'd have the advantage of being the lurker. She'd just investigate and decide what to do when she found out what was going on. No confrontations.

After tucking her feet into sneakers, she set off on a journey that had her heart thudding. Her throat was dry. She hadn't felt this way in longer than she could remember. Was she crazy to be afraid and to relish the feeling at the same time? The small penlight she'd grabbed from the kitchen drawer lit only a small patch of ground before her feet. Anything more could alert whoever was creating the noise. Her feet sank into the layers of leaves, from last fall and many falls before that. The muffled crunch of leaves seemed to signal to everyone in Flatlands that she was there, trudging through the saplings that brushed softly by her arms.

When her penlight lit a spray of feathers on the ground, she stopped. It wasn't a dead bird, no body anyway. Only the brown feathers to signify the lost battle.

She didn't believe dead birds were a bad omen anymore, but it never hurt to be a little more cautious after seeing one, just in case. Which made what she was doing even more foolish. Still, her feet took her forward instead of back to the house.

In a short while, the maples and oaks gave way to a thicket of pines. Some were slash pines, but many were what she called northern pines. Their spindly branches scratched and pulled at her clothes and hair. She shielded her eyes and continued on. It was hard going for ten more minutes, until the pines started mingling with the grand old oaks that surrounded the house where Silas grew up. Like the old oaks by the cemetery, these spread their branches in a canopy. Ivy covered their trunks and dripped from the branches.

Once in a while she found herself wandering to the Greek Revival house tucked into the forest. It was long past white, though it still looked in good condition. Someone had boarded up the windows in the last couple years, probably the Atlanta company that owned it. Sometimes kids partied there, and Katie picked up the garbage. She couldn't bear to see the place trashed up.

The sound grew louder, the high-pitched whining creeping up her spine. If someone hired by the company was working on the house, why after dark? And why didn't anyone know about it? The city council had been trying to buy the property the house was on, but the company never responded.

Unease skittered along her nerves when she spotted the light. Just an innocuous twinkle through the trees as she moved through the dark. The saw ground through another length of board and faded into silence again. Then the staccato sound of hammering. Not enough sound for many people to be making. Her mother's warnings echoed in her mind: *Stay away from strangers. Don't trust anyone.* As often as she'd heard that during her first nine years, she'd never had reason to be afraid of anyone. This was Flatlands, a quiet town established in the early eighteen hundreds that was separated from the surrounding towns by acres of forest. Folks spent their whole lives here. Nothing bad ever happened in Flatlands.

Nevertheless, the murder mysteries she liked to indulge in helped create a scene in her mind of illegal activities being carried out in the night, of the innocent person who stumbles across them and pays with his life. Well, she sure wasn't going to gasp in surprise or trip over a root and give herself away.

Even the moonlight was obliterated by the trees. Massive trunks covered in etched bark were spaced farther apart now. The thick canopy of leaves left the ground barren of growth. Something cool whispered past her cheek. She stopped, holding her breath before she realized what it was: a strand of the ivy.

She saw the house first, washed in light and rising out of the distance. Music floated through the air, a rock and roll station that faded in and out. Pressing herself against one of the rough trunks, she peered around it. Sawhorses were set up just outside the front door, a door that was now leaning against one of the massive columns. Three portable lights washed the front of the house and the work area in brightness. A black and gold sport utility vehicle was parked nearby, tailgate open. She got as close as she could to the house, which was closely guarded by the oaks surrounding it.

A man walked out carrying a length of wood. Her heart reacted first, not a startled jump but a different kind of jolt. He was tall and lean, his brown wavy hair reaching just past his collar. A blue handkerchief worked as a headband. He wore jeans and a long-sleeved plaid shirt that was left unbuttoned. She glimpsed a hard chest and taut stomach as the shirt opened with his movements.

Silas, a voice whispered in her head.

He stopped just short of the circular saw and, amazingly, looked into the trees surrounding the house. She hadn't made a sound, except a startled gasp in her mind. He set the wood against the sawhorses and turned down the radio. And he kept searching.

She was able to do nothing more than press closer to the tree.

Silas.

Could it be him, after all this time? It seemed a dream, a crazy dream that spun her insides and made breathing difficult. The last time she'd seen him had haunted her, Silas being taken away. Even though he had been cleared of any suspicion in his father's death, he'd still been an orphaned minor. Katie had pleaded with the Emersons to take him. The two Emerson boys who went to school with Silas said he was strange, unfriendly, that he'd probably killed his father, and no way would they live with Spooky Silas. So he'd been relegated to state protective services, and Katie had never seen him again.

Spooky and mysterious, yet tender and compassionate. He'd touched her little girl soul and left an imprint that hadn't quite gone away.

Silas walked toward the edge of the encroaching trees, then turned back toward her. He closed his eyes for a moment. When he inhaled, the memory of the lanky teenager evaporated. He was still lean, but his chest and shoulders had broadened. He'd grown even taller. The last time she had seen him, he'd been an adult to her young eyes. Now he was all man, and the thought stirred her in some inexplicable way.

When he opened his eyes, he looked right at her. She was still certain, despite her hammering heartbeat, that he couldn't see her. She shrank behind the trunk and waited for him to look elsewhere. Curly green mold that was plastered to the trunk pulled at her hair, but she didn't even move to disentangle herself. This wasn't the way she wanted to see him again. She wasn't sure she wanted to see him at all, wasn't sure it was wise. She'd wait him out, for as long as necessary, and go home.

"Katie."

Her eyes widened. It wasn't a question or unsure guess. Her fingers tightened against the bark. She wasn't sure what she felt the strongest: trepidation, embarrassment, or something she couldn't define. She squeezed her eyes closed and hoped she'd misheard, because that made sense. As it was, the pulse in her ears obliterated any sound. A second passed, then two, three.

Something skittered down her bare arm. Not a wayward vine. Her senses pieced together the feel of a finger grazing her arm and then the words, "Katie, you all right?"

She jumped and stumbled backward. The loamy ground cushioned her fall, though a bed of marshmallows couldn't have cushioned her pride.

"You okay?" he asked, reaching down to her.

"I'm fine." She couldn't see his expression in the shadows, which was probably a good thing. She accepted his hand, and he pulled her to her feet. She spent as much time as allowable brushing off the damp leaves clinging to her like leeches. When she looked up at him at last, he was watching her. "Hi, Silas."

"Hi, Katie." His smile was laced with question.

"I wasn't . . . spying on you exactly. I heard the saw and came over to see what was going on."

His low laugh vibrated through her. "It's okay. I was surprised to see you here." He started walking into the glow of light, turning to see if she was following.

"Me, too. Surprised to see you here, I mean."

Her insides were as jittery as Jell-O as she stepped up beside him. Closer up, she could see that his chest was sprinkled with sawdust. He smelled like a mixture of pine and man, interesting in a way she shouldn't have found interesting.

Now she could see that hint of smile he'd surely had when she'd fallen on her butt. She'd forgotten about those deep blue eyes, the way they slanted up complemented by the arch of his eyebrows. She'd forgotten how much his smile had meant to her way back when, like a rare gemstone glittering out of ordinary dust. He reached out, and she readied herself for his touch against her cheek. Instead, he removed a leaf from her hair.

"Good to see you again, Katie."

"Me, too. I mean, it's good to see you, too." She rolled her eyes, mortified at the way he was throwing her off. "How'd you know I was there?"

He shrugged. "Just a feeling."

All she could do was nod, though she wasn't sure she bought it. Still, she was the interloper here, so she had no basis to demand more of an answer.

He walked over to a cooler on the steps. "Want a drink?"

"I don't really drink," she said, imagining a bottle of beer. Instead he lifted out a bottle of water.

"At all?" he asked, looking so genuinely perplexed that she knew he was pulling her leg.

"I'm fine, thanks." The way her stomach was dancing, she didn't trust even water. "What are you doing back here? I didn't think I'd ever see you again." Looking at him as she spoke softened her words to the consistency of butter.

He studied her for a moment. "Did you want to see me again?"

"Yes," she answered too quickly. "I mean, I wanted to . . . I felt bad. I felt responsible for the sheriff finding out about your dad. If you hadn't taken me to see him about pressing charges, he probably wouldn't have found out."

This time he did touch her face, trailing a finger along her jawline before dropping his hand. His touch raised a trail of goose bumps on her arms. "It wasn't your fault. It was my decision to go in with you. My choice."

"But you did it for me."

"My choice."

But you never helped anyone else. Why me? "What happened to you?"

He leaned back against the column. A gold cross, two simple bars he wore on a chain, caught the light. She wondered if it was the same cross he'd worn before. "They sent me away to a foster family in Adgateville. I figured all they wanted was someone to tend the garden and fix up the house. I took off, went to Atlanta."

She leaned against the column across from him. "I tried to find out where you were. No one would tell me."

He took a drink of water and set the bottle down. "It's hard to be resourceful at nine. Were the Emersons good to you? I was afraid they were going to work you to death, too."

She narrowed her eyes. "How'd you know where I went?"

"It's easier to be resourceful when you're fifteen. I checked on you once in a while. Came back a few times."

"Came here? To Flatlands?"

The lines of his face had sharpened over the years. With his shaggy hair and easy posture, he still reminded her of a wolf. He nodded. "When I ran away from Adgateville, I came here first. I wanted to make sure you were all right. The Emersons wouldn't let me see you. I knew Ben Ferguson wouldn't help me. When I came back later, you were about to marry him."

For a moment, she felt a prick of guilt, as though she'd let Silas down by marrying Ben. Ridiculous, since Silas hadn't come to propose to her. She shivered at the thought of meeting him when she'd been eighteen. He probably would have been somewhere between the lanky teen and the man he was now. But she'd been promised to Ben; she'd belonged to him since she was nine in one way or another. And she owed him so much.

Followed by the guilt was a melancholy sense of something missed. Of opportunity lost.

"You could have come to see me then," she said.

He stretched, touching high up on the column. His fingers were long, but not terribly work worn. "No I couldn't."

She had the most perverse urge to touch him, to press her hand against the planes of his stomach and up to the ridge of his rib cage. With his body stretched long, there was a gap between his skin and the waistband of his jeans. She stopped her thoughts and promised to never read another *Cosmo* magazine again.

"Where are you staying?" she asked.

"Here."

She pushed away from the column and walked toward the open doorway. It looked cleaner now, devoid of the disintegrating carpet and draperies. Two wall sconces and three lamps filled the parlor with light. Odd that the electricity was on. Three boxes of hardware supplies lined the wall. The once-elegant room with its high ceilings adorned with intricate molding now looked sadly empty. She couldn't tell where he slept.

What she thought was a pile of brown carpet struggled to its feet and ambled over to inspect her. The big dog was a hound mix of some sort, old and cumbersome. His nose twitched as he covered her hand with dog moisture. His face was sprinkled liberally with white hair, as were his big feet.

"That's The Boss. He's named after Bruce Springsteen."

"You a fan?" she said, scratching the dog's head.

"He came with the name. I've only had him a couple of years. His owner died, and there wasn't anyone else who could take him."

Finished with his inspection, The Boss settled down at Silas's feet with a sigh.

"He might have arthritis," she said, taking in the way he couldn't seem to get comfortable. "You might want to have him checked over."

"He's already on medication for it, and my vet taught me how to massage his paws when the pain reliever doesn't seem to work." Silas ran his fingers lightly over the dog's head. "I wonder how much pain he's in. I'm not sure I could put him down, though."

"It's a hard thing to do, but sometimes it's for the best." She knelt down and looked into The Boss's cloudy eyes. "What bothers me most is when people can't bear to be with their pets during those last few minutes." She held his snout in her hand and stroked his nose. "After all they do for us, the least we can do is be the last loving face they see."

After a moment of silence, she realized how out of place she was for being so emotional about that. "Not that I'm condemning those people. I just see it from the animal's point of view."

He was still regarding her with those intent eyes. "You're right, though. It's a tough thing to do, but we owe them that much. I bet you have a lot of pets."

"Not really. Ben said after being with animals all day, he wants peace and quiet at home." She scanned the dusty oak floors. "Why are you fixing this place up? Some corporation owns it now."

"This was my home once. I didn't feel like staying at a hotel. Besides, I want to keep a low profile."

When she turned back to him, he was standing just behind her. Having him this close was doing strange things to her insides. She could feel the heat coming off him, elevating the temperature inside the house.

She kept her gaze on the gold cross that rested against the hollow of his collarbone. "Low profile, huh?"

"You'll recall I wasn't exactly popular here."

Spooky Silas. "I wouldn't know anything about being popular." She took a step back, feeling awkward as she crossed, then uncrossed her arms. "I'm not in the town loop myself. Not that I want to be," she added quickly, feeling like a failure at making friends. Feeling unlovable.

"You live at old lady Babbage's place."

She nodded, giving up asking him how he knew. "I was in the back yard when I heard your saw."

"Where's Ben?"

"Helping a farmer with a foaling mare."

"He good to you?"

It took her a second to realize what he was asking. "Very. He helped me through some tough years."

His eyes darkened for a moment, as though he blamed himself for not being there for her. Which was ridiculous since he didn't owe her anything, and he'd only been a kid himself. "Good. As long as you're happy."

"I am happy. Very happy." The words shot out of her mouth. "I have what I wanted all my life: security. Though Mama gave me a lot of emotional security, we didn't always have money for the bills. With the Emersons, I always knew I'd have food and a roof over my head, even if I did have to share that roof with six other kids and a room with two sisters who weren't particularly happy about the addition to the family. I'm sure they thought I wasn't going to pull my share of the load. I worked harder than any of them to prove myself."

He was standing too close, watching her too intently. She stepped back again. "Anyway, Ben was there through all of it. Marrying him was natural." Expected.

He merely nodded, keeping his opinion from his face. But the way he was looking at her . . . "As long as you're happy. That's all that's important." His soft voice belied that soul-searching look in his eyes.

"I am." She looked at the house again. "How long are you going to be staying here? Looks like for a while."

"I don't stay anywhere for long."

She tried to tamp down the disappointment that he'd be leaving soon. No, it was *good* that he was leaving soon. She didn't need this, this strange feeling of having him close. To add to her discomfort, he swept her with his gaze and said, "You grew up good, Katie."

She wrapped her arms around her waist. "Thanks." It seemed silly, not to mention unwise, to reciprocate the compliment, so she left it at that. Still, she wondered what he'd meant by it. She wasn't a scrawny kid anymore, but she wasn't overly attractive, either. "I"—she waved toward the doorway—"should probably get going. In case Ben calls or comes home. I don't want to worry him."

He followed her down the steps. "I'll walk you back."

"You don't have—" She abruptly turned around, sending him crashing into her. For a moment their bodies connected, her breasts to his chest, thigh to thigh. He grabbed her arms to catch her balance. She laughed, because it was the only way to release the pressure building inside her. "Sorry about that. I didn't realize you were so"—she took note of his hands on her arms—"close behind me."

He also seemed to realize he was still holding on to her and let go.

"You don't have to walk me back. You're busy, and I know the way. After all, I got here alone, didn't I?"

"I'd still feel better walking with you."

She could see the stubborn set of his jaw and gave in with a nod. She started walking into the bosom of the forest, and he walked with her.

"You always wander around the woods at night?" he asked a few minutes later.

"Not at night. When I have time on the weekend, I go for walks."

"Be careful, Katie. You never know what's out here."

Like you, she wanted to say. She was still caught up in his warning, the propriety of it. "I suppose that's true."

As she neared her yard, she started worrying that Ben might be there. He got so funny when he couldn't find her. He liked to keep tabs on her because he cared about her. She stopped just shy of the gazebo.

She didn't know what to say as she stood facing him. "I'd invite you in, but . . ."

"I understand."

She started to say something else when he brushed his

hand over her hair. Just a casual touch, the way a husband would touch a wife. As though she belonged to him. She shivered at the thought. "Silas . . ." The words died in her throat at hearing the pleading tone in that one word. She cleared her throat and her head. "It was good to see you again. Stop by the hospital sometime and say hello."

"Sure, I'll do that," he said in the way one does when he doesn't mean it.

This would probably be the last time she'd talk to him. She wanted to give him a hug, something to show him how much he'd meant to her all those years ago. Instead, she said, "I'm sorry about, well, about everything."

He gently placed his hands on her shoulders, moving close enough to force her to look up at him. His touch, casual though it was, sent a peculiar warmth down her body, as though someone had poured warm molasses over her head. "Don't blame yourself. I told you, what I did was my choice." He looked away for a moment, then back at her. "You probably don't even know what you gave me that day."

"Gave you? Trouble maybe."

He didn't smile at her lame attempt at a joke. "You trusted me, Katie. You were the first person to ever trust me." He brushed her chin with his knuckles and backed away. Then he disappeared into the night.

Silas watched her touch her chin as she walked into the house. He saw her briefly in the door window as she searched for him. She was gone just as quickly. He made it back to his house in half the time. He didn't want her to know how many times he'd made this trip, so he'd let her lead the way.

She might have trusted him before, but she had no reason to trust him now.

He went back to trimming the wood so he could reset the front door. Was Katie still listening to the sound of the saw? He never imagined that she could hear him from this distance or especially that she'd walk over to check it out. She hadn't lost her adventurousness, that was for sure.

Sawdust coated his forearm as he finished the cut. He hoped she hadn't seen how astounded he was to find her there. He'd been no less attracted to her than she was to him. He suspected that if they'd met when she was in her late teens, there would have been chemistry between them. She'd grown up to be a stunning young woman, though that was hardly a surprise. With her glossy brown hair and wide-set brown eyes, she wasn't a classic beauty, but she was enchanting all the same. She was still thin, and her arms were still long. Her birthmark was partially hidden by the shirt she wore. Perfect in her own way.

She was the reason he'd come back. Not for the attraction, he assured himself. God, how he'd wanted to just take her in his arms, though. He shook his head, sending a faint shower of sawdust spiraling to the ground. To feel her, to hold her . . . even touching her briefly had sent a rush through him.

He walked back to the doorway with the finished wood. The Boss was standing in the opening, as though contemplating whether he wanted to walk the distance to where Silas had been cutting. Silas set the wood against the doorway and sat down on the top step. The Boss wandered over and settled down with his head on Silas's thigh. Poor old guy. He was probably too old for Silas to be hauling him around with him, but he just didn't have the heart to give him away or worse, send him to a shelter. He had to know that someone would give him his arthritis medication, had to know that someone would stand by him when the time came to say goodbye.

Silas massaged The Boss's paws and then his back legs. "What'd you think of Katie, big guy? Pretty cute, huh?"

The dog let out a sigh, agreement if Silas ever heard it.

Katie. Even though he hadn't spoken with her in eighteen years, she'd been part of him for so long, he felt as though she somehow belonged to him. He had to remind himself that she didn't. There was no way he and Katie could get involved. Her being married presented one problem. All those years ago in Atlanta, living on the streets at times, he'd found God. Or maybe God had found him. Either way, religion had given him the hope and belief to fight his way off the streets, and then to deal with the horrors he'd witnessed since then.

He respected Katie's vow of marriage, even though she wasn't happy with Ben. Not really happy, anyway. From their encounter tonight, he knew that sweeping her off her feet wouldn't be hard. But that was not what he wanted. Putting her through that kind of turmoil would be too hard on both of them. His reasons for coming back were purely unselfish.

The Boss snorted, as if to contradict him.

"Totally unselfish, my friend." He glanced at the place where he'd found Katie lurking. He couldn't have her for himself, and that was something he'd accepted long ago.

Something else interrupted his reverie. He recognized it right away, the insidious way the evil quietly lurked at the edge of his consciousness. *Stop*, he ordered, knowing he could only allay it temporarily. It moved relentlessly forward, the anticipation of cruel pleasure, the thrill of the hunt, salivation at the prospect of fulfillment.

He'd been such a good boy, coloring inside the lines.

Black and white, good and evil.

Reward time.

Not now. Silas wanted to savor the effect seeing Katie had on him for a while longer.

But soon those bittersweet thoughts eroded, giving full rein to the sadistic ones that had haunted him for years. He knew the pattern, knew it was hopeless to shove them away. He walked to his vehicle. He felt the pull and knew he was powerless to stop it. Just like the other times.

He was glad Katie hadn't asked him why he'd come back. He wasn't prepared to tell her the truth or a lie. There were things he had to do first, one which was earning her trust. You couldn't just throw that kind of thing at someone the first time you'd seen her in eighteen years. *Hi, Katie. You're looking well. Me, I'm fine. By the way, someone wants to finish off your life in the most heinous way you can possibly imagine. And it's someone you know.*

~~~ CHAPTER 3

BLACK AND WHITE.

Some pompous psychologist might have diagnosed him with multiple personalities. Not so.

Day and night.

He was like everyone else, with a polite side he showed to polite society, and a selfish side he kept to himself. The good side longed to belong, to be loved, to color within the lines. The bad side longed to take what he deserved, teased at the edges of his life until he could no longer ignore it. And why should he ignore it? This one secret pleasure was his reward for being good the rest of the time.

Two sides of a coin.

This was his secret pleasure, and the secret was the sweetest part. He held it the way a man would hold the Hope diamond to his breast. If he told anyone, they would surely take it away. They would grill him for the details, how he'd killed them, why he'd killed them, where he'd taken the bodies. They'd try to pick his psyche apart, categorize his childhood fears and traumas, his stormy adolescence. They'd try to discover the reason for his behavior. There was nothing wrong with him. He simply liked hunting women, the same way other men liked hunting deer and boar. Women were infinitely more interesting than deer and boar.

Good and evil.

The sweetest part was that no one could stop him. Which was good because restraining himself was getting harder and harder. He prided himself on restraint, on holding back the urgent desires. Only five months since the last time.

She should have lasted him longer. When he first started, they sated his hunger for a year or more. He used to tell himself, *Just once more*, too. Like that had worked. And why should he restrain himself? Hadn't he earned the right to a little pleasure once in a while? If it was so wrong, why did it feel so right? So deserved? *Be a good boy*, a voice from his childhood intoned. *Color between the lines.* But the hunger started earlier now, a sweet hunger that coiled through his insides and brought him alive.

Fog settled into the culverts along the road as though waiting to catch its own prey. Old clapboard homes were spread out here in this rural area. Trucks set up on blocks adorned a yard here and there, along with the occasional rusty appliance. It was a lot like Possum Holler. This time of night, the chickens were settled into wherever they slept. He couldn't tell if the dark lumps on the ground were dogs or other debris. The houses nearby were dark. A dog barked in the distance. The moon was only a sliver, hardly enough to lift the gloom. The girl, however . . . the girl he could see quite clearly.

She was probably in her teens, with her arms crossed in front of her and her shoulders hunched as she walked away from a dingy house. She glanced up as his vehicle passed her by, then stared downward again. She wasn't his chosen, but he wasn't a man to pass up a golden opportunity.

He backed up. She peered in his window as he stopped beside her.

"You all right?" he asked.

She glanced back at the house. "I missed my curfew and I guess my mom's teaching me a lesson by locking me out."

Her shoulder-length blond hair was in disarray and her lush mouth was pushed into a frown. Pretty enough. Hunger bubbled inside him. "Is there some way I can help you? Our youngest is spending the night with friends. You could stay in her room tonight."

"Where do you live?"

"About ten miles from here, toward Gray. If you're hungry, my wife could probably whip up something for you.

You could call your mom in the morning . . . or wait a bit and make her worry. Locking her daughter out of the house for the night is a cruel thing to do."

"Tell me about it." She glanced back to the house. If anyone was watching, they'd have come out by now. "I was going to walk to my friend Gwen's house. It's about two miles up the road." She smirked. "If her mom'll let me stay. We don't get along too well. She thinks I'm a troublemaker." She smiled then. "I'm not, really. I only missed my curfew by a few minutes."

"That's a lousy deal. Your mom would never forgive herself if something happened to you. Look, I can take you to your friend's. At least I know you'll get there safe. I don't like the idea of a young woman walking around by herself at night. I'd sure want someone to help my daughter in the same situation."

She nodded. "All right, thanks."

The door closed with a sweet thud.

"I'm Clancy, by the way. What's your name?"

"Carrie."

He never gave out his real name, just in case the girl got away. Not that it had happened yet. One girl had run off and he'd been forced to shoot her. Bad thing, that. No joy in shooting a girl in the back.

She was chatting about her boyfriend and how her mother disapproved of him. Did one conviction of marijuana possession make him a bad person?

"Nothing wrong with getting high once in a while," he said, enjoying the look of surprise on her face.

"*You* get high? No way."

"What, you think because I'm an adult I can't have fun anymore?"

She laughed. "I thought a family man would have to give that kind of thing up."

"A man's entitled to some secret fun once in a while." He wondered if she could see his smile at the truth of that statement. "A reward for good behavior."

"Too cool. You sneak a toke and your wife doesn't even

know!" Her expression changed to something like his own. "You got some on you now?"

"I have some at my special place. Blue Moonshine."

"I've never heard of it."

"I order the seeds from California and grow my own. It'll take all your troubles away." This could be even more interesting. He let that sit between them for a moment, sensing her interest, watching her mull over the possibility. Then he casually tossed out, "We could go share a joint." He glanced at his clock. "But you wanted to go to your friend's house, and it's getting pretty late."

She was hooked, he could tell by the mischievous glint in her eyes. "You did say I could hang at your house, didn't you? I'm not even sure I can stay with Gwen. Her mom is such a drag."

His smile broadened. "It would be fun to get stoned with someone else for a change."

"Sounds good to me. That'll teach Mama. She locks me out, I get stoned with some family man. And when she doesn't know where I am in the morning, she'll really get worried. I bet this is the last time she does this to me."

"I'll bet it is, too."

He settled back in the seat and enjoyed the ride. She regaled him with stories about different drugs she'd done, nothing serious. Speed to get through finals, Quaaludes once in a while. He told her about his experience with angel dust and the times he'd done mushrooms.

He'd never done a drug in his life. He didn't like losing control.

He pulled onto a road that was nearly grown over with vegetation. As soon as the car was a suitable distance off the highway, and hidden from sight, he pulled to a stop at a metal gate that blocked the way. NO TRESPASSING! TRESPASSERS WILL BE SHOT! the rusty sign stated. Beyond that, the road disappeared beneath layers of leaves and growth. He quelled the urge to giggle in delight as the first look of apprehension melted her grin. Once he cut the headlights, they were thrown into darkness.

"Clancy, this is kinda creepy."

"Don't worry about it. I know the way by heart, and it's not far from here. There's nothing to be afraid of, I promise." Even though he always asked their name, he never used it. She was not a person with a mother and boyfriend, she was something for his pleasure. His reward.

Still she hesitated, staring into the blackness in front of the car.

"We can skip the joint if you're uneasy," he offered.

She pushed her door open. "Let's do it."

As soon as they approached the gate, the sensor was triggered, sending a message to his beeper. It always soothed him when it went off, as it did now. The moment anyone got near the special place, he'd be alerted.

From the gate, even in the daytime, his special place couldn't be seen. It was, contrary to what he'd said, quite a distance from the gate. The building was hardly visible in the gloom, but he knew exactly where it was. It was at night that he visited it the most. He unlocked the rusty hinge lock, opened the old wooden door and stepped inside.

The battery-powered light cast a dim glow throughout the small room. It smelled musty, but there was nothing to indicate what had happened there before, the pleas for mercy, the sex, or the blood. The walls were painted dark red to match the exterior. A battered table sat off to the side, a dilapidated couch sat against the wall. A twin bed with rust-spotted head and foot rails was tucked into the corner. All from junk sales out of town. Beneath the bed, where she couldn't see, was a bedpan. He'd learned that freeing them to relieve themselves gave them an opportunity to escape. More than anything, he was a man who valued his freedom.

The windows were boarded up. There was a small fireplace, but he never lit it for fear of drawing attention. Details like that got the others caught. He had no intention of getting caught.

The girl looked around. If they came here voluntarily, which was rare, they always took in the place. That gave him the opportunity to remove the handcuffs from beneath the sofa cushion.

"Pretty rough, huh?" he said with a chuckle. "I've thought about fixing it up, but I'm just not here enough to warrant it."

"What else do you do here?" She was looking at the bed.

"When you've got three kids, you need some downtime. We have a farm, and I'm with them all day. Sometimes I need a break, or I feel like I'll explode."

The mention of the kids took the edge off her expression. "Where's the stuff?"

He knelt down beside the bed and slid his hand beneath the musty gray mattress. "Right under . . ." His hand slid in deeper. "Wait a minute. I had most of a dime bag right here. Maybe it slipped through the frame."

She knelt down near him and helped him look. "Could someone have found it?"

"I doubt it. No one even knows this place exists, as far as I can tell. It's got to be here somewhere."

"There's an old bedpan under here," she said, distaste in her voice.

"Oh, that's where it is. I forgot, I'd stuck it there just in case. Can you reach it? Just shove it this way."

He reached beneath the bed and clamped the handcuff on her wrist. The disbelief was always the best part.

"Hey, what are you doing?" She jerked back, but he had a firm hold on the other cuff. "Oh, my God, what are you doing?"

She started to scramble to her feet. He knocked her on the bed and landed hard on top of her. A gust of breath whooshed from her lungs, leaving her temporarily weakened while he clamped the other cuff around the iron rod. The second pair of cuffs was within reach beneath the mattress. He grabbed it just as she started to struggle again.

"No, please don't do this. If it's sex you want, I'll give it to you. Just please don't cuff me . . ."

He cuffed her other hand, hearing the pleasant sound of

metal against metal as she started to jerk her hands downward. In a cold voice, he said, "It's not just sex I want."

"Oh, no, please, God, no."

He settled back, straddling her waist. This was the fear he enjoyed most, when they were manacled to the bed, knowing there was no escape, no hope. They were going to go through something terrible, and the best they could hope for was to get out alive. He sometimes told them he'd let them go if they behaved, and they believed him . . . for a while anyway.

She started screaming then. He could tell her that no one would hear her, that they were too far away from the road or any other house. But that sounded trite and overused, so he grabbed the rag he kept beneath the mattress and stuffed it into her mouth. He wondered if she could taste the other girls' saliva.

Her nostrils flared as she took in air in her panicked breathing. He simply watched her. Sweet anticipation surged through his loins. If only this part could last forever. He had been keeping them longer lately, several days sometimes, visiting them when he could. He drew such pleasure just thinking about them waiting for him. Keeping them indefinitely would be trickier. He doubted they could escape, but one never knew. That's how the others were caught, when one got away and identified them. They kept trophies, too, adding to the evidence. He was smarter than that. Sure, he liked having something to remind him of the pleasure they'd given him. He had a better plan.

He slid down her legs as she bucked beneath him. The leg cuffs were already clamped to the corner rail hidden beneath the mattress. He gently removed her green Converse sneaker and closed the cuff around her ankle. Then he did the same to her other foot.

He caressed the sneaker with affection. It was ingenious, really. A shoe was often tossed carelessly out a car window. There it sat for weeks, months, even years, lying among the other litter along the side of the road. Nobody thought twice about it as they drove past it every day. Nobody but him. He looked for them, the pleasure of anticipation building as he neared where he left one. Always a distance from the town where the girl lived. He'd remember everything about the girl, every delicious detail.

Until the need grew too large for the fantasy to sate it. Then the slow build up of anticipation grew again as he searched for the next girl, the next opportunity.

The best part was that his trophies were right there for everyone to see. Trash to them, memories for him. His secret. And if one was connected to the missing girl, it told them nothing about the crime or her whereabouts. He always washed them before carefully setting them in their spot. Sometimes the authorities found them and the news would report the great "lead." They would launch a search in the area to no avail.

Muffled cries brought his attention back to the girl. He slid off her and went to the drawer. Her eyes bugged out even more when he pulled out the twelve-inch knife. He approached slowly, knifepoint held facing upward. He liked the opposite of terrified surprise, too. When they were sure he was going to cut them, he cut their clothing instead. Very carefully, he sliced away the seams. He enjoyed every whimper, as the blade touched their delicate skin, as the point sometimes grazed them. But he never drew blood. It was too early for that.

Once she was naked, he set the knife down. Then he stared at her with dispassionate eyes that belied the burning lust in his soul. Her legs were spread to each corner of the bed, as were her arms. She was ready for him, like a bug in a spider's web, trapped without hope of escape.

"Now, the fun begins," he said as he stepped closer.

Silas woke with a jerk, but the dread started even before he found himself in his vehicle parked along the side of the road. Fingers of dawn light were creeping up over the line of trees to the east. One lone car drove past, sending the weeds into a frantic dance. The images of the night before crowded back into his mind, as vivid as they'd been while it had been happening: the terrified girl shackled to the bed, the feelings of pleasure as she struggled and pleaded with her eyes. The vile acts that followed. Nausea rose in his stomach, though he'd learned to keep it at bay. Still, he broke out in a cold sweat.

Every time the killer struck, he took Silas with him. Since that day in prison, when Charles Swenson had reached across the table and grabbed Silas's arm. When Silas had seen and felt the atrocities Swenson had committed, and worse, why he'd committed them. Silas had understood the man's mind, had felt all the shadows in his black heart.

It had opened a door he wished he could close. A door that allowed evil to flow into his soul. Since that day, he had witnessed the deeds of the man he called the Ghost. And every time he struck, Silas got closer to being there at the moment of the kidnapping.

With weary resignation, he climbed out of the vehicle and searched for the signpost he'd seen in the final image. He looked down the slope and saw what the killer had discarded: a green sneaker. He felt nausea rise again. It was still damp where the killer had washed it. It was the first time he'd been this close. Usually he had to go searching for it.

He was getting closer to the killer. Silas had never seen his face, only the heinous crimes he committed. And when he caught up with him, what then? How long could one stare into the abyss before the abyss swallowed him? And the question that haunted him most: What if the killer wore his face?

CHAPTER 4

THE ALL-ANIMALS Hospital hadn't changed much in the years Katie had known it. She had planted some rhododendron bushes along the front of the building and at the road, but the driveway and lot were still gray gravel. The building had been a house back in the early nineteen hundreds. Later, it had been transformed to a law office, and years later into the animal hospital.

Inside, the bright walls were nearly blinding. Ben liked everything to look clean and professional. That's why she wore her standard black polyester pants and white blouse. He wore his smock. Not that he had anything to worry about; they were the only veterinary hospital in Flatlands, and the only one within a great distance that serviced the rural areas and farms.

In all the years she'd been married to Ben, all the years she'd known him, he'd never changed. He treated the animals with love and gentleness and their owners with respect. That was what won her respect for him, that the residents of Possum Holler were treated with the same civility as those who lived in the nicer areas.

"Don't you worry a thing about that," Ben was telling one plump woman who'd brought her cat in after it had lost a fight with a neighbor's dog. "Bellflower will be fine, and you can pay me whenever you've got the money." That meant never, but it made the customers feel like they weren't getting charity. They had pride, just as her mother had had pride.

Katie smiled as she wrote up the slip and gave the woman the medications Ben had prescribed. "You remember my kitten, don't you? Gus, the one Gary threw against the glass window?"

"Oh, yeah, I remember . . ." The woman obviously also remembered that no one believed Gary had done it.

"He came out of it all right. He survived, even with brain damage, lived a good, long life. Bellflower will come out of this, too."

"Thank you. And thank your husband again for me. He's the nicest man in the whole universe, he is."

"He sure is." She pulled the paperwork for their afternoon patients. He was wonderful, every woman's dream. He was older, yes, but he wasn't out sowing his wild oats with the young bucks in town, either.

"The Williams's puppy is coming out of anesthesia," Ben said, walking out of the recovery room. Skunk had been hit by a car, an unfortunately common occurrence in the rural areas. "I think he's going to make it."

"Oh, good. I made them promise to fence in an area for him if he made it through."

The waiting area was empty, and Ben took the opportunity to slide up behind her. "I see shadows in your eyes, Katie. Aren't you happy?"

"Of course I am." He had a way of making her feel guilty for every bad feeling she ever had.

"I want to know what my girl's thinking."

She turned to him. "I'm okay."

"You know I want an open marriage, Katie. What's going on?"

"I just . . . sometimes I feel lonely. Disconnected from the world."

His mouth tightened. "Aren't I enough for you?"

"Yes, you're enough for me."

"What's the problem, then?"

"Just a mood, I guess. It's nothing."

"I love you. You know that, don't you?"

She nodded. "I love you, too."

Instead of lightening, his face shadowed. "Sometimes I hear the words, but I don't see it in your face."

She hugged him, trying to emphasize her words with a hard squeeze. "I do love you, Ben. You're my life." That was true. She did love Ben, in some way. She'd loved him since she was a girl, when he'd saved Gus, and then saved her. And he was her life. Maybe that was the problem. He was her whole life.

When the door opened, they stepped apart. Bertrice dropped her glitter-painted book bag and looked at them.

"What's wrong? I know that look. Don't tell me you're fighting. I get enough of that at home, with my mom threatening to divorce my dad every ten minutes. You two can't get divorced. You're like, the best example of a happy couple I know, otherwise I'd probably never get married."

Ben smiled. "We're fine, we're just discussing a patient."

Her eyes widened again. "Someone die?"

"No, but a puppy was hit by a car this morning. He's okay," he added at her crestfallen look.

"Cool. Let me wash off my makeup, and I'll take the dogs out." She emerged without the half-moons of purple over her eyes and matching lipstick. Her short brown hair ended in blond tips. She was a never-ending source of diatribes about the arguments she had with her mother (over makeup, boys, girlfriends, boys, and clothes) and the fights between her parents. She was helping out after school during this, her senior year, before deciding what she wanted to be in life.

Katie envied her beyond belief. What she wouldn't have given to have had teenage fights with her mom about anything. Or to have had a choice in what she wanted to do with her life. Not that she minded working with Ben. She'd had thoughts of going into nursing, and being a veterinary assistant was close to that in many ways. Since her mama died, though, Katie hadn't made one choice of her own.

"How was school?" Katie asked Bertrice later as they shampooed a Great Dane. She held onto the dog while Bertrice lathered. The dog kept eating the suds.

"Blech. Marcy and I got caught smoking in the bathroom, only I wasn't smoking, she was, but I still got called into the principal's office. Mom's gonna have a cow, 'cause she smelled smoke on me last week and thought I was, like, smoking. I told her, no way, and she said, 'I catch you smoking and you're gonna be, like, under house arrest or something.' "

"You weren't smoking, were you?" Katie asked with a raised eyebrow.

"Naw. I hate the way it leaves my mouth feeling, like an ashtray or something. I got detention, too, next Tuesday, so I'll be late." She got a twinkle in her eye and after checking to make sure Ben wasn't around, lifted the bottom edge of her striped tank top. A gold ring winked from her belly button. "Don't tell anyone, or Mom'll, like, skin me."

Katie was so tickled to be let in on a girl secret, she didn't even think of admonishing Bertrice. "Where'd you get it done?"

"Guy in Milledgeville does body art and piercing on the side. He's legit," she added at Katie's worried look. "Isn't it awesome?"

"Cool," Katie said, using one of Bertrice's favorite words.

Bertrice beamed and continued to scrub the dog. "You ought to get something done like that. For a change."

"Ben would skin *me*. Besides, I'm not into that kind of thing."

"What, like being fashionable? You've worn your hair that way for as long as I've known you. I'll bet it's always looked like that." Bertrice reached over with a soapy hand and took a strand of Katie's hair. "Have you ever done anything to it? Like highlighted it or cut it? You're starting to get the grays."

"Just a few." Katie glanced at her distorted reflection on the paper towel dispenser. She'd worn her hair straight and just past her shoulders since she was a teenager. "Ben likes it this way."

"And what about you?"

She shrugged. "If I had my way, I'd cut it short. Especially for the summer." Even in the distorted image, she could see the wine stain on her neck. "Maybe to my shoulders. Ben would kill me if I dyed it."

"Even to cover the grays?"

"Yep. He likes it just the way it is."

Bertrice rolled her eyes. "I like Ben and all, but I don't understand why you can't do what you want with your hair. He'd get used to it."

"I'll think about it." And that's all she'd do. She didn't even want to start the discussion with Ben.

"And what about your clothes? I know you wear this boring outfit for the hospital, but what about after work?"

Despite the gentle badgering, Katie was enjoying the conversation. She'd never had a girlfriend before. "I don't do much after work. Sometimes I pick out something at the K Mart when Ben and I go out of town. And he orders me things from catalogs." She pretended to love everything, the same way she'd pretended to love her one Christmas gift from the Emersons every year. Like the bra or the box of tampons.

"Cool stuff?" Bertrice looked skeptical already.

Now it was Katie's turn to see if Ben was in the vicinity. "Boring stuff," she whispered. "But I don't go anywhere, so it doesn't matter."

Bertrice eyed Katie's waist. "You wear what, a seven?"

"Or eight. But I've got a flat butt."

"No you don't." She glanced at her own behind. "At least you don't have a fat butt, like me. Anyway, I've got some stuff you can have. It's a little out of style, but, like, what does it matter? Step out of middle-aged-lady stuff and start dressing your age."

"Yes, ma'am," Katie said with a smile. But the prospect of getting something stylish, even teenage stylish, made her giddy. "I wish I'd had someone like you for a friend when I was your age."

"But you had sisters, didn't you?"

"Not really. I was the intruder. They were nice, but I didn't really belong. Don't get me wrong; I was lucky to have them, to have a home."

"I know what you mean. Sometimes I hate my mom, but then I think what I'd do if she weren't around." She gave Katie a sympathetic look. "Hey, we should go shopping sometime."

"Uh-oh," Ben said, walking around the corner. "Sounds like a conspiracy we can't afford."

Bertrice rolled her eyes. "You must make a fortune here, with all your customers."

"But he gives his services away half the time," Katie said, never wanting to begrudge Ben his generous nature.

"What else can I do? Turn away a sick or injured animal? It can't be helped."

"You've got a good heart, Dr. Ferguson," Bertrice said with a genuine smile.

"Katie, the town council is having a meeting tonight, trying to come up with strategies about the land."

That's what everyone called the acreage the town had been trying to buy for two years: simply, "the land." Now that the historical district had been fixed up, even with a board depicting where the old jail and courthouse used to be, the town was vying for more business. Without a historical claim to fame, it was tough to woo people to move to Flatlands. A lot of folks were moving closer to Gray or Macon.

"Celine Inc. still won't return our calls," Ben continued. "I think we're going to send someone up to find their offices. We're tired of playing games with them. Anyway, we can grab a bite at Pie in the Sky and then you can head on home. I'll catch a ride from Tate or Harold."

Katie nodded. She already knew asking him if she could sit in on the meeting would be fruitless. As the suds slid down her hands and down the drain, she felt the first impish glimmer light in her stomach. She pushed it away.

Ben preceded Katie into the diner that served as the hub of town despite its out-of-way location. Dinah Simpson had bought the ailing diner with the money her late husband left her. At forty, her short, black hair and stylish outfits, along with her lucrative business, garnered her more marriage proposals in one week than a woman got in two lifetimes, Katie suspected. The menu was an eclectic mix of down-home and *nouvelle* cuisine that Dinah copied from Atlanta restaurants. Every night the specials were something interesting, like salmon with mango salsa and grits or trout with dill and wine sauce. She'd classed up the joint with fancy wallpaper borders and a European decor, then sold out to greed by displaying area advertising everywhere one looked, even in the bathrooms.

"Hey, Ben!" Dinah greeted with a warm smile. "How's it going?"

"For a man going to the dogs, as good as can be expected," he answered.

Dinah and two men at the counter laughed, even though they'd heard the reply every time Ben walked in.

Dinah's smile cooled considerably when she laid eyes on Katie. "Hey," she said, then turned to wipe down a section of counter that already looked clean.

"Hi," Katie said warmly, then turned to the men. "How are you?"

They nodded, then resumed their conversation.

She joined Ben at a booth, and Linda sauntered over. "Hey ya, Ben. Katie," she added as an afterthought. "Iced tea?" She waited for Ben to answer, though he nodded for Katie to order.

"People don't like me," Katie said when the waitress left.

"Sure they do."

"You didn't notice the difference in response we get? It's so obvious."

He glanced over her head to see the specials written on a blackboard in fluorescent marker. "You're imagining things."

"Am I, Ben?"

He set his menu down and looked across the slate table at her. "Katie, what possible reason could anyone here have to dislike you?"

"I . . . don't know. But they do. I'm not imagining it."

She glanced around the diner. Those who met her gaze nodded briefly—no smile—before returning to whatever they were doing. Maybe the problem was that they didn't know her. She'd been born in Flatlands, but had participated in very little in town. She saw a pink flier in the window asking for volunteers to help at the county fair. But then Ben would be by himself, and she'd feel guilty all day and more for it.

Harold Boyd walked over and planted his beefy hands on their table. "Hey, ya'll. How's it going?"

Katie was pretty sure it wasn't just the pulsing tic on Harold's right eyelid that made her uneasy. He couldn't help that just like she couldn't help the wine stain on her neck. She nodded before returning her attention to the menu. Maybe it was his bearlike physique or the way he liked to hover just a little too close.

The men talked over some small-town gossip for a minute, and then Harold rapped his knuckles on the tabletop. "Got to head back to the barn." She was unnerved to find him looking right at her. "I'll see you around." He even touched her arm in an affectionate gesture before heading out.

"See, he's friendly toward you," Ben said.

When she drove home an hour later, she was convinced that she was nothing more than a selfish, dissatisfied woman. Everyone worshiped Ben, and he was a wonderful man. She, on the other hand, had leeched off him from the time she was nine, eagerly taking the security he offered.

When she passed her own driveway, she chastised herself again.

What are you doing, Katie?

Just going to see why he's back in town, that's all.

That was her thought as she turned down the long-unused driveway that led to Silas's house. The drive wasn't as long as it had seemed to her that awful day. A warm breeze ruffled through the lush green leaves of the maples and oaks. Then it got darker as the large oak trees took over. And then, there was the house.

The sawhorses were still set up outside, and Silas was reclining at the top of the porch steps with his dog. He looked like a man who had worked hard all day. And perhaps he had, because new windows were now installed in the front of the house. He was watching her as she pulled next to his car. Or was it a truck? A Lincoln Navigator, one of those SUVs. Very nice, which made her wonder what he did for a living. That's why she was here, because her curiosity was eating away at her. Curiosity didn't always kill cats, did it?

He pulled himself to his feet as she stepped out of her van. The Boss merely raised his head and woofed softly. Silas's gaze never left her as she made her way to him, like a wolf sizing up his prey

"Hi. I was on my way home and thought I'd come by and see how things were going." *Lame, Katie, so lame.*

He glanced toward the house. "It's getting closer to livable."

"They're having a town council meeting right now, that's where Ben is, to see what to do about this property."

"What do they want to do with it?"

"That's the big debate. Some want to put shopping centers to attract the area townspeople and travelers to stop. Others want to put some kind of amusement park, with miniature golf and the like. The only thing most of them agree on is that we need to do something. We've lost three businesses in the last year, and seven families have moved out of town to find better prospects."

He regarded her with amused curiosity. She found herself crossing her arms in front of her.

"What do *you* think they should do with this property?"

"I . . ." She blinked in surprise. "You know, I've never thought about it. No one ever asks my opinion on stuff like that."

He leaned against the massive column. "As I recall, you were happy enough to supply it anyway. When you were a kid, I mean. You were the feistiest kid I knew, a fighter if I ever saw one. You were also fearless; I saw the scratches on Gary's face."

"Fearless," she said in a low voice, trying to remember that girl. "I was fearless, wasn't I? And feisty." Her gaze fastened on the frayed bottoms of his jeans.

"What happened to you, Katie?" he asked after a few moments. His voice was low and soft, laced in Southern honey.

She looked at him at last. "People change, I suppose."

She could see a visible strain in his posture, as though he wanted to come closer, but held himself back. Which was a good thing, a really good thing. He hadn't changed much, other than filling out and looking even more interesting than he had before.

"People are s'posed to change for the better." He ran his hand back through the long waves of his hair. "What I mean is, people are s'posed to get stronger."

Should she be insulted by his words? She felt a twinge of something, but not anger. "What do you do, Silas?"

"I do freelance work for a newspaper in Atlanta. And you work for your husband."

"With my husband. I love working with animals. Since Gus's ordeal, I've become very interested in animal welfare. The people in town probably think I'm bossy."

Silas slid down the column and sat on the top step. He patted the area next to him. "What happened with your kitten?"

She eyed the spot warily, but her body took her to it. She kept a safe distance between them, an appropriate distance between a married woman and a man she didn't really know.

"God, I loved that cat." She smiled, remembering the way he slept curled up by her feet every night. "Do you know what he did, right before he died? He found me. It was right after Ben and I married. I was down in the basement moving some stuff around. Gus crawled down the steps . . . I didn't even hear him, not until he landed in a thump on the floor." Her voice went tight. *Stop being so damn sentimental.*

"He lay in my arms staring up at me with his crossed eyes. He had a condition known as strabismus, permanently crossed eyes." A laugh escaped. "Do you know how many times I had to tell people that he wasn't a Siamese? Aside from having a little trouble nabbing flies on the windowsill, he could see pretty well." Her laughter faded as she found herself back in the cold, damp basement. "I couldn't figure out why he'd come downstairs. He didn't do stairs well. He was purring." She wiped at her eyes. "Purring, like he was happy. He looked up at me the best he could, the way he always had. Like he loved me, with a slow blink. He raised his paw to me. And then he died." The last word was swallowed in a cry, and she turned away. "This is silly. He's been gone for nine years."

Silas got to his feet and went inside. She'd embarrassed him. Well, great, she'd embarrassed herself, too. But he came back with a wad of toilet paper. "Sorry, it's all I've got."

"Thanks." She dabbed her eyes and blew her nose. "It's silly."

"No it's not." His voice was soft, and it pulled her gaze to his. He touched her cheek, and that simple touch warmed her all over. "There's nothing silly about feeling pain. You've had a lot of pain in your life. I wish I could take it away."

She shook her head, because she couldn't take the feel of his hand against her cheek another moment without acting on it. "I've been lucky in many ways."

He rested his arm on his knee. "Maybe."

It was an odd remark, and its implications shivered through her. As though he knew her doubts, as though he could see right into her soul. She'd gotten so good at pretending. No way could he, who knew her hardly at all, figure out what she'd told no one. The Boss groaned as he hefted himself from the floor and moved closer to Silas.

"Still think about your mom?"

"Every day," she said without thinking. What was it about Silas that made her open up? "She was my age when she died."

"And you're feeling very mortal."

Her eyes widened. "Stop it."

"Stop what?"

"Whatever it is that you're doing." She remembered the rumors she'd heard about him being strange. "You're scaring me."

His expression went still and dark. "Don't be afraid of me, Katie. You trusted me when no one else did."

"Tell me why you're back."

"It was something I had to do." The intense way he looked at her . . .

"Maybe I should go—"

"Tell me about your mom," he said at the same time, stopping her.

"What?" The word came out a whisper.

He leaned forward, not into her comfort zone, but still discomforting all the same. "Tell me what she was thinking just before she died. That's what you're searching for, isn't it? You're afraid that whatever got to her will get to you."

"Either explain how you know these things or stop saying them."

"Just talk to me."

She would have gotten up then, if he weren't so right. The sun was filtering through the tops of the trees on its descent. It was still light out, even though it was evening. But here on the porch, tucked beneath the massive oaks, it was cool and shadowy. Just like the man sitting next to her.

"She seemed fine," she said at last. "At least from a nine-year-old's point of view. She had a hard life, worked hard. She seemed to live in a world of fear and distrust, though I never understood why. We were dirt poor, but I thought we had it all. Just the two of us together forever, I thought. She wasn't happy with me hanging out at the hospital with Ben. Or you. She thought it was inappropriate. I was mad at her, because seeing Gus meant everything to me." So had seeing Silas. "I wanted to punish her by sneaking out and staying the night with a friend."

"It's not your fault."

"Logically, I know that my sneaking away didn't cause her to take her life. But I can't help thinking..." She looked into the trees again. "If I'd been there, maybe I could have done something."

"There's nothing you could have done. If she was determined to take her life, she would have found a way."

Katie nodded. "I didn't even know what it meant then, taking one's own life. I kept waiting for her to come back. When I went to stay with the Emersons, I would sit outside by the fence and wait for her at the end of the day. When the sun went down, I'd get so mad at her. It meant she wasn't coming again." She turned away from the sunlight. "I still hate sunsets."

"I don't remember much of my mom," he said, surprising her. "Just vague images. I was three when she ran headlong into a semi. The semi was in her lane."

"I'm sorry, Silas. I never knew that."

"No one knew. My father collected the insurance settlement and moved here. He didn't want anything to do with the people in town. They caused him nothing but trouble, meddling in the ways he parented, telling him how to live. So he kept us out here away from everyone. It annoyed him that I had to go to school, because I couldn't help him with his carvings. The truant office annoyed him, too. My father blamed me, promised to make sure I got to school."

"Why are you telling me this?" Why this, this very personal recollection from his life, when he wouldn't even tell her why he was back in town?

He leaned back against the column. "Because I've never told anyone before."

She felt her insides cave in, but she held her passive expression. "Oh." She wished she hadn't interrupted him when he remained silent. "Did you hate your father?"

"He represented everything I hated. Apathy. Selfishness. Violence."

She winced. "He hit you, didn't he?"

"He slapped me around once in a while, made me sleep in the woods when he wasn't happy with me. He handled everything violently." He wasn't looking at her now, but somewhere past her. "He took me hunting with him. I hated it. He had a place north of here, an old barn out in the middle of nowhere. He'd take me out for the weekend and make me shoot animals. Not just for food. He really enjoyed it, the killing part. The first time he let me shoot—made me shoot—he thought it was some kind of honor." This last word he said with a sneer. "I couldn't shoot the deer. It was standing right there. He jammed my finger on the trigger." He crooked his finger, making her aware of his long fingers. "Hurt like hell. The deer fell. We took it to the barn and skinned it. I hated that place even more than I hated him. It smelled like death. My father, he enjoyed all of it. The power, mostly. That he had power over another living creature. What makes someone evil like that? What makes them enjoy taking a life?"

He wasn't asking her those questions. His gaze was on the woods beyond. Still, she felt herself responding to the trace of agony that laced his voice.

To keep herself in check, she said, "I think I found that barn once. Dark red, with the foundation of a burned house nearby?" When he nodded, she said, "It gave me the creeps. I'd gone in a different direction that day, walking by myself. I never went that way again."

"My father loved that place. I hated it."

"I wish you'd had the kind of relationship my mama and I had."

His expression softened. "Thanks, Katie."

She wanted to thank him, too. For letting her talk about her mama for the first time since she could remember. For wanting to take away her pain. For making her feel more alive than she'd felt in a long time. But that last part made her get to her feet.

"I'd better go."

He took hold of her arm before she could move away.

"Katie . . ." He took one step down, looking at where he held her arm, then at her. Since she was one step above him, he was face-to-face with her. "Be careful, okay?"

She hadn't expected anything, really, especially not what he'd shared. But a warning, least of all.

"What do you mean?"

He hesitated, searching her eyes. "Just be careful who you trust."

"Does that include you, Silas?"

"Definitely."

"You said not to be afraid of you."

"I don't want you afraid of me. But I don't want you to trust me, either."

A warning. She needed that like a fish needed a fiddle.

Her first thought, after chastising herself for going to see Silas, was what a contradiction the man was. Touched that she'd trusted him years ago and telling her not to trust him now. Why had he come back? She hit the steering wheel. It was driving her crazy.

Her thoughts were abruptly returned to the present when she pulled down her driveway and saw a strange truck parked there.

CHAPTER 5

A KNOT TIGHTENED in Katie's throat. Before she even opened her car door, Ben and Morton Thorpe stepped out onto the porch. The knot grew bigger. The meeting should have lasted more than an hour, usually two. Both men walked toward her with hurried motions.

"Good grief, Katie, where have you been?" Ben started before she could say a word.

"Just . . . driving around. It was nice to have the van to myself for a change."

"Your husband's been out of his mind with worry," Morton said, as though he were speaking to a little girl. Or maybe as he talked to his daughter, Geraldine. "You ought to be ashamed of yourself, putting him through that."

Ben patted him on the back. "Thanks for the ride, Mort. And for being here for me."

"No problem, Ben. Anything for you, you know that. I don't blame you a bit for being worried, especially with . . ." He looked at her with watery gray eyes. "Well, you can handle things from here."

They both stood in silence as Morton pulled out of the drive. Katie had lied to Ben before, of course. Little lies, about liking the clothes he ordered for her, liking the decor in the house. Lies designed to save his feelings. But this was a big lie. She couldn't quite admit why she was reluctant to tell Ben about Silas. What if he saw something in her eyes, something that shouldn't be in a married woman's eyes?

"Katie, what got into you?"

"I didn't mean to worry you. I just wanted to"—enjoy

her freedom, that's what she wanted to say. When she wasn't with Ben, she was stuck at the house without a car—"take a drive, that's all."

He rubbed the back of his neck. She thought about Silas's words: where had the feisty Katie gone? But her mama hadn't been much of a fighter. Maybe you grew out of the feistiness.

"I'm sorry, Ben."

He pulled her close. "You can't blame a man for worrying about his wife. And with you acting so strange lately, hiding all the poisons in the house, talking about your mama dying . . . I called you, just to make sure you got home all right. I got a little worried after hearing . . ."

"What?"

"A girl went missing up toward Haddock last night. At first they thought she'd run away. The girl's mother locked her out after she missed curfew, trying to teach her a lesson. When she didn't turn up at school the next day, they started worrying. Sheriff told us at the beginning of the meeting that there's still no sign of her."

"Just like that hitchhiker that disappeared up by Milledgeville five months ago."

"Without a trace. They don't know if the cases are connected. This Haddock girl has gotten into some trouble in the past, so it might be something like that. But her boyfriend said she wasn't in any mood to run off when he dropped her at her house." He brushed the hair from her face. "And if she did, she would have run to him."

"I hope she's all right. But what does that have to do with me?"

"I was just worried, that's all."

Maybe if some of that feistiness remained in her, she could have pointed out that she didn't have to know where Ben was every minute. But he always wanted to know where she was. He did carry a beeper in case she needed him.

"Everything's fine. Why don't you go on back to the meeting?"

"I'd have missed half of it by the time I got back."

"What if I go with you and just sit in the back all quiet like?"

He kissed her forehead. "You're not part of the town council, sweetheart. Only members can sit in on the meeting. Even Harold's joined in. He and Sam Savino have butted heads a few times, but then again, Savino is a butthead."

She sighed. She wasn't even part of the town, but if she voiced that feeling, he would only tell her how silly that was. Of course she was part of town; she'd lived here her whole life.

He held her face again. "Katie, is there a problem? Are you really worried you might take your life like your mama? If you're that unhappy, you need to tell me, 'cause I can't bear to think of losing you. I know . . . things aren't right between us in some ways. In that way. You've told me it's okay, but maybe it's not."

They rarely talked about his impotency. It wasn't his fault the horse kicked him, but Ben was crushed anyway. He tried to make up for it by being affectionate in other ways. He'd asked her how she felt about it. But he never told her how he felt about it.

"I'm okay with that, but . . ."

As usual, he gave her his whole attention. "Tell me what you're feeling, Katie. I want to make you happy."

"I am happy. But I'd like . . ." This was hard to say, especially since the last time she'd brought it up, nothing had changed. "I'd like for us to explore . . . other kinds of pleasure." She didn't want him to know she'd been reading *Cosmo* and finding out what other women experienced. All those intriguing sex positions were out of her range, but there were other things, like oral sex, that would probably do just fine.

"I give you foot rubs," Ben said. "You make all those pleasurable noises."

"It does feel good. But I'd like . . . more."

He dropped his hands with a sigh and moved away.

"You know I feel so inadequate already, and now you're asking me for things, I don't even know where you're hearing about these things, but Katie, anything like that just makes it damn clear that I'm not enough for you. That everything I do for you, this house and a good life and all my love, isn't enough."

She took his hand, feeling that familiar crushing sense of responsibility and guilt. "It is enough. But the doctor said there wasn't any reason you couldn't come back from the injury. I just thought . . . never mind. It's not important," she said, feeling a sting in her eyes and not sure why. She stepped back. "Maybe if I . . . changed my hair. Or my looks. Maybe you just got bored with the way I look, or with me, and that's why . . ."

"You look fine."

She wasn't sure if Ben had ever looked at her in a sexual way. He had always loved her, but had he ever wanted her?

Silas's eyes flashed into her mind, the sultry way he'd assessed her that first night. Not lustily, but . . . interested.

She took Ben's hand. "Let's give each other foot rubs."

"Do I have a daddy, Mama? All the kids at school have one, even if he doesn't live with them."

"You have a daddy, 'course you do." She laughed, but her face didn't match the sound. "He's not around anymore. Someday I'll tell you about him, sweetness. When you're old enough to understand."

"What do I need to understand, Mama?"

Katie's mama squeezed her tighter as they sat by the creek and watched twigs float on by. "It's not simple to explain to a six-year-old."

"Will you tell me when I'm seven?"

She laughed again, but still her face looked so sad. Then that fierce look came over her, and she pinched Katie's cheeks affectionately. "Do we need a man around?" Katie shook her head. "No, we don't. 'Cause it's the two of us, together forever. That's all that matters, right?"

"Right." Katie settled back in front of her mama. "Just us, forever."

During a quiet moment the next afternoon, Ben listened to Katie and Bertrice outside with the two dogs they were boarding. The girls were giggling, though he wasn't close enough this time to hear what they were talking about. It bothered him to realize that Katie never giggled with him, never even laughed much. Was it Bertrice who was putting these sexual ideas in Katie's head?

He sometimes wondered if she realized how hard he worked to keep her happy. She was his life, and all he asked in return was that he be her life.

He couldn't say that he'd fallen in love with her the first time he'd ever seen her. That would be immoral, after all, since she had been nine. But her dusty tear-streaked face looking at him like he was her hero had snared his heart. He'd wanted to make her world a better place. He'd done his best to make it happen. He tried to be the perfect husband. Sometimes it helped to remind her how much he'd done for her. Lately, it didn't seem to be enough. It scared him to think she'd leave him. He loved her more than anything.

The Great Dane dodged between them in their game of chase, sending Katie butt-down on the spongy grass. She was laughing so hard, she could barely get back to her feet. The strands of hair around her face were damp. She was pretty, prettier than he wanted her to realize. If she doubted her beauty, if she thought that maybe it was her plainness that kept him from sustaining an erection, then maybe she wouldn't go looking for an outlet elsewhere. That thought was worth the hurt look on her face when she tried to take the blame for his condition. In truth, sex just wasn't that important in his relationship with Katie.

He stepped out onto the porch, but the girls were having too much fun to even notice him. At least the cat that prowled the porch said hello, rubbing against his leg. He scratched behind her ears, mindful of the site of surgery.

The fenced-in yard was small, but plenty of room for a rambunctious Dalmatian mix and a Great Dane.

"I'm going to get an iced tea," he said. "You girls want one?"

Katie pushed her hair out of her face as she noticed him at last. "I'll walk with you. I've got to pick up some milk."

He liked the idea of her walking with him, and he held her hand as they crossed the street and headed up the cracked sidewalk.

"Meet you right here," he said as he headed into the diner.

She read the pink flier in the diner's window now begging for volunteers. Then she went next door to the grocery mart.

He liked that everyone greeted him when he walked in. It meant a lot to be accepted. Well, everyone greeted him except for the dark-haired stranger in the booth by the door. He looked familiar, but he wasn't one of Flatlands's residents. He figured he knew just about everyone. This is what the town council wanted, more strangers, more business.

Sitting in a booth nearby was the stranger who'd been born in Flatlands, Gary Savino. After disappointing his father by becoming a cop in Atlanta, he'd returned six months ago. Not to reconcile with his father, Sam, but to become a county cop. Word was, he was just as arrogant as ever, and Ben could believe that with the way Gary was slumped in a booth by himself. His dark hair was cut short, and his brown eyes watched everyone with silent recrimination. Judging, it seemed, who measured up and who didn't. As though that uniform gave him the right. Ben had caught him watching Katie on occasion, but in a different way.

"You ever find out what your wife was doing?" Dinah asked as she got Ben's sweetened tea ready.

"Get me two more for the girls," he said, nodding to the pitcher. "Driving around, she said. Sorry I missed the meeting. Katie wanted me to stick around after the scare and all."

Dinah set the Styrofoam cup on the counter. "I sure hope

that woman appreciates you. There are plenty of women around here who'd be glad to take her place."

Harold, who was sitting one stool away, said, "Dinah, if you're gonna flirt with anybody, do it with me. I'm not even married! I asked you to marry me, what, a hundred times and each time you said no." He crossed his bulky arms in front of him, doing his best to look hurt, which was an amusing prospect with a beast of a man like Harold. Especially with the tic that throbbed intermittently on his right eyelid.

She lowered her dark lashes. "I wasn't flirting, and I ain't in the market for no husband. I got everything I need right here." She lifted her eyebrow. "And in my drawer at home."

Ben cleared his throat, then eyed the display of handmade chocolate lollipops. "I'll get one of these for Katie, too."

Harold said, "Dinah, when you gonna stop trying to culturize us with this snooty music! Last week it was that island stuff, this week, instruments."

"It's contemporary jazz, and if you had a speck of culture, you'd have known that. All you all are is a bunch of farmhands wanting nothing but country music." Dinah picked up the remote and changed the satellite from the music station to the qualifying rounds of a Nascar race. She bagged up the teas and lollipop and handed them to Ben. "I'll put it on the tab," she said, the tab being a nonexistent bill. He'd helped her horse at no charge and she never forgot it. That's the kind of gratitude that touched him.

Sam Savino strolled in wearing his usual tweed suit. Ben could respect a man who prided himself on his professionalism. Ben, however, wouldn't count himself among Sam's friends; the man was as arrogant as a bear. He had impossibly high standards. They nodded to each other with barely a smile.

Sam stiffened when he saw his son in the far booth, then did what he usually did, which was ignore him. He slid onto one of the stools and said to Dinah, "How fresh is the iced tea?"

She glanced at the clock. "Two hours. I know, I know, I'll brew up a fresh pot."

Something made a chirping noise. Several men glanced at their belts to check beepers. Then Gary slid out of the booth, his shoulders stiffer than usual, and rushed out of the diner.

Katie was standing outside the diner staring so intently at the stranger she didn't even see Gary's eyes on her as he walked past. The stranger was talking to Geraldine Thorpe, who was working at the diner after school to help pay for college. She seemed more interested in the man in the booth than whether anyone needed a refill of sweet tea.

Ben stepped outside, and Katie blinked and laughed nervously. "Didn't even see you come out. Got the milk."

He took her hand and headed out. This time, the stranger was watching Katie.

"Who are they?" Silas asked his waitress, who was a cute brunette and a bit of a flirt.

"Oh, that's Dr. Ferguson. He's just the nicest person you'll ever know. He's the town vet."

"And who's that with him?"

Geraldine's warm tone of voice cooled. "That's his wife, Katie."

He stretched out beneath the table. "Sounds like you don't like her much."

She lifted her shoulder. "Don't really know her that well. She's nice enough at the animal hospital and all, but she never comes into town much, never participates in much. She's not really that friendly, you know? Bertrice says she's pretty nice—she works over there after school."

Silas wanted to ask more, but that would surpass casual interest. No one but Katie had seemed to recognize him. That was fine. The longer it was before they knew who he was, the more opportunity he'd have to nose around and ask questions.

"Is there any word on that missing girl?" he asked.

"No. It's scary. I hope she just ran away or something. I don't want to think there's someone out there kidnapping teenagers. We've always felt so safe around here. Nothing happens more than a guy beating up on his wife or getting drunk, that kind of thing. Once the Sherwin boys lit some firecrackers and threw them in our horse pen. The horses went crazy, I tell you. My pa was fit to be tied. Those boys spent a couple of days in jail over that."

The problem with the darkness that Silas lived in, with what he did for a living, was that whenever he talked with girls like Geraldine, he pictured their photo in the newspaper with the caption "missing." He summed up their features, their attributes, all the sweetness and ambition and talent wasted because some creep decided they should be dead.

He tossed his money on the table, including a large tip, and headed out into the sultry day. Katie and Ben were just two squiggles in the distance. An old junk barn across the street was closed up for lunch, and beyond that, the town turned rural.

He didn't like what he'd learned so far about Katie. She was isolated, both physically and socially. Even the hospital was set off by itself. Only the souls of the dead were near enough to hear her scream, if she had reason to. The safest thing he could do was stay away from her. It was a bad combination, her long-standing dissatisfaction, their attraction. He had no intention of interfering with her marriage, which was why he'd stayed away for so long. Until it became necessary to get closer to her.

But not too close.

CHAPTER 6

"WHAT DO YOU think?" Katie lifted her arms and twirled around. The yellow hip-huggers were a little too small, but seeing her hips encased in them, the thin slice of flesh between them and the flower-print top, made her feel sexy. Like one of those cover models on *Cosmo*.

Ben glanced up from the paper. She could already see his answer in his eyes. "Where'd you get that from?"

"Bertrice dropped off some of her old clothes while you were picking up the bags of soil for me." Bertrice had pulled in with the old Chevy she'd just bought. Geraldine and another teen were in the car, ready for a Saturday of driving around. "Just for something different." She smoothed her hands over her hips.

"You look like some hippie leftover."

"This is what's in style right now, or was recently anyway." The jeans flared slightly at the bottom and flowed over her bare feet. "Come on, it's at least different from what I usually wear."

"Katie, what's going on with you lately? Aren't you happy? Is that what this is about?" He gestured toward her outfit.

She sat on the footstool in front of Ben. He looked regal in the thronelike chair. "No, of course not. I'm just bored with—"

"Me," he stated flatly.

"No, I'm bored with myself. You must be bored with me, too."

"Don't be ridiculous." He set the paper down and rubbed her knee. "I like you just the way you are. I don't like these changes. They make me think you're dissatisfied with your life, a life I've worked very hard to provide."

"That's not true." The words stuck in her throat.

"This isn't about having a baby, is it?"

She shook her head and pushed out, "I'm fine with that." They'd had the discussion a few times. Early in their marriage, Ben wanted to wait so he could enjoy having her all to himself. And then the accident had happened. He said it would be too expensive to go to a fertility clinic. But oh, she did want a baby. Maybe not now, but someday. "Can I wear this tonight at least? Then I'll give it back to Bertrice."

He glanced down at the outfit, then returned to his paper. "If you must."

He sounded a lot like a father. She cut a glance to the dollhouse.

"Merry Christmas, darling." Ben uncovered the spectacularly intricate Victorian dollhouse.

She sank to the floor in front of it, reliving girlhood longings for something this beautiful. Every room was finished with the smallest of details. "It's . . . amazing." She reached in to touch the flocked wallpaper and knocked over a tiny glass lamp.

"For Pete's sake, be careful! Don't touch, just look."

She hadn't touched it since.

She went back to the kitchen to finish getting supper ready, feeling disappointment eat away at her. It didn't matter anyway; who else ever saw her except Ben?

She watched two of her squirrels chase each other up and down the trees near the feeders. They spiraled round and round, and through the open window she could hear their nails scrape against the trunks. One was No-tail, her name for him. The other was Missy-Lou. They didn't realize it, but they were her pets. She was so depressed after Gus's death, Ben said no more pets for her. She got too attached. Obviously that was true, since even just recently she'd cried over his death.

"That girl over Haddock way still hasn't shown up yet,"

Ben said from the living room, forcing her to leave the kitchen and ask him to repeat it.

"I hope she's only teaching her mama a lesson for locking her out. How terrible."

He snapped the paper open to a new page. "You might want to keep that in mind, that there might be someone out there hunting women, as you're driving around by yourself."

"I will."

She went back into the kitchen and stirred the gravy. One of her cardinal couples alighted on her bird feeder, and she watched them for a moment. The female, the duller of the cardinals, landed on the ledge first and started eating. The bright red male bumped her off, though, and she flew to a nearby bush and waited. Katie always wanted to tell her to go on the other side of the feeder, that there was room enough for both of them. The female flitted around, waiting her turn. Then the male took off, and she followed.

"Katie, you haven't eaten your lollipop yet," Ben said, again forcing her to walk to the living room to hear him.

She eyed the red-colored rose pop. "I don't want to spoil dinner. I'll have it for dessert."

She hated chocolate. None of the Emersons could believe that any child could dislike chocolate, but she did. Ben couldn't believe it, either, when he'd brought her an Easter basket one year. She'd eaten the chocolate rabbit out of guilt, exclaiming that for chocolate it wasn't bad. Now and then he still bought her a chocolate something or another. Sometimes a Valentine's Day box of the stuff. She always made a fuss over it, for the thought. It was a pattern she'd fallen into years ago and it was going to be impossible to break out of. She'd been pretending to like the Victorian decor for so long, how could she tell Ben that she hated it now.

She glanced down at the yellow jeans again and sighed. And when someone gave her something she actually liked, she was going to have to give it back.

What happened to you, Katie? Silas's voice echoed in her mind.

Damn him for asking! Marriage was compromise. Ben would never tolerate her being the way she was as a child. And that child had learned young that you paid for everything in life, every kindness and advantage. After her mother had left her in a chasm of darkness, finding security had become the most important thing in the world.

She caught a reflection of her waist in the toaster oven. She really liked this outfit. Damn it, she didn't want to give it back. Maybe she'd keep it and wear it when Ben wasn't around.

So there, Silas.

The dining area was in the kitchen and overlooked the small garden with her two newly planted azalea bushes and the gazebo. A soft breeze filtered into the kitchen. Birds were singing and chirping and sounding a lot like a pet store she'd been in once. At the distant humming noise, she couldn't resist looking out the window to try to spy the plane. At last it appeared in the opening of trees with the sun glinting off the metal. People were on that plane, going somewhere.

"Katie, I really wish you'd changed before dinner," Ben said, his unhappy gaze on her shirt.

The material was thin and stretchy. Because of the scoop neckline, she'd discovered her bra straps had shown, so she'd taken it off. It was just her husband around anyway. But he didn't look the least bit intrigued by the way the material sculpted her breasts and made the flowers look bigger. Maybe if she were more than a B-cup, he'd like them better.

"I'll change after dinner."

He punished her with silence. She thought about getting up and changing, just so they could talk.

What happened to you, Katie?

Damn you, Silas.

She remained at the table, feeling uglier by the minute.

Sometimes she just didn't like Ben much. It was a better feeling than not liking herself.

"Ben—"

"I really don't want to talk to you until you change. You look like a teenager, and it doesn't suit you."

Her muscles tensed, but she kept her seat at the table. God but she'd become a wimp. How had it happened?

Slowly.

She pushed the plate of baked chicken away. "I saw the poster asking people to help at the fair. They crossed off 'need help' and added 'begging for help.' " Still he didn't reply, instead working the crossword puzzle—in pen, as usual. "I want to help. I know you don't want to be all by yourself at the fair, but you wouldn't be alone for long anyway the way people around here love you. But you could help out, too. We could work together. How about that?"

"No."

Flattened with one word. "Why not?"

He set down the paper and looked at her. "I do stuff for people all day long. I don't feel like doing stuff for them at the fair. I want to enjoy it, and I want to enjoy it with my wife. I don't understand why you can't be happy that I want to spend time with you. Why are you obsessed with helping at this fair?"

She stood and picked up her plate. "Because I want to belong to this town. I know you think I'm imagining it, but I am invisible here. Everybody greets you like you're their best friend. I'm the stuff you stepped in."

"You're not going to let this go, are you?"

She squared her shoulders and felt the rush of independence. "No," she said just as succinctly as he had.

"Katie, I don't know what's got into you lately, but I am not going to tolerate it. You think about what you want in life, and how much I've done for you." He grabbed up the keys to the van and walked out.

If they had a spat, which was unusual, she always ran after him and gave in.

She let him go this time.

He would probably go to the diner. She looked at the four pieces of chicken and the bowl of mashed potatoes on the table. If she couldn't volunteer at the fair, then she'd do another charitable deed. After all, Silas probably didn't have a refrigerator.

Ben couldn't understand it. He'd done nothing wrong, nothing differently, yet Katie was changing. She hadn't even run after him to smooth things out.

He'd gotten to thinking that maybe she'd wanted him to leave, so he'd parked at the end of the driveway and walked back to the house. That's when he'd seen her walking into the woods wearing that whoring outfit. He'd gone farther down the road and pulled a short distance down the long, shadowed drive. The sunlight reflected on a car, though he couldn't see what kind it was.

He thought about going home and raising a fuss about her being gone, making her feel bad for wandering in the woods when she should have been home waiting for him to cool down. But it obviously hadn't done any good last time. Instead he drove into town and the comfort of the diner.

It was past the dinner rush, though still Saturday-night busy. He sidled up to the counter and ordered the blue-plate special, or the "featured menu item" as Dinah called it.

She gave him a curious look. "Where's your wife? Don't she cook for you no more?"

"Katie's going through something right now. I'm just trying to be a good husband, give her some space."

"She'd be a fool to make you unhappy. Why, what would she be without you?"

"I just hope she realizes that. And she will, I'm sure of it."

When Dinah turned in his order, he swiveled around on the stool and nodded to several people he knew. Marion Tate, self-appointed town busybody, was holding court with a group of people in the far corner. Her husband the sheriff sat next to her. Marion waved him over.

"How are y'all doing?" Ben asked everyone with a sweeping nod.

"How's it going?" Marvin Bale asked.

"It's going to the dogs, that's how it's going."

The table laughed pleasantly, amazing Ben that they never tired of the saying. As long as he got a reaction, he'd keep on saying it.

"Where's Katie?" Marion asked after surveying the diner. "Seems strange a married man eating by his lonesome."

"Marion, mind your own damn business," her husband muttered. The sheriff looked like Mel Gibson with a paunch. If his wife was the queen of Flatlands, he was surely the king.

Marion patted the table after giving her husband a pinched look. "You'll just sit here with us, no question about it."

Their dessert plates littered the table, along with blue ceramic coffee cups. "Looks like you're in the middle of something. Don't want to butt in."

"Nonsense," Marion said. "Marv, just clear that spot next to you. No man should eat alone, that's what I always say."

"Why, thank you, Marion. Appreciate your thoughtfulness." Ben went back to the counter to pick up his soda.

He met Sam Savino's grim gaze as he turned back to the table. Sam was there with his wife, Clarice. He was dark haired and olive skinned, traits he'd passed on to his son, Gary. His disowned son, that was. Ben wasn't sure if the perpetual sneer on his face was voluntary or just the way his face was made. Seeing as Gary had the same sneer, Ben figured it was the genes. Clarice was fair in looks and coloring, always quiet and looking as though the world had just pissed on her.

Ben stopped at their table. "Evening, folks."

Clarice only nodded and averted her gaze to her cream pie. Sam did what he always did: appraised Ben and made it clear he didn't like what he saw. "Don't you ever take your wife out to dinner?"

Ben blinked at the rude statement. "Sir, may I ask what you have against me? A man's entitled to know why another man doesn't like him."

"And a man's entitled to dislike someone and not explain why."

Ben took a step back when Sam pushed out of the booth. He hated feeling afraid, but Sam outweighed him by fifty or more pounds, and it was all muscle. "Let's go, Clarice," Sam said and pushed by Ben.

She glanced longingly at her unfinished pie, but followed dutifully.

"Don't worry about them," Marion said, obviously having watched the exchange. "Sam's a grump, always has been. He's got a big ole block of ice right where his heart ought to be. I thought he and Gary were going to get into fisticuffs the other day, right here in the diner. Can you imagine, a father and son who hate each other that much? And both of them on the side of the law?" She made a prim tsking sound.

Ben took a seat between Marvin and Harold just as Dinah brought out his salad.

"What's this lumpy white stuff?" Ben asked.

"Goat cheese. It's very chic. Just try it."

Eating goat anything didn't appeal. After Ben gave his salad to Harold, who ate everything, he said, "I don't want you thinking something's wrong. Katie's just going through a phase, is all. Everything'll turn out fine."

"Oh, good," Marion said on an exhalation, as though she'd been holding her breath to find out what the scoop was.

Sheriff Tate rolled his eyes. "Now everyone in town'll know about it."

"I just don't want people to worry about me," Ben said, feeling good that people did worry. But he didn't want to dwell on it. "So, what are you all doing here?"

"Working out the county fair details. We're really behind, and we've lost some of our usual volunteers. Pauline's got mono. Calvin broke his leg. Paul and Mary moved to Macon." Marion sent a smiling look his way. "I know you're busy with the farm calls and all, but what about your wife? It would give us the chance to get to know her."

"I can ask her again. I mentioned it a while back, when I saw the sign in the window. I said, 'Katie, you ought to see how you can help out.' But she said, 'I don't want to get involved in that silly fair.' I gotta badger her into just going to it."

Marion's shoulders raised two inches. Her face was red as she looked around at the others. "Well, I guess we won't ask her to get involved, then."

"Sorry, Marion. I didn't mean to make you angry. I probably shouldn't have repeated what Katie said."

"No, I'm glad you did. I might have asked her to help out."

"Well, we'll be there to support you on the big day, don't you worry about that." Ben took the plate of veal marsala from Dinah and dug in while the others decided how to line up the game booths.

And God, please look out for that missing girl from Haddock. Please let her be all right. Please look out for all those women in bad places. And please fix my heart so I'll be happy with Ben.

Patches of early evening sunlight danced on the leaves as Katie walked through the woods. The scent of warm leaves and earth had her inhaling deeply.

She hadn't prayed in a while. Too long. She and her mama had gotten down on their knees together every night and prayed for women who were victims. There were so many, in the news, famous and unknown. She clutched the plastic container with the chicken and the chocolate pop on top of it. She'd debated heavily on that. Would Silas take it as a romantic gesture, being a rose and all? Or should she tell him it was a gift from Ben and she hated chocolate so was giving it to him? Why was life so complicated?

Branches pulled at her shirt, and she wrapped her arms tight around her as she twined through the trees. The warm breeze ruffled through the bright green leaves. Birds whooped and called, and a woodpecker chattered as it glided gracefully from tree to tree. One bird even screeched like the sound effect from *Psycho*'s shower scene. Her sneakers crunched softly on the leaves and then the forest transformed to the grand oaks.

This time she didn't attempt to hide. She walked into the small clearing that surrounded the house. Silas was sitting on a rocking chair on the front porch watching for her, his feet up on the railing. The Boss was lying in the yard. He lifted his head and twitched his nose at her. Silas shrugged into a shirt and descended the steps in one smooth motion. She caught the glint of his gold cross against his collarbone as he moved through the filtered sunlight.

Coming here had seemed unselfish and innocent while she'd been convincing herself of her motives. But seeing the slice of bare chest and the mussed hair that brushed his shoulders made it seem like something more sinful.

"I brought you some dinner," she said on a rush of words, shoving the container at him. "And dessert," she added when he looked down at her offering. "I don't like chocolate." This wasn't coming out right at all.

He didn't take her offering. Instead, his smoky gaze took her in and made her realize how she was dressed. "That's a nice change from the way I've seen you dressed before."

A glance down revealed puckered nipples showing through the fabric. She crossed her arms in front of her. "It belongs to the girl who works with me. It's probably way too young for me."

A faint smile flickered in his eyes when he said, "Works for me."

Realizing he'd never taken the food, she covered her breasts with one arm and held out the container again. "We had some leftover food. I don't know if you have anything to heat it up with, but it'd probably be okay cold."

"I'm fine, thanks." He glanced beyond her to the general direction of her house. "Where's Ben?"

"In town."

He studied her for a moment, making her feel as though

he were reading her soul, knowing about the fight.

"I'd better get going," she said. It was dumb, bringing the food. And the way he was looking at her made it nearly cross the line into dangerous. She was married and had no intention of breaking her vow.

He nodded toward the porch. "Come up and have a drink before you head back. You look thirsty." Before waiting for her response, he walked back to the porch. His movements were fluid with lupine grace. And those eyes could definitely belong to a wolf sizing up his prey. He turned to find her still standing there. "Don't worry, I'm not going to eat you up."

She nearly choked at that, but pushed herself forward. "Maybe just a quick drink."

Could he know her throat was tight and dry? Could he know the reason wasn't the long walk? She followed, setting her rejected food on the railing.

A notepad covered in his scribbles sat askew atop a stack of folders on the faded boards of the porch. There was also a map, a cell phone, and a beeper beneath an open box holding two slices of pepperoni and mushroom pizza. He held out the rocking chair to her. Her legs were a bit wobbly, probably from the walk, so she sank onto the wooden chair.

"Pizza?" he asked when he saw her looking at the box.

"You don't take my food, so I won't take yours."

He lifted one edge of his mouth. "One has nothing to do with the other. Giving and receiving," he clarified. "Water or chocolate milk?" he asked, holding up a dripping bottle of each from the cooler.

She could see his own bottle of Nestle's chocolate milk on the railing. "Water, please."

He opened it and handed it to her. One of the cold drops of water dripped on her arm. He leaned against the railing in front of her, looking completely at ease. He picked up his bottle and took a swig. His neck was long, and she felt something shift inside her as she watched the muscles move as he swallowed. She looked away when he stopped drinking. She didn't understand these strange feelings that eased through her body the way wine did on an empty stomach. She took a drink. Because she could feel him watching her the way she'd been watching him, she got nervous and dribbled down her chin. She rubbed it with the sleeve of her shirt.

"Is that why you came here tonight?" he asked, nodding toward the food container.

"Yes. And . . . I just needed a walk." She glanced down at the array of paperwork on the floor. "Did I interrupt you?"

"A beautiful nymph materializes out of the forest as if by magic, and you think I'd mind?"

"I'm not beautiful." The words rushed out before she could even think to stop them.

He crossed his arms in front of him, framing a square of tan, flat stomach between his arms and the waistband of his faded jeans. "You really don't think you're beautiful, do you? What would you rate yourself on a scale of one to ten?"

Her fingers tightened on the worn edge of the chair arms. "That's silly. I don't rate myself." He waited, sending a shiver through her as he studied her. "Okay, a five."

"You're serious?"

"I don't want to talk about this anymore. Who cares about scales?"

"Nine."

"What?" Her throat tightened all over again, despite the recent wash of water.

"I'd say you're a nine. Definitely. Ten with makeup, I bet."

She opened her mouth to protest, but he was serious. She should never have worn this outfit over here. "It's just the clothes," she said at last.

He lifted an eyebrow. "I bet you look just as good without them."

Did he mean naked? She didn't allow herself to even think about it. "I'd better get back, in case Ben returns . . ."

She pushed out of the chair, only to find herself face-to-face with him. He touched her, running his thumb down her chin as he held her face. She heard herself inhale, but couldn't make herself move away.

To her horror, her chin trembled. His eyes were amazing up close like this as they looked into hers. Smoky blue, full of secrets and shadows. His thumb slid over her lower lip, making the trembling worse.

"You're not a five, Katie," he said, his voice as smoky as his eyes. "Whoever's been telling you that is lying."

She wanted to say that no one had told her that, it was just what she'd assumed given all indications. But she couldn't say anything at the moment. Her heart was hammering so loud it felt like an earthquake. How could he do this to her with just a simple, innocent touch that didn't make her feel innocent at all?

"I didn't come here to interfere with your marriage," he said.

And then in total contradiction of that, he slid his hand up her cheek and pulled her close. When his mouth touched hers, it felt as though her heart exploded. Like Silas had plugged her in and sent a surge of electricity to places long dormant. His mouth moved against hers for a few moments, and his nose brushed against hers.

He moved back, leaving her straining for more. Then embarrassment and shame washed over her just as desire had moments ago. She covered her mouth.

He turned his cheek to her. "Go ahead and slap me."

Slap him? Heck, she wanted him to kiss her again! She stumbled back, nearly tripping on the rocking chair. "Why'd you come back here, Silas? Tell me."

"I'm not ready to tell you yet, Katie. But I will."

She didn't like the grim look on his face. "Don't do that. Don't kiss me again."

She grabbed up her container; the chocolate rose dropped to the steps. She left it there and tried not to run. What worried her most was that Silas hadn't responded. But something else worried her more: the feeling that she was the reason for his return.

⌒ CHAPTER 7

KATIE RAN THROUGH the woods, using the exertion to clear her head. Kissing Silas . . . well, that wasn't supposed to have happened. She had to take responsibility for putting herself in the position. Maybe that's what she wanted.

But she couldn't have it.

Silas was an unknown quantity, and he made no effort to change that. He didn't settle down. That's all she knew about him. And what about the weird way he could tell what she was thinking?

Birds scattered at the sound of her pounding footsteps. The dying sunlight filtered through the trees once she exited the deep forest of evergreens. Now her shirt had pulls all over it. It was just as well. She wasn't going to wear it again.

That's what it was; the clothes made her do it!

A sheen of sweat covered her, and sticks tangled in her hair. She hoped Ben wasn't there. She needed some time to gather herself.

Though she didn't deserve the luck, it came in the form of the empty driveway. She tossed her clothes in the back of the closet and jumped into the cold shower. She was wrapped in a robe by the time Ben returned home.

She was sure guilt was splashed all over her face, but Ben pulled her into his arms.

"I'm sorry, honey. I shouldn't have gotten so mad at you. You can't blame a guy for wanting his wife to himself, can you?"

He pulled back and waited for her answer. She could

only shake her head, thinking she'd never kissed anyone other than Ben until tonight.

"I'm sorry, too, Ben." She couldn't tell him how sorry.

"I want you to volunteer at the fair."

"Really? Are you going to volunteer, too?"

"No, but don't worry about me. You do whatever it is you're going to do. You're right. Even if I'm not with you, I'll be among friends."

Her smile faded, but she plastered it back on. Maybe they'd accept her, and she could say that, too.

When the doorbell rang, she had the terrifying feeling it was Silas coming to apologize for kissing her. When Ben answered the door, she wasn't sure which was worse: Silas or Gary Savino.

She could see his official vehicle parked outside, the Explorer painted in the county colors. He was in full uniform, looking arrogant enough to rule the world. She'd done her best to avoid him in the last six months. She couldn't help remembering the time he'd cornered her outside the grocery store right after she'd married Ben. He'd wanted to talk to her about Gus. He'd pinned her against the wall, but she'd slipped out and run inside.

Gary's dark hair was slicked away from his face. He was muscular and wore shirts small enough to show off the muscles he obviously worked so hard for. His presence in the security of her home unnerved her.

"Mr. Ferguson," he said with a nod, then slid his dark-eyed gaze to her. "Katie." Just the way he said her name in that drawn-out way slithered down her spine. "Sheriff said you mentioned someone being out at the old Koole place, and he asked me to check up on it. I wanted to get some details." He flipped open his small notepad. Instead of looking at Ben, like most people did, he looked at Katie. "You think someone's at the house?"

She looked at Ben, totally lost. Had he known she'd been over there?

Ben said, "I saw a car in the driveway. Or at least the reflection of the sun against a bumper."

Is that all he'd seen? Her chest felt paralyzed. She pushed out, "It was probably the sun reflecting off the windows."

Gary hadn't taken his brown eyes off her, even while Ben spoke. "There ain't no glass in the windows. They're all boarded up."

"I'd appreciate you checking it out," Ben said. "Katie insists on wandering around in the woods, and with that girl disappearing up near Haddock, it worries me to death."

"Carrie Druthers was a troublemaker. Probably deserved what she got." Gary finally shifted his gaze from her to the house. No telling what he thought about the interior. He strolled around at his leisure. "Interesting place you got here. Kinda like a girl's dollhouse." His gaze alighted on the dollhouse itself.

Ben beamed at the compliment, if that's what it was. "I wanted to give Katie the kind of place she'd never had as a girl. Secure and cozy."

She just wanted Gary to leave, and she wanted him to leave Silas alone. "If we see anything suspicious over there, we'll call you."

Gary didn't seem to hear her. He finished his scan of the living area, including her with her candy-pink robe and slippers with the bunny faces Ben had bought her last Christmas. "Nice shoes."

Was he being sarcastic? She automatically tucked them within the folds of her robe. "I really don't think you need to check out the Koole place."

Ben asked, "Any reason he shouldn't check it out, Katie?"

Guilt bloomed on her face. If he knew and she lied . . . "Silas is there."

Silence fell like a leaden sunset. Both men looked as though she'd admitted she'd kissed the man. She shrugged. "When I went for a walk earlier, I discovered him there." Not a lie, technically. "I haven't seen him in years, didn't know he'd returned to town. Anyway, I didn't figure it was a big deal, him being there. He wasn't doing anything illegal and he did live there once."

Gary's expression hardened. "Doesn't mean he has any business being there now. It's owned by that snobby corporation, and even if they are jerks, Silas don't have any right to be there."

"But—"

Ben squeezed her shoulder. "Katie, let him check it out." Each word carried the weight of a stone.

Gary watched their exchange with interest. His hand rested comfortably on his baton handle. She shifted her gaze to Ben. He was telling her to let it go. After they'd just made up, after he'd acceded to let her volunteer at the fair, she didn't want to go against him.

What happened to you, Katie?

A memory slipped into her mind, that feisty little girl who insisted on reporting Gary. Who feared nothing. Who did everything with passion.

"He'll probably be gone in a few days," Katie said, moving out of Ben's grasp. "He's not doing anything wrong. Leave him be."

Ben's voice sounded hard. "He has no right to be here." He looked at Katie with cold eyes. "I don't trust him."

The leather holster on Gary's waist squeaked as he moved to the door. "Don't worry, Dr. Ferguson. The lowlife has no business being there. I'll see to it that he's gone by morning."

Ben nodded. "I knew you'd handle things."

Gary didn't warm to the compliment the way others did. He looked at Katie once more before walking out onto the porch. Once the door closed, Ben said, "Is that what this is all about?"

"What?"

"Your mood, your wandering around . . ."

"No!" She crossed her arms over her chest and walked into the kitchen. "I just want . . ."

"What?" He followed her.

She looked at her gazebo in the waning light. Her space.

Her garden. She wanted too damn much. "I just want you."
She moved into Ben's arms, wishing it were true.

He breathed out in relief, she suspected. "Good. That's
all I want, too."

Gary remained outside the door, trying to listen to their
conversation. Ben was pissed, that much he could tell. Katie
was up to something. There was guilt written all over that
pretty face. Surely she wasn't messing with Silas Koole.

He walked quietly down the steps to his truck. He'd
gotten the old Explorer when he'd joined the county sheriff's office, which entitled him to all the rural calls in the
far reaches of the county. He'd been to every corner, every
piece of crap house and doublewide and places nobody
even knew existed.

He glanced at the house one more time before climbing
into the truck. Just in case Katie was watching. Seems like
his life had gotten screwed up since tangling with her and
her stupid cat. His father may have taken his side to the
town, but he'd beaten the piss out of him privately. Sam
only hit him where it wouldn't show. He'd learned that with
Gary's mother. And who would believe such an upstanding
citizen as Sam Savino was a brute? Who would dare go up
against him? Well, Katie had tried.

Sam had called Gary trash and trouble and every foul
word in the English language. Even a few in Italian. He'd
shipped him off to a military school in Atlanta, and that's
where he'd stayed upon graduating. After one semester at
college, he'd walked out and never looked back. He was
tired of being the one who listened and obeyed. He wanted
to be the one someone else obeyed. Becoming a cop had
been the answer. Women dug the uniform, and people respected and listened to him. Everyone except his father,
who spit on him when he'd learned that instead of becoming an attorney he'd become a cop.

Everything had gone well in Atlanta until a few sissy
suspects had complained that Gary had hit them. His girl-
friend filed assault charges against him, even though she'd

hit him first. A woman accused him of using intimidation inappropriately. His superiors had been intimidated by Gary's ambition and determination. They made him take an anger-management course, and when he hadn't cooperated with the instructor, he'd been asked to resign nice and quiet like. That stupid course had changed everything, though, when he'd discovered the real reason for his anger. So he'd returned to Flatlands to confront his father.

Katie was part of the reason he'd come back. Her accusing eyes had haunted him over the years. He'd thought about her a lot, about what he'd done to her cat. About why he'd done it. Anger. Rage. Resentment that no one could understand. He had a confession to make, but only to Katie and only when the time was right. One of these days he'd get her alone.

He turned down the leaf-covered drive that disappeared into the murky forest. He'd always hated this place, but he'd hated Silas more. Spooky Silas the kids had called him. Gary couldn't even remember why. Maybe because he hadn't been intimidated by Gary back in school. He was the one kid who'd just stare at him, ignore his threats with a blank, cold look on his face. Then he'd stood by Katie when she'd accused him of throwing her kitten. The jerk hadn't even been there.

He glanced at his reflection in the rearview mirror. A fine line ran from the corner of his right eye to his hairline. Katie had done that when she'd attacked him. Because he'd picked at it, it had scarred. She'd put her mark on him. He was willing to forgive her for that if she forgave him.

The house loomed out of the woods, as creepy as he remembered it. He'd come out here a few months back, just to see if the old building was still around. As a deputy, he needed to know where everything was. The creepy part was that it wasn't as derelict as he'd expected. Like someone used it occasionally, kept it up.

This time, though, a car twice as nice as his own was parked in front of the house. Lights were on, and the first floor had windows. Silas was standing in the doorway looking the same insolent way he always did, like a wild animal protecting his territory. A big brown dog stood on the porch in front of him.

Gary waited in his truck for a minute or two, just to make Silas wonder. Then he took his time getting out, making sure his gun and baton were within sight. No way was this punk going to forget who had the power here.

Silas was already walking toward him, still not looking the least concerned. His hair was months overdue for a cut. Damned nonconformist. "What's the problem . . . Officer?"

Now he knew where he'd seen Silas before—in the diner. Now that he thought about it, the guy hadn't changed much since high school. Still tall and rangy, still taller than Gary, though less bulked up. Gary could take him, if it came to that.

"What are you doing on this property? It's private."

"I thought it was private until now."

Gary straightened his shoulders and rested the palm of his hand on the baton. "I'm gonna ask you again, what are you doing here?"

Silas didn't look intimidated, but he did answer. "I'm staying here for a few days."

"You're going to have to vacate the premises. You're trespassing."

"Why don't you contact the owner and see if he minds?"

"You some kind of smart-ass? It's a company in Atlanta, and unless you have their permission, you're trespassing. Period. I'll give you an hour to pack up and get the hell out of here."

Silas turned away right in the middle of his threat. He sauntered to the steps. "I'm not going anywhere."

Rage burned red in Gary's head. He was about to find out if he could take Silas. "Then I'm arresting you for trespassing." He pulled out his baton and his cuffs. It was going to be sweet joy to cuff the son of a bitch and shove him in his vehicle. And if he resisted, even sweeter.

Silas turned around with an annoyed look on his face. "You can't throw me off my own land."

"You don't own this land. You never did."

Silas sounded impatient as he said, "My dad bought it when we moved here with some insurance money. And I kept paying the taxes on it. They weren't that much. When I formed my company, Celine Inc., I made it a company asset. So get off my land."

Anger and humiliation raged in Gary. "Celine is your company? You're the one who hasn't been returning the town council's calls about buying the land?"

"You catch on fast."

Not a smack of shame in his face, either. It didn't matter to Gary one way or the other if the town bought the property. What did matter was this jerk ignoring authority, both the town council's and his. "What are you doing back in town after all this time?"

"I believe that falls into the none-of-your-damned-business category."

He felt his shoulders stiffen. "I've had reports of suspicious activity around your house." He glanced up at the structure. Silas had been doing some work on it. "If you tell me why you're here, that'll probably clear things up."

"I don't owe you or anyone an explanation of why I'm on my own property."

Blood pulsed in Gary's temple. Silas couldn't win. He pulled out his gun. "I'm going to have to see for myself."

Silas stood in his way and didn't flinch at all when the gun's barrel pressed against his ribs. "Not without a warrant."

Gary lifted the gun. "Meet my warrant." He shoved Silas out of the way and stalked up the steps. The big dog just stood there, too, like his master. Except the dog was old, too old to do anything.

"This is an illegal search, and you know it. You're out of bounds, Savino."

"Yeah, well, I never did much care for boundaries." He started with the folders on the porch. "What the hell?" Where had he gotten these pictures? He took those into the house. Silas watched him, but did nothing further to try to stop him. Good thing. Attacking an officer wasn't looked upon lightly.

The gun made him swallow thickly. It was hidden in a box of papers. He hadn't thought about Silas having firepower. It was a good thing he'd done the search.

He radioed Sheriff Tate and requested immediate backup.

Silas leaned against the column and tried to tamp down his anger at the violation of his privacy. There wasn't a thing he could do about it. If he touched Gary, he'd be hauled in for assault on an officer. He knew Gary was close to the edge, which was Silas's fault for not cowing under Gary's power. He could feel anger pulsing off the man.

The sheriff pulled up fifteen minutes later. Gary kept his eye on Silas as he showed Tate what he'd found. Now it was Gary's excitement Silas felt, the savage glory of a beast tearing strips of flesh off its prey.

Tate kept glancing over at Silas, appalled by what he saw. Hell, it appalled Silas, too. It was the yellow folder that bothered him the most; not the contents, but that Gary had found it. Read some of it. But Gary hadn't shown that folder to the sheriff.

After a few minutes, the sheriff gathered everything and walked over to Silas. "This is yours?"

"My *private* property."

Gary stepped up beside the sheriff. "I had probable cause to check the premises, sir. The man was acting suspicious."

"By doing what?" Tate asked in a low voice.

"He had a look in his eyes, sir. He was defiant, obviously hiding something. So I searched."

"But you didn't get a warrant," Tate said.

"But he would have destroyed the evidence," Gary said.

"I don't suppose any of this was in plain sight," he asked Gary in a near whisper.

"As soon as I walked up on the porch I could see those folders—"

Tate shoved the folders at Silas. "I'd sure like an explanation of why you've got this stuff, son."

"Maybe I'll tell you someday."

Silence hovered like a snake, ready to strike. The men waited, Silas waited.

Tate said, "We're going to have to verify that you own the property . . ."

Silas dug through another box and gave him a tax receipt he'd brought just in case. It showed Celine Inc. as the owner of the property. Then he produced a worn business card that identified him as the CEO of Celine. Since he was the only employee, there was no one they could call to verify. "Need anything else?"

"Got a license for the gun?"

Silas produced that as well.

Tate looked sheepish as he pushed the permit back at Silas. "Sorry we barged in."

"You can't let him get away with this!" Gary protested as Tate took him by the arm and yanked him toward the vehicles.

In a low tone, Tate said, "You don't barge into someone's house and go through their stuff without a warrant. Period. If you thought there was something in there, you should have called me first. And what made you think there was something going on?"

Gary pulled his arm out of Tate's grasp. "He looked guilty. And he is!"

Tate glanced back at Silas, who was openly listening to them. Then he turned back to Gary. "We'll talk about this at the station."

Gary shot Silas a venomous look before getting into his vehicle. He slammed the door and tore out, spinning leaves and gravel.

This was going to complicate things. Now people would know he was back. And the sheriff would be keeping an eye on him because of what they'd found.

By the time this was over, they were probably all going to know why he was called Spooky Silas.

* * *

The feelings started again right after dinner. This time Silas felt rage and frustration. He'd spent the evening putting his research back in order. Luckily they hadn't found everything. He'd been unable to resist trying to see it through their eyes. Their feelings of shock were clear enough. Their disgust. Definitely their suspicion.

The pictures were gruesome, yes. The kind a big-city cop would have seen too many times, but not a small-town sheriff. Gary, perhaps, in his years on the Atlanta force. Silas had put in a call to his contact in Atlanta to find out more about his stint up there.

It was nearly midnight when he'd become aware of the feelings. Not the feelings of the joy of the hunt this time, but pure rage. Silas wasn't sure which worried him more. He tucked his research into a back corner of what constituted his office and bedroom. He set his suitcase on top of that and walked to the front porch.

Wind howled through the trees and brought the forest alive with the sound of rushing leaves. Another time it may have soothed him. Tonight it was a backdrop to sinister rage. He glanced toward Katie's house, not that he could see anything. She was probably tucked in her bed with her husband for the night, safe and sound.

That's not where she belonged. She knew it, too, but she was powerless to do anything about it. So was he. Coveting another man's wife was one of the big Ten.

So was murder, a black thought reminded him.

He focused on kissing Katie rather than his darkest doubts. He hadn't meant to kiss her. He was only here to protect her, a totally unselfish purpose. He'd promised himself he wouldn't compromise her or put her in a tenuous position. Just his presence, unfortunately, had done that. He could feel her conflict and desire. Though he hadn't seen her, or at least talked to her, in eighteen years, he'd always believed she belonged to him.

He scanned the writhing miasma of shadows and leaves.

Someone was out there watching him. He could feel the anger closer than ever.

Even The Boss seemed to sense it. He lifted his head and looked to the darkness, his saggy lips dusty from the floor. Silas reached out and scratched his head before heading to the inflatable mattress in the bedroom.

Fully clothed, he lay in bed and listened to the sounds of the darkness. He'd been in the dark for so long, he wasn't sure where it ended and he began. It was that fine line that obsessed him. What pushed a man over it? What made him kill another human being?

The rage had receded, leaving behind emptiness. But the evil was there, hovering at the edge. The Ghost was on the move. Not hunting, but definitely looking for an outlet for his anger.

Silas got out of bed and called The Boss. He waited while the old dog creakily made his way down the steps. On his way to the Navigator, the dog sniffed something crinkly on the ground.

It was the chocolate lollipop Katie had brought over. She must have dropped it, and either Gary or the sheriff had run over it. Silas picked it up and tossed it to the edge of the woods. He didn't want any reminders of her offering.

He helped The Boss into the vehicle and climbed in. If the killer were on the prowl, Silas had a feeling where he'd go: where the green sneaker still lay on the side of the road. He'd been keeping an eye on it, not yet ready to anonymously call it in to the police. There'd be no evidence on it.

The Ghost left the shoe there so he could vicariously relive his crime. Serial killers usually kept their trophies nearby. The Ghost was smarter than that. He left his trophies on the side of the road, as innocuous as the rest of the debris scattered among the grass and wildflowers. He probably returned here from time to time, and if no one was around, masturbated to the memories.

Silas had tried to tell that to the sheriff's office when he'd found the first shoe north of here. In his anonymous tip, he'd told them to leave the shoe there and watch who slowed down or stopped nearby. They'd taken it away to run tests on it, tests that were inconclusive.

Silas had stopped notifying the authorities, collecting evidence and data himself until he had enough to connect the disappearances and find out who the Ghost was. Besides, how could he explain how he knew so much about the murders? How could he explain that he was inside the killer's mind without implicating himself?

He paused at the end of the drive and glanced in the rearview mirror. The dash lights played across the contours of his face and left his eyes in shadows.

Or was he afraid to find out the Ghost was himself?

Had he become the very thing he'd been researching all these years?

After all, *he* was constantly monitoring the sneaker, slowing down to see it just as the killer did. Though he hadn't once been moved to sexually stimulate himself over it. He could feel the killer's joy and lust, but Silas's core being was repulsed by what he saw and felt. That was little relief. He'd studied serial killers who felt the same way, compelled and disgusted at once.

Silas had gone to a church in every town he visited in his search for the Ghost. It was a test, to see if he'd become too close to evil to be allowed in. He'd slip inside during a lull between services, take in the religious symbols—the cross, perhaps a statue of Christ—and be glad he'd been allowed in once more. When he'd gone to Flatlands Baptist Church, the doors had been locked.

The highways were nearly deserted at this time of night. These rural areas closed down at dusk. Most of the outlying farms and homes were dark. The perfect place to make a girl disappear.

The shoe was there, just a few feet from the sign as it had been. The feelings were growing, anger and retribution. Soon, the payoff. The reward.

His fingers tightened on the steering wheel as the first of the flashes started. A room, old and dusty. A girl spread on the bed. Satisfaction at the terror on her face.

For all the persecution.

For everything that didn't go my way.

My reward.

Her scream tore through the night and faded by degrees. Somewhere inside Silas, there was enough of himself to feel the relief that it wasn't Katie, not this time.

He woke up two hours later in his vehicle, which was parked several yards off the road. He didn't know how he'd gotten there, didn't remember pulling off the highway.

She was dead. Carrie Druthers was gone forever, probably never to be found. Like the others.

His head was pounding and his body felt weak. He cleared his vision enough to drive back onto the highway and figure out where he was. He took a mental note of the route number before heading back to the house. Each time he had an episode, he had to be getting closer. Before long, he'd be face-to-face with the killer.

CHAPTER 8

KATIE WAS ON her third cup of coffee, and she still hadn't woken up yet. Luckily it was Sunday, and she and Ben had been able to sleep in until nine.

"How much wine did you drink last night?" Ben asked as he worked the crossword puzzle at the kitchen table.

"Just two glasses."

He didn't look up at her, just kept working the puzzle in ink. He had an amazing memory for knowledge. Katie suspected he had a high IQ, though he downplayed his intelligence. She felt rather dumb compared to him, but he never made her feel that way on purpose.

She'd told him most of the truth about her meeting with Silas, that she was curious about why he was there and grateful for the chance to apologize for inadvertently ousting him from town. She omitted the fact that she'd already seen him, and of course, the kiss. No need to mention that. After all, it was a fluke, something that would never happen again.

Ben had been stoic about it all, really. They'd had some wine, and he hadn't brought it up again. The tension, however, was still apparent. His manner was pleasant, but reserved. He was perfectly entitled to be disappointed in her. She felt the same way.

She scanned the local paper, a small weekly that was produced in Flatlands but covered the general area. "No news on the missing girl. I wonder if it's connected to the girl who disappeared over to Milledgeville."

"She's probably just taken off. I'm sure they're not putting all the facts in the paper."

She hoped it was something like that. Bad things didn't happen in their area. This was rural Georgia, small towns, people not locking their doors.

The knock on the door startled her. Sheriff Tate looked tired, though his uniform was as crisp as always. He tipped his hat. "Sorry to barge in on you folks on a nice Sunday morning, but I thought you might want to know what's going on with Silas Koole."

Her heart jumped. She'd caused him trouble again. "Would you like some coffee?"

"I'm good, thanks." Sheriff nodded to the chairs on the porch. "Out here's fine."

Her throat was tight as she took the rocker next to Ben's, while Tate leaned against the railing. He looked so serious, so grim.

"Sure am glad you had us check into Silas being over there to the old Koole place," he said to Ben, who looked inordinately pleased with himself. "I think we got ourselves a problem, a real dangerous one. I'm going to ask you to keep this to yourselves for now. But seeing as you're in close proximity to the Koole house, you'd best know." He looked at Katie. "Especially with the way you wander around here."

How did he know? She had scooted to the edge of her chair, tipping it forward. "What is it?"

Tate ran his hands down his thighs. "First of all, he has every right to be there. It's his property. We're going to check further tomorrow, but it appears to be his."

Ben said, "I thought it was some corporation in Atlanta that owned it."

"Yep, and it appears he owns the corporation."

That wasn't what Katie expected at all. Shaggy Silas who was living in that old place owned a corporation? "But . . . how?" And why hadn't he told her, the jerk?

"Don't know how he got to owning a corporation, and how he earns his money may well be another issue altogether. His old man bought that whole tract of land when he moved here. We thought he just rented the place. Seems that Silas has been paying the taxes all along."

Ben tensed. "So we can't make him leave?"

"Can't make a man vacate his own property unless he's doing something illegal there."

Ben asked the question that had haunted Katie for five days. "But why did he come back after all this time?"

Tate seemed to gauge their readiness for the news. "Maybe to find new hunting grounds."

She said, "Well, I guess a guy's got a right to hunt on his own property," though she knew he hated hunting.

"Not when he's hunting young women."

She went cold, all the way down to her fingertips. Luckily Ben had the presence of mind to respond.

"Are you saying . . ."

"Yep, that's what I'm saying. Maybe the girl up near Haddock, maybe the hitchhiker outside of Milledgeville . . . maybe more."

Katie finally found her voice. "Why . . . what makes you think that?"

"Gary went over there last night. Unfortunately, he went overboard, as he's wont to do, and started searching the place without a warrant. He found a lot of disturbing things, stuff Silas was working on." Tate shifted his gaze away, as though gathering himself to go on.

"He had notes, photographs, and newspaper clippings about teenage girls disappearing. At least half a dozen, going back a few years, maybe more. I didn't have a chance to read much of what he'd wrote, but he had graphic pictures of two girls' battered bodies. Like police photos. I was up most the night doing research and pulled up missing-girl reports all the way back to 1989. See, here's the thing: nobody thought to connect these disappearances. Some were thought to have run off, like the Haddock girl. They'd been in trouble, or were hitchhiking, things they'd oughtn't do. Others were considered random, a guy passing through. There's no pattern, nothing to connect them really. But he had notes on a few of them. And it turns out there is a pattern of sorts. All the girls just disappeared, without a trace. Back in 1986 and 1990, two bodies were found. The guy—if it's one guy—got good after that, and not one body has been found since. Some of the disappearances are connected by where they were taken. Others are connected by shoes."

"Shoes?" she asked, horrified at the picture Tate was painting. How it jived with Silas's secretiveness, his evasiveness. And his warnings.

"Two girls who went missing in the same area around the same time back in 1989 and 1990 also had another connection: one body was found without a shoe, and only the shoe of the other girl was found. That's not unusual in itself, far as I can tell. But in 1996 a girl went missing near I-16 south of here. Her shoe was found not far from here. Her mother was searching everywhere in the area, and she recognized the shoe. Her daughter had special arches inserted in all her shoes. Two years later, a girl goes missing from Ivey. A few months later, her shoe is found in Haddock, which, not coincidentally, is where the recent girl was taken, if she was taken. That tip was called in anonymously, something killers do sometimes. Could be the guy's calling card; he just leaves 'em on the side of the road."

Ben jumped to his feet. "Do you know what you're saying?"

"I'm afraid I do. No one would have connected the disappearances if it weren't for Gary finding Silas's files."

Ben looked happy about that. "Good thing I alerted Gary about Silas. We can probably stop the bastard right here, and it'll all be our doing. We'll be heroes, Tate."

"Afraid not, Ben. Because Gary's search was illegal, I couldn't take the files last night, can't arrest Silas, can't do anything until I have proof not obtained by illegal means. And I'm not sure we'd find enough evidence for a court's needs. My hands are tied. I can't even call in the FBI, because they'll be all over me for my deputy's overeagerness. But I'm on the case now. I'm working on connecting him, digging into his past, and finding out how I can nail him to the wall. I'm going to keep my guys watching him as much as manpower allows. If this is one man taking these women, he's damned smart. And Silas doesn't strike me as being a dumb guy."

"Surely you can find a way around the illegal-search business."

"Believe me, I've tried to come up with something. The bottom line is, we screwed up. Gary screwed up. Now we're going to make it right. This is big, real big. I want to nail this guy myself, bring some notoriety to Flatlands. But if I screw it up and he gets off on a technicality, my ass'll be fried six ways from Sunday."

"I can go in!" Ben said, straightening his shoulders. "I'm a private citizen."

"I don't want you to do anything, Ben."

"Why not?"

"The only reason I'm telling you all this is so you can be extra careful until we can gather enough evidence to bring him in. There's something else you should know, in case you get any crazy ideas: He has a gun."

"Damn it," Ben muttered, hitting the wall.

Katie felt as though she were in a daze. This couldn't be real. "I don't believe Silas could kill anyone."

Both men looked at her as though she'd just thrown up all over Tate's shoes.

In a venomous voice, Ben admitted, "Katie was over there talking to him yesterday. Could have disappeared like the others."

Now they were looking at her as though she were the stupidest woman alive. She wanted to slink into the house and wait until she could beg Ben's forgiveness . . . again. *What happened to you, Katie?* No way had she kissed a killer. "Well, I didn't," she said. "Silas stood by me during a hard time in my life. And he was nothing but polite when I spoke with him recently." Well, mostly. "I don't believe he's a killer."

Tate studied her for a moment. "Katie, I want you to think about this: Killers don't always look like creeps. The most successful are the nicest people you'll ever know.

Sometimes they're your friends, brother, or cousin. Someone you trust. Think of Ted Bundy, Jeffrey Dahmer. Koole had psychology-type notes on them with charts and time-lines, like he was studying them. They were probably nice to some people when they were kids. They were probably nice to people even when they were killing others. But Silas isn't a nice guy. He just stood there while we went through his things, this cold look on his face. I asked him to explain what we'd found. You know what he said? 'Maybe I'll tell you someday.' He's playing games with us is what he's doing."

Now *that* sounded like Silas.

"He was always creepy, even when he was a kid." Tate nodded to Katie. "After your mama died, and we had Silas in custody, he got away from us and went to your trailer. I was just giving the place another once-over in case we missed something, and he was inside. He wouldn't say what he was doing there. That's when we knew we had to get rid of him, ship him out of town."

Tate stood. "I gotta get back to the office. Stay clear of him, both of you. He's here for a reason. It's only going to be a matter of time before we get to the truth of it." He slanted another look at Katie, taking her in from head to toe. "You're a married woman with no business hanging around a man you don't really know. For that reason alone you ought to be begging your husband for forgiveness and making him feel every bit like the good husband he is to you. And I suggest you be very careful." To Ben he said, "We'll keep you informed, as long as you stay cool about this."

"I will, Sheriff. You'll have him wrapped up in no time, I'm sure of it. Thank you for warning us."

Ben watched Tate disappear down the drive. Then he turned to Katie and looked at her in silence. She wasn't sure how to respond. Was he angry? Scared? Without a word he went inside. She followed him to the office where he took care of the bills. He opened the bottom file drawer and reached into the back of the old files. She sucked in a breath when he pulled out a gun.

"Where did that come from?" she asked, feeling more uneasy by the second. "What are you going to do with it?"

He turned around and faced her, the gun sideways in his hand but pointed toward her. She'd never seen that hard glint in his eyes before. He walked closer, took her hand, and shoved the cold metal in it. He squeezed her fingers around it when she didn't automatically grab hold. She remembered Silas's words about his father making him shoot a deer by squeezing his finger on the trigger. Ben was hurting her fingers the same way.

"If Silas comes anywhere near this house, I want you to shoot him. Do you understand, Katie? He'll be on our property, a trespasser. You'll be within your rights."

"I can't shoot him," she whispered.

"Everyone knows you were consorting with him. It's shameful, to me and to you."

"I'm sorry I embarrassed you, but that's no reason to shoot a man."

"Don't be stupid. Shoot him because he's a killer." He pinched her chin. "Do not trust him, Katie."

"I . . . don't." That much was true. Mostly, she didn't trust herself around him.

He stepped back and the gun clattered to the floor between them. He swore and picked it up. "You idiot! It's loaded and ready to fire. It could have gone off. Come on, I'm going to teach you how to use it."

"I don't want to learn. I'm not going to shoot anyone."

He pulled her out the back door. "I'm going to the Greater Atlanta Academy of Veterinary Medicine's annual Atlanta conference. I leave tonight, remember?"

She remembered him mentioning it the week before, but had forgotten in light of everything else that had happened recently. Her squirrels tore off into the surrounding trees at their approach. After the gun went off, they'd hide for weeks. Maybe never come back.

"I suppose I could cancel it," he said.

"No, I don't want you to do that. You've been looking forward to it for months."

"Especially that discussion on advances in the treatment of feline viral diseases. I know how much cats mean to you."

"Why don't you take me with you? I wouldn't mind seeing Atlanta again. I've only been that one time."

He molded her into position with the gun in both hands. "You know we can't close the clinic for three days. One of us needs to be around to handle emergencies." He was even more adamant against bringing in another vet to cover their business. He was a private person and didn't want anyone nosing around his business. "Look, I'll just cancel. Hopefully I can get some of my registration fee back."

"What do you want me to do?"

Her words echoed in her mind as he showed her how to aim the gun. What *had* happened to her? She thought adults just lost their fight. Her mother was a survivor, but she wasn't a fighter. She'd back down on any fight. Katie could try to convince Ben to take her to Atlanta, but she realized something: she didn't want to go with him. She needed some time to think, to clear her head.

"What if there's an animal out there?" she asked, nodding toward the woods. "Or a person?"

"If it's a person, it's Silas sneaking around and he deserves to be shot."

The shot blasted through the peaceful Sunday sounds of nature. Birds scattered from nearby trees, and all Katie could hear for a few seconds was the muted aftershocks. He pointed out different targets among the trees, and she pulled the trigger. When they'd emptied the chamber, she couldn't hear a thing.

"I didn't think about earplugs," Ben repeated for the fourth time. "The gun's for emergencies, that's all. I've had it for years." He took the gun and walked into the house.

She wondered if Silas had heard the shots. Once her hearing had returned to somewhat normal, she asked, "What did you mean by Silas sneaking around here?"

Ben settled into his chair. "I didn't want to tell you, because I didn't want you to worry. But now I *do* want you worried. I've had a feeling lately of someone watching me. Last night even, after we went to bed. I walked around the house and looked outside, but of course I couldn't see anything in the dark."

"I didn't hear you get up."

"You were out, thanks to the wine. It was only a feeling, but I didn't like it. Until the sheriff finds something to nail that bastard with, I want you to stay put, you understand? No walks in the forest. No visiting the neighbors."

She felt a part of her resist. Maybe not the advice, which was wise, but how it was worded. An order. She wasn't sure what he saw in her face, but he reached out to her. She stepped forward and slid her hand into his.

"Katie, I worry about you, that's all. You're trusting. And while that's a wonderful thing, it can also be dangerous if you trust the wrong person."

She nodded, feeling that bit of fight leak out of her. He was right. He was always right. "I'll be careful. I promise."

He smiled. "That's my girl."

Her own smile was weak as she pulled away. "I want you to go to Atlanta, Ben."

"Are you sure? I don't mind canceling if it'll make you feel better."

"No, go. I know how much you're looking forward to it. It sounded like the girls who got taken were out walking or hitchhiking. I sure won't be doing that. But I'd like to talk about getting a second car again. When you go for a few days, I'm stuck out here in the woods."

The relative calm that had settled over Ben's face evaporated. "We'll talk about it later. I need to think about what the sheriff told us."

And that would be the end of it until she gathered up her nerve to ask again. Sometimes he brought up the money factor, upkeep on two vehicles when ninety-five percent of the time one was all they needed. And, after all, she wasn't actually bringing in any money. She helped Ben out, that's all. She didn't draw a paycheck, didn't earn a dime on her own. All their money went into the hospital's account, and Ben took a weekly paycheck to cover their bills.

Katie returned to the kitchen where she prepared soap to clean the walls. On top of the cabinet was a tin. Standing on the counter washing the upper walls, she could see it, but not from the floor. It was the change from her expenditures over the last year. She'd been tucking it away just in case. In case of what, she didn't know. *Cosmo* said all women should have their own money. That's when she realized how dependant she was on Ben. She had nothing, not a dime, not a speck of credit.

Silas would like the idea of her squirreling away money. *Silas.*

As she scrubbed months of grime off the top of the refrigerator, she pictured him tenderly holding her face, kissing her. Telling her she was a nine.

Silas was a man full of shadows. And secrets. But in her heart, she couldn't believe he was a killer. And yet, hadn't he asked her not to trust anyone, not even him?

Ben waited until late that evening before leaving for Atlanta. Katie looked pensive, but she didn't necessarily look worried. He wanted her worried. Not terrified, of course, but worried enough to be careful—and to stay away from Silas.

When he'd gone into the bedroom where she was packing his case, he caught her looking at her reflection over the dresser. She was holding her hair up high enough to show the wine stain on her neck. She dropped her hair when she saw him standing in the doorway.

"What'cha doing?"

"I . . ." She glanced at the mirror, her face flushing pink. "I was just wondering what my hair would look like shoulder length. For a change."

"Sounds like a Bertrice influence again. Besides, you wouldn't want your birthmark to show, would you?" Her face shadowed at that remark. He came up behind her and wrapped his arms around her shoulders. He was fifteen years older than she, and looking at them in the reflection, he could see every day of it. Not that he was bad looking. She just made him look even older, because she looked so young. Short hair would make her look even younger. "I like your hair the way it is. Not up, not in a ponytail, not braided . . . just like this." He ran his fingers through the soft strands.

"Don't you get tired of it? I do."

"Never." He kissed her temple, then went into the bathroom. She was still looking at herself when he emerged. "Are you sure you're going to be okay while I'm gone?"

"I'll be fine." She kissed him on the nose and closed up his suitcase. "You have a good time, learn a lot."

"Okay. If you're sure. I've got my beeper in case you need me for anything. Harold's going to give you a ride to work the next few mornings and Bertrice is set to give you rides home."

She stilled. "Harold doesn't have to give me a ride. I can walk through the woods and catch a ride home with Bertrice."

Ben lowered his head. "What did we just agree on about you wandering in the woods? I don't want to hear from Harold that you didn't take his ride, understand? It's a long walk I don't like you taking."

She reluctantly nodded. He kissed her on the mouth, much more suitable than the silly nose kiss she'd given him. "And no borrowing clothes from Bertrice. I want my wife to look like a woman, not a teenybopper."

"I won't," she said on a soft sigh.

"What are you feeling, Katie? Tell me."

"That I'm going to miss you." She hugged him hard, and he felt the worry ease out of him. Now he could focus on the upcoming conference.

It was dark by the time he pulled out of the driveway. He settled in for the long drive. The headlights caught his attention when he turned out of town. He realized they'd been behind him for a time now. The vehicle stayed exactly three car lengths behind him, whether he sped up or slowed down. It was enough space that he couldn't see what kind of car it was because of the glare. For twenty minutes the car followed as he wound his way to the Interstate. And then, just as Ben took the on-ramp, the car turned around and headed back toward Flatlands.

Katie spent most of the night wondering if Ben truly did feel as though someone were watching him. Was his paranoia affecting her, or did she have the same feeling now? Relief picked up her mood when dawn opened up an overcast morning. It disappeared when Harold arrived at her door to take her to work. Only he wanted coffee.

"I've already washed out the pot. Sorry." She knew she didn't sound very sorry as she stood in the doorway.

"I thought Ben said you'd have a cup of coffee for me, for taking you into work and all." He glanced into the house. "Have anything left over from breakfast?"

"No."

He was blocking her exit from the house. He weighed well over two hundred pounds, all of it muscle. He was probably near forty, and though he obviously worked out regularly, he didn't give much attention to the rest of his appearance. His head was a brown mop of unwashed hair, his cheeks bristly with shadow. And that hideous tic pulsed at his eyelid.

"So, you all alone out here, huh?" he said, taking in the yard.

She took the opportunity to slide around him and lock the front door. "Yep." She pushed aside food wrappers and two empty beer cans before climbing into his truck. The extended part of the cab was crammed with junk.

"Is it scary at night?"

"Not really."

"If I was a woman all alone out here, I'd be scared."

"I've got a gun." She rather liked the surprised look on his beefy face, even if she detested the gun itself. He didn't need to know she probably couldn't shoot anyone with it.

Harold scratched his head. He probably hadn't washed his hair in a week. "I heard they think the girl from Haddock might've been murdered. Or kidnapped at least. Same as the one near Milledgeville. I hear tell there might even be more, though no one at the sheriff's office is talking much. Being on the town council, I'm privy to a lot of information." He slid his gaze to her. "What'cha think about that? Scary, someone like that living round these parts. Could even be someone we know. Wouldn't that be something? Someone we see day in and out." His brown eyes glittered with interest, and the tic pulsed even faster. "That would make it interesting, wouldn't it? Too boring around here."

The truck lurched, forcing her to grab the strap by the door. "I hope it's no one we know." She was thinking of Silas, of course. "Do you know if they have any suspects?"

"They're sure looking at Silas Koole. He's back in town, you know." His grin widened. "Oh, that's right. You knew that. Heard you were . . . what's the word? Consorting with him."

"I wasn't consorting with him." Where'd he hear that word, anyway? And where had he heard about the consorting to begin with?

She was startled out of her ruminations by Harold's big hand slapping down on her thigh. "Don't worry none. We know you'd never cheat on the doc."

She stiffened and waited for him to remove his hand. He'd averted his gaze back to the road ahead as they passed the old cemetery. What to do? She didn't want him to think she was uneasy around him. He might play on it, and she had two more mornings to deal with him. But the heat of his hand, coupled with the inappropriateness of it being there, was unnerving.

Finally he lifted it to point out the barn just off the road. "If you get lonely during the day, come on over and visit for a spell." The sign over the closed double doors read One Man's Trash, and that's basically what it was. The gray, weathered wood looked as though it would fall over in a gentle breeze. The yard was littered with the things that didn't fit into the large building, including an old wagon, a hearse up on blocks, and a doghouse that was in the same condition as the barn. "I know you and Ben are into that fussy stuff. He hasn't bought anything from me in a while, though. You could come over and see what I've got."

She had shifted so his hand couldn't come back down on her thigh. She pressed against the door waiting for the hospital to come into view. "Thanks for the ride," she said as she pushed out of the truck. Even though he honked goodbye, she didn't look back. She'd mentioned to Ben her dislike of having Harold take her to work once before, but he said she was being silly. Harold was harmless.

Sure he was.

Harold watched her unlock the front door and close it behind her. She didn't even look back or wave. There was gratitude for you. People thought she was a snob. They were right. Here he came out of his way to take her to work, and not a speck of thanks.

Did she think she was too good for him? He knew where she'd been born—Possum Holler. He'd been out there a few times, picking up or delivering. She wasn't any better than him, though maybe marrying the doc had elevated her status in her mind.

He was going to make her see he wasn't just some dumb hick. He was going to see that she showed him some respect.

Throughout the day, Katie took care of routine things like rabies, DHLPPC, panleukopenia, and leukemia vaccinations. She dealt with a beagle's ear infection. Though her animal patients trusted her, their owners were always dubious about her skills when Ben was gone. She knew almost as much as Ben did, having worked with him for so long.

Ben checked in twice. At lunch, she closed down the

place and walked to the diner. Since their building was set back from the road a short distance, the shortcut went right through the cemetery. She hadn't actually minded being next to the cemetery too much until her last birthday. She wished her mama were there. She'd been cremated and her ashes sprinkled into the creek they'd spent so many wonderful afternoons at. Her mama would forever travel with the water, exploring the world the way she hadn't been able to do in life.

The new cemetery, over by the Methodist church on the other side of town, was kept pristine and trimmed. Nobody had touched the old cemetery for what looked like a hundred years. Once this had been the final resting place for the town's oldest and wealthiest families. Some had constructed detailed iron fences around their marble gravestones and crypts. Now, huge oak trees grew right around some of those fences, warping and breaking them. Gates hung crookedly, as though the ghosts had long ago risen and stormed out of their iron prisons. Ivy grew all over the moldy gravestones and slabs, as though trying to keep the remaining ghosts from escaping.

The cemetery sprawled over the small hill and dipped down to the far edge of their property. Some graves were only marked with jagged stones. Deep in the shadows unmarked mounds were barely visible, claimed by no one.

She found an odd peace here sometimes, a sense of time marching on. Sadness also permeated her in the way the sunlight permeated the canopy of leaves to sprinkle down upon the graves and the faded silk flowers left here and there. Even here, she didn't belong. She had no history here, no family in either cemetery. Some folks in town could trace their history right there, great-grandparents, grandparents, parents, heroes honored for wars as notable as the War of 1812. Though few families tended to the graves, she could feel their pride at their heritage. Or maybe it was her envy.

The walk to the diner took fifteen minutes when she didn't linger at the graves. Harold waved at her from his chair outside his old barn. His pit bull was sitting next to his chair watching her. Then she realized Harold was actually waving her over. She quickly averted her gaze to the ground and was relieved to near the busy parking lot of the small shopping strip that housed the diner.

The sign begging for volunteers for the fair was still in the window.

The conversation level was high when she opened the door. It was habit for everyone to check out the new arrival, and she expected all eyes to momentarily shift to her. She put a warm smile on her face and greeted the familiar faces. Most resumed their conversation without returning her smile.

"Hey, how are you?" she asked Loralei, the woman who cut her hair.

"Fine, how're ya'll doing?" she asked.

Katie rolled her eyes. "Going to the dogs."

No one laughed. No one even smiled. Loralei forced something like a smile and went back to looking at the menu.

With a sigh that tried to cover the hurt, Katie walked to the counter. She'd been planning on eating there, but she didn't feel welcome. She took the stool at the end of the counter. Dinah handed her a menu and said, "Be right with you."

Ten minutes later, she still hadn't been with her. Katie pretended to be interested in the placemat that fit twenty business cards. Even if it was tacky to advertise in such a way, she was envious that Dinah had her own money. Of course, her husband had had to die for it to happen.

Nearby conversations centered around Silas Koole being back in town—goodness how could they have not recognized him?—and the missing girl and rumors of connected disappearances.

She was startled to find Sam Savino staring at her. He sat by himself—no surprise there. Dressed in a smart three-piece suit, he outdressed everyone else there. She forced herself to meet his gaze and a trill of alarm sounded deep in her belly. There was something about him, something beyond the way he stared at her even though she was looking at him. She hated that it was she who looked away first.

She spotted Marion Tate having lunch with her cronies at one of the booths. She summoned her courage and walked over. All four women looked up with surprise.

"Hi, ya'll. Mrs. Tate, whatever you need help with at the fair, I'd be glad to help out."

There, she'd done it. Now Ben couldn't stop her, couldn't have her take back her offer once it was accepted.

"We don't need your help," Marion said without the faintest glimmer of a smile. "But thanks so much for offering anyway."

It was the most insincere thanks she'd ever gotten. Katie nodded toward the sign. "But the sign said . . ."

"Never mind the sign. We just got the last of the volunteers we needed. You're a little late."

Marion went back to whatever conversation they'd been having, leaving Katie to stand there red-faced. The first face she saw was Sam's. He'd probably overheard the conversation. She numbly walked back to the counter to find her stool had been taken. Her stomach was all knotted up not knowing what to do. Dinah hadn't even looked her way once. Some folks had overheard Katie's conversation with the women and were now whispering about it. She turned and left the diner with as much dignity as she could muster. With her arms around her waist and her head down, she walked back to the animal hospital and nibbled on a package of cheese and crackers.

What had she ever done to those people? She hated to admit how their indifference hurt, but it did. She was married to the most popular man in town, and they all hated her.

The highlight of the day was Bertrice telling Katie about her escapades over the weekend. The girls had gone to a tattoo artist.

Bertrice lifted her pant leg. "Isn't he too cool? I call him

Ed, for Eye Dude." That's exactly what Ed was, an eyeball with legs, arms, and a top hat. "Geraldine got a butterfly on her shoulder. She has *no* imagination. Kelly got a bracelet tattooed on her arm. Looks like barbed wire. Now we gotta hide these puppies from our parents. Well, Kelly's parents don't care, they're not even together anymore. My mom would skin me if she found out. She is so uncool. I'm going to be a cool mom when I'm her age."

Katie wasn't sure if her mama had been cool or not. She had no idea how she would age, what areas would become problems. If she made it past twenty-seven herself.

"Wanna come over for dinner?" Bertrice asked when they left for the day. "You being alone and all. I'm sure my mom won't mind."

Just the thought of sharing a dinner with Bertrice and her family, of mother-daughter chatter and arguments, was too much for Katie to bear. She was feeling way too fragile. "That's sweet of you, but if Ben calls and I'm not home, he'll worry. I'll be fine, really."

Bertrice shrugged. "Whatever. But you're welcome any night."

"Thanks, I . . ." She saw a pair of old sneakers tied together by their shoelaces hanging over the phone lines. Such an everyday sight in rural America. Now something sinister.

She had the worst urge to hug Bertrice goodbye and luckily overcame it. She waved as Bertrice pulled out of the driveway, and it was quiet again. She scanned the woods bordering her yard. In the shadows, a spray of leaves looked like a waving hand, the only thing moving at the moment. Then a breeze rushed through, bringing the forest alive with movement and noise. One of her squirrels climbed up the tree, its tail twitching. She tried to forget about Harold, Silas, and the trace of evil that lingered in the air. She tried not to think about Ben feeling as though someone were watching him. She had a long night ahead of her.

CHAPTER 9

KATIE HEATED THE leftover chicken and wished she'd taken Bertrice up on her offer of dinner. As painful as it would have been to watch her and her mom bicker, it would have been better than loneliness.

Katie had never minded being alone. She rarely was. Usually she got to relax and read her hidden *Cosmopolitan* magazines. Tonight it just gave her too much time to think. And notice every little noise outside.

She walked out the back door, but stayed on the step. A walk through the woods would have cleared her head, but now the darkness was steeped in evil. And Silas, he was out there, too, in the shadows. Her last fearless pursuit had been robbed from her. Instead of enjoying the rush of sound as wind pummeled the leaves, she realized the cacophony could cover footsteps. Instead of enjoying the shadows moving through the trees as a kind of living art, she now wondered if a living being was one of those shadows.

Miles above her a plane crossed the open space in the forest. As always, she wondered where they were going. She pictured families and businesspeople, some going to an exciting place, some returning from one. She had the strongest urge to get on one herself for the first time and just go anywhere. But she had no money of her own, no way to get to an airport.

Like a bug in a spider's web.

She glanced back at the corner window and could barely see the gloss of the spider's web. Is this how her mama had felt that last night? Trapped by circumstances, wondering if she was even worthy of what she had. Feeling isolated in a way no one else could possibly understand? She desperately wanted to understand the depth of despair her mama had felt to leave her daughter behind. Katie vacillated between guilt over having argued with and then leaving her mama that night and anger at her. That was the legacy her mama had left her, along with the certainty that she would also die young.

The sound of tires crunching against gravel shot her heart up into her throat. Headlights slashed across the leaves briefly before disappearing. She ran inside and went to the front window.

The sheriff's vehicle was barely visible. Was Tate back with more insidious news about Silas?

As soon as she opened the door, she wanted to slam it shut again. But Gary just strolled right in as though he'd been invited for supper. " 'Evening, Katie." He even sniffed the air and said, "Smells good in here. I'm not disturbing your supper, am I?"

She hated the way he said her name, drawing it out and adding a cup of sugar to it like they were old friends. It was the same way he'd said it all those years ago when she'd been too young to see through it. She stayed by the door. "What do you want?" Her voice sound shaky and weak.

He had the gall to sit in Ben's throne chair. His uniform was wrinkled, and his dark hair was mussed. "Sheriff has us working on the Koole case every spare minute. Protecting our fair citizens is mighty tiring. Do I smell coffee?"

"It's decaf."

Her intent was to dissuade him, but he nodded. "I'll take anything that remotely smells like coffee, thanks."

She couldn't believe it. Why hadn't she just told him to leave? Now she was actually walking to the kitchen to fix the jerk a cup of coffee. She didn't offer him sugar or cream, but apparently he didn't mind. He sipped from the mug without complaining.

Never before had Katie so sharply felt like her mama.

She'd seen stark fear in her eyes at the approach of a man. She wished she'd known what caused her mama's fear. Her father, perhaps? The man she would learn about *someday, when you're old enough to understand*. That day never came.

She positioned herself near the door again, angry for being less comfortable in her home than the intruder. "What do you want?" This time the words came out stronger.

"Shucks, used to be a visit from a lawman would be welcome from a woman all by herself out in the woods. Especially considering I'm the one who found out you got a killer as a neighbor." He snapped his finger. "That's right, he's your pal, isn't he?" He lifted an eyebrow. "Or maybe more."

"Leave, please."

He set his coffee mug on the table and settled back in the chair with a low chuckle. His blunt fingers curled over the curved wood of the chair arms. "Katie, you and me, we need to come to an understanding. I should be your pal, not Spooky Silas. You and me are more alike than you know."

Through a tight throat she said, "Leave or I'll call the sheriff."

He outright laughed at that. "You're gonna call the sheriff on me. Now that's a laugh and a half, it is. You're gonna complain because one of his deputies stopped by to check on you, make sure you're okay. To let you know Silas isn't over there right now, though we're trying to keep an eye on him." He pulled himself up to his six-foot-one frame and walked closer. "They'll think you're a paranoid priss."

They would. Who would believe her over Gary? They didn't last time.

She could smell fresh aftershave slathered over the sweat of a long day. God, she wished she were up in that plane right now. He studied her face, though she tried to keep the fear from her expression so he wouldn't feed off it. His intent gaze sent that same trill of alarm through her that she'd felt from Sam Savino.

"Soon you're going to find out that I'm your pal, not Silas. As soon as you can forgive me and stop looking at me like you want to rip out my guts and feed 'em to a dog, you're gonna see that I'm the only one you can really trust. Then I can forgive you for putting this here scar on me."

She stepped away and opened the door. Having an escape route was more comfortable, at least until she realized Gary could catch up with her in two seconds. He moved slowly toward the doorway, but he paused in front of her. She summoned the image of her younger self, afraid of no one, even if he was bigger and richer. She'd put the scar on his face then, the fine line from the corner of his right eye to his hairline.

He reached inside his shirt and pulled out a folded sketch paper. "There's something the sheriff doesn't know. Something I found at Silas's."

She expected to see some gruesome sketch like the photographs the sheriff had described. What she saw was even more disturbing. It was a pencil sketch of a woman kneeling at a small grave. The grave was in a patch of woods with a plant for every one of his eleven years of life. A small, flat stone sat in the middle of the plants, and . . . could it even be her teardrops he'd drawn on the stone?

She grabbed the paper from Gary's hand. "It's impossible!"

"It's you, isn't it?"

She couldn't even answer him. Yes, it was her. The day Gus had died and she'd buried him behind her garden. Nobody knew about the garden, not even Ben. She figured he'd think it was silly. And her feelings and grief for her cat weren't something she wanted to share with anyone, not even her new husband. She'd held in her feelings until he'd gone on a farm call.

Silas had been there. That was the only explanation of how he'd captured all the details, even what she'd been wearing. But how? Surely she would have heard him traipsing through the woods.

"There was more," Gary said once she'd absorbed the

sketch. "I didn't get a chance to read much of it, but he had a journal . . . about you. He had your wedding day, notes about how you weren't sure you loved Ben enough, but you owed him so much."

Her head jerked up at that, but not a word formed in her mouth. No one knew about her ambivalence. *No one.* Even though Ben always wanted them to share their feelings with each other, she never, ever shared that. "What else?" she finally asked.

"That's all I could read. There was too much to take in."

She looked down at the sketch again, bewildered and spooked. *Spooky Silas.*

"You didn't tell the sheriff about this?"

"I wanted to tell you myself. It's our secret, Katie. Didn't I tell you you could trust me? Only me?"

Before she could even form a response to that, because no way in hell did she trust him, the police siren shattered the air. Gary ran to the driver's side of his vehicle. After a moment, the siren went silent again. He walked back toward the house, but she closed the door. She could hear his boots on the wooden steps.

"Go away!" she said, fortified by the door between them. She couldn't face him anyway, couldn't begin to assimilate this with him standing there gloating.

"Katie, you know we need to talk about this." After a moment, he said, "I'm gonna keep my eye on you. Don't you worry about a thing. We'll talk again." Then he walked to his vehicle and left.

She tried to catch her breath as she stared at the sketch. How could he have been there? And more eerily, how could he have been inside her heart when she and Ben were exchanging vows at the justice of the peace?

A knock on the front door a few minutes later sent her out of her skin. Especially since she hadn't heard a car drive up. She wasn't ready to deal with Gary again, or anybody. She took the gun from the drawer and walked to the front window.

What her heart really didn't need at the moment was to

see Silas's rangy frame leaning against the column. He was wearing jeans and a black shirt. She stood at the window for a few seconds, deciding what to do. Ignore him would be the safest, all things considered. But she needed answers, answers only he could provide. She cracked open the door, somehow knowing he wouldn't barge into her home like Gary had.

He kept his distance, remaining by the column. "You all right?"

"Not really." She opened the door a fraction more and looked beyond Silas. He'd walked over—no vehicle. She pressed the gun against the wall next to the door. "I'm . . . well, I'm not in danger, if that's what you mean." Maybe.

He didn't look convinced. "Who was the guy who took you to work this morning? And where's Ben?"

"Ben's at a conference in Atlanta for a few days. That was Harold, one of Ben's friends." She narrowed her eyes. "How did you know?"

"Saw you in his truck. Harold who?"

"Boyd. Why?"

He hammered out the questions, "How long has he been in town? What do you know about him?"

"He's been here for several years now, owns One Man's Trash, that secondhand place on the corner. That's about all I know, or want to know, about him."

"You didn't look very comfortable with him."

"I'm not. He gives me the creeps."

"Any particular reason why?"

"I get the feeling he likes giving me the creeps."

He seemed to absorb that with interest, then nodded toward the empty drive. "Gary been bothering you?"

"You set off his siren, didn't you?"

He shrugged, reminding her of that insolent teenager she'd known so long ago. "I came over to see if you were okay and saw him in the house. You looked beyond uncomfortable, so I gave you a chance to get him out of the house."

She wasn't sure whether to thank him or not. It de-

118 TINA WAINSCOTT

pended on his motive for sending away law enforcement. And for coming over to begin with.

"Remember what I told you about not trusting anyone," he said. "I mean it, Katie. If you don't feel comfortable with someone, don't let them near you."

How could she explain that she *had* to ride with Harold? "Silas, tell me what's going on. The sheriff said he found stuff about girls who'd disappeared at your house . . . files and pictures and . . . sketches."

He raised his arm against the column and leaned his face against it. "Why'd you send Gary over there, anyway?"

"I didn't," she said on a rush, then wondered why she was so worried about what he thought of her. "Ben saw your truck in your drive."

"Did he know you'd been over there?"

"I wasn't sure, so I told him just in case. I keep causing you trouble, don't I?"

"It wasn't your fault. Neither time was."

He was looking at her in a way that made her feel all gooey inside. Not that appraising kind of way Gary did, or in Harold's leering way. This was different, sensual. The way a wolf surveys one of his pack. He nodded to the swinging bench in front of the window. "Talk to me through the window." Then he walked over and sat down.

She almost suspected he didn't trust himself with her. In any case, it was a good idea, talking through the screen. She set the gun on the couch next to her and opened the window. He sat sideways on the bench, his profile not much more than a silhouette. He was quiet for a few moments, as though figuring out how to word what he was going to say. She took the sketch from the coffee table and ran her finger across the worn edge. She would ask him about this once she had an explanation of the missing girls.

His arm rested along the top edge of the bench, only inches from her face. He turned to her and rested his chin on his arm. "Do you think I'm some kind of murderer?"

Hey, she was supposed to be asking the questions around here. "I don't know. Deep inside, no. But you have to admit you've given me nothing to base your innocence on, being mysterious about being here, being mysterious period."

She could feel his gaze right through the screen. "Why are you even talking to me then? If you've got the slightest inkling that I kill women, why would you let me within two feet of you?"

She folded her hands on the top of the sofa and propped her chin on top of them, only inches from his face. "I don't know. Maybe the deep-down feeling overrides everything else, at least until I hear it from you."

He flexed his fingers, and she heard a soft sigh escape him. "Katie, sharing doesn't come easy to me. I've always been a loner, you know that. Nobody knows me, maybe including me. I'll tell you what I can, what you're prepared to hear now."

"Are you going to tell me why you keep warning me not to trust anyone?"

"That's one of those things you're not prepared to hear yet."

"I see. Okay, start with the pictures and stuff."

"I told you about running off to Atlanta. I lived on the streets for a while, did odd jobs, did some things I'm not proud of, but I survived. I started writing about the things I saw on the streets and sending them to newspapers. After selling a few freelance pieces, *The Constitution* hired me full-time. I covered crimes and I wrote them better than anyone else. They liked my ability to show the crime from the victim's viewpoint. That's what I'm good at, expressing their feelings."

She wanted to know what things he'd done that he wasn't proud of, but she sensed he wouldn't part with that, either. "So you got off the streets then?"

"Yeah, I shared an apartment with a friend who was also trying to get her life together."

For some reason, that word—her—stuck Katie like a pin.

He paused for a moment, no doubt thinking of *her*. "A few years later, an editor of a publishing house saw my work and offered me a deal to cover a love-triangle story in the Hamptons. They obviously liked it, because they offered me another and then another. That's what I do, Katie. I write about murder, deception, the ultimate betrayal. I write about pain and destruction."

"You don't sound very happy about it."

"It's who I am. It's who I've always been. And I make a decent living at it."

She was so caught up in his personal story, she'd momentarily missed the connection. "So that's why you have all those notes and pictures?" The relief was plain in her voice.

"Yes. There were two disappearances outside the Atlanta area back in 1989 and 1990. They were loosely connected because of one body being found without a shoe and the other girl's shoe being found. There were a couple of other disappearances, too, but nothing was found. I'd become . . . interested in the case because of those."

"I thought crime writers got involved once the murderer was found."

"Not always. Sometimes we get involved if there's evidence of a serial or spree killer. But this was dropped because nothing else happened that matched or indicated a continuation. Only I didn't drop it. I pursued it on my own time, but found nothing. Eight years later I got involved in the case again." Whenever he paused, she wondered if he was deciding what to tell her and what to omit. "I started investigating disappearances in small towns southeast of Atlanta, going through old microfiche and talking to law enforcement. I found a pattern that no one else found. Some cases could be linked logically, but not all of them. Because the disappearances occurred all over, and mostly in small towns, nothing was connected. I decided to follow my instincts and start a full-scale investigation."

"The sheriff knows about the connections now."

"I figured he did, and that he also thinks I'm the one taking the girls."

"He does," she answered without thinking about it. Silas's explanation made sense, yet she knew he was holding back a lot, too. "Why didn't you tell me you owned the house and property?"

"I told you, sharing isn't easy for me. Even with you."

Those last three words were weighted with some emotion she couldn't place. But he had shared some. "So, you like to be trusted, but you have trouble trusting people, is that it?"

"Something like that." He traced a line across the screen between them with his finger, making her feel that he was somehow touching her. "You're the reason I kept the property and house. I've never been anywhere that felt like home. I don't even own an apartment in Atlanta anymore. I realized I spent more time at the office space I rented than at home, so I got rid of the apartment and made a bedroom there."

She put her hand against the screen. "Tell me why you kept this place, Silas. Why because of me?" She held her breath and waited for his answer.

He kept tracing that line back and forth, and he tickled her palm where her hand pressed against the screen. "You were the only good memory I had of this place. You were probably the only good thing about my life. I held you in the first moments of your life and I knew you were special. I was so touched that your mom trusted me to help her— well, truth was she probably didn't have much choice. She'd gone into labor at the trailer and the only other person who was around ran to call the midwife. She was so scared. After you were born I helped your mom from time to time, doing things around the trailer. The kind of things a five-year-old can do, I suppose, but I felt like I mattered, like I was helping. Then my dad caught wind of it and went through the roof. He figured I was taking time away from him to help Ellie, so I couldn't come anymore.

"Life sucked and the kids in town hated me and then you came to me to help you with the kitten. You were everything good and right with the world. You were pure and you were willing to fight for what was right."

She couldn't stand talking to him through the window anymore. She walked outside and sat down on the far side of the bench. "Tell me about my mama, Silas. Tell me about the day I was born."

"You were all slimy and looked a bit like a prune."

"Ew!" Their laughter faded together. She leaned closer and asked in a soft voice, "Tell me what she did. Was she happy?"

Silas had tucked his leg beneath him and sat sideways to give her room to join him. He reached over and touched her chin before letting his hand drop. "She was in total awe of you. You came fast, but she had a hard time of it. But you wouldn't have known that when she held you, when she saw you. Even slimy and pruny, you might as well have been an angel. We both just stared at you until the midwife got there. Then she cut the umbilical cord and cleaned you up and you really did look like an angel. And as I watched you grow up, you became beautiful and smart and strong. I don't want you to get the wrong idea. I didn't lust after you. I just wanted to protect you, to keep all the world's harm from you."

She could see his face better now in the dim light from the house. But it was his voice that touched her, the way he spoke about her. She felt everything inside her melt. If only she'd really grown up to be beautiful and smart and strong. If only Silas could have protected her from harm.

"Was my father around then?" she asked, because saying anything else was too dangerous.

"I never saw anyone around who could have been your dad. Ellie never talked about him, either. I asked once, and she said, 'There is no dad,' and it screwed up how I thought things were supposed to happen for a long time."

They both laughed, though it was a softer laugh. Katie would probably never know who fathered her, and she wasn't sure she cared. All right, sometimes she cared a little.

He ran the tips of his fingers over the top of her hair, sweeping it out of her face. Even that innocent gesture made her shiver. "I thought I'd be like a big brother to you, you know, take care of you and all. It didn't work out that way."

She could hardly breathe as the feel of his fingertips contradicted his words. She wasn't feeling at all sisterly about him. She wanted to crawl in his lap and put her arms around him. She tightened her fingers around the top of the bench to keep herself in place.

"Why do you keep notes on serial killers?"

He looked up for a moment, thinking. "I can't really explain it. It's like an obsession, I guess. I want to know what makes a human being cross the line into inhumanity. What makes him not kill one day and kill the next."

"Why is crime writing who you are, Silas?"

He rested his hand only inches from her hand on the back of the bench. "When you live in the dark too long, the dark begins to live inside you."

Before thinking about it, she covered his hand with hers. "Then walk away. Look into the light."

He started to lean forward, as though to kiss her. His mouth, in fact, hovered over hers for a fraction until he completed the movement and got to his feet. He reached behind his neck and unclasped the gold chain. He held the chain in his grip, and the cross swung like a pendulum at the end. "Your mom gave this to me the day after she had you. She wanted me to have it as a thank-you for helping her. I hid it from my dad for years, knowing he'd hock it for cash. I'd planned to give it to you later, and then when I came back to town years ago. It didn't seem like the right time, and I'm not sure how Ben would have reacted anyway. I want you to have it now."

He held it out to her. She watched the cross swing toward her, then back to Silas. Her heart caved in at the gesture, and at the thought of having something of her mother's. "But it's yours," she said in a hoarse voice. "She gave it to you."

"I was just keeping it for you. Wear it to ward off evil."

She'd seen him touch it in a subconscious gesture and

wondered if he really felt that way about it. "Put it on me. Please."

He hesitated, then stepped forward and reached around her. She was woman enough to admit that's what she wanted, him to stand close and make her feel . . . well, like a woman. She also wanted the symbolism of him putting it on her, transferring the gift. He smelled awfully clean for someone who had no running water. She wondered if he bathed in the creek that ran through their properties. His chin nearly touched her nose as he finished the clasp and stepped back.

It still felt warm from his body heat. She touched the bars of the cross. "Have you worn this for long?"

"Since my father died."

"Wait, I have something for you, too."

She went into the house to the tune of his protests. After rummaging in her jewelry case, she returned with a quartz crystal. "Crystals are supposed to have special powers. Let's believe this one will chase away the darkness."

"I can't take that. You keep it."

"But why? You gave me this."

"It's just . . . I can't." He closed his hand over hers with the crystal in her palm. "I want you to have this, too." He handed her a wrinkled piece of paper with a phone number on it. "It's my beeper."

"Why do you have a beeper?"

"So my editor can get hold of me while I'm on assignment. It's easier than giving him a lot of different numbers. And I don't have a phone here, just my cell phone, which I don't keep on all the time. If you need me, page me. Leave a 911 and I'll be right over."

She wrapped the paper around the crystal. "You won't owe me anything if I give this to you, you know. If that's what you're worried about."

"What do you mean?"

"It's a gift, that's all. I don't expect anything from you."

He still didn't take the crystal. "That's what a gift is."

"There's a price for everything, Silas. What they say

about there being no free lunch, it's true. Everything has a price tag on it, an expectation. That's obviously what you think, that if I give you something, there's some sort of expectation. I'm just saying there isn't."

He looked into her eyes and said, "God, Katie." He ran his hand back through his hair and looked away for a moment. "I'd better go. Being around you is . harder than I thought it would be."

He started to step away, but she grabbed his arm. "What do you mean? Am I a horrible person? Tell me Silas. I need to know. Is that why no one in town likes me because there's something wrong with me?"

He closed his eyes, and she saw the muscles in his jaw tic. "There's nothing wrong with you."

"There must be. You just said being around me is hard."

He opened his eyes and took her wrists in his hands. Her knuckles brushed against his stomach. "Being around you is hard because . . . I don't want to want you, Katie. I don't want to lose myself in you. I don't vant to kiss you again. That's not why I'm here."

"Why are you here?" she whispered, her voice breaking at everything he'd said. He wanted her. He wanted to kiss her.

"To warn you to be careful. To make sure you're safe."

"From what? You're confusing me. Safe from what?"

His gaze scanned her face, and his voice was low and deadly. "From someone out there who's hunting women for sport, the man who killed Carrie Druthers and a lot of other women just because he enjoys doing it, because he can. He's been watching you, Katie. And it's someone you know."

When the phone rang, all the blood rushed to her head and nearly wiped her out. She sagged against Silas for a moment before catching her balance. "I've got to get that. It's probably Ben."

Her shoulder bumped against the doorjamb as she made her way inside. "Hello?"

"Hi, honey. Just checking to see if everything's all right. You sound a little breathless."

"I was in the shower. Ran to get the phone." She was facing the kitchen, not wanting to see Silas while she spoke to Ben. "I'm fine."

"Has Silas bothered you at all?"

She nearly jumped when he appeared in the open doorway. He pushed the door closed, locked it, and walked toward her with a determined look on his face. He looked bigger inside her house than he had on the darkened porch. His hands brushed by her shoulders as he passed her and went into the kitchen. Then he walked outside and closed the door quietly behind him.

"Katie, what's wrong? You didn't answer me. Has Silas been there?"

She swallowed, though it felt like goose feathers coated her throat. "No, but . . ." Headlights slashed across the living room again. "Someone's here."

"Keep me on the phone. See who it is."

She walked woodenly to the door and saw Gary's Explorer. She went to the window where she'd just been talking to Silas.

"What do you want?" she asked, holding the phone where Gary could see it.

"I was just heading home and checked again. Silas's car is there, but he's not. Which means he's around here somewhere. Do you want me to check around the house?"

"No, I'm fine, thank you. The house is locked tight and I've got Ben's beeper number if anything comes up." But it wasn't Ben's number on the paper still clutched in her damp palm.

"He's a long while away, Katie. You should be calling me if you hear anything."

"I will. Thank you." She closed the window.

"Was that Tate?" Ben asked.

"It was Gary. He's already been by once."

"Well, you didn't sound very grateful that he was checking on you. Thank him right now. Before he leaves."

"I don't like him, Ben."

"He's doing his job making sure you're okay. Now thank him." Ben's voice went firm, as though he were talking to a child.

She glanced into the kitchen. "No, Ben, I will not. Good night."

She dropped the phone on the couch as though it were a hot potato and released a deep breath. She'd stood up for herself. She'd seen a glimmer of that feisty little girl who had impressed Silas so much. The phone started ringing again, and she answered it with a wan, "I'm sorry I spoke to you like that."

She stood in the doorway and looked out at the darkness. If Silas was out there, he was well hidden. He'd obviously seen Gary pull up and didn't want to be seen there with her. Thank God for that. Gary would delight in telling Ben about her visitor.

She finished her conversation, adding yet another apology at the end. The glimmer had faded. She curled up on the couch and touched the cross. Silas's explanation of his research sounded plausible. But he was right; he was dangerous. Because she'd stood on the porch with him knowing he was holding secrets and pain close to him. Because she'd wanted to kiss him. He'd not only awakened the feisty girl inside her, but he was also awakening a woman she didn't even know.

She glanced out the window, hoping he would return. What did he mean that someone meant to hurt her? Someone she knew? She shivered. Was Ben the only man she could trust?

---○ CHAPTER 10

SILAS WATCHED HAROLD pull down Katie's driveway. He'd give the guy five minutes, then he'd follow. Luckily, within three minutes the old truck emerged. She was sitting as far away from him as possible.

He'd rather be the one taking her to work, but that would cause more trouble. This way, he could make sure she was all right without interfering. Besides, being alone with her was not a good thing. Last night had proved that, if he'd needed the proof.

The police tail was on him, too. Gary was enjoying the game of chase, and probably soaking up the fact that it looked as though Silas were following Katie. Everyone had their obsession. He was apparently Gary's. Once she was safely at the hospital, Silas played a little game of his own and lost Gary. He knew some of these back roads better than anyone. Roads that hadn't existed in years. Then he circled back to town and headed to Gary's apartment.

Silas had ideas on who the Ghost was. Some of them he didn't like, but he couldn't exclude anyone . . . even himself. Gary's persistence parlayed him into the role of suspect. And while Gary was no doubt checking on his past, Silas was going to do some checking of his own.

One of those things he wasn't proud of in his past was now going to come in handy. He pulled out the lock-pick kit, and after a moment, the apartment Gary lived in was open to his perusal. The place was bachelor messy with beat-up furniture and faded carpet. A mechanic's magazine covered three *Playboys* on the coffee table. The satellite dish was tuned to one of those adult channels.

There wasn't anything criminal about a guy amusing himself. Silas needed a lot more than that. He found an old gun under Gary's mattress. Hiking boots in the closet with leaves and mud in the treads. Could have been hunting or hiking. No other shoes but his own. But the Ghost was too smart to leave something like that around. That's why he left them on the side of the road, pointing to no one.

What did bother him was finding a picture of Katie in the dresser drawer. She'd been standing in a group of people, maybe with the Emersons on a family outing. She'd been about twelve or thirteen. Her picture had been trimmed away from the rest of the people, singling her out.

Silas had relocked the door just in case, but was still surprised to hear a key being inserted into it. There wasn't much room to hide in a one-bedroom apartment. He dove under the bed. It was most likely Gary's shoes he saw walking purposefully into the bedroom. He heard noises, and then heard him take a leak.

That's when Silas noticed the picture he'd dropped on the floor in front of the dresser. He hoped Gary wouldn't notice it, too. His boots went right by it . . . at first. Before Silas could even draw a breath in relief, Gary backed up and stood by the picture. Then picked it up.

"What the hell . . ."

Silas couldn't believe he'd been found out so fast when he felt the mattress lift. The fact that it dropped back down wasn't so comforting, either. Gary had taken his gun and thrown open the closet door. Silas started surveying his hiding place. The bed sat up high, with wooden frames down the sides. He pulled himself up against the bottom of the bed by holding on to the boards of the frame. His fingers poked through the flimsy fabric. He braced his feet in the far corners and sucked in his breath. If Gary found him, he'd probably get away with shooting him under some pretext or another. Who would care if he shot a suspected serial killer?

*   *   *

Katie had brought a sandwich with her to avoid a repeat of yesterday's visit to the diner. She had another task in mind for lunch anyway: a visit to the library. It was a long trek in the hot summer sun once she cleared the shady comfort of the cemetery. The long, black pants didn't help, nor did the colorful vest she'd worn over her white shirt. She wondered what people would think if she'd worn the yellow hip-huggers and flower shirt. Harold was outside working on the old wagon. She avoided meeting his gaze.

Silas wanted to kiss her. He wanted her.

Those thoughts had kept her up most of the night. It was the first time she'd seen that kind of desire in a man's eyes. The kind of desire that made a woman feel sexy and warm all over. She passed the shopping strip that housed the diner. Before she could stop herself, she scanned the busy parking lot for Silas's vehicle. It wasn't there. People walked together toward the diner, chatting and laughing. The sign was still in the window pleading for help at the fair. She was an outcast in her own town. She touched the gold cross as she held up her head and walked on by.

By the time she reached the library, she was covered in a layer of perspiration. She pulled her hair back with her hand as she walked inside the cool interior, then remembered the birthmark and released her hair. It obviously bothered Ben. Mostly she'd gotten used to it.

The librarian gave her a prim nod before going back to whatever it was she was doing. Katie took out books from time to time, mysteries mostly, though she didn't know anyone who worked there. Like most of Flatland's residents, they seemed to regard Katie as an outsider not worthy of getting to know.

She sat down at the new computer system and tried pulling up Silas's name. She even spelled it several different ways, but nothing came up. Then she went to the true crime section. It was a sizable section, even in their tiny library. The titles reminded her of Silas's words the night before about murder, deception, and the ultimate betrayal. She saw books by Lisa Pulitzer and Ann Rule, by an assortment of others, but nothing by Silas Koole. She even asked the librarian to see if the on-line book stores had anything. Nothing.

Disappointment was two-pronged. She'd wanted to know more about Silas through his writing. And if he was lying about writing those books, there was probably a darker reason for his having those notes.

But what reason could he have for knowing intimate details of her life?

When Katie was ready for Bertrice's stories and laughter to break up the afternoon silence, she glanced at the calendar and realized the girl had detention after school that day. Most of the hospital's appointments were scheduled around Ben's absences, leaving only routine things for her to deal with. Otherwise, it was dead slow.

She passed some time checking their food and medical inventory. She was filling out an order form at the reception desk when the door burst open and Gary stepped inside. She felt an uncomfortable twist in her stomach.

"A dog ran out in front of my vehicle," he said in a rush. His hair was tousled and his skin damp with sweat. "Help me bring him in." Then he walked back outside again.

She followed, not sure whether to trust him or not. The prospect of an injured dog, however, overrode her fears and propelled her on. He'd opened the tailgate of his explorer, and she saw the golden retriever lying on a board in the back. Blood stained the plywood, though Katie was relieved to note there wasn't a lot of it. Gary was already maneuvering the board so she could take one end.

"I tried to swerve around him, but I couldn't," he said as they carried the dog inside. "I got the board from a construction site."

"Let me take a look at him and see what he needs."

She always had to push past her fury at animal owners for not keeping their pets secure. The puppy last week was evidence of that danger. She often saw packs of dogs roaming the streets. Once she'd even seen a potbellied pig roaming with its dog friends.

She looked at Gary and hated the thought that slammed into her mind. Had he purposely hit the dog as an excuse to come here? Then her instincts kicked in and she instructed him to help carry the dog to the exam room.

The dog wore a blue collar, but no tag or license. "Do you know whose dog this is?"

"I'm not sure. There are a couple of farms out where I hit him. He probably belongs to one of them."

She removed the collar and started examining him—no, her—for injuries. The dog tried to get up, but Gary gently held her down. She resisted the urge to meet his gaze in a silent thank-you. She didn't want him that close to her, but she needed his help.

"All I can see are road burns and a few lacerations. This one's pretty deep." She was talking to herself, logging each area into memory. "You're one lucky girl." She shaved the hair away from the injuries and cleaned them. The dog tried to get up again, but Gary held her in place. She stroked the dog's face, which luckily had escaped injury. "It's okay, sweetie. I know it stings, but it's going to be okay." The dog licked her hand.

"It can't understand you, you know," Gary said.

She started to explain it wasn't the words themselves that were important, but the tone they were spoken in. But he wouldn't understand kindness or the pain she felt for these animals. She went back to work, using a disposable plastic pistol that looked like a toy ray gun to staple the deep wound closed. All the while, she spoke softly to the dog, who resigned herself to the ministrations with a sigh. Once Katie had her bandaged, she gave the dog an Amoxicillin tablet and an injection of Torb for the pain.

She didn't want to notice that Gary was stroking the dog's fur as he watched her work. She didn't want to see how gentle he was.

"You're good at what you do," he said as she washed up and removed the smock she'd put on earlier.

Compliments came so rarely, but she couldn't let this one soften her. "You sound surprised."

"I thought you were just Ben's helper."

Those words ate into her confidence like acid. "She's stable for now. Maybe you could put out a bulletin for her owner. Thanks for bringing her in."

She hoped that would suffice as a dismissal. He was in uniform, which meant he was on duty. Didn't he have someplace else to be?

Gary walked up to the table, his hand resting only inches from hers. "It's a man's duty to protect a helpless animal."

Her face flushed hot with anger that had been seething for eighteen years. "Don't even talk to me about kindness to animals. Not after what you did."

He surprised her by grabbing her hands. "What I did to your cat was wrong. But there was a reason I did it, a reason that involves you."

She jerked her hands away. "You're *blaming* me?"

"No, of course not. When the time is right, I'll tell you."

She crossed her arms in front of her. "Tell me now."

He surveyed her stance and the stiff expression on her face. "The time isn't right."

"Any apology or explanation you might have is eighteen years too late anyway. I want you to go."

Even he seemed surprised by the vehemence in her voice. "I'm trying to make amends here. You and me, we need to come to an understanding. I did a bad thing. I had a rage management problem. There was something inside me, something I didn't know about then. I understand what it is now. I took it out on your cat. All I'm asking is for you to forgive me." He moved closer. "Forgive me, Katie. That's the first step."

And then what? Kill her? More than anything, she was aware of her situation. Alone. He had a gun. He was a lot bigger. And no one would believe her, not even Ben, if he assaulted her.

Silas's words came back to haunt her once again. *He's been watching you, Katie. And it's someone you know.* Fear clutched her heart, squeezing the strength right out of her.

"I'm not going to hurt you," he said, taking hold of her arm.

She jerked it back so hard that she toppled a tray. Bloody tweezers and other instruments scattered across the linoleum floor. He still had a hold on her arm, even after all that.

"Stop being afraid of me," he ground out. Intensity burned in his brown eyes. "I can't stand your fear and anger anymore. I want it to stop. It's just you and me, Katie. Don't you understand?"

She shook her head. Her eyes felt as large as tennis balls. He just looked at her, as though deciding what to do with her.

"What else do you want from me?" he asked.

"What I want from you . . ." The words "is to leave" became "is to go out there and tell all those people who didn't believe me that I wasn't lying."

His fingers were digging into her arm even as he shook his head. "I would, if I wasn't a deputy. What would they think of me if I told them what I'd done, and that I'd lied about it?"

"What would they think if they knew how you were bullying me?"

He didn't seem to hear that. "If it helps any, my dad beat the crap out of me for throwing that kitten."

"He believed me?" she whispered in disbelief.

"He wasn't sure what to believe, so he walloped me anyway. He liked doing it."

His grip had lessened some with those words, and she finally wrenched free. "Your father beat you?"

His laugh was bitter. "Ironic that no one would have believed me either if I'd said anything. Not my father, not upstanding Sam Savino. He has a rage management problem, too." Gary's laugh was bitter. "Runs in the family. But he has a nasty tendency to take what he wants no matter what the consequences. He told me I was worthless and then showed me just how worthless time and again." His eyes narrowed. "So you see we had that in common, too."

She moved to the opposite side of the table, the dog between them. She wasn't sure she believed him, either. He was good at lying. "We have nothing in common. Not then, not now."

He moved close again, taking note of her dipping down to the floor and picking up some of the fallen instruments— including one of the scalpels. She wasn't holding it out as a threat, but her fingers locked around the handle.

"Yes we do. And when you forgive me—and you will forgive me someday—we'll sit down and talk."

"Hey, what's going on in here?"

Katie nearly fainted in relief as Bertrice popped her head around the corner. She clearly didn't know what to make of the situation, especially as she took in Katie's rigid stance and the scalpel in her hand. Gary spit out an expletive, but gathered his composure.

"Gary was just leaving," she said on a breath as she joined Bertrice in the doorway. "Weren't you?"

He didn't reply, just gave a last look at the dog and sauntered out. Katie still gripped the scalpel. As soon as she heard the front door close, she forced herself to set it on the counter.

"You look as white as an egg," Bertrice said. "You okay? What was he doing here?"

Making light of the whole thing seemed the best way to handle it. And, she realized, wouldn't put her in the position to be disbelieved. "He hit this dog . . . accidentally." Maybe. "He and I don't particularly get along. It goes back to when we were kids."

"Too bad." Bertrice glanced toward the door. "He's kind of a hottie."

"A hottie?"

"Yeah, you know . . . good-looking. Hot. Especially compared to all the dorks in school. And that uniform . . . The girls talk about him a lot. I'd heard he lived here before."

Katie found herself staring at the door, too. "I wish he'd

stayed away." She looked at Bertrice. "Don't go near him. He may be a . . . hottie, but he's dangerous. Not to be trusted. Promise me you won't have anything to do with him."

Bertrice nodded in agreement, though her raised eyebrows showed she thought Katie was being extreme. "Are you all right?"

"I'm going to call it a day. Other than Gary, it's been a slow afternoon, and it's nearly four anyway."

"Are you sure you're all right? You can come home with me tonight if you want."

"I appreciate that, but I'll be fine. I just need some quiet time alone." As much as she'd love the company, she was in no mood for polite conversation. She was still shaking. "Let's close up."

Bertrice and Katie secured the retriever in one of the recovery pens and closed for the night. Katie would have to walk back to the hospital to check on her later, and that wasn't something she was looking forward to.

As soon as Katie opened her front door, the hairs on her neck went up. She wasn't sure why. The house was quiet. A thin stream of watery light washed over the couch and the dollhouse. She stood there for a few minutes absorbing the silence. And that's all it was, silent peacefulness. Still, she opened the hidden drawer in the phone table. The gun felt as though it weighed forty pounds. She advanced into the house. The kitchen looked normal. So did the bedroom. The office door was closed. That was mostly Ben's domain. She stood outside the door and listened.

She almost missed the faint shuffling sound. For the second time that afternoon, her heart jumped up into her throat. It was beginning to seem as though she lived in fear of something or another. Maybe it was just her imagination. A faint sound, this time the squeak of a drawer closing. *Be strong, Katie. Be feisty.* Holding the gun tight in her hand, she took a breath and pushed open the door.

* * *

"Sir? Would you pass these down, please?"

Fingers snapped in front of Ben's face. The man sitting in front of him was holding out a stack of papers to be passed on down his row to the other conference attendees.

He'd been deep in thought, but not about the latest in veterinary instruments. He'd have to catch up by reading the notes. He was a fast learner, so he wasn't worried about missing anything.

But he *was* worried about Katie. He'd called her that morning at the hospital, and she'd sounded down. He sat in the last of the day's seminars and wondered what he could do to bring back the happy woman he'd known since she was a girl. What could he do to make her his again? Everyone was grateful for his kind deeds, the way an animal repays kindness with its loyalty. Why wasn't Katie? At least he'd curtailed her insistence on helping with that damn fair. It was mean, but he liked things the way they were. Look what just one person was doing to his wife. Bertrice was poisoning her mind, giving her unsuitable clothing. Seeing Katie in that getup . . . it wasn't right. She wasn't supposed to look that sexy. He didn't like feeling jealous of a teenager, of the way she made Katie laugh. Ben hadn't made her laugh in . . . well, he couldn't even remember the last time.

His gut twisted at that thought. He had to keep her close and away from all the vamps in town. No one could blame him for wanting to keep his wife pure. She was his. She'd always been his. He'd made a perfect life for the two of them.

Silas was the bigger problem. Katie had sneaked off to see him at least once. She'd sounded weird on the phone the night before, too, which might have meant he was there. Could she be that stupid to let a possible killer into her home? The thought knifed him in the gut.

He got up in the middle of the lecture, gathered his briefcase and notes, and walked out. A few people looked up, but he didn't meet their eyes.

Tate picked up his line a few minutes later with a brusque, "Hello, Ben. What's up?"

"I'm just checking in on the Silas Koole situation. Katie's there all by herself, and I'm a little worried about her." It also bothered him that she'd been rude to Gary. Katie wasn't rude to anyone, at least she hadn't been until Silas had returned to town. She'd even tried to keep Gary from investigating Silas.

"We haven't turned up anything conclusive yet. Nothing but a parking ticket and two speeding tickets. The business is his, as is the property. Gary's taken a personal interest in this whole situation. Glad to see the boy take an initiative, though I think it's bordering on obsessive. In any case, he's keeping a close eye on Katie. He's also been watching Silas."

"I don't understand why he's not in jail yet. The man's obviously guilty."

"We can't prove that, Ben. I know you're uptight about this, but the law is the law. I've spent every spare minute checking into the facts of this case. I've been talking to law enforcement in every county where a girl has disappeared, trying to tie Silas in with the time of disappearance. Here's something I have found, though. He has talked to, or tried to talk to, many of these girls' families *after* their disappearances. He tells them that he's researching a book on the case, that he's a crime writer. We're checking on that right now. If he's lying, we're on to something for sure."

"What's he asking the families?"

"One woman I spoke with said he walked around her daughter's room, touched some of her things, and said she definitely wasn't planning to run away like the authorities suspected."

"Did he take anything?"

"Not that she knew of, but here's what I'm finding out, reading about serial killers: they like to return to the scene of the crime. And they like to have a souvenir of their victims. If Silas is talking to these parents under false pretenses, he's playing one sick game. And I want him taken out. What we need is a body, something to prove the girls are dead.

"I want to nail this bastard. That's what's going to put Flatlands on the map, not buying Silas's stupid land and putting in some stupid park. People will flock here to see the town where they finally put an end to a vicious killer."

And Tate was going to enjoy being the one who caught him. The pleasure of that prospect oozed from the man's voice.

"So you're keeping an eye on Silas all the time?"

"When manpower permits. Gary's even doing it on his own time. But there's something else you ought to know . . . Silas has been enjoying a game of cat and mouse. He's been giving Gary and my other guys the slip now and then. And he's followed Katie and Harold to work both mornings you've been gone."

Ben swallowed hard on that. "Has he gone to the hospital to see her?"

"Not that we know of."

"Get rid of him, Tate. Either nail him or run him out of town. He's got to go."

"Now, Ben, we're doing the best we can. I'm doing this by the book, because when we do nail him—and we will— I want him in jail for a good long time. No more mistakes."

"Fry him, Tate. Make sure they fry him."

KATIE PUSHED THE door open and affected the kind of stance she'd seen television cops take. The gun was out in front of her. Adrenaline pounded through her, making her vision pulse with it. The empty room was a letdown. She scanned the office, only now able to take a breath. The bifold doors were open. The drawer in the metal desk was also open. Ben was meticulous about how he left this office.

It was more than that, though, that set her on edge and kept her standing in the open doorway: the feeling of someone being inside the room. She could hear nothing but the pounding of her heart. Maybe she was losing her mind. Paranoia did things like that to a person. She certainly had reason enough to be paranoid as of late.

The feeling persisted, though. She kept looking around the office, taking in the places where someone could be hiding. Inside the closet, maybe. Behind the desk. What would she do if she found someone there?

Throw up most likely, the way her stomach was jolting around inside her. Why would anyone be in here looking through their files? Logic happily invaded her mind, nearly replacing her instinctual fear. If a killer were on the prowl, he wouldn't be in here. And from what she'd heard, this killer didn't grab his victims from their houses.

Relief poured through her. She lowered the gun, though her fingers were still white where they gripped it. She'd have to pry them off for sure. She backed up to the kitchen area. If Ben could see her tonight, he'd be laughing at her. Her legs were wobbly when she walked to the table to sit down. Even before she'd pulled the chair out to drop into it, she looked at the kitchen door.

It was unlocked.

She braced herself with the table, blinking to make sure she wasn't imagining it. It was definitely unlocked. Her ears perked again for any sounds out of the ordinary. She took a deep breath, lifted the gun again, and walked back to the office.

Nobody's here, she told herself. *I left the door unlocked.* Even as she tried to convince herself of that, she knew it wasn't true. She always locked the doors when she was alone, even before she had a reason to.

She stood in the doorway again, waiting it out. In a moment of panic, she looked behind her, realizing she was so focused on the office, she was leaving her back wide open. Her heartbeat had picked up to supersonic speed the moment she'd seen the door unlocked. How did anyone overcome fear when it nearly debilitated you?

She'd been standing in the doorway for nearly ten minutes, hearing nothing but her waning heart spasms and the ticking clock. If someone were in there, they knew she was still standing there. She had herself nearly talked out of someone being inside again after another five minutes of silence. But she also knew she'd never relax unless she looked in the office just to make sure.

She took one step in. *Nobody's here, nobody's here,* she chanted with each subsequent step. *I'll laugh about this in just a few minutes, laugh at how scared I was. Over dinner, if I can eat, I'll laugh, and I won't even tell Ben. I'll—*

She made a choking sound when she saw the arm. It was real, there was someone crouched behind the desk, and he was going to kill her. It was too late to back out now, too late to call for help.

Silas stood with an annoyed expression on his face. "I didn't expect you to be home this early."

Her knees sagged, and she stumbled back and sank onto the striped loveseat. For a moment she felt all the blood leave her head. He started to walk over, but she gathered

herself in a way that amazed her and pointed the gun at
him. He paused, then raised his hands in mock surrender.

She pushed herself to a standing position. "What are you
doing in here?" Her voice sounded shrill and on the edge
of hysterical.

He did at least look contrite as he leaned against the
edge of the desk with his arms crossed in front of him. His
surrender sure hadn't lasted long. "I didn't mean to scare
you. I thought I'd be out of here before you got home. This
is not my day for breaking and entering, that's for sure.
I'm obviously out of practice."

He looked way too relaxed for a man being held at gun-
point. She checked her stance. The gun was pointed right
at him, at his stomach to be precise. He was wearing jeans
and a brown and green plaid shirt, probably to blend into
the woods for his getaway.

"What do you mean, it's not a good day for breaking
and entering?"

"Gary nearly caught me in his place, too. It's a long
story, but suffice it to say I'm glad I didn't let myself get
pudgy."

She caught herself looking down at that not-at-all-pudgy
body of his. Her gaze snapped back to his face. "What are
you doing here?" she asked again, this time raising the gun
to the vicinity of his chest.

He shook his head, looking for all the world . . . *disappointed in her?* "Katie, I'm glad you have a gun, I really
am. But you've got to be ready to shoot someone. That's
what I've been trying to tell you. Holding a gun on someone is one thing; being willing to use it is something altogether different." He made a quick move toward her, and
she jerked back. "That's what I'm talking about. If you
come home and find a man in your house, you can't be
afraid to shoot him. Even if you know him."

His chilling words from the night before slithered
through her mind. She raised the gun at his face now. "I'm
not afraid to shoot you."

"That's because you have no intention of shooting me.

It's not even loaded, is it?" Her expression must have given her away, because he only shook his head. "If you're in a bad situation, even with someone you thought you trusted, are you willing to shoot him to save your life? That's the bottom line, Katie. What if I have a gun, too?"

He did have a gun. Gary had found it. She glanced down at him again, looking for any telltale bulges. She wasn't taking any more chances. She advanced closer, her gun still aimed right at him. "It's loaded, Silas. And I'm willing to use it if necessary."

Keeping the gun aimed with one hand, she patted him down with her other hand. He was all muscle beneath the worn, soft cotton of his shirt. She kept darting her gaze to where she was patting and back to his face. He seemed to suffer her ministrations without much trouble. In fact, she was having more trouble than he as she got to his jeans. She had to kneel down, pressing against the thick fabric, avoiding the front section.

He groaned when she patted his inner thigh, then twisted her right off her feet. It happened so fast, she didn't have a chance to even react. In a flash, she was lying on the floor, he was straddling her, and she had no idea where her gun had even gone.

"Katie, for God's sake, you've got to get better at protecting yourself. You left yourself wide open, and look what could have happened."

He was lecturing her! This penetrated the haze of her fear first, that and his weight on top of her. He was leaning over her, his hair falling on either side of his face. "This is dangerous."

It was very dangerous, because, of all the crazy emotions running through her, desire shouldn't be one of them. There was something sick and delicious about being pinned beneath him.

She pushed at him. "Let me up!"

His gaze swept over her face and down to where his body fused with hers. He abruptly got up and turned to help her up. She waved away his help and got to her feet on her own. "Is that what this is about? Scaring me?" She picked up the gun that had slid across the carpet.

"No, Katie, that's not why I'm here."

"I want answers, Silas. No more games. You're making me crazy, telling me to be afraid, not telling me why, sneaking into my house . . ." *My heart.* "I could have shot you! And you wanted me to! Are you crazy like they say?"

For a few long moments, he just looked at her. She swore he could read every thought in her head. He ran his hand back through his hair and sighed. "Maybe I am, Katie. Maybe I am."

"Your books weren't in the library."

"I write under a pseudonym. Johnny Black."

She'd seen that name in her search. Relief chased away a tidbit of her fear. The rest mingled in her stomach. "You said you broke into Gary's place. You think Gary's the guy taking the women?"

"Could be."

He revealed infuriatingly little information. "But you don't know."

He shook his head.

"You said someone was after me. Someone I know."

She saw the shadow of fear in his blue eyes. "I'm sure of that much."

"You know who it is?"

"Wish I did."

The weight of the gun made her drop her arm to her side. "Why are you here, then?" She looked at the desk and saw a folder open to their credit card statements. "You can't think . . ."

"I'm not eliminating anyone until I can prove they're innocent."

She laughed, though it sounded edgy. "You are crazy. Ben's not a killer. Gary, maybe. He's been harassing me ever since he discovered you were back in town. He came to the hospital today. You would have been proud of me: I held him off with a scalpel."

"But could you have used it on him? That's what worries me. I'm glad to see some of your feistiness is still in there." He touched her collarbone, rubbing his finger back and forth. "I can see it in your eyes, too. But it may not be enough."

"Is that how you knew I wouldn't shoot you? You could see it in my eyes?"

"Part of it. I don't want to get into that just yet. Not with you already thinking I'm crazy." He turned toward the file on the desk. "I was looking for dates, matching up the times Ben's out of town with the disappearances."

"He pays in cash. The credit card is only for emergencies and ordering things. That doesn't mean anything," she added at the quirk of his mouth.

"Maybe, maybe not."

She took a step closer. "How do you know this killer is after me?" Her voice dropped an octave. "How do you know so much about me, Silas? It's driving me crazy, wondering how you know . . . things no one else knows." She left the room and returned with the sketch. "This, Silas. How did you come to have this?"

When he looked at the sketch, he had the same expression he'd had when she caught him. "Gary gave that to you, didn't he?"

"It doesn't matter how I got it, but yes, he did. He said you had notes about my life. About . . . the day I married Ben."

He took in the turmoil in her expression and ran his fingers down his face with a sigh. "That's the part I don't want to get into just yet. I'll explain everything when the time is right."

"You and Gary, when the time is right. Are you both in this together?"

"What do you mean?"

"He said there was something inside him when he threw Gus, something he didn't know was in there. He's also going to tell me when the time is right." She wanted to curse when the phone rang. "Don't you dare go anywhere. I want answers."

It was Ben. "Honey, I tried you at the hospital before five and you weren't there. Then I called the house and you didn't answer. I got worried. What's going on?"

A frisson of annoyance went through her. She walked back into the office, and like a ghost, Silas was gone. "I didn't feel well, that's all. Gary brought in a dog that he'd hit, and once I had her stabilized, I just felt dragged out. It had been slow up until then, so I closed early and came home. You probably called here when I was on my way."

As she talked, she walked through the house checking all the rooms. No sign of Silas. He could have been a figment of her imagination if the file wasn't still open on the desk. She picked up one of the bills.

"You sound funny again. Is someone there?"

"No one's here but me." That was apparently true.

"Has Silas been around? Have you seen him, Katie?"

She let the bill drift down to the desk. "Just around town."

"He followed you to work both mornings. I can't emphasize enough how dangerous he is, sweetheart. Tate thinks Silas is the guy taking women. Please keep yourself safe until I come home. Okay? Promise?"

Her hand automatically went to her cross. "I will." Stupid promise. Silas had been right there, and she'd let him get the upper hand.

"You know you mean the world to me. If anything ever happened to you, I don't know what I'd do. Do you love me, Katie?"

Her hand squeezed the cross, digging the edges into her palm. "I do love you, Ben. I always have, always will." What would he do if she ever left him? The one time she'd left her mother . . .

"I love you, too, Katie. More than anything. I'll see you tomorrow."

Once she'd hung up, she walked to the kitchen window and searched the woods. It was still light out, but she couldn't see Silas anywhere. Once again he'd given her the slip and left burning questions unanswered.

* * *

It was nearly nine o'clock by the time Katie had fixed dinner, returned everything in the office back to normal, and made sure every window in the house was locked tight. She wasn't sure how Silas had managed to open the kitchen door, and that made her completely uneasy.

Then she remembered the dog at the hospital. She had to check on her at least once during the night. Ben hadn't even asked about the dog or how she'd handled it. He'd only cared about Silas hanging around.

All that adrenaline she'd used earlier had drained her energy, but she readied herself to walk to the hospital. She'd done it a few times, when Ben was tied up with a patient and she needed to get home to start supper. But he hadn't liked it.

She doused the lights in the living room and stepped onto the porch. She decided in favor of not being visible to having the security of the light when she returned. She'd left the office light on to guide her back.

The woods were alive with an evening wind that rattled the leaves and made it sound like heavy rain. The air was warm and slightly humid, and the breeze was a welcome addition. It also masked her footsteps, another bonus. Of course, it masked anyone else's footsteps, as well.

She hated feeling this trepidation over doing something she'd done for years: walk through the woods at night. But it was there, like a ghost, looming in the darkness around her. Silas's voice whispered about danger. Ben's voice warned her about Silas. Even Harold's voice asked if she was afraid, being out here in the woods all by herself. She pulled her black sweater tighter and headed into the trees.

She'd only taken a few steps when she realized what she was hearing wasn't wind in the leaves but the sound of a car coming down the drive. These trees weren't big enough to hide behind, but she ducked behind a trunk anyway. She wasn't surprised to see Gary's vehicle pull up to the house. He looked full of himself as he swaggered up the porch steps. He knocked several times, then walked around the perimeter of the house. He even tried to peer in the windows, making her wonder if he'd done that before.

He looked around at the woods, but unlike Silas, didn't find her. She shivered again at Silas's spookiness. Luckily, Gary didn't have whatever power Silas did. He finally got into his vehicle and left.

Her penlight led the way through the woods. Soon, the trees thinned out. She could smell pine and the scent of the fire that some kids had started a year ago when they were playing with matches. They'd had to evacuate the animals while the fire blazed. Luckily, it had been contained quickly, without going near the cemetery or their building.

Light glowed dimly from the recovery room, where she'd left a night-light on to soothe the dog. The front light lit up the entry. She went inside and locked the door. And then, just in case, she checked each room.

The dog woke up when she snapped on the light. "Hi, there, Goldie," she soothed as she opened her gate. "That seems like a good name for you." Her tail thumped in agreement, and she leaned forward and licked Katie's hand. "I wish you could tell me what happened." She checked her lacerations. No sign of infection or shock. She sat with her for a time and gave her some loving before returning the room to its peaceful, dim state.

The wind had kicked up even more by the time she walked outside again. Rain would be good, but not until she returned home. But it was a dry wind that blew her hair in her face. She glanced to the north, where the cemetery sprawled out in the glow of moonlight. She didn't know why, but she was drawn to it. She wasn't afraid of ghosts. As a child, before the bad thing happened with her mama, she used to come here just to prove to the other kids that she wasn't afraid. She hadn't been afraid of much back then.

The only ghosts she saw were her younger self. *Chicken! I'm not afraid of ghosts. See, there's nothing here.* She'd run all around the cemetery, and then tripped on a hole. She could still hear the echo of kids' laughter.

She walked to the edge where the first cluster of graves

sat. Moonlight danced on the gravestones like fairies. Though she couldn't see the details, she knew the black iron fence surrounding this group had a lamb sitting under a tree molded into each section. She also knew someone left flowers here every once in a while. The scent of fresh earth tainted the air, even though no one had been buried here in many years. She lifted her nose, trying to trace the scent.

"Looking for ghosts?" Silas's voice said through the darkness.

She surprised herself by not jumping in fright. At first she couldn't even see him. Then, slowly, he materialized out of the huge oak trees at the corner of the plot.

"Looks like I've found my first one." She congratulated herself on sounding calm and cool, when that was the last thing that she felt as he walked closer. "Did you follow me here? Or do you regularly hang around graveyards?"

He stopped only a few inches from her. His face was in shadows, and his lips were shiny as though he'd just licked them. "Would you believe the latter?"

"Not really."

"Good. Don't trust anyone."

"If you were following me, why'd you let me know you were here?"

"I wasn't expecting you to walk this way. I didn't want to scare you."

That was so laughable, she did let out a burst of laughter. "But sneaking around, breaking into my house, and warning me that someone's trying to kill me, someone I know, that isn't meant to scare me."

He didn't share her humor, warped though it was. "That's different. What are you doing walking in the woods at night, anyway?"

"No one's been abducted from the woods yet as far as I know. I had to check on a patient."

"Did you bring the gun?"

She glanced down at her empty hands. "No. I'm not used to being a gun-totin' individual."

He slid his hands down her arms and took her hands in

his. "Don't take any chances, Katie." The graveness in his voice almost overrode the way his hands made her feel. In the distance she heard a car drive by, reminding her how far from civilization she was.

She squeezed his hands, maybe because she didn't want him to get away again. "Tell me what's going on, Silas. I need to know for my own sanity."

He squeezed back, pulling her close enough to feel his body heat, but not his body. "It's easier to tell you like this . . . in the dark."

"Why?"

He released one of her hands and trailed his finger down her cheek. "Because you're going to look at me like they all do, and I don't want to see that in your eyes."

She felt her chest squeeze at the vulnerability in his voice. "Why do I matter?" she whispered, wanting to matter so bad, it hurt.

He closed his eyes and tilted his head back. "You've always mattered, Katie. More than you'll ever know."

He'd told her nothing yet, and still it was as though he'd reached right in and taken her heart in his hands. He met her gaze, though she could see nothing of what lay beyond those dark shadows. Moonlight danced over his face, too, as the wind shifted the leaves above them. For that moment, she saw a glimpse of his soul mirrored in his eyes. Moonlight fairies skittered across her face and over their joined hands.

"Do you know what empathy is?"

She nodded. "When you can understand what someone is feeling."

"Because you can read their expressions and body language." She nodded again, and he continued. "I know what people feel, because I *feel* what they're feeling. The closer I am physically to someone, the stronger the feeling is. That's how I knew you couldn't shoot me."

She started to pull away, but he held on tight. "You can read my mind?"

"No. Usually, I get a sense of what someone's feeling,

sometimes why they're feeling it. But I can't read their thoughts."

"Is that why . . . they called you Spooky Silas?"

He nodded. "I've had this . . . I don't know what to call it, ability, I guess, for as long as I can remember. I picked up feelings from my parents. Of course, I didn't realize it was anything . . . different. I thought everyone had it. When I told kids I knew they were upset or mad or whatever, it freaked them out. I figured out pretty soon that what I had made me strange. Even my parents, especially my dad, got freaked out by it. I learned to hold it in most of the time. And to stay away from people so I wouldn't feel anything."

She couldn't help but wonder what he felt from her now. Even she didn't know what she was feeling when it came to Silas. "You said you had an uncanny ability to capture the victim's feelings in your books."

She saw a glimmer of a smile on his face. "You remembered."

"I remember every word you've said. I just don't understand most of it."

He shook his head. "I don't understand all of it, either." He took a breath, released it slowly. "I get residual feelings, too. Sometimes I go to the victim's place of residence and pick up whatever feelings they were having in that room last. There are times when I know the girl simply ran away, that she was going through a lot at home." He let that sink in for a moment. "Do you think I'm spooky now?"

"I don't know." That was the truth. "But . . . how could you have known about the day I buried Gus? That sketch is, well, it's exactly how it happened. Even down to my clothes. Were you there?"

He bowed his head, raising their joined hands toward his chin. She felt the brush of his stubble against her knuckles, and then the startling feeling of his soft mouth against her skin. Her heart hiccupped, closing off her breath.

He looked up at her finally, though he didn't let go of her hands. His thumbs grazed over her fingers as he spoke. "Remember when I said that I held you right after you were born and knew you were special?" She nodded. "Something happened between us that day. It was like I . . . bonded with you. I didn't understand it at the time, but I knew it had something to do with my ability."

He'd wanted to protect her and keep her from harm. Something scurried through the leaves behind them, but she didn't even look. She couldn't take her eyes off him.

"I wanted to stick close to you, but my dad didn't give me much free time. And we were never in the same school together. As we grew older, I started to realize what it was that bonded us: your feelings. I felt what you felt stronger than with anyone else. Even when you were nowhere near me. When you were scared, I could *see* what was happening through your eyes. Do you remember when you were seven and those boys saw you walking down the road by yourself? They circled you and told you to pull down your panties."

She remembered too well. "There was no one around, and then . . . you walked by, lingered. That's all you did. They took one look at you and left. They were afraid of you."

"Spooky Silas," he said without a trace of humor. "But it was enough to get them to leave you alone. I made sure you got home all right."

"I remember wondering why you didn't walk with me."

He looked toward the graves. "When I was cleaning up the house after my father was gone, I found some . . . pornography." He enunciated the words. "Child pornography. It made me sick. I was only a kid myself, but I knew it was wrong for my dad to be looking at little girls."

"You didn't want your father near me?"

"I didn't want to be like him."

Those words struck her in the chest. It took her a moment to draw the air to say, "So you stayed away from me."

He nodded, swallowing hard. "I'm not like that. But I was a kid, I didn't know if that kind of thing ran in the blood. I don't think he actually molested children. I think it was some kind of sick hobby."

The impact of his earlier words was just now sinking in.

This time when she pulled her hands away, he let her go. "Silas, what you're saying . . . your seeing through my eyes when I'm scared—"

He wrapped his fingers around one of the iron columns. "Or whenever you feel anything strongly. When Gary threw your kitten—"

"You saw it happen? That's why you believed me, because you saw it?" When he nodded, she said, "But why didn't you come to me then?"

"That's why I was trying to get the damn truck working. I didn't know exactly where you were. And then you showed up."

She remembered how surprised he'd been and how he'd asked about the kitten before even hearing the story. "And when Gus died . . ."

He looked up at the canopy of trees over them, stroking the length of his neck. "You were so broken up. I was in Atlanta. I knew you'd just married Ben, and it wasn't my place to comfort you. But you just cried"—his voice went low, and he looked at her again—"and cried."

Her throat went tight. "I waited until Ben left on farm calls before I let out my grief. I knew he wouldn't understand. I wanted to be alone." She looked into his eyes, those dark, mysterious shadows. "But I wasn't alone."

"You're never alone, Katie. Not really."

She shivered at those words, at their implications. It sounded crazy, unbelievable. And yet, hadn't he been around during those times when she'd needed him as a child? And hadn't she thought of Silas when he wasn't around?

"I felt your fear when you were holding off Gary with a scalpel." His mouth twitched. "But before I could get to you, I felt your relief."

"My own personal hero," she said sardonically.

"I'm not a hero."

A low, moaning sound drifted from the far reaches of the cemetery.

"Cows," she said quickly, as much to convince herself

as to assure him. "The sound carries well at night."

"Now that's spooky."

She found herself laughing at that. She reached out to the column for support, pulling back when she felt the warmth of his hand already there. "I don't know what to think." She turned to the plot and wondered if anyone there had gone through something like this. Vines and other plants grew up between the stones and twined partially up the posts. She balanced her hands on top of the spikes, making circles against her palms. "You probably know better what I think than I do."

"You're a little scared, a lot unnerved, and a touch freaked out. How'd I do?"

She could hear a faint smile in his voice, a smile she couldn't return. "I'll go along with that."

He grew silent for so long, she thought he'd disappeared again. But she could see him leaning against that column. The moonlight fairies didn't quite reach him there, but she thought his eyes might be closed.

"Not again," he said in a strange, low voice.

"What?"

He pushed away from the column. "Let's get you home."

He started heading through the woods, though he paused when he realized she wasn't following. "What's wrong?"

"Let's just go."

The urgency in his voice was unmistakable. He took a step toward her, grabbed her arm, and started walking again.

She shook free of him, tired of being told what to do and going along silently. "What is going on with you?"

He looked beyond her. "He's on the prowl again."

"Who is?"

"The Ghost . . . the killer."

CHAPTER 12

WHEN THE FEELINGS started, Silas didn't want to believe it. Not already, not so soon after Carrie's disappearance. The Ghost was escalating too fast. He was losing control.

"Please tell me what's going on," Katie said, slowing down to make her point. She was beautiful, standing there among the trees with the wind blowing her hair around her face, framing it. Spots of moonlight washed over her face, letting him see the fear and confusion he'd caused.

He took her hand and was gratified that she didn't pull away this time. Even now, some part of her trusted him. He relished it, and he feared it. "We have to get you back now. I'll explain later."

"Not again!" She let out a sound of exasperation. "I'm going to hold you to that. You haven't come close to answering all my questions."

He twined his fingers with hers, absorbing the feel of her warmth and even her calluses. But he wouldn't let himself look back at her. He had to stay focused on winding around the trees and undergrowth, and then the darkness as they entered the thicker part of the forest. He wasn't sure if the rushing sound in his head was the trees or . . . *him*. Everything was starting to blend together, sounds, sights, and feelings. Maybe this time he'd catch up with the Ghost. He got closer and closer each time, waking up from the strange spell nearer to the scene where the girl was taken. And whatever he discovered, he didn't want to be anywhere near Katie. Just in case . . .

The house was dark when they stepped into the clearing,

except for one light in the office. Urgency pulsed through his brain, through his whole body.

When they reached the porch, she turned around in front of him. "Silas . . ."

"Where's Ben staying?"

"What?"

He took both her hands in his. "Where is he staying?"

"At the Marriott."

"Call him, Katie. Right now."

"You can't think . . . it's not Ben, I swear it's not."

"I just want to make sure." He followed her inside. "If he answers, we can eliminate him."

She grabbed up the phone and searched for the number. Before she dialed, she said, "You said you'd tell me what's going on."

"There isn't time right now. Dial."

She hesitated, looking into his eyes. "You look . . . different. Your eyes are all dilated. They look black."

"Dial the number," he said in something that sounded like a growl.

She did, but kept her eye on him as though she suspected he might turn into a werewolf. "Room 464 please." She waited, and then said, "Hi, Ben, it's me. I just called to say good night. Everything's . . . fine here. Windy tonight. I'll talk to you tomorrow. Bye."

"Voice mail?"

She nodded. "He's probably down in the lobby bar having a drink with the other attendees." She forced a laugh. "He makes friends everywhere. I can beep him."

"Do it."

Ten minutes later, Ben called. After she hung up with him, she said, "He'd been in the lobby in a quiet corner reading over his notes. I could hear people in the background."

Silas nodded, feeling relieved she wasn't living with a killer. "Lock your door. I'm going to track down Harold and Gary."

"Silas . . ." She grabbed his arm this time. She looked windblown and scared. "What's happening?"

"I've got to track down the devil."

He stepped outside and became one with the dark.

One part of his life was bleeding into the other. It wasn't right, not at all. Separate, it was always to be kept separate. Divided completely.

Now they knew about him, about this part of him anyway. They still didn't know, couldn't prove, that he was one and the same. No one would ever tie him to anything. They were too stupid to ever find out what happened to the bodies. Too stupid to find evidence to convict him. He was too smart to get caught.

The first time the hunger had grabbed hold of him, he'd turned a date into rough sex. He'd learned quickly after getting his hand slapped—figuratively speaking. Either control his impulses or make sure they weren't around to report him.

The first time he'd killed, he'd been shocked. Repulsed even. And terrified. He'd been sure he'd get caught. But he hadn't. The next time it went easier. That's when he realized it: he was meant to do these things. That's why he had the impulse.

But things were getting messy. They'd connected the girls' disappearances. He'd been so clever, too, making sure they were spaced apart in time and distance. Many of his crimes had been attributed to the girl running away or a run-in with a random maniac. For so long, it had been perfect.

They also knew about the shoes. That bothered him most. No longer his secret pleasure. How had they found that out? Only a couple of shoes had been found, and no one thought the murderer had left them there on purpose. Everyone in town was speculating about it. He'd overheard two of the deputies snickering about the guy masturbating over the shoe. He'd become a joke. Just hearing them had made his stomach churn. He wasn't like that!

He wasn't sick. He just liked his pleasures in different ways than other men. He'd always been different. Special.

He was going to show them just how stupid they were.

How they were no match for him. He was living under their noses, yet they'd have nothing to pin on him. Even when he took one of their own.

It was early, only ten-thirty. The road that ran by the edge of town was quiet. One truck came the other way. Far ahead two fuzzy red lights disappeared into the distance. And just off the side of the road, he saw what he was looking for, what he'd been waiting for.

He deserved this. For everything he'd been through. For the disappointment he'd felt over the last girl. He'd tried to figure that out, why he'd felt empty after her death, empty and let down. Maybe she'd come too willingly. Maybe she'd died too quickly.

He turned around and pulled to a stop by the girl who was walking home from the diner as always. He smiled. Geraldine. He liked her. Maybe this would give him the rush he needed, taking someone he knew.

Something else piqued his interest: Geraldine was with a friend. He hadn't seen her at first, because she was wearing black. Two women . . . risky. Different.

He rolled down the window. "Geraldine, what are you doing walking way out here?"

Beyond the swale and tall weeds that overtook the fence were the vast cotton fields her father farmed. He couldn't see any sign of the house in the distance.

Geraldine walked cautiously closer, then smiled. "Hey. Aw, we're just talking. Dana's got boy troubles."

He'd seen the other girl before, but didn't know her. "Should you be walking out here by yourselves, what with those girls disappearing and all?"

Her brown hair spilled over her shoulders when she braced herself on the door. "We heard about that. But it ain't happened around here. And we're being careful, walking away from the road and all."

"I'd hate for something to happen to you. Why don't I give you both a ride home? Better to be safe than sorry, don't you think?"

Geraldine looked at Dana, who subtly shook her head.

"We still got some talking to do," she said. "But thanks anyway."

No matter how much success he'd achieved in his life, rejection still cut down to the raw tendons exposed during his early years. It brought back every person who'd ever turned away from him, every word that sliced into his soul, every time he'd reached out to someone and found no one there.

He used that pain to interject hurt into his voice. "You don't trust me, do you?"

"Of course I do. We're just not ready to go back, is all."

"Good, I'm glad you trust me. Because I happen to know something about this man who's taking women. Something that hasn't been released to the public so they won't panic."

Geraldine rested more comfortably in the open window. "Like what?" Dana walked up beside her.

"Like he might be here in town. Now don't go telling anyone yet. There's more, but I can't tell you yet."

In the dim light from the dashboard, he saw her easy expression darken. "Did they find that girl from Haddock?"

"That's the part I can't tell you."

"They did, didn't they?"

He paused as one who knows inside information and must decide how much to part with. Then he gravely nodded. "It wasn't pretty, either. He tortured her bad, raped her."

Geraldine glanced at Dana. "And they think he's here? In Flatlands?" Her panic edged through.

"Being involved in the investigation, I can tell you it's a real possibility." He splayed his hand on his chest. "I consider it my job to make sure you get home all right. I don't want to hear tomorrow that you both disappeared, and here I could have saved you. I don't want to see your pictures on missing posters."

Geraldine opened the door and slid onto the seat next to him.

"I have a bunch of junk in the back, but I think you both can fit on the front seat."

After hesitating, Dana slid in beside her and pulled the door closed. He let out a breath of relief. He'd already gotten himself into a lie he'd have trouble explaining if they hadn't gotten in. Big mistake.

The girls smelled sweet, a soft fragrance that was at odds with the curves beneath their blouses. He loved the anticipation, loved knowing he'd be privy to every curve on their bodies before long. Now that they were in his vehicle, he would soon have complete control over every aspect of their lives. Dreams about boys and makeup and college would be replaced with a nightmare they couldn't begin to fathom. His palms got sweaty on the wheel just thinking about the surprise on their faces when it dawned on them.

He pulled onto one of the roads that led to the cotton farm so he could turn around. "Where do you live, Dana?"

"Possum Holler," she answered after a pause.

Where Katie used to live.

Everything would change at the place where two roads converged. There was one lone light, blinking red. If someone saw him, he'd have to change plans. After all, he really had no business being there at that time. As soon as he went straight, the girls would know something was wrong. At first they'd protest, then he'd shut them up. By then he'd be driving so fast, no one would see into the vehicle at all.

He smiled as the blinking light beckoned, casting a red glow on the black asphalt. *Come closer, closer.*

What a marvel, that life could change in the blink of that light. In the distance, he saw headlights coming from the west. Too far away to see anything. He shot through the intersection.

"Hey, wait!" Dana said, looking back. "Possum Holler is on 74."

"And you ran the red light," Geraldine pointed out.

He glanced over at them. No alarm. Dana looked concerned, nothing more. Yet.

"I thought it was out this way."

"I think I'd know where I lived," she said with sarcasm.

"Sorry. Guess I get disoriented out this way at night."

"You should know your way around this area," Dana said.

"You'd think." He slowed down just a bit. "Let me look for a place to turn around."

"Right there—you were going too fast."

They passed another road that trailed off to the west. He slowed down a bit more.

"There's a house up there," Geraldine said, pointing at the cottage with the lights on inside.

"I don't like to turn around in people's driveways when they're that close to the road," he said as he passed it. "I'd think it'd be unnerving to have someone pull up this time of night."

"Maybe we could just do a U-ee in the road," Dana said, searching for another turnoff.

He suspected she was annoyed more than anything at this point. "I'd be afraid another car would come by and hit us. Besides, it's illegal. I take my responsibility to keep you safe very seriously. Don't worry, we'll find something up ahead. Go ahead, keep talking about boys or whatever you were discussing."

Dana rolled her eyes. "Yeah, right, with a man in the car?"

"It's just girl stuff," Geraldine said.

He kept slowing down so they'd think he was at least trying to find a turnaround spot. He already knew civilization thinned out from there. The forest grew thick on either side of the road for miles.

"I know a road up here a ways. It'll be a safe place to turn around."

He'd already unlatched the gate. When it was open, it blended into the vines surrounding it. All they'd see was the dark road leading to hell. Their hell, his heaven.

He kept his eyes on the road ahead, but sensed their growing unease. He did nothing more to soothe them. When he saw his landmark, a state road sign next to a sign asking drivers not to litter, he slowed down.

"Hang on, I'm going to swing around."

Dana grabbed the strap and Geraldine braced herself against the dash. He swung into the road that was barely discernible, especially at night. But he didn't turn around. Before they even realized it, they'd plunged into the black opening of the forest.

"Hey, where are you going?" Geraldine said, swiveling on the seat.

"I'm turning around," he said in a flat voice.

He turned on the interior light, not wanting to miss a thing. The girls didn't want to think the worst yet. No one did. Being taken against their will happened to other people.

They were holding hands now . . . waiting. The barn came into view as he came to a stop. Dana was quicker than he thought, grabbing for the door handle.

"Stop!" he said, pulling the gun from between the seat and the door with his left hand and snagging Geraldine's arm with the other. "I hate when I have to shoot them right off the bat."

Reality dawned on them, freezing their faces and filling their eyes with disbelief and terror. The transformation, that's what he loved. The utter and sweet control to turn their charming little lives into a nightmare. He enjoyed watching it happen, logging it into his memory for the future when the other side of him lived within the confines of the law.

Two would be a challenge, he'd known that. He didn't let go of the girl's arm; the other girl he'd control with the gun. "Get out. Slowly. If you try to run, I'll have to shoot you. If you cooperate, I'll be easy on you."

"You're not going to let us go, are you?" Geraldine whispered. "Because you won't take the chance that we'll turn you in."

She was smart. He slid across the seat, nudging her ahead of him and holding the gun to the other one. She looked ready to bolt, but her deer eyes shifted between the gun and the grip he had on her friend.

"We'll see."

Every step was a thrill as he readied himself for pleasure. He pushed them ahead of him into the building. It smelled musty, as it usually did. The girls huddled together against the far wall whimpering.

What to do with two of them . . . he looked around the single room, then back to their huddling forms. He pointed to one of them. "You, cuff her hands to the bed."

Their gazes went simultaneously to the bed. He'd left the cuffs there this time, and he enjoyed anew the terror blazing in their eyes. Both girls shook their heads.

He walked closer to them, and they pushed close against the wall. He didn't want to leave himself open by cuffing one of them himself while the other was free. He pressed the end of the gun to Geraldine's cheek. "Cuff her."

She started crying. "Why are you doing this to me? I know you! I served you at the diner just the other day!"

"You know one side of me. Now you're going to get to know the other side."

Her sobs deepened. He gripped the back of her neck and shoved her toward the bed. She fell onto the lumpy mattress and curled into herself. The gun now pressed against Dana's face. "Okay, you cuff her, then."

He thought Geraldine would be more of a fighter. Dana was crying, but she was still looking for a way out. He saw the survivalist gleam in her eyes. She slowly walked to the bed. Her hand trembled when she took one of Geraldine's wrists. Geraldine screamed and pulled back. Dana met his eyes, perhaps searching for a speck of mercy. That gleam dimmed, and she turned back to her friend.

"I'm sorry," she whispered brokenly as she slid the cuff over her friend's wrist and clamped it shut.

The reality of that set Geraldine into a fit of screaming and thrashing. Dana shrank back against the wall, pain wracking her features. He pointed the gun at her. "Cuff her other hand!" She slowly pushed away from the wall and approached her friend. Geraldine fought her, though Dana wasn't trying too hard. He was tempted to shoot off a round to show the girls he meant business, but making that kind of sound was reserved only for a last-ditch effort. The screaming, however, would go unnoticed, though it usually got to his nerves before long.

He shoved Dana against the wall, grabbed Geraldine's

wrist and cuffed her himself. She continued to scream and thrash. He grabbed Dana next and cuffed her wrists to the foot rails. Both girls were at opposite ends of the bed. Both were screaming and kicking now, even kicking each other by accident.

He jerked their shoes off, then the socks, and stuffed a sock in Dana's mouth first. She bit him in the process, but luckily hadn't drawn blood. He balled up the other sock and turned to Geraldine.

Her voice was thick with fear and crying. "Why are you doing this? Why, why, why?"

He smiled. "Because I want to." And then he stuffed the sock in her mouth.

An hour later, he stood looking at them. Their feet were tied to the rails, and their naked bodies overlapped. This should be a sweet moment, looking at what he now owned, knowing he could do whatever he wanted with them. Yet, something was lacking inside him again. He thought knowing his victims would give him a thrill. It left him cold as he took in the mix of hatred and fear on their faces.

He'd made his first mistake, that's what was wrong. He'd let his anger get the upper hand. As soon as someone realized they were missing, a massive search would ensue. A search he'd be part of. Naturally, he could be the one to cover this area, but he couldn't take the chance of leaving the girls there. He would have to dispose of them now.

What would Katie think if she knew? What if she were there right now, watching him? Maybe she would enjoy holding someone's life in her hands, controlling them completely. He pictured her sitting there, but the picture turned to Katie cuffed to the bed rails.

But if she knew . . . would she understand? Could she forgive him his sins?

Silas had seen the two young, naked bodies on the bed. He'd seen the butterfly tattoo on one girl's shoulder. He knew her, had seen that fresh face before. Geraldine. God, this had to stop. Flashes had bombarded his brain like gunfire: the two girls, their terror, that road that disappeared into the woods. Accompanying the flashes were the feelings, the anticipation, the pleasure at their terror. He touched them, tortured them with his violation, and terrified them with the way he enjoyed their distress. Everything came in vivid detail, overtaking his own senses.

He hadn't killed them yet.

Silas always tried to follow it at first, trying to find the clues that would show him where the girls were. He held on for as long as he could, until the images overwhelmed his brain and blacked him out. But it hadn't gone as far this time. He'd only just begun the games.

When Silas woke, it was still dark. He wasn't in his vehicle. He blinked to get his bearings, rubbing his hands over his face. Something sticky transferred from his hands to his face. He couldn't see anything. The moon was blotted out by thick clouds. He touched the tip of his tongue to his hand. Blood.

He jerked to his feet and stumbled before catching his balance. As his vision tuned in to the dark, he saw a highway that disappeared into the night. He was standing a few yards from it, wildflowers and weeds up to his knees.

The Navigator was farther down in the swale, its nose end buried in the bushes. He started to run his hand over his face in exasperation, but remembered the blood.

Where the hell had it come from?

It was too dark to see himself, but he dimly became aware of a throbbing pain in his arm. He was sticky down to his elbow. He yanked off his shirt and wrapped it around his arm. As his mind cleared, he remembered the shoe. He nearly stumbled as he made his way to his vehicle. The engine wasn't running. He pulled out a flashlight and started searching the area.

He found an old milk carton, three beer bottles, and an old, dirty diaper before finding it. A glittery pink Sketchers sneaker with a thick heel. It was wet, so wet it glistened in the light. He searched the highway again, though whoever had thrown this here was long gone.

Or was he?

He shuddered at the thought. Charles Swenson had changed him that awful day, there was no doubt about that. But how much?

He walked back down to his vehicle and searched it. No signs of a struggle or that two girls had been inside. It was only a small relief. He'd probably just missed whoever had thrown that shoe there.

Could you handle knowing the killer is you?

He tried to shake those words out of his head. He was the best prime suspect, according to his own evidence. He'd been in the area when the girls had been taken, drawn there by an irresistible force that rendered him unconscious. He'd seen the victims. Though he hadn't found every shoe, he'd found a few of them. The last two times he'd woken up shortly after the shoe had been left there. If he were a cop, he'd arrest himself.

There hadn't been the conspicuous patrol vehicle parked on the road near his driveway when he'd left. Soon he'd found out why—Gary had been called away on a domestic disturbance call. Harold hadn't been home, either.

Would you turn yourself in? that insidious voice asked.

Of course he would. Or he'd drive north to the Smoky Mountains and sail off a cliff.

Did Dr. Hyde remember what Mr. Jekyll had done? He climbed into his vehicle and started it. It took some maneuvering, but he finally got back on the road. He drove until he found a highway marker, then pulled out a map to find out where the hell he was.

He narrowed it down to Juliette. Miles away from Flatlands, and he remembered nothing of the drive. Something else: Anne Clasp had disappeared from Juliette a year ago.

He ignored his throbbing arm and searched for the hidden road he'd gotten a glimpse of. The night revealed none of its secrets, nor did his mind. He'd have to return during the day to search.

The first thing he did was check on Katie. It was late, and he figured she'd be asleep. He didn't want to talk to her, just make sure she was all right. He cut his lights halfway down her drive, left the engine running, and walked the rest of the way. Her bedroom light was on, as well as the front porch light. He felt a step closer to that evil being as he walked around the side and looked in the bedroom window. The blinds were closed, of course, but he could see through the tiny holes. Her leg jiggled nervously. He saw a corner of a book, and the tip of her finger. Relief flooded him; she was all right.

He owed her an explanation, and she would darn well hold him to it. That spirited little girl he'd known wasn't far beneath the surface. Although he was glad, he didn't much like when she used her feistiness on him. But now wasn't the time to tell her anything, not shirtless and bleeding.

Bone-tired, he dragged himself to his vehicle. As soon as he got home, he let The Boss out and unwound his shirt from his arm. Dots of blood oozed from a fine cut down the outside of his arm. Using his good arm, he opened the first-aid kit and doused the cut with peroxide. Then he put on antibiotic and wrapped gauze around it.

He had no memory of getting that cut, no idea how it happened. Worse than the sting of the peroxide was the fact that it added yet another arrow of guilt pointed right at him.

Later he settled onto his air mattress, The Boss lying at his side. He gently rested his injured arm on the dog's back and moved his fingers over his coarse hair. The dog barely lifted his head. He searched his mind for anything that would be the key to finding where the girls were hidden. Somewhere in this area, but that included hundreds of acres of remote forestland. He'd look tomorrow as soon as he escorted Katie and Harold to work.

Katie.

It felt as though someone had dropped an anvil on his chest. He shot to his feet. Katie had flowed into that miasma of images and thoughts, of terror and pleasure. The Ghost had wondered if Katie would forgive him. And he'd pictured Katie on that bed instead of the girls.

That kept him up the rest of the night.

* * *

Grover Thompson hauled a bucket of leftovers from Thelma's canning out to the pig stalls. That woman's insomnia was going to drive him crazy. Here it was four in the morning and no breakfast even started. The place smelled like peaches and blackberries, and not a stitch of food for himself. She'd sent him out with the peelings and a promise to start breakfast.

Thump. Thump.

He heard the strange sound first, and then the commotion in the pig stalls. Not loud, but enough to indicate they were excited about something. The pigs used one of his old barns once the cows got moved into larger quarters. An opening led out to the troughs and mud pit. All the pigs were gathered around that opening eating something in the troughs.

He opened the gate. It creaked, reminding him for the umpteenth time to bring out the WD-40. What the heck were they eating at this time of morning? They were crunching and slurping as though they hadn't eaten in days. He flipped on the light, which didn't faze the pigs one bit.

He trudged through the muddy ground to check it out. From the corner of his eye, he caught movement in the shadows. By the time he turned around, the pen was doused in darkness again. He dropped the bucket and wished he were younger, stronger. The pigs were making such a ruckus, he couldn't hear if someone was approaching.

The pain was so sharp, he thought he'd imagined it at first. He felt it knife into his back and twist inside him. He couldn't even call out; the pain had sucked the air from his lungs. As he dropped to his knees in the muck, he saw the shadowy figure standing beside him. The mud was warm and comforting as he rolled onto his side. Above him was the person who had done this to him for no reason. He saw the figure raise his arms, and then it was all over.

~~~ CHAPTER 13

KATIE SPENT THE night in groggy wakefulness. She waited for Silas to return and explain his strange behavior. How could he announce that the killer was on the prowl and just take off?

She set the book down on the bed. Silas *was* spooky. Now she knew why the kids had been so freaked out. She felt the same way. Worse, she felt violated. It was one thing Ben always wanting to know what she was thinking. It was a totally different matter to have someone know your feelings without your permission.

She pulled out the sketch from beneath her mama's picture on her nightstand. He'd been there with her, that was the only explanation. She put her hand to her chest. Not with her, but inside her. The more she thought about it, the more it made sense in a . . . well, a spooky kind of way. She'd always trusted Silas, even though everyone else clearly feared him. And he *had* been around during the most tense and scary moments of her life, in one way or another. She glanced at her mama's smiling face. Even then, when Silas had been in the custody of the county social services, she'd felt him beside her.

What had he been doing at their trailer after her mama's death?

She tried to read some more, but she had the eeriest feeling someone was watching her. The bedroom door was closed, and her blinds were shut. No one could see in, but the feeling persisted. She'd felt this disorientating feeling before, of not trusting her world anymore, of not knowing herself, either. After her mama died. One day everything was fine, and the next, her world had shattered. Someone said it was a horrible way to take your life. Later she'd understand what that meant. For years she went through the sequence of events in her mind, her mama pulling out the Blue Devil, contemplating. Then opening the top and readying herself . . . pouring it down her throat.

She had talked to the doctor who was also the medical examiner in Flatlands. He'd been delicate in explaining it to her, as delicate as he could be. Lye, the main ingredient in the drain opener, burned on contact. It tore through her esophagus and compromised her airway. She died from asphyxiation. What he didn't say was how desperate she must have been to use such a painful method.

More haunting than the image of her mother contemplating that painful end to her life was wondering if she'd felt this same disorientation and despair. Katie thought she'd gotten used to the idea of being trapped and of hating herself for being so unhappy with a wonderful man. Then Silas had come along and turned everything topsy-turvy. Spooky Silas who probably knew everything she'd been feeling about him.

She threw the book across the room, then went still. She'd heard another sound. Scratching. Her heart again jumped into her throat as she picked up the gun and opened the bedroom door. The house was dark except for the slice of light coming from the bedroom. She doused the light and walked back to the kitchen. She heard the scratching again, right outside the window. When she turned on the outside lights, it stopped.

She left the lights on and returned to bed, huddling into a ball again.

Katie climbed into Harold's truck the next morning, grateful it was the last time she'd have to do it for a while. Dammit, she was talking to Ben about getting another car.

Harold took one look at her, holding her coffee to her chest as she drank, and said, "You look like hell. Was you out looking for the girls last night, too?"

Her heart dropped about three inches. "What girls?"

"Geraldine Thorpe and Dana Westbury." He put the truck in gear and headed toward the road. "Shame about them, ain't it?"

"They're . . . gone? Like the others?" Her voice sounded raspy enough to get his attention.

"Look like you seen a ghost or something." He pulled onto the road. "Yep, gone like the others. Morton called the sheriff last night, said Geraldine didn't come home after work. One of her brothers saw the two of them walking away from the diner. He offered them a ride, but they said they had girl things to discuss. That was the last anybody saw of them. Except whoever took them, of course."

Harold wasn't looking at her like he usually did. He was concentrating on the road, or deep in his thoughts. He looked as ragged as she did. She could hardly breathe as Silas's urgent words floated through her mind: *He's on the prowl again.*

"People . . ." She cleared the tightness from her throat. "People were looking for them?"

"Bunch of us went driving all over. There wasn't hide nor hair of them. We'll be looking again all day, I'm sure. Maybe we'll find them now that it's light out."

"Just like Carrie Druthers," she said, more to herself.

"And a girl in Juliette last year. She'd been sneaking off to meet her boyfriend and disappeared. The boyfriend said he never saw her, but the police figured it was him. Now, they're wondering. The more we talked about it, the more girls we remembered hearing about going missing. People are talking about a serial killer loose in this area." He glanced over at her. "That's some excitement, huh? A real, honest-to-goodness serial killer right here in Flatlands."

"Why do you think he's here in Flatlands?"

"Tate has a map of all the disappearances. They're all around here. He thinks this is his home base."

Why was Tate involving someone like Harold in the investigation?

Katie tried not to notice the tic, but it pulsed as he lifted his eyebrows and said, "I'll bet it's someone we know. Maybe someone we pass a friendly comment to once in a while. Do you pass a friendly comment with anyone, Katie?"

She couldn't even answer that question, not with the gleam of interest in his eyes. She turned around and saw Silas's Navigator following a short distance behind. He'd damn well better stop and talk to her after Harold dropped her off. That's when she noticed the blood on his shirt.

"Is that . . . blood?"

There was a faded patch of red on his plaid shirt. He glanced down. "Oh, yeah, I cut my hand a few months back." He imitated the gesture that may have put the blood there, pressing his hand to his stomach. "Cut it deep, too, and there wasn't anyone around to kiss it and make it better. Imagine that."

It was easy to imagine, but she wasn't commenting.

"Remember, I won't be on the other side of the cemetery if you need me," he said when she climbed down from his truck. "I'll be looking for those girls." He pulled out of the gravel parking lot.

She was too busy watching Silas's vehicle drive slowly past. His face was indiscernible. The side of the Navigator was scratched. This she noticed as it drove past and disappeared. That's when she remembered that piece of paper with his beeper number on it.

As soon as she checked on Goldie, she beeped Silas with a 911. He called within a minute.

"Come back here and tell me what's going on, Silas Koole."

"You're all right?"

"No, I'm not all right. I'm confused and worried and . . . hell, you ought to know just how I feel!" The curse word took her aback.

His voice was low when he said, "Katie, don't say that."

"It's true, isn't it?"

"I don't always know what you're feeling. Only when

I'm near you or if it's an intense emotion." His voice was fading out.

"Did you find Gary? Geraldine Thorpe and her friend are missing, you know."

"I know." There was a pause before he said, "Gary was on patrol. They'd sent him on a domestic disturbance call way out in the boonies. He wasn't responding to his radio when I tried reaching him. I pretended to be a neighbor who'd seen someone lurking around his apartment."

"What about Harold?"

"He wasn't home, either. He lives way out on the east side of Flatlands, in some dump set off from the road. The house was dark, and his truck wasn't there."

"Come back here and talk to me."

"I can't. There's something I have to do."

"Look, Ben's going to be back sometime today, and then I won't be able to talk to you until he leaves again this weekend. You can't let me sit here wondering what's going on and why you took off like you did last night." *And what you did while you were gone.*

She heard faint music in the background. "I can't talk right now." He hung up.

"Damn you!" She banged the phone down on the unit, imagining it was his face. She glanced at the appointment schedule. Nothing for a few hours. She closed up and headed to the library.

"I thought Dr. Ferguson was going to be back today," Mrs. Miller said, pulling her Pekingese closer to her chest.

Katie had spent the morning reading about Charles Swenson, one of the most heinous serial killers in the history of all serial killers. Silas had detailed the events in Swenson's life that pushed him over the line. She felt vulnerable in the face of utter evil, sinking into the heart and soul of a man who enjoyed mutilating and killing women. Even if he had been fried two years ago. What she didn't need was Mrs. Miller's fearful gaze as she looked at Katie.

Particularly when the woman looked an awful lot like her dog.

"He's on his way home now, but he's going to help look for those girls." When Katie had told him on the phone that morning, he cut his trip short to return. "I can handle the vaccinations, Mrs. Miller. I've been doing it for years."

"I'm sure you have, dear, but I only trust Dr. Ferguson with my Petunia. I'll call to reschedule." She turned, nearly tripped on the leash that dangled to the floor, and quickly departed without another glance back.

Katie threw down her pen and crossed her arms over her chest. This helpless frustration had been building all day. She walked in the back to visit Goldie.

"At least you trust me, don't you?"

Goldie licked her nose and chased away the dark feelings. The dog was limping around the recovery room, but her brown eyes were bright and full of life. Katie always judged a dog's mood and outlook on what she called their doggie smile. When a dog was relaxed and comfortable, it panted and looked like it was smiling. Goldie did that now and aimed the smile at Katie. She felt ridiculous when her eyes watered in the gratitude and warmth of being someone's hero.

"Hello, Katie."

She spun around. It was Gary, looking tired and grim. He walked right up to her, inches from her face, then knelt down and scratched the dog's head.

"She looks okay."

Katie called Goldie over to the bed in the corner to get her away from Gary. "She's doing good for getting hit by a car."

"You think I hit her on purpose, don't you?"

She kept her gaze on Goldie. "I don't know."

The groan would have touched her if it hadn't come from Gary. "If you'd let yourself get to know me, you'd see I'm not like that anymore. I like animals. I stopped in to see how she was doing."

"That's nice of you." Her words sounded as hollow as

a pipe. "You can see she's doing just fine. Have you found out who owns her?"

"We've been too busy trying to find Geraldine and Dana."

She slipped by him and out to the reception area. She wanted to put the desk between them. "Have they found anything?"

"They're gone," Gary said in a low voice. "Just like the others. People want to believe anything but the truth. They're even looking for sinkholes. But they'll never be seen again." His words sent a shiver down her spine.

"You think Silas is doing this?"

He leaned against the desk, making her back up—and chastise herself for showing fear. "Katie, it's him. He's been around the area every time a girl has disappeared or at least shortly afterward. We're learning a lot about serial killers. They like to be part of the investigation, to pretend to help. Silas writes about it, interviews the families." His gaze went to the book on her desk. "That's him. He lives this stuff." He tapped the book. "He is this stuff."

She thought of the shadows in Silas's eyes. Did they hide the pain of a killer? "I can't believe he's a killer."

"You know him that well?"

"No." She didn't know, for instance, who the woman he'd lived with was and what she'd meant to him.

"Katie, you're making alliances with the wrong man. You look at me like I'm the biggest creep in the world. Like *I'm* a killer. I'm a cop, for God's sake! One of the good guys. And when I say Silas is behind this, I see a wall go up in your eyes. Be careful who you trust, little girl."

"Silas told me the same thing."

"I'm sure he did. But remember this: he was seen talking to Geraldine just days before she disappeared."

"She was his waitress!" She remembered seeing him exchanging laughter with the girl, remembered feeling a little jealous about it. "I've seen you talking to her, too. And Harold. Probably everyone in town for that matter."

He ignored that. "And now she's dead."

"You don't know that for sure."

Gary fisted his hand at his chest. "I can feel it. They're dead, and God only knows what he does with their bodies. It's like they disappear. He probably chops them up and feeds them to that dog of his."

"Stop it! You're just speculating."

"He's nowhere to be found today. We didn't have anyone to keep him under surveillance. Last night I had to take a call, so I couldn't keep an eye on him." Which gave Gary opportunity, too, she realized. "I checked his place; his stuff is still there, but he and the dog are gone. So are all his files. I'll bet that son of a bitch is long gone. And if he is, I'm going to hunt him down. The next person who'll disappear will be Silas Koole." His face went red with rage and his jaw clenched.

She didn't doubt that if Silas walked in just then, Gary would try to kill him. "Let the authorities handle him." She tried not to let her concern for Silas show in her voice. Or the fear that he'd really left without saying goodbye. Just like last time. Like her mother. "Don't take matters into your own hands. You don't know for sure that he's guilty." The thought of vigilante justice made her blood freeze.

"I have to get back to the investigation. He's crossed the line. He's taken our own, and he's going to pay this time."

The day went downhill from there. Mrs. Westbury, Dana's mother, walked in with a flier she'd made. Her eyes were bruised and swollen, her voice thick and raw when she asked, "Could you please hang this up somewhere?"

Katie nodded, taking the flier from the woman's trembling hand. She dared to give that hand a gentle squeeze. "I'm very sorry about . . . what's happened."

The woman's blue eyes were on the edge of being wild. "If you were really sorry, you'd ask that boyfriend of yours where he has them."

Katie backed up a few inches. "Silas didn't take them. And he's not my boyfriend."

The woman's laugh was on the verge of hysterical. "Maybe you're both in it together. Maybe it was you who lured them to him. They would never have gone with him otherwise."

They trusted him. Katie tried to calm her down by touching her arm. "I know you've been under a lot of stress, but—"

Mrs. Westbury jerked her arm away as though Katie had burned her. "You don't know stress until your girl is taken away from you! You can't imagine how it rips through your heart, wondering what she's going through, if she's alive. He has them! And you know where he is, maybe even where they are. Tell us! Tell us!"

Katie ducked as the woman starting punching at her. She grabbed at her wrists and held them in a grip. Mrs. Westbury collapsed to the floor in sobs. Katie could only stand there and look at her. She didn't dare put her arms around her or offer her comfort. She felt helpless and cold.

The woman looked up at Katie, then down at herself. She pulled herself up, and again Katie had to hold back from helping her.

"I don't know how you sleep at night," Mrs. Westbury growled, making her wobbly way to the door. "God help your soul."

Katie stared at the door for several minutes once she was alone again. And then she leaned against the counter and started crying. When Goldie, who was allowed to roam at will, came over and licked her face, she hugged the dog closer and didn't feel so alone.

"Mama, where does this creek go?" Katie sat next to her mama on the edge of the water, dipping their feet into the chilly water. It wasn't a deep creek; she could see the rocks beneath the surface, could make her way across without going deeper than her shoulders.

Her mama had a funny look on her face as she watched the water splash up over the rocks at the edge and keep going. "I don't know, honey. Maybe it goes all the way to

California. Maybe even farther. At least it gets out of here."

Katie scooted closer, having trouble imagining anything going as far as California. "Don't you like it here, Mama?"

Mama gave her that sad smile. "Doesn't matter if I do or not; this is the place we're stuck at."

She didn't like when her mama talked like that. She was watching the water again, a longing expression on her face.

"We could leave."

Mama laughed softly. "I wish we could. I wish I could build a raft and head down this creek, see where it takes me."

"But you wouldn't leave without me, would you?"

Mama folded her into her arms. She was bony, but she gave nice hugs anyway. "I'm not going anywhere without you, pumpkin. Bet on it."

CHAPTER 14

KATIE WALKED INTO the kitchen the next morning and came to an abrupt stop when she saw the box of rat poison on the counter. Her heart dropped down to her toes at the sight of the yellow box that had appeared as if by magic.

She'd put all the poisons away on her twenty-seventh birthday. But there it sat, taunting her. She called out to Ben, but he was apparently in the bathroom and didn't answer. Goldie, her very first houseguest, watched her with interest as Katie climbed on a chair and stuck the box back in the cabinet over the refrigerator.

Ben had been surprisingly fine about the dog staying with them—temporarily, he'd emphasized—until they could find her owners. He'd come home late after helping with the search, and Katie had explained why Goldie was lying at the foot of their bed.

Resuming her morning routine, Katie walked outside to feed her animal family. Missy-Lou and No-tail chattered from their respective trees, waiting impatiently for their breakfast. "Coming, coming," she sang out. Goldie had followed her out, however, and the squirrels were none too happy about it. "She's only a temporary guest." No-tail continued to make his warning noises, with twitching tail. She dumped the combination bird seed/cat food into the bin. "Oh, you had a run-in with a dog, huh? Is that what happened to your tail? Well, I can see why you're so distressed, then."

Goldie watched the squirrels with interest. Katie had already gotten attached to the beautiful dog with bandages. Goldie walked to the corner of the house. She barked three times, looked at Katie, then barked again. The trash was once again spilled out of the can. When they'd heard the critters rummaging outside early that morning, Ben hadn't jumped up to chase them away.

Katie was surprised to see a young raccoon sitting out in the open. More surprising was that the raccoon was looking at her as though pleading for something. Raccoons didn't beg. Nor did they approach humans. Its little paws drooped at its chest, and its breathing was raspy. It inched closer, sending Goldie scampering cautiously back. Its little mouth gasped open and closed.

She called Goldie back into the house and found Ben sipping his coffee in the kitchen. "There's a raccoon out there and it looks like it's in pain."

"Don't worry about it." He glanced around. "Why isn't breakfast cooking?"

"It's wheezing and kind of hunched over. We can't just let it die out there."

His eyes were devoid of the usual compassion where animals were concerned. "Yes we can."

She glanced to where the yellow box had been. "You poisoned it?"

"I heard them out there before I went to bed and put some hamburger out."

"With poison in it?"

'I'm tired of them leaving a mess for you to clean all the time. They're just raccoons, Katie. Rodents. Don't look at me like I'm some monster. I did it for you."

"I'd rather clean up the garbage than kill an animal that's just following its nature."

Her stomach churned while she got dressed. The thought of cooking bacon didn't help, either. She pulled out the pan and set it on the stove, but didn't turn it on. Instead, she checked on the raccoon again. It looked in even more agony, pleading with those black button eyes.

"Ben, please put it out of its misery."

He finished his glass of orange juice. "It'll die soon. Come on, we're late as it is."

"I can't leave knowing it's suffering."

He walked to the phone table and pulled out the gun. Her heart lurched. This was the best way to put the poor thing out of its misery.

He handed her the gun. "I'll meet you out at the van. Make it quick." He left her staring at the vile weapon. For that moment, she hated him, pure, unadulterated hatred. He'd gone outside and left her to deal with his mess. She wasn't sure she could kill a living creature. She started to put the gun away, but stopped. She couldn't let the poor thing suffer, either.

Her hands were shaking as she loaded a bullet into the chamber. Numb, she walked out back. Her eyes were tearing up as she stared into that little bandit face.

How long had Mama suffered before dying? Could Katie have put her out of her misery? Like her mama, there was no hope for this creature now that the poison was in its system.

She held her arms straight and aimed the gun. She had to blink several times to clear the tears from her eyes. She was trembling. The weak part of her said to walk away, but she couldn't go to work knowing the raccoon was suffering. She steadied her arms.

"God, please forgive me."

She pulled the trigger.

Ben dropped Katie at the hospital and went to the diner to pick up something for breakfast. He couldn't understand why she was so angry with him; it was only a pesky raccoon. But she'd hardly said a word to him during the drive. He couldn't believe she'd shot it. He'd figured she'd leave it there. He didn't want to shoot it, either.

Tate and Gary were sitting at the counter with a marked-up map spread out before them. Empty sugar packets and drops of cream littered the table, evidence of a long morning already under their belt.

"Anything yet?" Ben asked, sitting down beside them. They both shook their head morosely. Tate said, "Between everyone who's been looking, we've covered every square inch of Flatlands. Every officer within three hundred miles is looking for them."

Gary shook his head. "They ain't gonna find them. It's him striking again. They never find the bodies."

"Shut up, Gary. I don't want to hear you talk like that."

"What about Silas?" Ben asked. "Found him yet?"

"Yeah, he came back into town late yesterday," Gary said. "He knows something, but he ain't talking. We took samples of the mud and leaves from his tires, trying to find out where he went."

The sheriff said, "He was more cooperative this time, let us check the house and surrounding grounds, even his vehicle."

"But he wouldn't tell us where he'd been, or how his truck got scratched up," Gary said.

"Whoever this killer is, he's damn smart. I have to admit I'm impressed."

Gary slapped his hands down. "How can you say that, Sheriff?"

"Just because I'm on the side of good doesn't mean I can't appreciate evil. Sometimes evil can be more beautiful than good. And sometimes it can be smarter."

Dinah walked over with more coffee. "How's it going, Ben?"

"I need a breakfast sandwich to go. Katie and I had a fight this morning."

"Over Silas?" she asked.

"She shot a raccoon." That got everyone's attention.

"What?" the sheriff said, his cup midway to his mouth.

"That doesn't sound like Katie," Gary said, as though he knew Katie so well.

Ben shrugged. "Like I said, she's been acting different lately. Raccoons have been getting into our garbage for a few months now. She's fed up with it. This morning she shot one, then insisted on burying it before we left."

Dinah made a face before going back to put in his order.

"But my problems are nothing compared to the girls.

I've got a couple of surgeries this morning, but I can help with the search again after that."

The raccoon haunted Katie all morning, almost as much as those girls still being missing. Bertrice was misty-eyed when she came in mid-morning. The school had hosted a prayer session for the two girls and dismissed the students early. Yellow ribbons had been tied to street posts and trees all over town.

"Some people think they're already dead," Bertrice said. "They're acting like they're never going to come back." She looked at Katie. "I was supposed to be with them that night. But my mom grounded me because of the detention. If I'd been there . . . maybe they wouldn't have been taken. The guy never took two girls at a time before. He wouldn't have tried to take three of us."

Katie put her arm around Bertrice's shoulders. "It's not your fault."

"No, it's my mom's fault. I hate her for keeping me home."

Katie turned Bertrice toward her. "Don't hate her. I know you're mad at her, but don't hate her. I said the same thing about my mom. She wouldn't let me keep a kitten I'd fallen in love with. I told her I hated her. A few weeks later she was dead."

"My mom isn't going to die," Bertrice said, though her face had gone pale.

"I didn't think mine would, either."

When the door to the hospital opened, Katie almost fell over. Silas walked in with The Boss on a leash. The big dog's head was tilted to the right, and he kept flapping his ears.

Silas was wearing baggy jeans and a denim shirt with long sleeves. At the collar she could see a white undershirt peeking out. His hair was thick and shiny, slightly damp from a shower. He looked at her as though he wanted to ask her something. Had he felt her hatred toward Ben and the shock of shooting the raccoon?

"The Boss has a tick deep in his ear canal. I tried to get it out, but I don't want to damage his ear drum."

"Bring him on back." Katie led the way into the examination room. Ben was in the storage area, or at least she thought he was until he appeared in the doorway. "Tick in the ear canal," she said to him, trying to sound casual.

Ben surveyed Silas with cool eyes. That frost remained when he tugged the dog onto the platform that would raise him to their height. He turned The Boss's head without his usual gentleness and pulled up his floppy ear. Katie held the dog steady, wondering what had come over Ben lately. He always talked to his patients in calming tones, but he said nothing now. She handed him the long tweezers and held the tiny flashlight. As Ben lowered the tweezers into the ear canal, she had the bizarre thought that he'd poke the dog's eardrum.

She was definitely getting paranoid. Ben had never hurt a creature in his life. Until the raccoon, that was.

"It's okay, big fella," she said, lowering her mouth to the top of his head. "It'll be over in just a second."

She met Silas's gaze. His eyes were warm with gratitude. When she guiltily looked at Ben, his gaze was on her. He shifted it to the dog's ear again and pulled out a fat wriggling tick. He dipped it into a dish of alcohol and its movements stilled in death.

"Thanks," Silas said, walking closer.

Katie touched the welt the tick had caused with a swab of alcohol, then dabbed on some antibiotic ointment. She rubbed The Boss's head, her face level with his. "That was a good boy, yes, what a good boy you are." She needed to make up for Ben's coldness. When she glanced at Silas, he was watching her hands caressing his dog's fur with a smoldering fire in his eyes.

Ben lowered the dog while she was still petting him. Silas took the leash and led him out to the waiting area. Bertrice wrote up the bill, and Katie gave him a small tube of ointment and a couple of swabs.

"He sure has a lot of nerve coming here," Ben said as soon as Silas left.

"Why?" Bertrice asked. "I mean, we're the only vet in town."

"Haven't you heard that he's probably the guy who killed your friends?"

Bertrice was watching Silas's Navigator turn out of the parking lot and raising a cloud of dust. "Someone at school said he was a suspect, but I don't believe that."

Ben met Katie's gaze as though accusing her of poisoning Bertrice's mind. "Why? Is he too good-looking to be a murderer?"

"Well, he is a hottie. But that's not it. I think they're trying to pin it on him because he's, like, new or something. No one knows him. But he wouldn't still be around if he'd done it."

"Don't be too sure of that," Ben said in a hard voice. "If I were an attractive young woman, I sure wouldn't trust him." This he said to Katie. "By the way, I found out who owns the retriever."

Katie went from tense to disappointed. "You did?"

"I figured you'd want to get her back to her owners right away. I did some calling out to the farms where Gary hit the dog. I know most of them. The Cartwrights will be in this morning to pick her up. I'm sure they appreciate how well you've taken care of her."

But when they came to take Goldie away, it wasn't Katie they thanked profusely. It was Ben.

"Katie, what's bothering you?" Ben asked her that night when he returned from the latest round of searching.

She didn't want to share what bothered her. She'd tried to discuss the raccoon poisoning, but Ben's official position was it was only a rodent and to drop the subject. He'd taken all the credit for Goldie's recovery and happy demeanor. Not outright, of course. He'd never once said he'd treated Goldie. But he hadn't dispelled their presumptions, either.

Her gaze zeroed in on the box of poison that was once

again out on the counter. "Ben, why is the box out again? You're not going to poison any more raccoons. I won't allow it."

He narrowed his eyes at her. "I saw evidence of mice out by your gazebo. Do you want to let them just eat the wood away? And scamper across your feet?"

"Please just put it away." She turned toward the window where two moths were banging against the glass in a desperate effort to get in. The spider waited in the shadows, hoping one of them would catch on the sticky web.

Ben came up behind her and rubbed her shoulders. She could feel his warm, moist breath as he spoke against her neck. His voice had tones of incredulity when he said, "You called me when I was in Atlanta. That meant a lot to me, that you called me. I'm always the one who calls."

Even though he was saying something nice, his words grated like a fork across her skin. "You know I always want to be there for you, don't you, Katie?"

This time he waited for her answer. She caught him watching their reflection in the window. She eased the edge from her expression. "You are . . . always there for me, Ben."

"Am I still your hero, Katie?"

She swallowed hard. For years she'd pushed out the words he wanted to hear. This time she said, "Heroes don't poison raccoons."

His fingers tightened on her shoulders. She saw his gaze harden in the reflection. "I did it for you. You didn't like hearing them out there at night, and you were always mad when you picked up the mess they left behind. I was trying to make things all right for you. That was the only way I knew how; we'd tried everything else. That's all I ever think about, Katie, making things better for you."

It felt as though someone were tightening a clamp inside her chest. She squeezed her eyes shut. How could he make her feel responsible for the raccoon's death? He did it a lot, she realized, made her feel low and undeserving. Then he'd say something to smooth it over and the hurt would go away.

But the hurt never really went away. She just shoved it under the carpet of his kindness. Like dirt, it only accumulated unseen. "You don't have to make things better."

"Yes I do. I never feel like I'm doing enough to make you happy. It's like I'm not quite good enough to be your husband. I try to make everything good for you. But it's never enough, is it?" He turned her around to face him.

"Yes it is," she forced out. "It's me. Maybe I'm too selfish. Maybe I don't deserve you."

His expression eased, and he bracketed her face with his hands. "Of course you deserve me. We belong together, Katie. Always and forever. I can't help it if I made you my world. Can you forgive me?"

For what? she wanted to ask. Instead she said, "Of course."

He walked over to the counter and handed her a pink bag. "I brought you something from Atlanta."

Not chocolates, thank goodness. She pulled out a white dress with a black ribbon circling the empire waistline. It looked like something a little girl would wear. She'd look terrible in it.

She tucked it back into the bag. "Thanks, Ben. That was sweet."

"Katie, I want to have a baby with you."

She drooped against the stove in shock. "Wha . . . what?"

"That's what this is all about, isn't it? Your moods, your unhappiness. You've talked about having a baby, and I kind of dismissed it. I didn't want to go through the embarrassment of tests and procedures. But I see how selfish I was. I just want you to be happy, Katie. That's all I've ever wanted. I don't want to lose you."

For years she'd longed to have someone who belonged to her wholly, who would love her unconditionally. Now that he was offering her that baby, she was all tangled up inside. "I'm not sure I'm ready now."

He pulled her against him and said in a thick voice, "Don't tell me it's too late. That I've lost you."

"I'm just not sure I'm good mother material." What kind of role model did she have? A mother who professed her love and then killed herself? Mrs. Emerson, who treated her children like employees? Maybe she was too cold to be a good mother. And the thing that scared her most: What if her own child didn't love her?

"You'd make a great mother," he said, pulling back to look at her. "What do you say?"

"I don't feel right talking about a baby with those girls gone." Still, the longing pulled inside her. "Maybe later."

He tipped her chin up. "Are you sure you're all right?"

"I'm fine," she said, though she didn't sound the least bit convincing.

Apparently Ben bought it, because he kissed her. "Why don't you treat yourself to a bubble bath, ease some of your tension? I'll fix dinner."

"You will?"

"Between the girls' disappearance, Silas creeping around, and the fact that you've been off balance since your birthday, I think you're over the edge. You're taking everything too seriously these days. Too personally. Relax." He kissed her cheek. "I'll take care of everything tonight, even cleaning up."

Was she over the edge? Could she be blowing everything out of proportion? It was likely, what with her mother's suicide haunting her and Silas taunting her. Fear and guilt could mess with a woman's mind and make things seem worse than they were.

She kissed Ben back. "Thanks, honey."

When she came into the kitchen forty minutes later, Ben had set the table with candles and wine. Something was sizzling in the pan on the stove. She was wrapped in her robe, her hair still damp.

"This is lovely," she said, taking in the marigold he'd snagged from her garden and placed in a vase.

That's when she saw the poison still sitting on the counter. And in the pan were two large hamburger patties spitting grease into the light above. Her stomach clenched. It was crazy to think he'd put something in the hamburgers. She knew it made no sense. She wasn't a pesky rodent. But that paranoia shuddered through her and brought fresh images of that raccoon in pain and the hatred she'd felt for Ben.

He set a hamburger on each plate, *sans* bun, next to a pile of rice. Then he placed the plates on the table and took his seat. "What's wrong?"

"I . . . I don't feel well all of a sudden. Maybe I sat in the hot water too long."

"You're probably just hungry. Sit down."

She glanced at the yellow box with the dead rat on it. Had it been moved since she'd gone into the bathroom? She could already feel the pain searing through her insides, as though she'd ingested the poison. He looked impatiently at her, and she sat down.

"Good. Now eat."

The grease oozed from beneath the burger and pooled bloodred on her plate. The rice started to absorb it. He was already eating, but he paused when he saw her studying her burger. "Is it too rare? I know you like it more cooked."

"I've gotten used to eating it rare." Because whenever he cooked on the grill, he always forgot to cook hers the way she liked, and she never wanted to bother him to cook it more. But eating an undercooked steak or burger was different than eating something she suspected was poisoned.

She glanced at his burger. "How does yours look? Maybe it's more cooked."

"It's even rarer," he said without looking.

He was waiting for her to take a bite. "Go ahead and try it. If it's too raw, I'll throw it back in the pan for a few minutes."

"It's fine." She bought time by salting and peppering the burger. She cut into it with her fork. More blood oozed out and infected her pure white rice. This was Silas's doing, making her doubt her husband. Ben wasn't a serial killer, and he wasn't a wife killer, either. She raised the fork to her mouth.

He stuck another chunk of burger into his mouth and talked around it. "I was thinking maybe I should cancel my farm calls this weekend. You know, with all the stuff going on, the girls being missing . . . and Silas hanging around."

She set the fork down. "Silas isn't hanging around here."

"I know that." He smiled. "I mean, hanging around town."

"But Tate said that this guy, whoever he is, only hits a town once. He won't take another woman from Flatlands. Serial killers have methods. They don't change them."

"How do you know about serial killers?"

She thought of the books tucked beneath her side of the bed. "Just hearing everyone talk about them."

"Silas writes about them. Tate bought five books to read up on. He said Silas is a good writer—too good. He knows the minds of killers well. Like his own, I'd bet." He glanced down at her plate. "Katie, you haven't touched your burger. I made dinner so you could relax. And this is how you say thanks, by not eating it?"

Her stomach lurched. He had a way of making her feel so . . . obligated. Not with harsh words, but with sweetness. She scooped up a forkful of rice and stuck it in her mouth. In the end, it wasn't her choice to make whether to eat the hamburger or not. She rushed to the bathroom and threw up.

There were nights when Katie instantaneously slipped into a deep sleep. Tonight should have been one of them. Ben had seen her to bed, laid a cool washcloth over her forehead, and turned off the lights. But hours later, she lay there looking up at the fan that resembled a huge spider ready to descend on her.

She didn't think Ben had really tried to poison her. The panic, well, that was a reaction to everything that had been going on lately. For the third time in her life, her world was folding in upon itself. The first time had been when Gary threw the kitten. Silas had been there for her then. When her mother died, Ben had been there.

Who was there for her now? No one. Even with Ben snoring softly beside her, she was beginning to think he was no longer on her side. Not emotionally anyway. She couldn't trust Gary, couldn't trust Silas, and apparently, she couldn't even trust Ben, though that wasn't his fault. Bertrice was too young to understand any of this, and she had her own problems to deal with, namely her friends' disappearance. So Katie was alone, really alone.

She turned over on her side. Silas still had a lot of questions to answer. Mostly, why he was so sure she was in danger. The killer had struck here in Flatlands and would move on.

It's someone you know.

She automatically touched her collarbone, but the cross was sitting in her jewelry box. She wanted to wear it in the worst way. To remember her mother, not Silas. It seemed that Silas haunted her every thought lately. Those smoky blue eyes floated through her mind constantly. The way he looked at her . . . wanted her. That guilty admission had turned her inside out. She wanted him, too. She'd never felt this way, even with her husband. Even when they had had a sex life, Ben never stirred this hunger inside her.

She quietly pushed back the covers and sat up.

"What's wrong?" Ben said in a sleepy voice.

"Can't sleep. I'm going to fix some warm milk."

"Want a pill?"

"No, I'm fine. Just restless."

She padded into the kitchen and turned on the stove, then poured milk into a pan. She sat down at the table to wait a few minutes. That's when she noticed the whisper of light beneath the office door.

This time she didn't grab the gun. If it was Gary, she'd scream. If it was Silas . . .

Her heart picked up another notch at that thought. She

turned off the heat and opened the door. Only the desk lamp was on, casting an eerie glow across the desk and floor. The room was empty, but she again *felt* a presence. Whoever was in here had probably heard her walk into the kitchen. She walked in and looked where Silas had hidden before. Nothing. The bifold doors were slightly ajar. She pushed them open. Even though she'd known someone was in here, the sight of Silas in the shadows still startled her. She swallowed back the gasp.

"You're supposed to be asleep," he whispered as though she were a disobedient child.

"And *you're* not supposed to be breaking into my home."

"Touché." He was dressed in black from his jeans to his T-shirt. Stripes of light crossed his face, making him look like a wolf waiting for his prey. "Are you all right? I've been getting some pretty strong feelings lately."

"I've been better." She didn't want to talk about the raccoon. "What are you doing here?"

"I need to verify some information."

She closed the office door as he set an old metal box on the desk. "Ever seen this before?"

She had to walk close to hear his soft words. "No. Where was it?"

"Buried in the back of the closet beneath some other boxes. It was locked."

"I don't mess with the stuff back there. Most of it belongs to Ben. The rest is old paperwork."

He opened the lid on the box. He'd obviously already picked the lock, just as he had to get in here.

"Ben's not sound asleep," she said. "You have to get out of here. If he catches you, he'll probably shoot you."

He didn't look too concerned about his own safety. But he took in her face and asked, "Would he hurt you?"

"No, never." She didn't want to tell him about her paranoia, either.

He started pulling out papers, but stilled when she touched his hand. "Silas, tell me what's going on. What happened to Dana and Geraldine? You knew, didn't you? Knew they'd be taken."

"I knew someone would be taken. I had no idea who or where it would happen." His gaze took in her hand still closed over the top of his. "Until he stopped to give them a ride. Then I recognized Geraldine."

"You were there?"

"In a way. I'll explain it later, when the time is right. I don't want to get you in trouble with Ben if he finds me here."

Always he was concerned for her. He took her hand in his, rubbing his thumb across the back of her fingers. That's when she noticed the gauze bandage peering out from beneath one of his rolled-up sleeves.

"What happened to your arm?"

"It's just a cut." He squeezed her fingers. "Remember when I told you that the Ghost is someone you know?" She nodded. "Geraldine and Dana knew him, too. He was someone they trusted."

It was someone who lived in Flatlands, then.

"How much do you know about Ben? About his past?" he asked.

"I thought we'd eliminated him when he called."

"I never eliminate anyone until I'm sure. But it's not a killing tendency I'm looking for."

"What, then?"

"I have a guy doing some background checks. I had him check Ben first, since he's closest to you. Something didn't add up. What do you know?"

"Not much. He doesn't like talking about his childhood. I know he was in foster care for a large part of it."

He dug through the box and took out a yellowed piece of paper. A birth certificate, she saw when he held it under the light. *Benjamin Arnold Ferguson,* the certificate read. Born in Milledgeville, not far from Flatlands. Ben had never once taken her there. He didn't go there himself. Bad memories, he said, and not much more.

Silas pointed to the birth date. She blinked, and then took the paper herself.

"He looks pretty good for an eighty-six-year-old man."

"This can't be right."

He shuffled through some of the other papers in the box. "Diplomas, high school and college, all with corresponding dates to the birth certificate."

"There must be some mistake."

He took her chin and lifted her face to his. "Katie, be very careful. Remember what I said about not trusting any-one."

"And here I am, harboring a criminal in my home." His eyes were more shadowy than the room itself. "Silas, tell me what's going on. You're the one who seems most likely to be committing these crimes. You tell me I'm in danger, but won't tell me how you know. And you warn me not to trust anyone, including you. Then I find you breaking into my home, not once but twice."

He lowered his face to hers and whispered, "Then why haven't you screamed your head off?"

"Because . . ." That womanly awareness trickled through her. "I'm crazy."

While Silas's thoughts were often a mystery to Katie, she could clearly see desire in his eyes. He was standing so close, she felt the heat of his body. It didn't seem to matter that she was standing in her own home with a man who shouldn't be there, wanting him to kiss her when her husband was only two rooms away. He cupped her face with both his large hands, running his thumbs over the cor-ners of her mouth.

She found her voice, which sounded hoarse. "I'm not everything that's good and pure with the world anymore. I haven't fought for what's right in longer than I can remem-ber. I'm not that little girl. I haven't been in a long, long time."

She felt his fingers tighten. Then he leaned down and kissed her. She saw his eyes close before he'd even started the kiss, as though he'd given in after a fight. His mouth was warm and soft against hers. She couldn't breathe, could do nothing more than lose herself in what she was feeling. An electrical charge sizzled through her chest and then down to her extremities.

She was kissing Silas. Or rather, he was kissing her, softly, slowly. She leaned closer, becoming a participant instead of just receiving. She captured his upper lip between hers and moved back and forth. His fingers slid up into her hair, and he opened her mouth and deepened the kiss. She sucked in a breath, but her own hunger kicked in. Her tongue danced with his, tasting him and making her feel as though she were spinning on a merry-go-round.

She became a woman right there without shedding a piece of clothing. Just kissing him took her from being a little girl to a woman with needs and desires long denied. She could feel her molecules changing. Her arms went around his waist, and she pulled him close enough to feel the evidence of his desire. He wanted her. It astounded her that she could produce that kind of reaction in him.

He was breathless when he pulled her against him and kissed her shoulder. He whispered her name, a plea maybe, though the hopelessness in his voice was unmistakable.

"Silas, stop living in the shadows," she whispered into his ear. "Let me help you."

He buried his face in her hair and squeezed her tight. "I can't."

He lifted his head at the sound. "Ben," she whispered, hearing him call her name. Her heart raced for a different reason. Silas slipped into the closet at the same time that Ben opened the door.

"Hon, what are you doing?" His curious tone bordered on the accusatory.

It was hard not to look at the closet doors, but she managed. "I . . ." She glanced at the box sitting out on the desk. "I couldn't sleep. So I came in here because . . ." Her first thought was to make up some benign reason and hope he didn't see the box. She didn't like rocking the boat, especially with Ben who could make her feel so guilty and selfish. "I have never felt as though I really know you. I want to know you better so I did some snooping and found this." She pulled the box closer and flipped open the lid.

He didn't look the least bit disturbed that she'd been snooping in his personal papers. "Katie, all you had to do was ask. I don't like talking about my past, you know that. But if there was something you wanted to know . . ." He walked close to take her hands in his, but she pulled out the birth certificate.

"Why is the date wrong?" She pulled out the diploma. "And on these?"

"They're my father's."

She blinked at the simplicity of his answer. He hadn't given it a thought, hadn't even looked at the papers in her hand. "Your father's?"

"The man who kindly donated sperm to create me and then left my mother to try to raise me alone."

"You said you didn't know your father."

"I did, just not personally. When he died, I took these papers because . . ." He looked away, and his voice got thick. "I wanted something of my father. Something to say who I was." When she could find nothing to say in return, he took the papers and returned them to the box. "Just ask me next time, Katie. I'd be glad to show you or tell you anything. I have nothing to hide from you."

"I'm sorry," she found herself saying. Then she realized he intended to return the box to the closet.

"I'll put it back," she said, taking the box. "I'm the one who took it out." She opened the right side of the closet and leaned into the shadows of the left side to set the box on the shelf. Silas was inches away. He was the man she wanted to know more about. His secrets, his demons, and his dreams. She wanted it all, no matter how dark.

She pulled herself from the closet and closed the door. "Let's go to bed," she said, turning off the lamp.

The room was plunged into darkness. Only a thread of light from the kitchen trailed in. Ben was looking at the closet. She paused by the door, her heart lodged firmly in her throat. "Ben?"

He led her out of the room, and she closed the door. "Katie, you're the one I don't know anymore. I have given you everything a man can give a woman . . . well, almost everything. Most importantly, I've given you love when no one else would. Since your birthday, you've been acting strange. And now that Silas is back in town, it's gotten even worse. I want my old Katie back."

"The old Katie never had to kill something. The old Katie didn't know her husband was capable of poisoning another creature, no matter how pesky."

She wished she had the guts to sleep on the couch. Even if she had, that left Ben to possibly go back into the office and see what she'd found in the box.

"I did it for you," he said, no remorse on his face.

"Don't ever kill anything for me again. And stop saying you did it for me."

~ CHAPTER 15

KATIE TOOK A bite of her meat loaf, the lunch special at the diner. Her portion had been significantly smaller than Ben's, but she wasn't very hungry anyway. They sat at one of the booths by the front window. Dinah's place was as busy as always, though most people were still talking about the two girls. They'd raked over every inch of Flatlands to no avail. Just like the other girls, they'd simply vanished. Everyone wore yellow ribbons for their safe return—everyone but Katie, who'd never gotten one.

Sam Savino and his wife sat in a booth nearby. He wasn't wearing a ribbon, either. Those dark eyes were on her, making her feel self-conscious.

"Every time I see that man, he's giving me strange looks," Katie said.

Instead of refuting that, Ben said, "No, he's looking at me. I don't know why, but he hates me."

But those hard eyes were looking right at her.

"Come with me this weekend," Ben said. "On my farm calls."

He must really be feeling insecure. He hadn't even mentioned her snooping through his things, and now he was inviting her along. Last week guilt would have made her accept. Nothing inside her was strong enough to want to patch things up now. What she wanted was some time alone to sort out her feelings, which was why she hadn't let him cancel the calls.

"Thanks for asking, but I've got some things I want to get done this weekend."

"I'll help you with them next weekend."

"I appreciate that, Ben, but I'd really planned to get them done this weekend. And besides, I wouldn't feel comfortable staying at the house of someone I don't know." Ben's customers usually put him up on his weekend trips.

"What about the killer who's on the loose? I don't want to leave you alone."

"I'll be fine. He's probably long gone by now. He only strikes one town before moving on." But it was someone she knew.

"Silas is still here."

Katie set down her fork. "There's no proof he's the one doing all this. It's just easy and convenient to pin it on him."

Ben's voice rose loud enough for anyone in the vicinity to hear him. "Why do you insist on defending Silas? He's done nothing to deserve anyone's loyalty. He didn't respond to the town's pleas to buy his property, not even the courtesy of a return call. He comes back to town after eighteen years and won't tell anyone why. He's got pictures and notes about young women being murdered—"

"He writes true-crime books."

Ben shook his head, disappointment dripping from his voice and expression. "Still defending him. Are you that stupid, Katie? A man that interested in murder is as warped as the killers he writes about. After everything I've done for you, how can you take his side?"

The people at the surrounding tables all stared at her with cold looks. She turned back to Ben and lowered her voice. "I'm not taking his side. I just don't like how everyone's judging him."

He only looked at her with that deadened expression. When neither had touched their food for several minutes, Maybel, their waitress, asked if they needed anything else. Asked Ben, not Katie.

He put his friendly face back on. "We're just fine and dandy, Maybel. No dessert for either of us."

"You hear about Grover Thompson?"

Again Maybel only addressed Ben, as though Katie weren't even there. "No, what happened?"

"He's gone. Just like the girls, disappeared into thin air. He took some slop out to the pigs and that was that. The bucket was found just outside the pig barn; he'd never even gotten to the pigs."

"Do they think it's the guy who took the girls?"

"I asked the sheriff that, but he said probably not. Those serial-type killers don't usually swing both ways. MO's different. Thelma's sure it's aliens that got him."

"I've heard them talk about the UFOs out there. I've taken care of Grover's animals for years. I'm going to have to pay Mrs. Thompson a visit and see if there's anything I can do. Damn shame, it is. Hopefully he's just trying to put the scare into her for some reason."

Then he pulled himself out of the booth and walked to the counter. Dinah walked right over and they exchanged a few words. Though Katie couldn't see Ben's face, she could see Dinah's. It was venomous. Compassion filled her expression when she turned back to Ben and patted his arm.

Maybel brought the bill over. Katie held out her hand, but Maybel flung it and made Katie crawl under the table where it had landed.

"Sorry 'bout that," Maybel said with enough sincerity to make Katie wonder. "So, when are you gonna give the doc babies? Ya'll have been married forever. Ain't right, not having babies by now. It's the least a woman can do for her man, you know. He'd make a great father."

Katie was so stunned by the personal question she couldn't answer at first. How strange, too, that she'd asked after Ben's offer. She cleared her throat and said, "We've decided to wait a little longer."

"Uh-huh," Maybel said before turning away.

Ben returned, his face neutral as ever. He threw a generous tip on the table and picked up the bill. "Ready?"

Katie slid out of the booth and wondered again if she were losing her mind or taking things too personally. She followed Ben to the front register, where Dinah processed their bill.

"You hear about the fire?" she asked Ben, pointedly ignoring Katie. "Started last night at the north edge of the Oconee Forest. Already burned a hundred acres."

"Heard it on the radio. Damn shame," Ben said, shaking his head. "But I'm glad it's not where I'm taking my farm calls this weekend." He turned to Katie. "Are you sure you don't want to come with me?" He nodded his thanks to Dinah and led the way out. Several people nearby waved to Ben as he walked past.

"I . . ." She wanted to draw out the answer until they got outside, but he paused at the glass door and waited for her to finish. Very polite of him. Two weeks ago she would have given in. This time she said, "I'm sure."

Thelma Thompson had been canning since Grover disappeared night before last. The cousins had helped as much as they could, what with having their own farms to tend to. Her own son couldn't be bothered to come back from college and help his mother. He had some important job for the summer, more important than farming or his family apparently. He was sure Grover had just run off for a few days.

She hauled the bucket of peelings to the pig pit, keeping her eye on the sky above. It was the same time it had been when Grover had taken this same path. She was going to be careful. The aliens wouldn't get her, too.

She'd seen the lights over the last few years, just like Grover had. Folks made fun of them when they talked about aliens flying overhead. Not a one believed them. The durned police wouldn't hear of it, either. But how else could one explain a whole person disappearing without a trace?

Some folks said it might be the killer who was taking the women in the area. But even the sheriff who came to take her statement thought that was unlikely. He had asked about the state of their marriage, with apologies. Thelma had wondered about that, too, but only for a moment. Grover wasn't the sort of man who'd stage something like this. Why, he knew where the door was. Besides, this farm had been in his family for three generations. No way would he walk away from it. Even the sheriff had agreed. She'd even heard someone say it was the pigs that got him.

Thelma laughed aloud as she neared the pit. Aliens it could be. But pigs? That was silly.

She switched on the lights and hauled the bucket to the troughs. Their big, beautiful pigs converged on her. She lost her balance for a moment and grabbed onto the side of the trough. The pigs dumped over the bucket she'd dropped and snorted through the peelings.

Something shiny caught her eye on the ground between the troughs. She angled her hand down into the muck to reach it. Maybe the aliens left it behind. Maybe it was proof-positive that Grover was way up there in the skies above.

It was long and hard and covered in mud. She left the pigs to ravage the bucket and walked over to the spigot. In the dim light she saw that it was pale, and that the glitter that had caught her eye only adorned one part of it. She walked over to the light—and screamed.

The finger dropped back to the ground and sank into the muck.

Ben said little as Katie got up early, fixed his breakfast, and sent him off to the country. Not even a thank-you. Then again, fixing breakfast, keeping the house clean, all of the household tasks fell within her responsibility. Even though she worked as many hours as he did at the hospital, she felt obligated to handle the house, too.

As resentment rushed to the surface, she realized it had been there for a long time, coated in a layer of gratitude. She'd long assumed that since she wasn't attractive or lovable, she had to make up for it by being complacent. Earning her keep.

She'd been brutally honest two nights ago with Silas

when she'd admitted she hadn't been good and pure for a long time. That's when he'd kissed her. Whenever she thought about that kiss, she involuntarily pressed her fingertips to her mouth.

Silas hadn't asked for anything. He hadn't offered much, either. Today he was going to give her something—the truth. All of it.

She pulled out the dress Ben had bought for her in Atlanta. It was as ugly as anything else he'd ever bought her. Still, she'd have to wear it once in a while or he'd mention it in his hurt way. She hung it in the back of the closet, where she found the other outfit Bertrice had brought over: purple jeans and a top with peace signs emblazoned in a colorful print.

She felt the same way she had when she'd put the other outfit on: liberated and a touch sexy. She stood in front of the dresser mirror and tried to see herself through Silas's eyes. That was impossible, of course. She wasn't beautiful, but when Silas looked at her, she felt beautiful.

She pulled the gold cross out of the jewelry box and put it on. It looked right there, a symbol of her mother. She wouldn't hide it from Ben any longer.

Her hair, washed that morning, hung limply over her shoulders. When she'd lived with the Emersons, they'd kept her hair short for easy maintenance. Since she married Ben, he'd insisted she keep it past her shoulders. She wanted something different. Her heart thrummed as she took the scissors from the sewing kit and held them poised over a hank of hair. Ben would be disappointed. She could well imagine the look on his face.

Four inches of brown hair rained into the sink. She trimmed the rest as evenly as she could and finger-curled the ends under. Although only a few ounces of hair were gone, it felt as though a hundred pounds had lifted off her. She picked up the picture of her and her mother and compared her laughing image there to the one in the mirror. She was getting closer to that Katie. All she needed was a reason to laugh so unabashedly.

Only after she'd curled her hair did she discover her birthmark now showed clearly. Ben would hate that. She traced her finger around the edge of the fist-sized stain and wondered if Silas would hate it, too. She had no makeup, not even concealor or foundation. Something else Ben hated.

"You're not going to kiss him again, Katie," she told her reflection. "It's not right. You have to decide what you're going to do with your life." Her throat went tight at the prospect of doing anything. What could she do? Leave Ben? And go where? The same vicious cycle.

What about Silas?

"He's just trying to protect me. Doesn't that sound familiar? Maybe that's all he wants, is to be my protector. Look what that got me last time."

Something in Silas's eyes said he wanted to possess her, too. The thought of him possessing her stirred her in a way Ben had never stirred her.

She slung an old backpack over her shoulder. The gun was inside; she was beginning to feel like a gun-toting individual, though it still wasn't loaded. As she headed out the door, she wished she still had Goldie to keep her company on the walk. It saddened her that Ben wouldn't even share her with a pet.

Her hand stilled on the doorknob. He didn't want to share her. Is that what it was about? He often told her she belonged to him, words that had once been endearing and were now cloying. In every way she could think of, he kept her to himself. Not intentionally. He'd already lived out here when she married him, already had the veterinary hospital that wasn't close to much. But the first time she'd mentioned having a baby, his response was, *I'm not ready to share you yet.*

Which meant his offer to try to have a baby with her was given out of sheer desperation.

She locked the door behind her. As she descended the steps, she heard a vehicle coming down the drive. Her whole body reacted when Harold's old truck came into view. The back was crammed with junk as usual.

Her instinct was to run inside the house, but he was already out of the truck before she could react. Her fingers tightened around the square post in front as he approached with an amiable expression on his face.

"Katie, how are you doing this morning?" He glanced at his watch. "I guess it's noon now."

"What can I do for you?"

He glanced toward the house. "Is Ben around? He asked me a while back if I ever run across paintings. Says you have a couple of blank walls he'd like to do something with. I got a couple I picked up yesterday that might fit the bill." He walked back to the truck and pulled out two large oil paintings. Both were nature scenes done in garish colors.

"He's . . . not here right now. Why don't you come back later? Or better yet, I'll have him stop by your place and take a look at them."

He was already at the bottom step with a painting in each large hand. "Well, since I'm here, why don't we go inside and see if they look good? That's the best way to tell, don't you think?" He started up the steps.

"Look, I was on my way out, so if this can wait . . ."

He glanced around at the absence of the van. "Need a ride somewhere?"

"No, I'm walking. But thank you anyway. I've got to get going—"

Harold took the remaining step toward the front door. "Look, I brought these out here for you, so let's see how they look, and then I'll be out of your hair."

No way was she going in that house with him. "I'm late—"

He tried the doorknob, finding it locked. When he took in her surprised look, he said, "What the hell is wrong with you, anyway? Ain't I good enough to be inside your house? Is that it?" He walked closer.

"No, it's not that, it's just that—"

He threw the paintings down. "That sure is it, isn't it? You're a regular snob is what you are. Don't have a nice word to say to me ever, don't thank me for giving you rides, and don't show any appreciation at all for driving all the way out here to show you my paintings. You think you're too good to talk to me. Well, let me tell you something: You aren't."

Katie backed up as he moved forward. His breath smelled like stale beer. "I don't think I am. Really."

"It's time you showed me some respect. As an equal." The muscle in his eyelid pulsed faster as he took a step closer.

The sound of a vehicle coming down the drive sent her scurrying down the steps. *Please let it be Silas.*

It wasn't.

The sheriff's SUV rolled to a stop behind the truck. Tate took his time getting out of the vehicle and sauntering to the bottom step where she remained. In her unease she'd forgotten about her appearance until he stopped short and blinked in surprise.

"Wow, Katie, you're looking something else." Not a compliment, just a frank appraisal.

She'd worn a bra this time, but still covered her chest with her arms. She glanced back at Harold, who was coming down the steps with the paintings.

"Howdy, Tate. Stopped by to show Katie some paintings I got in. Guess she didn't like them." He tossed them into the back of the truck.

"Didn't know you offered in-home shopping."

"For special customers, I do. Ben's bought a lot of stuff from me over the years. Have a good day." With a final challenging look at her, he climbed into his truck and left.

That challenge was whether she was going to mention their conversation to Tate. "Have you ever checked into Harold? I mean, as being the one who's taking the girls? You do think it's someone local, don't you?"

Tate laughed. "It's someone local all right. But Harold? He's a big guy, but he's no devil. Katie, I think you have it in for everyone."

Well, what had she expected? "What's up, Sheriff?"

"I know you're here by yourself and wanted to check on you, is all."

She was glad he did, even if he wouldn't consider Harold a threat.

"How'd you know Ben's out of town?"

"He calls, asking us to make sure you're all right. I think what he's really after is making sure you're not with Silas. We're getting closer to nailing him, you know. We finally got some evidence." And he was going to enjoy telling her. She reevaluated her previous thought about him looking like Mel Gibson. He had the intense, almost-over-the-edge blue eyes, but he wasn't nearly as good-looking. And he looked dog tired.

Her throat tightened, and she involuntarily covered it with her hand. "What evidence?"

Those eyes narrowed in amusement. "See, even you're not sure about him, are you?" He walked up to the steps where she leaned against the column. "We finally figured out how the clever son of a bitch hides the bodies. You probably heard about Grover Thompson being missing the same night the girls disappeared. Went out to feed the pigs and *whoosh* he was gone. Last night his wife found a finger."

He caught her wince. "But it wasn't his finger, no siree. It was most likely Dana Westbury's finger. The tests aren't done yet, but her mama said she wore sparkly nail polish and the fingernail had the same kind. We cut open the pigs and guess what we found? Body parts, or at least what was left of them." He took a step up. "He cuts them up with an axe. He cuts them up and feeds them to the pigs." He ground in each word, and she couldn't help recoiling. "That's what your friend does."

She didn't want to think about that finger, or the other images that came to mind. "That's . . . horrible."

"Yes, it is. But he's smart, you see. Gotta admire him for that. Knows pigs will eat anything flesh and bone. Now we just gotta figure out what he does with the clothes and jewelry." He had closed the distance and now stood only a foot in front of her. She could smell male sweat and Old Spice. "Don't you admire him for that?"

That steely gaze held her for a moment, but she finally broke free to ask, "You said Grover was missing. Maybe he's the one doing this."

"When we searched the barn, we found him buried in muck way toward the back. He went out to feed the pigs and caught Silas in the act. Understandably, Silas had to kill him."

Not Silas. It was another image, more terrible than the rest in its implications: the cut on his arm.

"He probably stalked them the same way he stalks you. He does stalk you, Katie. He's like your shadow, following you to work, peeking in your windows. He's gone to the Baptist church a couple of times, too. I saw him go inside for a while the last time. Maybe trying to atone for his sins. Or maybe he's challenging God to stop him. 'Stop me if You can. I'm the other side of You, the darkness to Your light. The evil to Your goodness.' You think that's what he's doing, Katie?"

"No."

Tate was getting some kind of perverse pleasure out of this little interrogation. But what he was doing was making her fear *him*, not Silas. "Interesting that you accused Gary of hurting that cat of yours when he was innocent. And now you're siding with evil. Don't you find that ironic?"

"No," she said again, afraid to say more.

"Then there's something else you should know. I'm only telling you this for your own good. I'm just trying to figure out why you trust Silas with your life. Don't you realize that every time you're alone with him, you risk never coming back?"

"I can't say why I trust him. But I do."

"Another woman trusted Silas, and she's probably dead, too."

"What are you talking about?"

"Her name was Celine Carrigan. She disappeared from the Atlanta area in 1988. Guess who reported her missing?"

"Silas." The word came out a raspy whisper.

"Smart girl. Not only that, they lived together."

She swallowed hard. "They were friends. He told me about her." Well, sort of.

"Did he mention she disappeared?"

"No," she had to admit. "Did they . . . find her shoe?"

"No. But they don't always find shoes. Sometimes he hides them well."

She digested the information. "Celine," she said at last. "Isn't that the name of his company?"

"Bingo. You're smarter than you look. Who can figure out a woman's mind? I've been trying for years with no luck. They fall in love with men who are incarcerated for violent crimes. They're drawn to the dark side."

"We all have a dark side; and a light side."

That made him smile. "Yes, we do."

The uneasy feeling that had started with Harold and then Tate's arrival now sent the hairs on the back of her neck standing at attention. "How do you know Silas is looking in my window? The only person I've seen peeking in is Gary."

His chuckle was even more unnerving than his smile. "Accusing Gary again? You never learn, girl who cried wolf. The only accusation you'll make that people will believe is when you point to Silas. And if you keep hanging around with him, you may not be around to point any fingers." He tipped his hat. "Good day, Katie."

She leaned against the column as he walked to his vehicle. She hoped she didn't look as drained as she felt when he gave her another glance before getting in. She straightened her shoulders and held his gaze until he got in and drove away.

Only then did she walk on shaky legs toward the woods. The sun was warming the leaves and filling the air with the scent of pine when she headed toward Silas's. She kept stopping suddenly to see if footsteps followed. Other than the birds hopping from branch to branch and the groundhog she'd spotted earlier, she seemed to be alone. Her thoughts were far more terrifying than anything physical.

She kept telling herself that Silas wasn't a murderer. She'd gotten guff for that belief, but down deep she believed it. And yet, everything seemed to point to him. Even Silas had warned her about himself.

The whining sound sent chills scurrying down her spine. She remembered the sound from that first night when Silas had reappeared in her life. A saw.

It was Tate's voice in her head saying, *Cuts up women with an axe. Could be a saw, you know. I'll bet that's what he's doing right now.*

She thought about sneaking up on Silas to see what he was doing. But that was impossible, because he always knew what she was feeling if it was a strong emotion. She tamped down the fear and continued forward. When she neared the house, she pulled the gun from her backpack.

The whining noise muffled as it cut through something. She shuddered. He was inside this time, not out where she could see him. She breathed in relief when the saw started again. He hadn't felt her. Yet.

With the gun pressed against her leg, she crept up the stairs. The Boss was sprawled across the threshold. He lifted his head with some amount of effort. She kept out of view where she could see Silas standing at a homemade table of sorts. As she tried to see what he was doing, he turned around.

She couldn't help but catch her breath at the sight of him. It brought back everything they'd shared last night. He wore the blue headband again. Not a speck of blood, not one body part anywhere. The only body was the gorgeous one with the low-slung white jeans and plaid shirt open to reveal a damp chest.

He cut the saw and set it down. His dark blue eyes lit with warmth and something she wasn't sure she wanted to define as he took in her outfit. "Katie." His expression changed when he saw the gun pressed against her leg. Instead of asking, he merely leaned back against the table and waited for her to explain.

"How'd you get the cut on your arm?" she asked.

He glanced at the gauze bandage wrapped around his right arm. "I don't know." He pushed away from the table and walked slowly around to her right. Like a wolf stalking his prey.

She turned to face him. "What do you mean, you don't know?"

"Katie, what's this about?" He nodded toward the gun. "You know you're not going to shoot me, so put it away."

She lifted the gun at him. "You don't know that for sure."

"Yeah, I do," he said in a resigned voice. He walked up so close, she felt the brush of his shirt against her. He took her wrists in his hands and held them between them. "I know you better than you know yourself, I bet. I know you're afraid of me, but you hate being afraid of me. I know you're lonely and confused and feeling a little more than guilty about our kiss last night." He released her hands and tipped up her chin. His voice went lower. "I know you want more of that kiss. I know it's the first time you've felt this way." He touched a strand of her hair that curled under her chin. "I know you're looking for some part of yourself that's been missing for a long time and you don't know how to find it. You're looking for that little girl you used to be, the one who felt life and passion and freedom."

"Silas . . ." The gun dropped to the floor.

"Shhh." He touched her mouth with his finger. "There's more. Someone has you scared of me and you need answers to assure yourself that you haven't kissed a serial killer. Am I right?"

She could only nod. God, how had he done that, gone right to her soul and pulled out every doubt and desire?

"I didn't want to put you in this position. I never wanted to, and that's why I never spoke to you whenever I came to town." His finger had remained against her lower lip. "I knew . . . this would be between us." He closed his eyes. "And Katie, if there was ever a bad time to want you, it's now. And you don't even want to think about wanting me, not now . . . not ever."

She swallowed hard on those words, seeing that no matter what he said, he did want her. She would never forget the sight of desire in a man's eyes. "I hate that you know what I'm feeling. Ben's always talking about sharing feelings, but I've recently realized that I'm the only one sharing feelings in our marriage. Just when I'm starting to hold back my feelings, and keep them to myself, you come along."

"I'm sorry, Katie, but you've been inside me for so long, I couldn't even try to shut you out."

Those words slithered through her and tightened her stomach. She had to push onward. "Who's Celine?"

He took a step back, but recovered his surprise quickly. "I suppose it was only a matter of time before they found out about her."

"If you'd told me everything up front—"

"You weren't ready to hear everything then. What would you have done if I'd dumped all this on you at our first meeting?"

"Run scared," she had to admit. She'd been different then. Silas had changed her. Instead of being comfortably unhappy, she was uncomfortably happy. And completely messed up. "So who's Celine? Is she the friend you lived with in Atlanta?"

"Yes."

"You named your company after her. She must have been important to you." She couldn't quite admit that she wanted to be the only important person to Silas. If she'd lived inside him, if he'd felt her across hundred of miles and years of separation, shouldn't she be the only important woman in his life? She pushed aside those selfish thoughts.

"She *was* important to me. She changed my life in some ways. We hooked up in Atlanta and along with a couple of other people rented a run-down place to live. Eventually the others moved out and Celine and I handled the rent on our own. We looked out for each other."

There were other questions Katie wanted to ask, but she settled with, "Did she know . . . about your empathy?"

"Anyone I know for a period of time finds out one way or the other. It bugged her, too." He studied her face. She tried to look down, but he tilted her chin up. "Did I love her? In a way. We gave each other what we needed. I protected her, and she gave me affection. We were together for about five years. She'd been in a real bad situation for most of her life and had run away five years earlier when she was fourteen. She came down with me when I tried to see you."

"She knew about me?" Katie asked in a croaky voice.

He nodded. "She said I was in love with you. I told her she was wrong, because I was twenty and you were only fourteen. I was too afraid of being like my father."

"The child pornography you found."

"But it wasn't like that. I didn't feel lustful toward you."

And had he toward Celine? She couldn't let herself picture them making love or let herself feel jealousy.

He glanced away. "She disappeared in 1988. Just like that, *poof,* she was gone. I went to work as a bartender at a bar around the corner one night. She worked there, too, as a waitress. She'd worked the afternoon shift and we saw each other briefly before she went back to our apartment. She never made it home."

She heard the pain in those last words. "What happened to her?"

"I never found out. I hounded the police to find her. They did a cursory investigation, but figured she'd just taken off. So I kept looking. I started investigating, taking notes and interviewing people who were on her route home." His voice went so low, she could hardly hear him. "She'd vanished without a trace. I know someone took her, but I have no idea who or how." He cleared his throat. "I kept a journal as I went along. I wrote an article for the newspaper, hoping they'd run it and get some leads. They liked my writing style and thoroughness. That's how I got into what I write. And that's why I named my company after her." She could see the pain across his features. "Did you think I'd killed her? Is that why I got an uneasy feeling from you just a bit ago?"

She sorted through what she'd been thinking and feeling. "I didn't think you'd done it. I just wanted to know the story. Wanted to know who Celine was." She paused when she saw how her trust had warmed his expression. "You still miss her?"

The warmth left as fast as it had come. "There's no use missing someone who's gone."

She reached out and grabbed his arm. It startled him, since he'd been looking in the other direction. As she opened her mouth to say something, she felt him. Not his feelings, exactly, but an odd sensation that invaded her senses. There was a vague sense of pain and a larger sense of him, of Silas inside her the way she'd been inside him.

"I feel you, Silas. I feel you," she said, enunciating the words. He pulled his arm away, but she was still stunned by it. "Let me share your pain. You've been sharing mine all these years. It's only fair." She started to reach for his hand again, but he gripped her wrist.

"Nothing's fair in life, Katie."

"Oh, I get it. You're supposed to be the protector. That's your role, with me and with Celine. It's okay for you to shoulder all that yourself, but God forbid if anyone tries to protect you once in a while. Or comfort you. It's that giving/accepting thing again, isn't it?"

"Giving's easy. You just give. That's it, real simple."

"And what's so difficult about accepting?"

"Taking, and all it implies, makes things complicated. I don't know how to deal with that part of it." He picked up the gun from the floor. "You wanted to know how I got this cut. Demanded to know, as I recall." He handed the gun to her.

His swift change of subject had her almost dizzy, but she nodded and put the gun in her backpack. "They found Dana's finger at a farmer's pigpen. The killer is cutting them up and . . . feeding them to the pigs."

"Oh, God." He closed his eyes and looked as horrified as she probably had when she'd heard the news. A minute later, he opened his eyes and looked at her. "And you think that's where I got this cut?"

She let out a long sigh. "I don't know what to think anymore. I guess I don't have to tell you how confused I am. You're right, I don't want to believe it's you, but things keep pointing at you. Tell me what's going on. Why did you come back here, why are you trying to protect me? Why are you so sure it's someone I know?"

"Who told you about Celine? Gary?"

"No, Tate." She fidgeted with her cross. "Would you think I'm crazy if I said I was afraid of him?"

"The sheriff? No, I wouldn't think you were crazy. Why are you afraid of him?"

She relayed their conversation. "It was creepy. But maybe I can't trust my judgment anymore—"

"Considering you're here with the one person who seems most likely to be a killer," he finished her unspoken words. "Trust your instincts. I'll see if I can dig up anything on Tate."

She was grateful that he hadn't dismissed her paranoia out of hand the way everyone else did. But there was more she needed to know, and she couldn't let her gratitude soften her. "Why do you think the killer is someone I know? Tell me, Silas. I'm ready to hear it."

He seemed to assess her, and she stood tall and strong to show him how ready she was. He let out a sigh and sat down on the top step, nodding for her to join him. "Because of my empathy feelings, I've avoided people for a long time. Unless it has something to do with the book I'm working on, I don't want to know the feelings of the people around me. Even simple things like flying on planes can be emotionally wracking, picking up broken hearts and financial worries and lust. When I touch someone, it's even worse. I don't just pick up their feelings, I feel them. They course through my blood the same way they course through their blood."

"But you touch me," she said in a soft voice.

"It's different with you. I'm used to feeling you." He pulled his gaze away from her after once again taking in her new look. "It's hard enough working with people who have lost their children, but that's what I do. Three years ago I was interviewing a serial killer named Charles Swenson along with an FBI agent."

"I'm reading that book now."

"Don't read it. It's worse than anything you can imagine."

She tried a smile. "You don't mean your writing, I hope."

He didn't return the smile. "Katie, it's ugly. It's dark. He was one of the most vicious serial killers in history."

It touched her that he was protecting her and yet . . . "But it's what you write."

"Some of us belong in the dark, trying to sort it out and understand it. Trying to figure out what makes a man cross the line into evil. You're not one of those people." The Boss walked over and sat down heavily near Silas. When he lifted one of his big paws, Silas started rubbing it with deliberate strokes, though he kept his gaze on Katie. "Swenson killed twenty-two women, maybe more. You can't even imagine in your worst nightmares what he did to those women."

She shivered. "I haven't gotten that far. Worse than cutting them up and feeding them to pigs?"

"Much. I was only an observer in the interview. The FBI was trying to find out what he'd done to the bodies. Swenson had teased us about revealing their locations, though he never did. Since I was working on the book about him, I was allowed to sit in on the interviews. There were several of them spanning almost a year. Swenson would look at me—just look at me. All that time, he never said one word to me. I couldn't feel anything from him. He'd masked his emotions." His gaze drifted out to the yard. "Like he knew I could feel them.

"On our last interview, he reached over and grabbed me.

He locked his fingers over my arm and looked at me with"—the memory clouded his eyes with revulsion—"satisfaction. The FBI agent pulled his gun and ordered him to let go. I heard it as though it were happening in some far-off place. All I could see were Swenson's memories. They flashed through my head, one pounding in right after another." He ran his hand down over his face, his gaze still directed inward. "And I could *feel* his joy, his lust, his carnal hunger . . . I could feel everything. I staggered back and passed out. When I came to, I went to the restroom and threw up." Even now his expression was grim, and his tan skin was pale.

"Why did he grab you? Did he ever say?"

"No, though I never saw him face-to-face after that. I was too afraid to initiate contact again. He knew, Katie. Somehow he knew I was reading him. When he touched me, he . . . changed something inside me. I can't explain it exactly, but it opened a door. Until he died two months later, I dreamt about his crimes. It didn't help that I was writing about them, too. It was like I was connected to him the same way I'm connected to you. When he died, I'd finished his book and was back on this case. I was consumed with it, researching it on my time, living and breathing it. It had been two years since the last girl had been taken, or at least that they knew about. Later that year, another girl disappeared near Ivey." He finally turned his gaze to hers. "And I saw it happen. I felt it."

"But Swenson was dead."

"It wasn't Swenson. When he died, the weird connection I had with him somehow . . . transferred to the guy I was trying to hunt down. Maybe because I was emotionally involved with this case more than any other."

"Because of Celine?"

"Yeah, because of Celine."

"Do you think this is the guy who took her?"

"I don't know for sure. He's the only one who can tell me that." He ran his fingers back through his hair in one quick motion. "I can feel when he starts to get antsy. It starts slow, and as it builds, I get these flashes of him prowling, though I can never figure out where he is. When he finds his victim, his emotions are so high, so finely tuned, I'm in his head and I understand why he's doing it. He feels justified, entitled. He likes the power he has over their lives, and especially relishes the moment when they realize they're in danger. He gets off on the surprise factor as much as the power factor."

Silas switched paws, keeping his focus now on the gentle kneading motion. Still, she could see the pain and horror of what he'd seen. Her own chest felt so tight, she could barely breathe.

"I've been with him now for eight of his kills."

"Eight? In just three years?" She couldn't keep the shock from her voice.

"Including Geraldine and Dana, yes. Like most serial killers, he's escalating. As they become more desperate to satiate their lust, they make mistakes. But this guy thinks he's smarter than everyone else. I call him the Ghost, because he never leaves behind a trace."

"But he left a finger."

"He was probably caught in the act and it slipped away from him."

"You didn't see—or feel—that?"

"No."

Those words, along with his serious expression, gave her the willies. She looked at the gauze on his arm. "Have you seen him . . . cut them up?"

"No. That's the letdown part for him. I'm only with him as his excitement grows, and when he takes the woman. When he ties her up and rapes her. He's keeping them alive longer too. Sometimes for a few days. But he always gets tired of them. He probably has no emotion at all when he kills them. That part's probably inconvenient."

"Oh, God, Silas. Have you gone to the police with this?"

"Do you know what they'd do to me if they discovered what I knew about the crimes? I'd be as dead as Swenson. I've given them anonymous tips."

"Tips?"

"Where to find his trophies. All serial killers take a trophy, some part of the woman, her body or jewelry or hair, to keep the fantasy alive for him after she's dead. A lot of times that's how they're proven guilty. Dahmer kept pieces of his victims in his freezer. Ed Gein upholstered his furniture with human skin and decorated his house with skulls he hung on the walls. He made things from body parts, like a belt made of nipples. There was a guy who murdered for his shoe collection. But this guy, he's different. He doesn't want a particular object to relive the fantasy. For him, it's leaving something in plain sight that gets him off. And because shoes are commonly found on the side of the road, that's what he uses.

"I started seeing him leaving the shoe, but I couldn't always spot a landmark to help me find it. He's covered this entire area, always leaving the shoe somewhere far from where he took the victim. And usually where another victim was or will be taken."

She leaned forward and took the Boss's foot in her hand and started massaging it, trying very hard not to picture a belt made of nipples. "The other night in the graveyard, you said he was on the prowl again and took off."

"When he goes on the prowl, I do, too. At first it's to try to find him. But something happens as he gets closer and then finds his victims. It gets so strong, it knocks me out, just like that first time Swenson grabbed me. I wake up sometime later, usually in my vehicle. Lately . . ."

She waited for him to continue, but the haunted look on his face made her prod him. "What?"

"Lately . . . I've been waking up closer and closer to where he's been. I probably just missed him this last time. Maybe next time, or the time after that, I'll come face-to-face with him."

"And then it'll be over. You'll turn him in, and he'll be put away." He didn't look relieved. "You said I knew him. That I was in danger. Is he stalking me? Tell me. I want to know it all."

"I don't know if he's stalking you. But once, when I was getting the flashes, when his urge to kill was just starting . . . I saw you. He was looking at you. That's why I came back."

CHAPTER 16

GARY WATCHED KATIE and Silas sitting out on the porch. He'd been staking out Silas since that morning. Despite everything he'd told her—all designed to scare her away from Silas—she still seemed to trust him. And like him.

And she was still scared of Gary, still hated him. She had to understand what was at stake, though how could he tell her when she didn't trust him? She'd never believe his confession if she didn't trust him. It was starting to look like he was going to have to force it on her.

He wished he could hear what they were talking about. He'd parked near the road and walked down the drive. He couldn't get any closer than the bend that hid him. His binoculars let him see them, but not enough to read their lips. Enough to see that she looked scared.

After a while, they stood. He touched her chin. She let him touch her. Gary couldn't tell whether they shared a bond like brother and sister or something sexual. Either way, it burned him. He wanted to pound Silas into the ground.

Silas dropped his hand and glanced out toward the road. Gary was sure he couldn't have heard him, couldn't see him. Still, Silas walked out into the yard and headed right at him.

Spooky Silas. This sure as hell was spooky. Gary ran down the drive, keeping to the far left where the trees shadowed the drive. He hopped into his vehicle and sped away.

Silas heard the engine start out by the highway, but there wasn't any way to catch up and see who it was.

"What's wrong?" Katie said, coming up behind him.

"Nothing."

"I may not be empathic, but I do know a lie when I hear one."

When he turned to face her, determination bristled from her. Oddly enough, her words warmed him. She didn't think he was a freak. He'd felt her concern as he'd told her his story, but not horror. That's when he'd felt something else: rage and jealousy. Not from Katie.

"Someone was watching us. And they weren't too happy that we were together."

"Ben?" She *did* look concerned about being caught there by him. He felt a mixture of fear and guilt.

"I don't know. Do you want to go home and check?"

She glanced toward the woods, then back at him. "No. I want to see your notes. I want to know everything about this murderer."

"Some of it's pretty graphic."

"I don't care. I need to know."

She had been kept back for too long. He wasn't going to hold her back anymore. "Come on."

Before he opened the first folder, she said, "I'd like to see a picture of Celine."

He blinked at that. "Why?"

"I don't know. But I would."

He dug through a box of old case notes and found a picture of the two of them. He handed it to her. She took it gingerly and studied it. She'd probably think how young he looked, and in that particular picture, how happy. He had been happy then. For the first time, he was in control of his world, and he was at peace with it. Soon after that picture had been taken, that world had been irretrievably damaged.

"She was pretty," Katie said, handing the picture back.

He nodded, taking in Celine's laughing face. Dark, long hair, brown eyes. Seeing that picture and Katie in the same moment, he realized that Celine looked a lot like her. Did she see it, too?

If she did, she didn't say. He put the picture back and pulled out the more recent folders. She tried to hold in her reaction to the photos of the two girls whose bodies were found, keeping the horror from her face. But of course he knew exactly how she felt. Still, she kept reading, kept studying everything. She touched several of the pins on the map, traced his charts and tried to follow his statistics.

She closed the last folder. "Is this what you do when you're working on a book? Have all these notes and stuff around?"

"I have to immerse myself in the case."

"Why do you do this, Silas? Why do you live so close to the dark?"

He was glad she couldn't read his mind as flashes of his childhood played through his head: shooting that animal, being kicked out of the house at night for some misdeed, feeling the blood lust as his father skinned his prey.

"It's where I'm comfortable." He turned to those woods where he'd spent many nights alone. Then he thought of the victims whose terrors he witnessed. "And because it lives inside me."

She started to reach for him, but he moved away under the pretense of gathering up the folders. "There's a quote from Friedrich Nietzsche that FBI profilers live with. It goes something like: 'Whoever fights monsters should see to it that in the process he does not become a monster. And when you look into an abyss, the abyss also looks into you.' The profilers I've worked with over the years look into the abyss of the killer's mind, trying to understand them. One agent was emotionally traumatized by Ted Bundy, who drew him into the abyss. They walk the fine wire between good and evil. I've been inside this killer's mind. I have, while in his mind, understood why he kills. I've felt his triumph and joy. What does that make me, Katie?"

"A tortured man."

He looked inside those big brown eyes of hers and saw salvation. And he couldn't take it. He didn't want to drag her down into the dark—into the abyss—with him. "I think this is what I'm meant to do, figure out what makes a man—or woman—cross the line. We all have evil inside us, or at least the capacity for it. We all feel rage and hatred." She nodded at that. "I need to understand how that rage transforms to murder." He continued to sort his folders and put them back into the box where he stored them.

She read some of the lists of known serial killers and the events leading up to their first kill. "You've done a lot of studying on the fine line between good and evil."

"Ted Bundy seemed to be pushed over the line by not being able to possess the one woman he wanted. Another man was pushed into rage killing when his wife threatened to never let him see his sons again."

Her fingers tightened on the folder. "Are you looking for the line that keeps you from crossing over?"

He couldn't meet her eyes, couldn't breathe for a moment. For years he'd been driven to read everything he could on serial and spree killers. He'd done graphs and charts, telling himself it was for his writing. She had crystallized that search in one simple question.

"Who are the men in your life?" he asked after several long moments.

She didn't let go of the folder right away, but eventually she released her hold and her breath, as well. "Ben, of course. Lately, Gary's been bothering me. Sheriff Tate has been coming around with regard to this whole investigation. He and I have been at odds since that day long ago. Harold took me to work those few days, and he's icky. And . . . you."

That last word was filled with a sweet combination of question and finality. He tried not to get hung up on it, focusing instead on the other part. "What's Gary been doing to bother you?"

"Popping over a lot when Ben's gone. He keeps saying we're alike, that I should only trust him. He . . . thinks you're the one taking the girls, and he tries to make me afraid of you. And he keeps asking me to forgive him for throwing Gus. He tried to explain why he did it, that his father was emotionally abusive but no one would believe it."

Silas was frozen on that one word: *forgive*. "He wants your forgiveness?"

"He says I have to forgive him because we're alike. There's more that he wants to tell me, but only after I forgive him. I don't think I could ever forgive him."

"Katie, I want you to be very careful around him."

She must have picked up the deadly tone in his voice, because her eyes widened. "What is it?"

"That's what the killer was thinking when he took the Flatlands girls. He wondered if you'd be able to forgive him if you knew."

She swallowed thickly. "Me?"

"You. Don't be alone with him if you can help it."

"Believe me, I'm trying."

"Gary's one of my leading suspects," Silas said. "He's had a history of rage problems. I can remember him picking on the younger kids even before he threw your kitten. He was always like a pressure cooker with the steam seeping out beneath the lid. Joining the police force in Atlanta didn't seem to help much. I finally managed to find out what he'd been up to there. They eventually made him take an anger-management course. He flunked out, so he was asked to leave the force." He glanced up at Katie. "Has he tried to get physical with you?"

"He gets in my face sometimes, grabs my arm, but he's never actually tried anything. He keeps trying to tell me something about himself."

"Maybe you should let him. Next time he tries, play along with him. See what he's got to say. But only if you're in a safe situation." He tapped his fingers on the steps. "He was also in Atlanta at the time of some of the disappearances. It's circumstantial evidence, of course. But still something to consider.

"As for Harold, I've had my police contacts in Atlanta checking on him. He's another one to stay clear of. If Ben knew his past, he sure wouldn't be asking him to take you to work."

"Why?"

"Back in 1980, he was charged with raping his girl-friend. He served time and got out on good behavior. A few years later, he moved here. He hasn't been into any trouble since, at least not that he's been caught at. I've checked his house—nothing there. But I can't get into the barn with the pit bull he keeps as a guard."

She'd wrapped her arms defensively around herself when he'd mentioned the rape. "I was so unnerved by Tate's visit, I forgot to tell you about Harold's visit."

"What visit?"

"He stopped by ostensibly to show me some paintings. Wanted to come inside, in fact, insisted on it. Then he called me a snob. He got pretty angry with me, said I'd better start respecting him as an equal. That's when Tate showed up."

"Did you mention it to him?"

"I didn't think there was much point to it. Harold was as nice as pie when Tate showed up, like he was doing me some favor by bringing those ugly paintings over. No way would Tate believe he'd just been threatening me."

Silas nodded at the truth of that. Tate wanted to believe what Tate wanted to believe.

"When you talk about trusting my instincts—God, I feel so paranoid even saying this, first the sheriff—"

"I'm not going to judge you, Katie."

The tension eased from her face. "I get a weird feeling about Sam Savino, too. He stares at me wherever I see him. Just stares. It's creepy."

"But he hasn't tried anything?"

"Hasn't said a word to me. But Gary said Sam used to hit him, that that's where he gets his rage problem from. I don't know whether to believe him or not, but . . ."

"But your instincts say he's telling the truth?"

"Yes. I can see that anger in Sam's eyes, as though he hates everyone. As though he hates himself."

"I haven't actively considered Savino a suspect, but I'll check him out. That's going to be tougher with his wife at home all the time. But I'll find a way in."

She looked worried. "Just don't get caught."

"You're the only one who seems adept at catching me." His smile faded as he turned back to the suspects. He nodded toward her backpack. "Is that gun loaded yet?"

She shook her head. "I hate weapons."

"Katie, you better learn to love that gun. It may save your life. And you have to be willing to use it on someone you know."

He'd meant to tell her everything, including his own doubts. But he couldn't, not when she was looking at him like she wanted to save him from his own demons.

"Do you mean Ben?"

"I'm not ruling out anybody."

She looked at the box of folders. "The man doing all this . . . he rapes the women, doesn't he?"

"Yes." He tried to keep the pain out of that one word, but it seeped in anyway. "The sex isn't why he takes the women. He goes for the power and surprise elements, and that fuels his sex drive."

"It's not Ben." The words came out in a clipped rush.

"How do you know for sure?"

"He can't . . ." She turned away from him, twisting her hands. "He can't stay hard. There was an accident."

Silas felt a strange mixture of outrage and relief. He'd always hated the image of Katie and Ben making love that sometimes haunted him.

She still hadn't met his eyes. "It's not his fault. I think . . . it's me."

"What do you mean, it's you? Do you dunk him in ice water?"

She nearly laughed, but the shame was clear on her face. "The doctor said he should have been able to . . . you know. Obviously I'm not . . . sexy enough to excite him." Those last words came out as a whisper.

He wanted to laugh at the absurdity of that. Especially

taking her in wearing those deliciously tight purple pants, the top that molded her curves and branded her breasts with peace signs. Thankfully he held it in, because she looked so very serious about it.

Now he understood why she'd looked so touched when he said she was a nine. She believed, really believed, she was unattractive. "Did Ben tell you that's why he's impotent? Because you're not pretty enough?"

"No, he would never say something like. He's much too kind."

But he let her think it. Silas wanted to kill him for it. She was looking at him for confirmation—or denial—of that. If he said one word, one complimentary thing to her, it would be all over. Because it wouldn't be with words that he'd prove the point, but actions. Actions that would lead them down a road better off not explored.

Silas's cell phone chirped from the makeshift desk and he identified himself. "This is Reverend Maplethorpe returning your call. You wanted to ask me about Ben Ferguson?"

"Yes, sir, I understand he lived there during his youth."

"He died here, too."

"Actually, it's his son I'm interested in."

That got Katie's attention.

"Ben didn't have any children. You must have the wrong Ben Ferguson."

"It's possible, but I'd like to meet with you and make sure. Are you available today?"

"I've got men's fellowship until two. I'll be at the church until six tonight."

"I'll come at two. Thanks, Reverend."

She was now standing in front of him, suspicion in her eyes. She probably didn't realize that by crossing her arms in front of her, she pushed up her breasts. The shirt had a V neck that showed a tantalizing bit of cleavage. He quickly averted his gaze to her face. He wasn't supposed to be admiring her cleavage, or her slender shoulders, or anything else about her. He was here to make sure she was safe, nothing more.

"Silas, what's going on? I heard Ben's name on the other end."

He tucked the phone into his pocket, then grabbed his car keys and the box of files. "Just some research."

She followed him out onto the porch, where he called The Boss to attention. Slowly, he got to his big feet, and Silas wondered again how much pain the poor dog was in.

"I thought we eliminated him," Katie said.

"It's not his potential as a killer I'm interested in. There are some things that don't add up. Hopefully it's nothing. Come on, I'll give you a ride home." He put the boxes in the back seat. "So no one goes through my files again."

The Boss managed to climb up with Silas's help and settled on his sheepskin bed. He waited until she got in on the passenger side before closing her door.

Once Silas slid in, she said, "I'm going with you."

"You don't even know where I'm going."

"I don't care, I'm going." She crossed her arms and tried to look as stubborn as possible. "I'm not getting out of this car."

He leaned back in his seat and sighed. Finally he started the engine and pulled away.

Gary was parked along the road; no surprise there. He'd probably been the one spying on them. He didn't even pretend to be doing anything other than that. As soon as Silas passed him, Gary started his vehicle and turned around.

"Hold on."

"What are you doing?" she said, grabbing onto the strap when he gunned the engine.

"Same thing I do whenever I want my privacy."

Gary had just made the U-turn as Silas cut behind where the old convenience store used to be. He drove behind the pile of junk dumped there over the years and headed down the road that led to the old party spot for the local teens. That's where he always lost Gary. He headed to the right, leaving the dirt road behind. The mat of pine needles didn't give away his path, and the trees were spread just far apart enough to allow him to finagle the obstacle course with some amount of speed. A few minutes later, he emerged next to another road, and off they went—tailless.

"You're good," she said, glancing behind them.

"I wish I were," he said, wishing he hadn't said it aloud. Before she could comment, which he could tell she was going to, he said, "You were ashamed that you hadn't fought for anything in a long time."

She obviously saw the dodge for what it was, but gave in to it. "I don't like who I've become. I don't even *know* who I've become. I'm Ben's wife and his assistant and that's about all. You made me realize how far I've wandered from that girl who used to fight the giants for what she believed in. The girl who felt so much, whether it was joy or anger. I can still feel the rage when Gary threw my kitten against the glass window. But I haven't felt anything like that for a long time. I've been thinking about that girl lately." She slid a look at him. "I miss her."

"She's coming back. In fact, I'll wager she never really left. She was just buried under obligation and duty."

She looked out the window. "I thought I loved Ben, I really did. He was everything in my life. Maybe that was the problem. He was all I had. What he offered, I took. I'd lost everything that mattered to me." She slid her finger across the glass. "My mom, my home . . . you."

That last word lodged in his heart and made him blink. "I . . . mattered to you?" He couldn't resist asking, couldn't stop himself even though he knew better.

"In a way I can't explain, yes, you did. Maybe it's this connection we have. Even though I can't feel what you feel, maybe it bonded us somehow. Maybe I had a crush on you."

He didn't like the way her eyes sparkled at those words, and how that sparkle sent a charge of pure electricity through his body. He didn't like the way she looked beautiful and vulnerable at the same time. "Do you love Ben?" he asked, wanting to get away from what she felt for him.

"What I feel for Ben is complicated. I feel something for him. I'd hoped it was the marrying kind of love or that it would turn into it. Maybe it was only gratitude. But I know it's not the kind of love a wife and husband share. Not for me, anyway. And maybe not for him either. I feel more like a possession." She glanced his way, then quickly looked away when she caught him watching her. "It's not soul-shaking, knee-quaking, feel-it-in-the-pit-of-your-stomach love. It's not a kiss that steals your breath away. It's not exchanging a look that makes you quiver. Have you ever experienced that kind of love?"

His fingers tightened on the wheel. "No." He kept his gaze straight ahead. He hated the silence that settled in the vehicle, but he couldn't tell her the truth. He'd felt all of that with her, and yet, it was beyond that. It couldn't be described.

"Do you think I'm still that girl?" she asked at last.

"Yeah, I do. I wasn't sure at first. Whenever I saw you around town, I couldn't see a trace of her. But she's coming back."

She smiled, and the light seemed to spread through his body. "Yeah, I think she is, too."

He had to look away from that smile or he'd end up off the road. "I'm not sure I want to know why you don't think yourself pure and good anymore."

She pulled her knees up to her chin. He could feel her guilt more than anything else. "Kissing you puts me squarely out of either category."

His mouth twisted wryly. "I wonder where wanting to kiss you again puts me."

Katie sat on those words for a long time, not sure how to respond to them. Silas obviously didn't expect a response. He turned on the stereo and let rock and roll music fill the silence. She tried not to think about that kiss, focusing instead on the vehicle.

"I've never seen so many buttons, switches, and dials in a car before," she said.

"I don't even know what half of them do."

The car smelled new and leathery. She'd never been in a new car before. Luxurious though it was, Silas went to no trouble to keep it clean. The Boss's paw prints marked the beige leather seats. Leaves adorned the carpet. In the back, an atlas and bowl of water for the dog were among some of the other stuff piled on either the seat or the floor.

A battered pewter cross hung from the rearview mirror from a cheap leather chain.

"Found it on the beach," he said, noticing her gaze on the cross. "Thought it might be lucky."

She reached into her backpack and pulled out the crystal. "To chase away the darkness." She set it in one of the cubbyholes in front of the glove box.

"Katie, don't give me that."

"Why not? I told you, I don't expect anything in return."

He closed his eyes briefly. "It has nothing to do with that. It's just that . . ."

"What? Every time I've tried to give you something, you turn it away. One time it was only food, for Pete's sake!"

She could see his struggle in deciding to tell her. He loosened his shoulders by rolling them back.

"I have trouble . . . accepting things. It makes me feel funny."

"Funny how?"

"Just funny. Inside, here." He rubbed his knuckles against his stomach. "I've always been that way."

"Didn't you get gifts when you were a kid?"

"No. Not after my mom died, anyway. Maybe it's because of the one gift I got at birth. My empathy," he clarified. "Maybe I think all gifts are going to affect me weird. I don't know, I'm guessing." He glanced at the crystal in the ashtray. "I don't have many friends, so I'm not used to getting gifts. It's usually not an issue."

"Uh-huh." She didn't get it at all. Except the part where he wasn't used to getting gifts. "Surely you've had girl-friends through the years."

"I've met women here and there, usually while I'm working on a book. I'm never in one place long enough to have a girlfriend."

In the instant she felt that jealous spike over Celine, she

realized that he could probably feel it, too. "I hate that you can feel what I feel."

"That's another reason I don't date for long. Women say they want men to read their minds, but they don't like when I read their feelings. I've learned to keep my thoughts to myself over the years, but they slip out. It's easier to just stay on my own."

But Celine had hung around. Why had she wanted to see a photograph of her anyway? Now she could picture that pretty woman cuddling up with Silas.

They were heading east and were already long out of Flatlands. Since reading the files, she kept imagining those girls walking along these roads. Stopping to talk to a stranger who offered them a ride. Disappearing forever. Some of the signs they passed were for towns where a girl was taken.

"How can you stand to do what you do?" she asked. "Writing about murder, I mean. What's it like?"

His fingers tightened on the wheel slightly, but he kept his gaze ahead. "I start to see everyone, particularly women, as potential victims. I imagine what their headline would be, how their life would be summed up. I did that with Geraldine, too."

"Do you see me that way?"

"No. I won't let myself."

She tried to hold back the shudder. "What about talking to killers like Swenson? When I read about his life, in your book, he seemed so real, so normal otherwise."

"That's the scary part of what I do. I actually understand where they're coming from. Not that I condone it, but I see that in some ways they're just like us. They eat, sleep, dream, and fear. It's what they dream and fear that separates us and them. I've looked evil in the face, and it's human. He's charming, handsome, rich, intelligent. He's a police officer, the man next door, the guy at the deli. He could befriend any of us, any of our daughters. He could *be* any one of us."

Those words chilled her, especially spoken in a low,

thick voice. He spent way too much time in the dark. She picked up the crystal and dropped it into his shirt pocket. "It's not a gift. It's a loan."

The corner of his mouth quirked. "A loan, huh?"

"To chase away the shadows that live inside you."

He pulled out the crystal and set it back in the cubbyhole. His fingers lingered on it for a moment before he put his hand back on the wheel. Getting him to accept anything, even as a loan, seemed futile. She wondered if he had trouble accepting nonphysical gifts . . . like love. Had he ever been offered it?

"What exactly are we investigating?" she asked, steering her thoughts away from that line of thinking.

"I don't want to get into the details yet in case it's a mistake."

"Does this have to do with the birth certificate and diplomas?"

"Yeah," he said. He clearly wasn't convinced they were Ben's father's.

"Ben talks about his past very little. All he said was he'd been orphaned at a young age and lived in various foster homes. He never mentioned his father before. But he wasn't lying. I mean, he didn't look guilty at being caught."

"Did he get mad at you for snooping?"

"Not at all. He said if I wanted to know anything, to ask.'

"People in town think he's some kind of god, at least that's the impression I get."

She nodded. "He's very kind and generous. Maybe too much. I don't understand why they all seem to dislike me so much." She hated the way her voice got thick when she admitted, "I offered to help out at the county fair. They've had signs in the diner window for weeks now begging for help. Ben didn't want me to, because he wants me with him at the fair. But I offered to help anyway."

"Good for you."

Even his genuine pride didn't lessen the disappointment. "They turned me down. Flat. I know they still need help; that sign is still in the window."

"I'm sorry they treat you that way. I know how it feels to be an outcast. It hurts."

She met his gaze then, feeling closer to him than she had to anyone since her mama. She felt other things, but she tamped them down before she could acknowledge them and before he could feel them. "Thanks, Silas," was all she could manage to say.

Reverend Maplethorpe led them to a small room off the main sanctuary. He was stoop-backed, though he got around well enough for a man of his age. The room was crowded with children's projects in mid-completion. Globs of dried glue and glitter dotted the white table where they sat.

"You wanted to know about Ben Ferguson," the reverend said once they'd sat down. "I'm not sure why. He's been dead a long time."

Katie met Silas's gaze, trying to keep the surprise from her own. But he meant Ben's father, she realized.

Silas said, "I can understand your question. Katie is Ben's wife. Ben Junior, that is. She's working on his family tree as a surprise. All she knows is that he's from Milledgeville and not much more than that."

The reverend looked perplexed as he took in Katie. "Ben Ferguson didn't have a son."

"That . . . can't be right," she said. "Are we talking about the same Ben, the town's vet, born right here in 1915."

"I'm quite certain it's the same man. He did have a young man who worked with him for several years, was as close as a son. His name was Larry Howard."

While Katie shook her head, Silas asked, "Tell me about Larry."

The reverend steepled his gnarled fingers and took a deep breath. "Larry's story could have been one of those sweet, romantic stories you see on television. He was left on the church steps just before the Sunday service. Except he wasn't exactly a baby; he was three years old. His mother, or we presume it was her, tied his hand to the front door so he wouldn't wander. We tried to find out where he'd come from, but to no avail. My wife—she's passed on now—and I decided to let him stay with us. We couldn't have children, and Larry seemed like a gift from God. We found out differently within a few months.

"He was the most incorrigible child I have ever seen. He hated to be touched, wouldn't be cuddled, and he cried all the time. We tried our best with him, but my darling wife just couldn't handle him. After two years, we put him back into the system. It broke our hearts, but we found out it was the best. For us, anyway."

"Why?" Silas asked, overly interested in the story of a stranger who had no bearing on their lives.

"He went through seventeen foster homes throughout his adolescence, and each one ended badly. With one family, he hung another foster child from a deck by his feet. He claimed he had no intention of dropping him, just scaring him. And he did try to be good. He organized a search party for a neighbor's lost dog. He saved a litter of kittens from drowning when someone put them in a bag and threw them into the creek. I think he liked animals better than people. I gathered from my talks with him over the years, he understood them better."

The reverend's preaching voice had emerged. "That's where Dr. Ferguson came in. He was our town's vet, a very nice man whose wife had recently died. Larry had hit a dog with his bike, and the doc had stopped to help. The two bonded. Dr. Ferguson was the first person to get through to Larry. Indeed, the doc probably saved his life. He hired him on after school and eventually let him move into one of his rooms. Larry graduated high school, barely, but he did graduate. He continued to live with the doc, working and learning about veterinary medicine. Everyone was happy that he'd finally found stability and was staying out of trouble. Or maybe they were relieved. We were."

The reverend was absently scraping off globs of glue with his thumbnail. "And then tragedy struck again for Larry, and most certainly for Dr. Ferguson. It was Larry who pulled his mentor from the lake where he'd drowned. Witnesses saw him trying to give the doc CPR, but it was too late. Larry was devastated. He tried to get work with one of the other vets in town, but there just wasn't a place for him. He stayed at the doc's house for a few months. No one had the heart to kick him out, and he was keeping the place up. Then the doc's niece, who inherited the place, came down and put it on the market. Larry, he tried to buy it, but none of the banks would take a chance on a kid with no family and no job. He left town, and that's the last we ever heard from him. We sometimes wondered where he ended up."

"Not far from here, as it turns out," Silas said.

"You can't think——" She couldn't even say the words. "Do you have a picture of him? It's important," she added at his hesitation.

"I'll see what I can find." The reverend pushed himself up and went to the room adjacent. He returned ten minutes later with a faded picture of a little boy dressed for school with one front tooth missing. "It's the only one we have."

She looked at the boy with the forced smile. It had been a long time since Ben had been this age. "When was Larry born?"

"We didn't know for sure, of course. We weren't even sure Larry Howard was his real name. He told us his name since there wasn't any name on the note. We figured he was born in . . . say 1959." He looked at Katie. "Did you say he was your husband?"

"Yes," Silas answered for her. "You'll be glad to know he's turned into a fine citizen, a veterinarian, actually."

The reverend smiled. "I'm very pleased, and I'm glad to know he considered the doc his father. He probably won't remember me, but please send him my regards. Tell him to come by sometime. I'd love to see how he turned out."

Silas shook the man's hand. "We'll let you know as soon as we find out for sure."

CHAPTER 17

BEN HAD HAD an uneasy feeling all day. He kept looking in the rearview mirror to see if someone was following him. Katie should have come with him. He should have worked harder to make her come. That's what bothered him most. All this time he'd had complete control over her. His offer to take her with him should have been met with surprised gratitude. Not just surprise. And certainly not with rejection.

That rejection stung. He'd done everything he could to ensure he'd never be rejected again. Sam Savino was the only person who had rebuffed him, though Ben didn't much care if the man liked him or not. He wanted Sam to like him, but it didn't matter in his life.

Katie mattered.

He'd called earlier, but she hadn't answered. He was going to have to figure out some way to deter her wanderings through the woods. He wouldn't even let himself think about her being with Silas.

Once he reached the Mattsons, he tried home again. No answer. It was late afternoon. He had to issue shipping papers for three of their horses and check over the new foal. Maybe he'd cut his trip short. Wouldn't she be surprised to find him at the door tonight?

The faint scent of smoke tainted the air. In the distance, a gray cloud hovered in the sky. Occasionally Katie had seen a helicopter carrying an orange bucket of water to the fires to the north. The radio DJ talked about the close calls with several homes and the acres of forestland being burned to ashes.

"There has to be some mistake," she said for the fiftieth time. "I mean, I just can't believe that my husband, the man I've been living with all these years, isn't who he says he is."

"Maybe *your* Ben isn't Larry Howard, but he's not Ben Ferguson. Will you at least admit that?"

"No." That meant her whole married life had been a lie.

"Maplethorpe said Ferguson was a veterinarian in Milledgeville. There's only one vet named Ben Ferguson. Have you seen any other paperwork to corroborate his identity as Ben Junior? I sure didn't see another birth certificate or diploma with his name on it."

"His degree on the wall at the animal hospital. I'm sure that has the right date on it."

"It's probably a forgery. Or has an altered date. But think: does it say 'Ben Arnold Ferguson *the second*'?"

"All right, dammit. He's not Ben Ferguson."

He sat on that victory for a moment, and then threw out something even worse than the lie of Ben's life. "Have you thought about this: He isn't really your husband."

"Well, of course he is. We took our vows—" The words died in her throat. "I'm legally married to Ben Ferguson. A dead man."

"You're not married to anyone."

She couldn't help meeting his eyes on that. Since Ben— Larry had used a false name on the documents, that would null and void them. "I'm not married," she whispered.

"Are you going to confront him?"

She chewed on a hangnail. "Of course I am. I just have to figure out how. How did I find out about this, for instance?"

"Without your seeing me?"

"Exactly. I don't want to hurt him. He's already accused me of"—she glanced at him—"taking your side. Defending you. He thinks you're the one taking the girls, too."

Even through his annoyance, she saw a glimmer of

warmth at her admission. She didn't want to delve into it at the moment. "If he's not Ben Ferguson, and not my legal husband, he's not even a licensed veterinarian. But he knows so much about it. He's good at it."

"He worked with the real Ben for a long time. I'm sure he learned a lot. Let's see what he has to say. I can confront him if you want."

"No, I—"

A loud pop preceded the car's swerving toward the shoulder of the highway. Silas kept control as they shuddered to a stop just off the road. He'd automatically put his arm in front of her to hold her back.

"You all right?" he asked, pulling his arm back after a moment. When she nodded, he checked on the dog. The Boss leaned between the seat and licked Silas's face.

Silas climbed out, followed by Katie. The front tire was blown. The smell of burning rubber permeated the air. He dropped his head forward and rubbed the back of his neck.

"You have a spare, don't you?" she asked.

"Not at the moment. I've been doing a lot of driving through back roads lately, and I got a nail in my tire last week. I wore the spare out by the time I got the tire put on, and I haven't gotten around to getting another spare. Luckily, I have road service and a cell phone." He got the phone out of the car and dialed the number on his card. After a few minutes of conversation, he disconnected. "The good news is, they know where we are. The bad news is, it's going to be a couple of hours before they can get to us. They're backlogged right now, and they've got to get us a tire first."

She glanced toward the western sky. The sun was heading downward; it was later than she thought. She was definitely going to miss Ben's call that evening. And it was sunset, the worst time of day.

"I guess we wait," she said. To the east, the sky was darkening into a storm that would hopefully move north and drench the fires. "Do you think it'll rain here before they come to rescue us?"

He surveyed the sky. "I don't think so."

He opened the back hatch and pulled out a blanket and The Boss's tub of water. He left a sticky note on the car for the tow truck to honk its horn three times if he got there early. Then he took her hand.

"Let's go for a walk."

With The Boss trailing them, they walked a short distance down the road that led off the highway. Signs indicated a controlled-burn experiment area just off the road. The trees were tagged for identification. The ground was gouged as though rivers had once run through the rolling terrain. He led the way into the charred area. Farther back the section of woods had been burned two years before and wasn't as blackened. Small trees grew up and lent their bright green leaves as miniature canopies. Slash pines dominated the tree life here, far outnumbering the maples and oaks.

She saw where he was headed: a small opening where the last of the sun's rays poured down through the trees. Her chest hitched as he led her by the hand to it. He glanced over at her, and she narrowed her eyes at him. Could he feel *everything*? Still, there was an increasing tightness inside as they reached the area and he let go of her hand to spread out the blanket. The Boss happily wandered around, sniffing the ground and glancing up into the trees. It smelled of warmed pine needles and charred bark that blended with the scent of smoke from the fires in the distance.

She sat down with her back facing skies that were splashed in orange and pink. Silas sat across from her, his head tilted as though he were contemplating her.

Obviously he was, because he said, "You know, you're missing something beautiful."

Well, she wasn't, not really. But she couldn't actually say she had a nice view anyway. "I can't watch sunsets. You know why."

He nodded. "So you're going to go through your whole life never watching a sunset."

"Maybe." She picked up a branch and snapped it into pieces. "I know it's silly. Thinking I'm going to die this year is silly, too, but it doesn't stop the feeling."

"That's because you never saw your mother age beyond twenty-seven. So you think it's the end of life."

She contemplated that for a moment. "Maybe that's it. Did you feel that way? You lost your mother young, too."

"I never really knew her. And I never related to my father; I separated myself from him, in my mind. But I understand what you're feeling."

"Because you can feel what I'm feeling."

"I'm sorry, Katie. I know it bothers you, but I can't turn it off. Especially with you." He reached over and tucked a strand of hair behind her ear, feathering his thumb across her cheek as he did so. "You've been inside me for so long, I can't imagine you not being there. I've felt your sorrows and your doubts and I've seen your life through your eyes. Being here with you makes it even stronger." He let his fingers trail down to her shoulder, and his thumb caressed her collarbone where the cross lay against her skin. "I can feel the jump in your heartbeat and the tightening of your throat. I can feel what you want and how you're afraid of wanting it." His voice was low and silky as he described almost everything she felt. "Or maybe it's what I feel. Maybe your feelings and my feelings are all tangled up inside me."

She curled her fingers over the hand at her shoulder. "I am afraid, Silas. I'm afraid of you being inside me, and I'm afraid of you not being there. I'm afraid of what I feel for you and what you feel for me. I'm afraid of how wrong it is and that I don't even care how wrong it is. I'm afraid of how I don't even know myself anymore."

She'd never seen his eyes this smoky blue as he seemed to look right into her soul. He moved closer and took her face in his hands. "I know who you are, Katie."

"Who am I?" she whispered.

"You're good and pure and everything you were when you were young." He ran his knuckles down her throat and pressed them against her chest. "Inside, you're everything you once were. You're strong and brave and compassionate. And you're beautiful." His other hand stroked down her cheek, and his voice had a breathless quality to it. "You're that incredible combination of sexy and cute, and I only came here to make sure you were safe, but since that first day you showed up at my house, all I can do is think about making love to you. I'm glad you can't sense my feelings, or you'd have run away from me a long time ago."

She remembered that first day she had seen him last week. Maybe she *had* known what he was feeling. Her face felt hot, and her eyes stung. "I'm not running away now."

Her chest felt so tight, she could hardly breathe. She saw the struggle in his eyes, temptation warring with doing the right thing. He twisted her around and pulled her up against him.

"Watch the sunset with me." His arms tightened around her, holding her possessively. His face was next to hers, his chin resting lightly on her shoulder. "And when you watch it, don't think about your mother not coming to get you. Think about that sunset being you: warm and beautiful and filling the world with light and color. Think about the palette of colors that you are, blues and reds and yellows. Paint the picture of what you want to be."

I want to be yours. The words drifted through her mind as she wrapped her hands around his arms and settled back against him. "What's your palette? If I'm the sunset, are you the night? Are your colors black and dusky blue or no light at all?"

When he didn't answer, she turned to look at him. Their cheeks rubbed together and she felt the slight bristle of his.

"Maybe you *can* feel me, too," he said at last.

She turned around to face him, kneeling in front of him. "I want to feel you, Silas." She put her hands on his shoulders and leaned her face close to his. "If I am the sunset, I fade into the night. I'm not afraid of the dark."

"I am," he whispered, all too serious.

She put her hands on his face, realizing she'd never

touched his face before. "Let me bring some of my light into your night." She kissed him before he could say something else to put distance between them. She knew what he was doing—trying to protect her from guilt, and from him. She didn't want protection. She wanted him.

He immediately deepened the kiss, his surrender. If he would not take her gifts, maybe he would take her body. And then, later, he would take her love. She felt their kiss right down to her soul. His fingers slid through her hair as he tilted her head back and devoured her mouth. She devoured him back, engulfed by passion she didn't know existed within her.

He kissed her ears and then down over the place where her birthmark stained her neck. He stripped off her shirt and bra, and she unbuttoned his shirt and peeled it off, careful of the bandage on his arm. He skimmed his hands over her breasts, his eyes taking her in as though she were the most beautiful thing in all the world.

She couldn't help the shuddering breaths at each touch. He ran his finger along her chain and pressed his thumb against the gold cross. He guided her down to the blanket, and then showed her his appreciation with his mouth. She arched into his touch and choked back the tears of feeling beautiful for the first time in her life. His hands tightened at her waist as he probably felt her gush of emotion, but he responded only by intensifying his actions. She responded to that by digging her fingers into his thick hair and whispering his name. He ran his hands over her pubic area, and even through her jeans she felt warmth stirring inside. After a few moments, she couldn't stand it anymore. She wriggled out of her jeans so there wouldn't be so much fabric between them.

He took in her body with his eyes, seeing everything but what her white cotton panties hid. And apparently he liked what he saw, because he made an amazing little sound in his throat and tore into her mouth again. His hands blissfully returned to explore her panties, cupping her with his warmth, then tracing her curves with his fingertip. When his finger traced just inside the edge of her panties, she felt herself quiver where the blood already pulsed out of control.

Silas was pretty sure this wasn't what he'd intended when he'd led her into the woods. Almost ninety-nine percent sure. He'd felt her trepidation when she thought that's what he had in mind. He thought he'd been safe then, because he would never push something on her she wasn't sure she wanted.

Where had this Katie come from then? The one who'd burned away his good intentions. The one whose mouth was nearly swallowing him. The one whose flesh was soft and nearly naked beneath his hands.

Nobody had loved her like this. He could feel her amazement, her absolute awe at the feelings coursing through her. He didn't need their connection to feel her reaction to his every touch. *Doesn't he touch you?* he wanted to ask. But the answer was obvious. Her need nearly overwhelmed him, and he did all he could to hold back his own desire. His body strained to rip off those plain cotton panties and plunge into her, but that's not what this was about. When he felt her hands at the button of his jeans, he sucked in another breath to hold himself back.

He shucked the jeans and his briefs in one shot and was taken aback by the awestruck look on her face as she took him in. He wasn't a Chippendales specimen, but the way she looked at him made him feel like an Adonis.

"Oh, Silas, you are amazing," she said in a breathy voice. She was still lying on the blanket, and he was standing over her.

He knelt down over her and took her mouth again. She tentatively slid her hands around him, but soon was exploring his backside. She got even braver and rubbed her pelvis against his. It nearly staggered him, that and her hunger. With Katie, he felt both her feelings and his own. They tangled together the same way their bodies did. It was heady and delicious the way he could both hear her intake of breath and feel the pure pleasure coming from her when he cupped her with his hand. When she moved against him, he decided it was time to remove the last barrier between them. He slid her panties down her legs, and she kicked them off.

He didn't have to ask if she was sure. He knew it as surely as he knew he would have had a hard time turning back now. He was lying on his side next to her. He pulled one of her legs closer and explored her damp, feminine area with his finger. Her chest rose and fell heavily and her toes curled as she got closer to the edge. Her eyes were wide, and her fingers tightened on his arm.

"Silas . . . what's happening to me?" she said on a jagged breath. "I feel so . . . weird."

"I believe you're about to have your first orgasm."

He paused for a few moments to prolong the anticipation and finally sent her over the edge. He could feel her pounding orgasm and the awe to go along with it so strongly, he almost went over the edge with her. Instead he catalogued her flushed face and her stretched body, all of the physical aspects to her pleasure. His fingers skimmed over her stomach, her ribs, and her breasts, every inch soft, womanly perfection.

Her eyes slowly opened, and they were still smoky with desire when they found him. All she had to do was reach for him, and he positioned himself over her.

"Put your legs around me," he said.

He loved the way her legs felt wrapped around his hips. "Relax," he whispered when he felt the tension in her body. She let out a breath, and he eased inside her. When they fused together, it was a dream of perfection. He had to admit he *had* been dreaming about making love to Katie, from the time he'd seen her as an eighteen-year-old. He slid into her slowly, eased by her dampness. She took a sharp breath, and when she let it out, he fully filled her. Her brown eyes glittered, and he could do nothing but kiss her again as they moved together.

Even though he filled her, she filled him, too. All that goodness she thought she didn't possess anymore lit the dark corners of his soul and chased away the shadows.

"Like making love to an angel," he whispered, not meaning at all to say the words aloud. But her soft sigh in response made it worthwhile. He'd never felt this pure sense of fulfillment coming from a woman he'd slept with before. Not just sexual fulfillment, but wonder and something he didn't want to explore too closely. This kind of passion was new to her, and it both scared her and swept her away. He didn't want to overwhelm her, so he kept the pace slow and steady. She'd squeezed her eyes shut, but opened them and looked at him. There was a glow in them that burned right through him.

"Silas," she whispered, drawing out the word.

Her fingers tightened on his bare back, and she took a quick series of breaths. He felt the buildup of pressure, felt her surrender to it, and let himself go right along with her.

He braced himself with his arms as they drifted down to earth. Every time she inhaled, her breasts pushed against his chest. He could smell her sweat, a sweet, light smell that he'd never forget. Her neck was damp, and he nuzzled that place where her birthmark adorned her skin.

She slid her arms around his neck and pulled him closer, until their combined heat made them part. He lay on his side, his head propped up with his hand, and looked at her.

She looked away for a moment, making him realize how long her eyelashes were. She wore no makeup, and didn't need any. Her cheeks were flushed, her skin glowing. He brushed his fingers down her hair.

"I like your hair like this," he said, letting the bottom curl around his finger.

"It was impulsive. Like doing this."

He lifted the corner of his mouth in a smile. "I liked this, too."

But that stole the glow from her face. "I'm sorry if I wasn't very good."

"Katie, you've got to be kidding." He tipped her face to make her look at him. She wasn't kidding. "You were great. And it wouldn't matter anyway. This wasn't about sex."

She finally met his gaze with eyes so full of vulnerability, it nearly broke him. "What was it about?"

He swallowed hard. "Don't ask me to define it. There's no way I could describe how I feel about you." But his chest hurt thinking about how much he wanted her.

She closed her eyes. "Silas, do you . . . love me?" When he didn't answer, she opened her eyes.

He'd never thought about what he felt for Katie, what he'd always felt for her. He'd never pinned it down to that one word.

She cleared her throat. "Because I felt something from you, too, when we were . . . making love. Just now."

He took her hand and focused on her fingers, which was easier than looking into her eyes. "I've cared about people . . . not many, but I have cared for a few people in my life. And then there's you. I don't just care about you, Katie. It's really all tangled up inside me, what I feel for you." He could feel her frustration at his nonanswer. He pulled her hand to his mouth and kissed the back of her fingers. Thunder rumbled in the distance. "I love you, Katie. I've loved you since that first moment I held you. When I came back to town after you'd turned eighteen, I probably wanted to see what could become of it. Not that I would have admitted that at the time, even to myself. But you were about to marry Ben. I could feel that you cared about him, even if you weren't in love with him. And he definitely loved you. I realized then that it wasn't going to be that kind of love between us."

He felt pain spike through her. "Why didn't you talk to me then? When I was eighteen."

The feeling of loss flowed through him, reminding him how he'd felt then. But he wasn't sure if it was coming from him or her. "You needed Ben. He was your rock, your savior. You didn't need two saviors."

"Is that all I am to you? Someone to save?"

He finally met her troubled gaze. "That's all I've ever known with you until now."

"And now?"

"Katie, we can't let this get complicated, not now. That's why I didn't want this to happen. That and the fact that you're married—emotionally married, anyway. I never wanted to cause you any guilt or confusion."

"Well, too late, fella. Because I love you, too."

He pulled her to her feet. "No you don't."

She raised her eyebrows at his statement. "Oh, I see. You're allowed to love me, but I can't love you. Is that it?"

"That's it."

"That's pretty selfish, don't you think?"

He handed her clothes to her. "I'm not the one you should be loving."

"Do you think that if I love you, you have to love me back? Is that it?"

"Love isn't about expecting something in return." He ran his hand through his hair. "I've loved you all these years and never expected anything in return."

She surprised him by reaching out for his hand and pressing it to her soft mouth. He tried to resist the urge to pull away, but couldn't.

She let out a sigh. "But you've got something in return, and you won't accept it. That's it, isn't it? You can't accept love, just like you can't accept gifts. I just did the same thing you've done to me more than once, kissing your hand, and you couldn't handle it. Does it make you feel weird that I love you?"

He grabbed up his own clothes and started getting dressed. "Yes, it does. Maybe I'm just weird. Spooky Silas, that's what they called me. I am spooky. Maybe I've got so many other people's feelings running around inside me, I don't know what my own feelings are. Maybe I don't even have any."

She opened her mouth to say something, but three short blasts of a horn in the distance stopped her.

"Tow truck's here," he said. "Let's go."

* * *

They rode through the dark night in silence once they were back on the road. Katie kept pushing away her feelings about what had happened in the woods because she didn't want Silas to pick them up.

"It's not fair that you can feel me and I can't feel you," she said at last.

"Life's not fair." He didn't look at her, though his fingers tightened on the wheel.

"Wow, that's profound. Thanks for sharing that with me."

That got his attention.

"I used to think I was unlovable," she continued. "Okay, sometimes I still do. I mean, even my mom couldn't bear to stay alive for me. I wasn't reason enough to hang in there, to fight her demons for." She leaned against the door so she could face Silas. "Do you feel that way, too?"

"There's nothing unlovable about you."

"But there is something unlovable about you, is that what you're saying?"

His fingers tightened again. "Yes."

"Because you're in touch with this killer?"

"It's why I'm in touch with him. Because there's something inside me that was open to him. It's the same thing that drew me to crime writing. It's like the instinct to look at an accident as you drive by, even though you know you might see something horrible. Because you might see something horrible. But you can't look away. That's what writing crime is like for me."

"What if . . . there was someone looking with you? Someone to pull you away if you stared too long?"

"Remember that quote I told you? How when you stare into the abyss, it also looks inside you? I wouldn't drag anyone into that darkness with me. And what if . . . what if I've already looked too long?"

She couldn't feel what he was feeling, but she could clearly see that something haunted him. "Silas, you know everything about me. Tell me what's going on inside you."

He shook his head before she'd even finished the sentence. "Not until I know for sure." He pulled onto an old dirt road that wound back into the woods. The Boss poked his head between the seats checking out the reason they'd stopped. Silas scratched his head, and The Boss settled back on the seat with a sigh. Silas looked at her, weighing something. "I've struggled over whether I should tell you something—something that would change the way you feel about your mother's death. It was part of the reason I came back when you were eighteen, to see if you were ready to hear it."

She leaned toward him, wondering if he could feel the pressure weighing down her chest. "What? Tell me."

He searched her face as thunder rumbled behind them. Out of the corner of her eye, she saw a flash of lightning.

Finally he said, "She didn't kill herself."

She nearly lost her balance, as though his words had physically hit her. "What are you saying? The Blue Devil drain opener was right there, she swallowed it . . . oh, God. Somebody made her swallow it."

He was still holding on to the steering wheel as though to keep himself from touching her. "I didn't know that I could pick up someone's feelings after they'd died, but I felt a strong need to go to your trailer afterward. I was staying at the sheriff's house at the time, waiting until they finished the paperwork to send me off. I sneaked out early one morning and walked to your trailer. They had the crime-scene tape across the door, but I broke in and went inside. I didn't know what I was expecting to find. I walked through the trailer, and I could feel a lingering trace of your terror, what you'd probably felt when you found her. Then I felt a different kind of terror. A struggle. More than being afraid of whoever was in here with her, she was afraid for you, for what would happen to you. What I knew for sure was she had no intention of dying that night."

Katie couldn't talk for a few moments. She envisioned her mother's struggle and the pain of the lye going down her throat. He reached over and took hold of her arm.

She pushed away the images, not ready to deal with

them yet. "The sheriff said they found you at the trailer. Did you tell them?"

"I knew what they'd think if I told them everything. But I asked them to check into it, to look further. I said I didn't think it was a suicide. All I got them to do was question me. Where was I that night? Did I know Ellie well? They tried to pin it on me. They took fingerprints and searched the trailer to find something to link me to the scene. But they found nothing."

"Were you afraid I'd think you'd done it, too?"

"I didn't know. But you were too young to understand any of it then."

She sat back heavily as her bones seemed to drain right out of her. "She was murdered. Who would have wanted to kill her? She wasn't raped. Didn't have anything to steal. She never bothered anyone. She was the most scared person I knew; she didn't trust anyone."

"Someone had hurt her once. I could feel it whenever she was around a man."

"This changes everything. I've got to find out who did it. Was it the same person who'd hurt her before? Was it a boyfriend? My . . . father?"

"Do you know who your father is?"

"She never told me."

Her mind was still sorting through the facts and implications. Someone had killed her mother and gotten away with it. Maybe someone she knew, someone she'd said hello to once.

Silas put the vehicle in gear and headed toward Flatlands again. The rain started, a heavy downpour that isolated them inside the car. She curled up on the seat and tried not to imagine what her mother's last moments were like. She understood his difficulty in deciding whether to tell her or not. Living with the fact that her mother had committed suicide was different than living with the fact that she'd been murdered. Especially if no one believed it.

What it did was remove the shame layer by layer. Everything she'd felt since she was nine peeled away to reveal different feelings. Still loss, still anger. Not directed at her mother, but at a faceless stranger.

It didn't lessen the pain, though, that their last conversation was laced with anger. That Katie had left her mother alone that last night, and that possibly the killer wouldn't have come into their trailer if she'd been there.

"It's not your fault," he said.

She pressed her hands on either side of her face. "Stop getting into my head and my heart! Leave me alone!"

He didn't reply, only continued driving in silence. But he was there inside her. She could feel him, just as she'd felt him during other traumatic times. He said he couldn't help it, and she believed him. But it didn't make it easier to live with.

He slowed down as they turned onto the road their houses were on. "What are you going to do about Ben? About what we learned?"

She pushed through the haze of her dark thoughts. "I'll have a day to think about it before he returns."

"You know I'll be here if you need me."

"Silas, I don't want you there. I need some time to sort out my feelings."

He only nodded; but of course, he could probably feel her confusion.

When they pulled down her driveway, she was even more uncomfortable to see lights blazing through the trees. She hadn't left the lights on.

Silas cut his lights and stopped. "Stay here." He got out and walked around the bend. When he returned, he said, "Ben's there and so is Gary. What do you want to do?"

She bit her lip and contemplated her options. Showing up with Silas wasn't going to be a good thing. "Ben knows I sometimes take walks through the woods at night. He hates it, but I still do it once in a while. Pull back out onto the highway and drop me off there. I'll walk back."

But he parked the car and walked with her. They stood at the edge of the woods looking at the house. Both men were obviously inside.

"Are you sure you can handle this?" he whispered in her ear.

She fought the urge to shiver as his warm breath tickled her. "I have to. I'm not going to be afraid like my mama was. Look where it got her."

He gave her hand a squeeze and stepped back. "If you need me . . ." He let the words drift off. "Forget I said that."

"I know." She knew he'd be there, knew she only had to call him. She walked forward into the wash of light and up the steps. Her heart was tight when she opened the front door. And her knees nearly buckled when she took in the living room.

~~~ CHAPTER 18

EVERYTHING HAD BEEN trashed. The couches were slashed and upturned, the bookshelves cleared of their contents. The coffee table was lying on the carpet, its legs broken from the tabletop. The porcelain replicas were scattered on the carpet in a thousand pieces. The flocked wallpaper had been torn in places.

Before she could take in any more of the house, Ben broke out of his daze and took her in his arms. "Katie, I've been worried sick. I had an uneasy feeling all day, like something wasn't right. I kept calling and you weren't here, so I came home . . . to this. You can imagine what I thought."

She tried to sort through everything, first that something *had* been wrong, because she'd been making love with another man. Then that their house was a shambles, that someone had done this. After that, the truth she now knew about Ben.

"I'm sorry I worried you."

He pulled her tight against him and stroked her hair. "I don't want you to leave the house anymore. I can't handle this." His hands tightened. "You've been doing way too much wandering lately."

It was probably only her imagination that it sounded faintly like a warning. Guilt had a way of tainting things. "I won't wander again," she caught herself saying in an attempt to salve that guilt. *But we're not married.*

He tugged sharply at the waistband of her purple jeans and gave her peace-sign top a look of pure disdain. With lowered eyes, he dismissed her as he shifted his gaze away.

"Any idea who would have done this?" Gary asked as he walked up to them. His gaze took her in with a knowing glint. He'd seen her with Silas earlier.

"None."

"I know who it was," Ben said. "Silas Koole."

"It wasn't Silas," she said, too fast. "Was anything stolen?" She started taking inventory. That's when she saw the smashed dollhouse. Not one miniature item had survived the savagery. This wasn't a robbery. It was an act of hatred and rage. She headed into the kitchen. A window was broken and shards of glass winked from the linoleum floor—point of entry. The kitchen hadn't been as damaged as the living room. The office wasn't touched at all, but the bedroom had been trashed in the same way.

"Nothing obvious," she said. "Whoever did this wasn't out to steal anything. He was angry. He did this to send a message."

Gary surveyed the wrecked bedroom from beside her. "That's what it looks like to me, too."

When she met his gaze, she saw no trace of malice there. But he'd no doubt been angry when she and Silas had given him the slip.

"I need you to take a good look around and tell me if anything's missing. Then I can finish my report."

Ben headed out to the living room, and she started looking through the heaps of clothes and towels and sheets in the bedroom. There were shreds of paper all over the floor. Confused, she started picking them up. That's when she saw what was left of the paperbacks she'd gotten at the library—Silas's books. Whoever had done this had found her hiding place under the mattress. Her jewelry box had been dumped out onto the dresser. Not that she'd had much, and nothing of value. Her cross and her wedding band were the only real gold she owned. The band on her finger seemed to burn into her skin, to grow tighter and tighter until she felt like tugging it off. It was only when she involuntarily touched the cross that she realized Gary had remained in the doorway.

"Who hates you this much?"

She blinked at those words so simply stated. "You think this was aimed at me?"

"You and Ben, of course." His voice lowered to an intimate level. "You piss anyone off lately?" That knowing glint on his face had remained.

"No one knows me well enough to hate me." But she wondered if Gary hated her this much. Or could he be creating another reason to get into her house, be involved in her life? "This looks like the work of someone with an anger-management problem."

A muscle on his upper lip ticked. "Any ideas on who that might be?" he asked in a soft, low voice. He studied her the same way Silas had when he weighed how much to tell her about her mother's death. As he opened his mouth, Ben walked in. Gary closed his mouth, contemplated for a moment, then asked him, "Why do you think Silas Koole did this?"

"He's been watching us lately, me and Katie. He's waiting for his chance to get rid of me . . . and to take Katie like he's taken the rest of them."

"I'm not sure he had the opportunity." He looked at Katie. "He was out of town all day."

"Doing what?"

"Wish I knew." Again, those accusatory eyes. "He lost me. I've taken the pictures of this place. When I run the place for prints, if any strange ones come up, I'll get his prints. I don't mind telling you that I'd love to put that son of a bitch in jail. It would do my heart some real good."

Katie said, "It wasn't Silas. I know because . . . I was with him all afternoon."

The silence fell like a thousand pounds of mud. For a few moments, no one moved. She wished she could rewind the moment and take back the words, but she knew she wouldn't. She couldn't allow Silas to be arrested, and it was very possible his prints would be found in the house. This would be easier to explain, but not by much.

"We were doing research," she said, forcing herself to

meet Ben's hard gaze. "I'll explain it to you later."

She couldn't tell who was angrier with her, though Ben's anger was laced with disappointment. Not that she could blame him. She wasn't particularly proud of her actions, and yet, she wouldn't go back and erase them, either.

Gary said, "I still want to dust for fingerprints."

"Don't bother," Ben said, not taking his eyes off Katie. "You probably won't find anything anyway. Whoever did this used gloves if they have an ounce of a brain. I've got other things on my mind now. Bigger things."

"Call me if you need anything else, then." Gary hesitated for a moment. "Are you going to the funeral for Geraldine and Dana tomorrow?"

"I hadn't heard about it," Ben said.

"They just scheduled it, now that we know . . ."

"Oh, God," Katie blurted out, thinking of those pigs again. "Of course we'll be there."

"The service will be at the cemetery at ten o'clock. They're figuring on most of the town showing up. See you there."

He backed out of the door. She heard his engine rev and then fade into the distance. She wondered if Silas was anywhere nearby. She wondered if he could feel the searing pain in her chest and the taste of betrayal in her mouth. She had fallen in love for the first time, had experienced real sexual pleasure for the first time—and it wasn't with her husband.

"Katie, sit down and explain what the hell you were doing with Silas."

He didn't give her much choice. He kept moving toward her, making her step back until she came up against the sofa and dropped onto the front edge. With an exasperated sound, Ben pushed the couch upright and then pushed Katie down on it. Shards of filling and fabric lay everywhere.

"I . . . needed answers, Ben. About you. Finding that birth certificate, and the diplomas, and you never talked about your father before, so it seemed strange that you'd keep his papers. Since I don't have a car of my own, I had to ask someone to take me to Milledgeville. So I asked Silas."

It was a variation of the truth. She was almost more ashamed that she'd so easily believed Ben's story.

"You went to Milledgeville," he said. "With Silas."

She took a deep breath. "Yes. I know about Ben Ferguson . . . and Larry Howard. You have some explaining to do, too. You're not a licensed veterinarian."

The icy façade of his face melted away to reveal deep sorrow. He knelt down in front of her after clearing away debris. "I suppose I should have just told you the truth Thursday night. I didn't want you to know because . . . I'm ashamed. I should have known that as my wife, you'd understand. But I want to be your hero, Katie. Your perfect man. And perfect men don't have sexual abuse in their background. I've never told anybody this. I just wanted to bury it in my past and hope no one found it. But you did find it. You and Silas." For a moment that iciness slipped back into his eyes, but it vanished just as quickly. "I can't tell you how much you've hurt me by going behind my back like this. You're my wife, the one person in this whole world that matters to me. The one person I can trust."

Her mouth tightened at those words. She'd wronged him, and there was no excuse for that. She'd take full responsibility, because Silas had done his best to stop it from happening. "I'm sorry I let you down. But I did trust you, and you lied to me. And now I have to know everything. No more lies." She realized how unfair that demand was in light of her own lies. But she hadn't stolen someone's identity; she was just trying to find it in the first place.

He took a deep breath and let it out in an anguished sigh. "You know I had a troubled childhood. You probably know about my being left on the church steps, tied to the doorknob like some animal. I don't remember much before that time. The reverend took me in. He's the one you spoke with, isn't he?" She nodded. "I thought so. They tried, I guess. But they were busy, and I was left with the other kids during all the services and classes. And maybe the reverend didn't know, but his wife would stick me in the nursery by myself for hours at a time, when it was convenient for her. I was sick a lot, and it was too much for her to handle. She locked me in that room so she could get things done. That I remember clearly, being in that prison and feeling like I'd been abandoned all over again."

She fought the urge to touch his arm in comfort. During all the years she'd known him, she'd believed him without question. It made sense, and of course, they'd only heard the reverend's version of events. But now he'd lied to her, and she'd lied to him. It changed everything between them.

"They did abandon me, in a way. Just as I was starting to feel like I finally had a home, they shuffled me off to another family. They didn't want me, either. I think the reverend just made them feel guilty, so they took me in. Like the Emersons took you in. Surely you can understand what it was like to be in a place where no one wanted you."

"I can, but I never tried to kill one of my siblings, either."

He winced, then shook his head. "That was a big misunderstanding. We were playing a game. No way would I have let him go. But I guess I scared him, and then he wouldn't admit that we'd just been playing. So off I went to another home. Because they went in thinking I had problems, they treated me like a criminal. They locked me in my bedroom at night and watched me like a hawk the rest of the time. Like they were waiting for me to screw up. No surprise that I didn't last long anywhere. It was a vicious cycle. I just wanted to be loved." He grabbed her hands. "That's all I've ever wanted, Katie, to be loved. Like you. That's why we're meant to be together. We're the same. Two lost souls in a sea of cold, uncaring people. You and me, together, forever."

She thought of Gary saying they were the same, and then feeling that Silas was where she really belonged. Her insides felt as pulled as taffy.

"What about Ben Ferguson?"

"He was the first person who gave me some direction.

He gave me a job at his clinic, and then let me live with him."

She pushed out the words, "Are you saying he molested you?"

He swallowed thickly and nodded. "I hate talking about this, but I can see you're going to make me do it. And maybe it's better that you know. Then you'll know everything. The only reason I didn't tell you was because I didn't want you to stop loving me. I didn't want you to think there was something wrong with me." His voice cracked, and he squeezed her hand tighter. She squeezed back, wishing she didn't feel so doubtful about his story. Wishing she could be totally supportive.

"I loved Ben, I really did. He was like the father I never had. And then he started touching me. First it was hugging, which was something I'd rarely had in my life. I loved being hugged. But those hugs transformed into something ugly. And I felt ugly."

"Why did you stay with him?" she asked in a whisper.

"Because I had no other place to go." He was crying now, the first time she'd ever seen him cry or show real emotion. "I knew no one would believe me if I told them. Ben was liked by everyone. His family had been one of the founders of Milledgeville. I made a choice, Katie. It may not have been the best choice, but we all make sacrifices. I stayed because he gave me a home, security, and a job. All I had to do was let him touch me once in a while. He'd crawl into my bed sometimes and hold me through the night. I'd lie there stiff as a log. Sometimes that's all he wanted. He was lonely, he said. His wife had died." He crawled up on the couch with her and gathered her in his arms. "Please don't hate me for the choice I made."

She could hardly react. She was too stunned by his earlier words, by not only what he'd gone through, but what he'd given up for home, security, and a job . . . sacrifices. It was her story.

"I don't hate you," she said, stroking his hair. "But tell me what happened when Ben died."

He was curled around her like a child, his head pressed against her chest. "Me and Ben went swimming sometimes. He'd been having heart trouble lately, though I didn't even want to think about him dying. I knew what he was doing to me was wrong, but he was my lifeline. It was a chilly afternoon, but we went to the lake anyway. No one was there, just the two of us. I stayed away from him. I just wanted to enjoy the cool water and sunshine and not be touched. I came up for air and heard him splashing. By the time I got to him, he was unconscious, floating in the water. I dragged him to the shore and tried to revive him. I'd seen CPR done on television and tried to do it like the paramedics did it. Some people heard my screams for help, and they tried, too. But he was gone."

His warm breath soaked through her shirt as he spoke. "I was lost. Everything had been ripped from under my feet. Like when your mom died. That's why I understood what you were going through. They let me stay at Ben's house for a while, but I knew his niece was coming to clean out his house and sell it. No one would give me a job or a place to stay, and I couldn't buy the house. I was desperate, Katie, you've got to understand that. By then, I knew a lot about being a veterinarian. I was a fast learner. I'd read Ben's journals and textbooks, asked him endless questions. He even took me to some of his conferences. I loved animals. Sometimes I think they're better than people. They never hurt you or betray you. If you're kind, they're forever loyal."

It all made sense then. *She* was supposed to be that grateful dog. That loyal pet.

He took her intent expression as interest and went on. "I was going through the house, trying to find some money to help me live until I figured out where I was going to go. And I found his birth certificate and diplomas. It all came together, like a light bulb going off in my head. I changed the dates on the certificates at the hospital, the ones we post on the walls. And I started looking for a job.

"I'd planned to go farther away than this, but I heard

the veterinarian here was dying of lung cancer. They needed someone desperately. The guy only wanted his family to be taken care of after he died. He didn't look too closely at my certifications, only saw that I was qualified. He sold me the business with the provision that I pay his family over time. The rest you know." He looked up at her with a face slick with tears. "Tell me you don't hate me for lying. Tell me I'm still your hero, Katie."

"I don't hate you for lying," she said, pushing his hair out of his face. "But you're practicing medicine without a license."

"I know everything the doc knew. I keep learning, keep reading. My patients never complain, and how many veterinarians do you think would be clamoring to open a practice here in Flatlands? Then what happens to all those people who need my services? Especially the ones who can't afford it?"

She knew that much was true. He was dedicated and conscientious. He was smart. Turning him in would only create problems for everyone, and what would happen to dogs like Goldie or kittens like Gus? He was already so wracked up, she couldn't bring up the fact they weren't legally married yet.

"Do you think I'm tainted now? Am I a terrible person?"

"No, you're not terrible. You did what you had to do to survive. We all do that."

Whenever he talked about what he'd do without her, she always feared the unspoken threat of suicide. She'd left her mama, and her mama had killed herself—would Ben do the same? But her mother had been a survivor, and she hadn't taken her life after all. How strong was Ben? Obviously he was a survivor, too.

He clung even closer to her, wrapping himself around her as he pulled her down onto the couch. "Tell me I'm still your hero, Katie," he whispered desperately.

She squeezed her eyes shut. "You're my hero, Ben."

* * *

He sat in the predawn darkness outside the Victorian cottage. When he'd arrived, the crickets and other night creatures had become quiet. Now they accepted his presence and continued with their songs.

Did Katie suspect him? The way she looked at him, he had to wonder. That mixture of fear and paranoia on her face pleased him somehow. Not as much as the moment of surprise, of revelation. But he'd been so dissatisfied lately, even her mild emotions turned him on.

Perhaps the moment would come when he'd see that look of shock on her face. Maybe that would bring the thrill back. Until then, he'd wait in the shadows, as he'd always done.

After a tumultuous night of vivid, disturbing dreams, Katie woke Sunday morning still on the couch. She could hear Ben in the kitchen and smelled bacon frying. He was making breakfast?

She pulled herself upright and was reminded again of the house's condition. Everything else crashed back in, too. It felt as though someone had dropped her life into a box, shaken it up, then tossed it back. And worse, they had a funeral to attend. She stumbled into the bathroom and washed her face. The woman staring back at her wasn't Katie at all. Her short hair was disheveled, her eyes bloodshot. Her husband had become a stranger, and a stranger had loved her beyond her wildest dreams.

She took a shower and put on the only black clothing she owned, pants and a black and red shirt.

"You cut your hair." Ben was standing at the stove mixing up eggs.

She ran her hand self-consciously over her wet hair. "I needed a change."

He turned back to the eggs. "Do you love him, Katie?"

She didn't need to ask who he meant. Still, the blatant question threw her off. She felt the word *yes* form in her throat. "I'm not sure how I feel about him." Wanting to shift the conversation away from Silas, she said, "Your past is part of who you are. Do you realize that's the first time you've shared some of your soul with me? You claim you want open communication in our marriage, yet I'm the only one who communicates. When you ask me what I'm feeling, there are sometimes things I don't want to share. So I bury them in order to not hurt your feelings. I'm just now realizing that I don't have to share them or bury them; I can keep them to myself." Except where Silas was concerned, darn it.

"Tell me what you need, Katie. Haven't I always tried to give you what you need?"

She thought of the way Silas's fingers had brought her more sexual pleasure than Ben had ever brought her. "I want to make my own choices. I haven't made a choice since my mama died." The words about her mother's death hung in her throat. That was something she wanted to hold close for a little longer. Not that he'd believe her. "I don't have any control of my life." She busied herself with pulling the bacon out of the hot grease and laying it on the paper towel.

"God, you've changed. I'm not even sure I know you anymore."

She had changed, and she wasn't sure how much Silas had to do with it. Like that door Swenson had opened in him, he had opened a door within her. All she knew was she didn't want it closed just yet, not until she explored what was on the other side.

"Don't forget we've got the funeral this morning," she said.

"How could I forget?" He glanced down at her outfit. "Could you wear the dress I bought you? It would mean a lot to me right now."

She started to protest, but realized it wasn't a big deal to give in on that small point. "All right."

"Where'd you get this?" Ben asked while they ate a short time later, startling her when he took the cross in his fingers.

She'd thought about taking it off when she'd gone to change, but left it on.

"It's my mother's. Silas gave it to me. She'd given it to him when he helped her through her labor. He wanted me to have it." She took the cross back, not wanting Ben to touch it for some reason. She needed some time away from both Ben and Silas, time to herself. Maybe she'd get a hotel room for a weekend. "Ben, maybe we should—"

He kissed her, stealing her words about separating right out of her mouth. He tried to open her mouth with the tip of his tongue. It felt so wrong and strange.

"Is it because of the molestation? That's it, isn't it? You don't want me anymore because I let him . . . do those things to me."

"God, no. I don't care about that. I mean, it's horrible that it happened, but it doesn't change what I feel for you."

"And what is that, Katie?"

She opened her mouth, but no words came out. She bought time by eating a forkful of scrambled egg. "That's what I need to figure out for myself. You've been telling me how to feel—how I should feel—for so long, I don't know anymore."

"I know you love me, even if you're going through something I can't understand. I'm going to give you some space. We can set up the office as a second bedroom if that's what you want. As long as you don't see Silas, I'm willing to let you sort through all this. You know why? Because I know you're going to realize how much I've done for you, how much I love you, and that you belong with me. Your home, your job, everything is here with me."

Even as Ben spoke of giving her space, she could feel the spider web tightening around her. *He'll never let you go,* a voice in her head whispered.

As she was about to take him up on the offer of the trial separation, her stomach lurched. She held on to the table and waited for the nausea to pass. Just as it did, another wave hit her.

"What's wrong?" he asked. "You look all white."

Sweat sprang out on her skin as she fought to control her stomach. And then she gave in and ran to the bathroom.

Monday afternoon Gary sat in the back booth at the Pie in the Sky and let himself sulk for a few minutes. For one thing, he hated Mexican day. All the specials were ethnic food, and Dinah had the satellite music station tuned to the Fiesta channel. He focused on that for a while and not on the snubbing he'd just gotten from his father. His mother had looked at him, perhaps in a longing way. But she'd never stand up to Sam from her place as his doormat. Not even for her son.

Everyone in town thought his father shot him looks of pure hate because Gary had gone into law enforcement. But their animosity had taken a turn for the worse when he had confronted his father about that day long ago, that horrible event he'd witnessed and buried in his subconscious. It came back in that stupid rage-management course he'd taken, the long-buried memory of the crime his father had committed.

He didn't need any head shrink to tell him his anger problems stemmed from his father. But he'd thought it was only how impotent he'd made Gary feel. And the shame . . . how Sam insisted his mother hang Gary's soiled sheets out the window so everyone would know he was still wetting the bed at eight.

It was the hidden memory that really ate away at him. His own father had brutalized a woman.

When Gary had returned to Flatlands to confront him, Sam had denied it and called him the same names he'd called him as a child. And who would believe him, a reject from the Atlanta police force, over Sam, a respected DA? Just like always.

The impotency had enraged him, but for once he'd held himself back. There were other ways to empower himself. Like joining the Flatlands sheriff's office. Seeing Katie had sealed the decision.

Not seeing her at the funeral had worried him. Ben said

recent events had caused an upset stomach. When he heard Ben walk in the diner, he peered around the back of his booth to see if she was with him. She wasn't. Ben joined Harold and Marion, who were sitting behind him. The first order of every conversation he'd heard so far was the funeral, how beautiful and sad, and then the fires that were slowly moving toward Flatlands. He was about to head out when Dinah walked over and asked Ben, "So what's going on with that wife of yours? She come to her senses yet?"

Marion whispered loudly, "Marv said she spent the whole of Saturday with Silas. Ben, how terrible for you."

Gary thought the sheriff had a big mouth as Marion dispensed with the details of the vandalism done to the Ferguson house. But no one was interested in that for long. They wanted to know about Katie and Silas.

Dinah said, "Did she say what she was doing with him? I just can't imagine . . ."

"She said she was doing research with him, I suspect for the book he's working on. The one about the guy who's taking the women in this area."

"Stupid woman," Marion muttered. "It's Silas Koole! And she couldn't even come to the funeral, sick, my fanny. She just didn't want to be bothered. Probably thought it was silly."

Harold said, "She thinks she's too good for the likes of us."

"I can't imagine why you're even still with her," Dinah said. "She won't give you babies, won't participate in anything for the good of the town."

"I can't leave her. I love her. I'll stay with her as long as she'll have me," Ben said in a dragged-out voice.

Gary grabbed his bill and slid out of the booth, not even looking at the gabfest. He paid and headed over to the hospital hoping he'd have time to talk to Katie before Ben returned. He had a lot to tell her.

She'd been resting her head on the counter when he walked in. He hated the fearful look that seized her expression every time she saw him. That was quickly replaced by a fierce look that reminded him of that day he'd thrown her kitten.

He tipped his hat. "Afternoon, Katie."

"We found Goldie's owners. The dog you hit," she clarified when he didn't understand. "Everything turned out all right." She paused. "If that's why you're here."

"I'm glad she's okay. I felt bad about not being able to avoid her. But that's not why I'm here."

"I'm not interested in anything you have to say about Silas."

He leaned comfortably on the counter, making her move back. "You're in love with him, aren't you?"

"It's none of your business how I feel about him. That's between me, Silas, and Ben."

"And everyone at the diner."

"What?"

"We'll get to that in a minute. We've got something more important to discuss."

She crossed her arms in front of her. "Fine, discuss it, then leave."

He assessed her, taking in her black polyester pants and plain man's shirt. Her eyes looked bloodshot, her face drawn from her illness. Her short hair revealed that birthmark on her neck. He remembered the outfit she'd worn Saturday night, the jeans that outlined her hips and the top that showcased what the shirts she usually wore hid. And though she swallowed thickly, she stood there and withstood his perusal.

"You've changed, Katie. Since Silas has come to town, you've changed. I thought you were like my mother, who spent her life being my father's doormat. When I came back to town, I watched you. Ben was always with you. You walked at his side like a puppy. I heard him change your mind about what you wanted to eat for dinner and I heard him talk you out of volunteering at the county fair. I could hardly believe you were the same girl who attacked me even though I was twice her size and a boy to boot. But from everything I've seen and heard about you, something has changed drastically."

He'd seen her eyes widen when he'd recited things he'd overheard, but otherwise she stood tall with her chin up.

"I think you're ready to hear what I've got to tell you. It's about my father."

Her expression changed from defiant to worried. "Tell me about everyone at the diner knowing my business first."

He was about to argue with her, but he took a breath and nodded. If Ben was eating with his cronies, he'd have time to tell her everything. "All right, we'll cover that first. There's something you should know about Ben."

"And what's that?"

Gary turned around to find Ben at the open door, holding a sack that smelled like one of those awful Mexican specials. Ben's face was neutral as he set the sack down on the counter between him and Katie. She blanched at the pungent smell.

Gary turned toward her so that Ben couldn't see his face. "He's doing everything he can to make you safe. He's one of the best guys in town, and you couldn't be in better hands." His expression negated every single word.

Ben said, "I appreciate the kind words, Gary." And his expression negated those words as well, much to Gary's surprise. "I plan to do everything I can to make sure my wife is safe. And I expect you to put Silas behind bars where he belongs. Now, if you'll excuse us, we've got lunch to eat."

Gary paused in the doorway for a moment. She was watching him, confusion tinting her expression.

CHAPTER 19

KATIE WAS GLAD when Bertrice came in a few hours later, at least until she saw the sulk on her face.

"What's wrong?" Katie asked.

"Nothing." One word that said, *Everything, but I'm not discussing it with you.*

"I'm sorry I missed the funeral," she said, just in case that's why Bertrice was sulking.

"Ben said you were sick."

"Believe me, I would rather have been at the funeral, but I couldn't stay more than a foot away from the bathroom all day. Must have been some kind of stomach flu. I'm still dragged out."

Bertrice only nodded and went back to her sulk. The truth came out when they were washing one of the dogs they were boarding. Katie had given her space, assuming that Bertrice was dealing with her friends' deaths or had had it out with her mom and wasn't ready to share it yet.

And that's why it was so surprising, and painful, when Bertrice said, "I thought you were my friend."

In fact, Katie even looked behind her to see if Bertrice was talking to someone else. "I am your friend. Why would you even say such a thing?"

"You told my mom about my belly ring. Then, of course, she had to inspect me, like some farm animal, and she found the tattoo. I'm grounded until my eightieth birthday. I trusted you."

Katie's throat went dry at the searing disappointment in Bertrice's eyes. "I never told her. Why would I do something like that?"

"Mom said you were concerned about my downward spiral. If you were concerned, I wish you'd just talked to me. And the only thing I'm down about is my friends."

Katie set the shampoo bottle on the concrete floor and let the Dalmatian shake himself dry. "I'm not concerned about any downward spiral. You're a teenager, a typical teenager. In fact, I envy you for being so typical, for having such a normal life."

"Maybe it was that envy that made you call her, then. I wasn't even going to say anything, but I had to."

"I'm glad you did. I never called your mother. I've only talked with her a couple of times and that was to tell her you were running a little late."

"Don't lie to me. You know, the people in town think you're, like, such a bitch, that you don't care about our town or anything. I've always said you were nice, that you weren't anything like what they were saying." Bertrice stood. "Maybe I was wrong."

Katie could hardly breathe with the crushing pain in her chest. "I swear to you I never called your mom. She must have been mistaken."

Bertrice's pouty mouth stretched into a frown. "You're the only one I told besides Geraldine and Dana, and they certainly didn't tell her. I've thought it over and it had to be you. I can't work with someone I can't trust. And I really can't work with a liar."

She ran toward the door leading into the hospital. Katie couldn't move; she was too stunned, too hurt to even think of following her inside. But it wouldn't matter; the girl had made up her mind. A few minutes later, she heard Bertrice's car tear out of the dirt parking lot.

When she finally finished drying the dog and led him inside, she felt numb. She'd just lost one of her best friends, one of her few friends. That left Silas, she realized, a man who couldn't accept her love and who wouldn't stay around anyway.

"She quit," Ben said when Katie walked into the reception area. "You're just leaving a trail of warm, fuzzy feelings lately, aren't you?"

"It was a misunderstanding. She'll be back."

He continued scribbling on one of his patient files. "No she won't. We really don't need the extra help anymore. I think we can make do with the two of us." He set down the pen and looked at her. "If you're staying around, that is."

"Where else would I go?"

Those words brought the first smile to Ben's face she'd seen in days.

The day of the county fair two days later dawned hot and rain-free, as usual. The town council had considered rescheduling the fair what with the funeral and the fires moving closer to Flatlands, but everyone thought it would do the town's spirit some good to congregate. A memorial was being set up in the girls' honor, with a candlelight service scheduled for sundown.

Ben had once again talked Katie into doing something she didn't have the heart to do—attend the fair with him. For appearances' sake, he said. What she really wanted to do was hide under her blanket all day.

"People are doing a lot of speculating about you, about us. I think it'd be good for you to make an appearance and try to look happy with me. Maybe you can talk to Bertrice."

Or her mother, Katie thought, deciding to go. She hadn't mentioned Bertrice's other comment about people saying she was a bad person. So it wasn't her imagination after all.

She looked through her closet to find something that she'd bought for herself . . . something she liked. Wearing an outfit Bertrice had given her seemed inappropriate. She settled on jean shorts and one of the white men's shirts she'd cut the sleeves off of.

The fair sprawled throughout the park and some of the surrounding streets as it usually did. But what wasn't usual was the pinkish-gray smoke in the distance and the tiny ashes that floated through the air. The aromas of roasting hot dogs and smoked pig mingled with the smoke from the fires.

Katie hadn't been eating much lately. Her appetite had nearly disintegrated. Every time Ben offered to make her something to eat, she remembered her bizarre suspicion that he'd poisoned the hamburgers and her stomach turned. And the emerging suspicion that he'd made her sick Sunday so she couldn't attend the funeral. What she couldn't figure out was his motive.

She walked beside Ben as they wandered among the tables and games. Kids threw darts at balloons, bobbed for apples, and raced around chasing each other. They were immune to the tensions hovering thicker than the smoke in the distance. Everyone wore yellow ribbons. Bertrice had gotten one for Katie before she'd quit, and she wore it on her shirt.

"Hey, Ben," Harold said as he approached them. "Katie," he added as he took her in without a trace of malice on his beefy face. He looked at her yellow ribbon—or maybe her chest, she wasn't sure. "The big discussion is whether it's in bad taste that Maurice is roasting his usual pig . . . in light of, well, you know. What do you think?" he asked Ben.

"I suppose he could have picked something else, like chickens. I'm sure he didn't mean anything by it, and it is his tradition."

"It's deviling that not one speck of evidence points to Silas Koole. Everybody knows he did it." Those hard eyes settled on her. "Except you. You're his little defender. Wonder how you'll feel when he turns that axe on you."

"That's Katie's choice," Ben said. "She's into making choices these days."

"Ah, well, here's a choice for you: would you rather be killed by someone you know or by a stranger?"

She was startled by the question and that it was aimed at her. "I'd rather not be killed at all."

Both men laughed, but she had the sense it was at her and not with her.

Dinah and Maybel joined them. "Hey, Ben. How's it going?" Dinah said. Both women slid her a look of disregard. "Sure is smoky. But I think this'll be good for everyone, getting out and socializing. Seems like all we think and talk about are those poor girls. At least we know what happened to them now, as horrible as it is. But I think one person here has a lot of nerve showing up." She sent a pointed look Katie's way before nodding toward the water dunk tank where Silas stood talking with Bertrice. "It enrages me that he's allowed to walk around free."

Katie said, "There's no evidence that he killed anyone."

"And what are you, the president of his fan club or something?" Maybel said.

Dinah patted Ben's arm. "Must be hard living with a traitor in the ranks. But we're here for you, you know that. We'll see you around. We've got to get over to the cakewalk. It's our turn to help out."

It definitely wasn't her imagination. These people despised her. But why? Her gaze went to Bertrice and Silas, who both looked over at her. Bertrice looked away and continued talking to Silas, who hadn't shifted his gaze from her. She felt some easing of the tension inside her, and at the same time, a different kind of charge ignite in her stomach.

Bertrice's mother, Treena, tapped her daughter on the shoulder, then pulled her away. They argued for a few seconds, with Bertrice glancing toward Silas. Of course, her mother didn't want her to socialize with a suspected killer. Bertrice stomped off in another direction, and Katie walked over to Treena.

"There she goes," someone muttered.

"I feel so bad for Ben."

Katie didn't even look to see who was talking. She glanced at Silas, but trained her gaze back to Treena, who just now realized Katie was heading in her direction. She started backing away.

"Treena, I'd like to talk to you."

"I've got a booth to take care of. Some of us have to help keep this thing going, you know."

"I just need a few minutes." Katie followed the woman who was weaving through people. "Why does Bertrice think I told you about her belly ring?"

"Look, I've heard about you. You like to tattle on people. And while I'm glad I know about the ring, I wish it had been my own daughter who told me. Excuse me."

Katie grabbed Treena's arm to halt her escape. "I didn't tell you about that ring. Who did?"

"Let go of me!" Treena yelled, catching everyone's attention in the vicinity.

Katie had no choice but to release her, and Treena backed through the crowd and headed off. Those who had gathered around just stared at her.

Sheriff Tate wasn't in uniform, but he stepped up beside Katie. "You causing trouble?"

"She was assaulting Treena!" someone shouted.

Tate's wife shot her a venomous look from what had become an audience. This was like a nightmare. Katie swore they were closing in on her. She glanced toward Ben, who was flanked by two other women as he just stood there. She couldn't see Silas.

"What is wrong with you people?" she said, circling around to take them all in. "How can you hate someone you don't even know?"

"We know enough about you," Marion said. "And we don't like what you're doing to Ben. You're trash and you always have been. Possum Holler trash."

Maybel had stepped up to the inner circle. "You're ungrateful and selfish. Even the Emersons said you didn't appreciate what they did for you, giving you a home after your mama killed herself. Ben has given you everything, and you spit in his face time and again. Who are you saving your babies for? A killer?"

"Look, she's even wearing his necklace," someone else whispered.

Katie could hardly breathe. It was as though their anger had sucked the oxygen from the air. They may as well have stabbed her in the tenderest places deep inside. How did they know so much? She pushed her way out of the crowd and walked toward the edge of the festivities.

"Hey, you're not allowed in this area," one man said when she stepped over the ribbon enclosing the fireworks section.

She kept on walking, right out to the streets that were nearly abandoned. Ben had been telling her for years that the people in town didn't dislike her, that it was her own paranoid imagination. That had not been her imagination.

When she was a safe distance away, she dared a glance backward. She expected a mob to be following her, carrying pitchforks and calling for the burning of the witch. No one followed. She didn't slow down her pace, though. Sweat poured off her as the sun burned down and danced off the asphalt. She wound through the streets and out of sight of the fair altogether. The tears were pushing to burst out, but she held them in. Fear edged in, too. God, she was that little girl all over again, with no one to love her or help her.

She heard an engine and glanced behind her. Silas's Navigator cruised the empty streets toward her. She ducked into a small alleyway, and his engine faded away. She'd only taken a few turns through the streets when she came face-to-face with him.

"Why are you running from me?" he asked, exasperation lacing his voice.

"I told you I needed some time."

He ran his fingers through his hair as he tilted his head up. "I threw a lot at you."

"And I threw myself at you."

"Don't be embarrassed about that. What happened between us was the most astounding thing I've ever experienced."

She met his gaze on that, hating the flutter in her stomach. "You said . . . it was like making love to an angel."

"It was. It was like having your light inside me." He brushed her hair back from her face. "I know you need some time away from me. No, I didn't feel it," he said when she gave him an annoyed look. "I believe the words 'Leave me alone!' were enough."

She overcame the urge to apologize and nodded instead. "Maybe I'm a selfish person for wanting to push away the people who want to help me."

"Not really."

She met his gaze. "Maybe I'm selfish for wanting something I don't have, and not wanting what I do have."

"We're all selfish in one way or the other. We all want things we can't or shouldn't have."

"What about you, Silas? What do you want?"

"I want you . . . to be happy."

She wasn't afraid that Silas was a serial killer who fed his victims to pigs. She wasn't even afraid—bothered, yes, but not afraid—that he could read her innermost feelings. What scared her down to the bone was that she'd found the one person who filled her soul, and he was so lost in the dark that he couldn't see how much she loved him.

"What happened at the fair?" he asked after a few moments of silence.

"I was trying to clear up a misunderstanding. It backfired. Look, it's no big deal. I just need to be by myself. Can you understand that?"

Stupid question. He could understand everything about her probably.

"I just wanted to make sure you were all right."

She smiled. Her protector. "I'm all right."

She watched him walk to the corner of the building, take one last look at her, and then disappear around the corner. When she heard his engine fade away, she continued on.

She reached the quiet coolness of the cemetery at last. Her fingers wrapped around the iron spikes that circled one section of gravestones. She felt as dead as any of these people. But even dead, they fit in more than she did. She slid down to her knees next to the fence, curled up, and closed her eyes.

Silas stood in the shadows of the oaks and watched her. He felt her agony and confusion, but there wasn't anything he could do about it. She obviously didn't want to be with him, didn't want the comfort he could provide. She didn't want that comfort, because she knew she'd break down and cry if he so much as touched her. She was too close to the edge.

He'd known she was heading to hang out with the ghosts, so he'd given her time to get there before walking over. He slid down to the base of the tree and stretched out. She wasn't crying at least. He wouldn't have been able to stay away from her if she'd been crying.

Now she was sitting among the dead. He could only see the top of her head where patches of sunlight washed over her. He'd give her time alone, and when she left, he'd make sure she didn't know he'd ever been there. For now, he watched over her. She was right; that was his role. He'd loved Katie from a distance for most of his life. He wasn't sure he knew how to love her close up.

⟶ CHAPTER 20

THE NEXT MORNING, Katie and Ben drove to the hospital as usual.

"I looked for you," Ben said for the fiftieth time. "I drove all over the place looking. So did your buddy, Silas. But even he gave up after a while. He parked by the cemetery for hours. Guy's spooky, just like they say."

She lifted her head at that revelation. He'd been there, watching over her, just like always.

"Say something, Katie. You can't just not talk about this." He let out an exasperated sigh at her continued silence.

Ben had come in later that evening, once she'd gotten home. And amazingly, he'd tried to convince her it was all some big misunderstanding.

"Gary was looking for you, too. Maybe you were right to be wary about him."

Now he believed her! She got out of the van without commenting. When they'd listened to the radio, he had tried to talk to her about the fires that were moving closer. The air was thick with the smell of smoke, and the winds had picked up. Residents of the Flatlands were warned to be on the alert and monitor the radio for further reports.

She had barely turned on the computers and coffee maker when their first customer pushed open the door: Silas.

He was carrying The Boss, which was no small feat. She rushed forward and held the door open.

"What happened?" she asked, taking in Silas's disheveled appearance and the dog's short, panting breaths.

"He went out this morning and came back like this."

"Ben!" She led the way to the examining room, and

Silas laid The Boss on the metal table. The dog shuddered and twitched, and she saw the pain in his brown eyes. When she looked up at Silas, she saw the pain there too as he watched his dog.

Ben walked in and visibly stiffened when he saw the two of them together.

Katie took The Boss's vitals. "There's something wrong with the dog. Silas, how long was he outside?"

"About an hour. He dragged himself to the front steps. I don't know when he started acting like this."

"It looks like he got into something, or maybe it's a snake bite." She met his gaze. "It doesn't look good."

"Do you want us to proceed with treatment?" Ben asked Silas.

Silas met Katie's eyes. He knew the real question was, try to save him or let him die? "Proceed."

"Then you'll have to leave," Ben said in a cold voice.

After a pause, Silas left the room. Ben checked the dog's mouth while she checked for signs of snakebite. When she found nothing, she started an IV drip of lactated Ringer's solution. She and Ben worked well together in cases like this. They both maintained a calm, efficient speed. He showed more compassion this time as he checked the dog. The Boss was having a hard time taking a breath. His mouth stayed slightly open and his tongue lolled out. Something bothered her, but of course, everything about his condition bothered her. She was about to induce vomiting when the dog's vital signs started dropping. They were losing him.

"Silas!"

"What are you doing?" Ben hissed.

Silas appeared in the doorway with a worried expression.

"Be the last face he sees," she whispered, and he rushed to the table.

He positioned his face in front of The Boss's and massaged his paws. "Goodbye, buddy," he whispered.

The Boss closed his eyes, shuddered one last time, and slipped away.

Ben glared at her over the improper procedure.

An apology, an explanation, hovered on the tip of her tongue. Instead, she looked at Silas and said, "I'm sorry."

The pain was evident in his features, and she felt it so fiercely, she wondered if the connection between them went both ways now. It was probably her pain.

"Do you know what happened to him?" Silas was looking at Katie, but slid a glance to Ben, who answered in a clinical voice, "My guess would be an internal bleed-out from a ruptured splenic tumor. I could do an autopsy, but it's expensive and it doesn't change the outcome. He was an old dog." He gently closed the dog's eyes.

She couldn't help but reach out and touch Silas's arm. "You did everything you could."

He stared at her hand, a raw mixture of pain and need in his eyes. Had anyone ever held him when he'd hurt? When he'd lost Celine? He'd probably never been held or comforted, which was why he was reluctant to allow anyone to do it now. He pulled away from her touch as though he'd read her mind.

Her heart melted when he walked out carrying his dog. The Boss's legs jiggled with each step Silas took as he headed to his vehicle. He returned a few minutes later and paid the bill in cash. Ben had already escorted the next patient into the examination room.

"Was it a bleed-out, Katie?" Silas asked quietly.

"I don't know."

Ben returned to stand guard as Katie returned his change. "We can cremate him if you want," he said.

Silas didn't even answer, just turned around and walked out. She wanted to go after him, to give him a hug and make him accept it.

"Katie, I need you to prepare Mrs. Turner's cat's vaccinations."

"Was it a bleed-out, Ben?" she asked, stopping him as he returned to the examination room. It didn't feel right.

"That's what I said it was, didn't I?" His eyes looked cold and as gray as the steel of the examining table.

In her mind, she saw the dog panting, and then The Boss turned into a raccoon pleading with her to help it. It was the same panting action, the same pain in his eyes. "He was poisoned. Just like the raccoon." Cold dread filled her chest as though someone had poured cement mix down her throat.

"Maybe he got into the stuff I left for the raccoons."

"That dog has never been near our house. He stays near Silas at all times."

Ben looked right at her and said, "Get the vaccinations ready." He returned to the room. "All right, Mrs. Turner, we'll have Fuzzy ready for another year in no time at all." His voice was once again warm.

Her hands shook as she readied the shots. Ben gently stroked the white cat while he spoke with Mrs. Turner. Then it was Katie's turn to hold the cat while he administered the shots.

"Weigh her and see what we've got," he asked in his nicest voice. She set the cat on the table and noted the cat's weight. "Up a pound and a half. Might want to think about putting her on a senior diet now that she's slowing down." He gave the cat a friendly pet. "Don't want her to get to be called Tubby."

Mrs. Turner chuckled and patted her own sizable stomach. "Fuzzy's not the only one who needs to go on a diet." She settled up her bill, and Ben hoisted the bag of cat food.

"Did I ever tell you that my brother is a veterinarian? He's been practicing in Macon for thirty years. You kind of remind me of him, you know, when he was younger."

"That's very nice," Ben said with a sweet smile. "What's his name?"

"Ken Buchanan. Do you know him?"

"Don't think so."

"He's dying of cancer. Untreatable they say. They give him nine months. I'm going to miss him. It'll be nice to have you around as a reminder."

He patted her shoulder. "I'd be glad to be your surrogate brother, Mrs. Turner."

"I'm going to Macon tomorrow for their annual Independence Festival. It'll probably be his last one."

Their conversation trailed off as the door closed behind them. Katie tried to remember where the box of rat poison had been recently. When he stepped back inside, she was waiting for him.

"Ben, we need to talk."

His expression was as open and friendly as it had been for Mrs. Turner. "Yes?"

"Good morning, Dr. Ferguson," Mrs. Lane said as she guided her German shepherd into the waiting area. "Thanks for getting us in this morning. With this fire coming in, and possibly having to put poor Duchess in a shelter, I want her vaccinations up to date."

Ben guided Mrs. Lane and her dog into the exam room. Katie was going to confront him about The Boss. But it wouldn't matter whether he confessed or not—it was over between them.

Even though The Boss had been old, even though he'd been a hassle to take on his travels, his loss left a hole inside Silas. He'd gone home to give him a proper burial.

Silas would never forget Ben's sense of smug satisfaction and vengeance when his dog died. Ben had had something to do with The Boss's death. As strongly as he felt Ben's malevolence, he felt Katie's compassion. She'd wanted to comfort him, to protect him from pain the way he tried to protect her. As much as he'd wanted to accept that comfort, he'd wanted to run from it, too.

He searched the yard for the right place to inter The Boss. He found the perfect spot nowhere near his house, but at the old cemetery. The place hadn't been touched in years, evident by the sprawling vines and the broken, rusted fences. Something about the place comforted Katie, and in an odd way, comforted him, too. No one would ever notice the new grave.

The smoke was getting thicker as he chose a spot toward the back of the cemetery and started digging. The smothering heat, combined with the smoke, broke him out in a sweat within minutes. He stripped off his shirt and continued, wishing The Boss had been the size of a small poodle rather than a small horse. He kept trying to tell himself this was for the better, remembering the pain the dog had been in. His chest tightened when he positioned him in the hole. He thought of his dog's devotion, of the way he licked Silas's hand in gratitude when he'd massaged his paws. And he realized something: he'd accepted The Boss's love. From a dog, not a person, but he hadn't felt strange about it.

He blinked away the moisture in his eyes as he tossed in the first shovelful of dirt. The orange dirt mingled with the dog's brown coat, and Silas had the urge to brush it away. He'd always kept The Boss clean. He dug the shovel into the pile of dirt and deposited the second load. He almost expected the dog to get up and shake it off. But he didn't move. He'd never move again.

He wiped his face with the back of his arm and continued until he couldn't see The Boss anymore. When he patted the dirt flat, he said a prayer for a good dog's soul. He hoped he was wrong about Ben being responsible. He hoped for Ben's sake. And for Katie's sake. Any man who'd kill a dog for spite could hurt the woman who wanted to leave him.

Silas had wondered about his father, whether his joy of killing animals and slapping his kid around could transform into something more violent. Perhaps that started his fixation on what made someone cross the line.

He was a boy again, feeling his father's joy at the kill, feeling his finger being squeezed over the trigger. Through the recesses of his mind, he saw the barn his father used for slaughter. Something kick-started his heart. For years, he'd pushed it from his mind, probably like Katie pushed away sunsets. Now he forced his thoughts around it, picturing the weathered and moldy exterior, the dim interior.

The barn. The eerie feelings it elicited weren't only from

his childhood memory. More recent events colored it blood-red—the Ghost's feelings of perverse joy.

The memory of those other feelings lured him back to his vehicle. It was time to put them to rest one way or the other. It was time to face the truth no matter what face that truth wore.

"That dog was poisoned. I need to know how he got into poison."

It was afternoon before the deluge of last-minute vaccinations ceased momentarily.

Ben had just pulled off a pair of rubber gloves and tossed them into the trash. "Honey, I think you've been way too preoccupied with poison lately. You've been paranoid and argumentative. I've been as patient as a saint through all this, but how much is one man supposed to take? You're accusing someone who saves animals for a living of poisoning a dog. Do you realize how silly that sounds? How paranoid? I don't like Silas, I admit that. He's been causing trouble between us since he came back to town. But I'd never hurt any dog. Dogs never turn their backs on people. They don't shun love, mislead, or hurt. They're loyal to a fault." He took her hands in his. "I love you, Katie. Even though you're putting me through a lot of pain and insecurity, I love you. How can I prove that to you?"

She looked into his eyes and saw love and warmth and earnestness there. It looked as real as the white walls around them and the rack of dog food behind him. It was as real as the look of cold hatred he'd worn when he'd spoken to Silas about The Boss.

"Give me a divorce."

He started to open his mouth, but he'd clearly not expected her to say that. "What?"

She wasn't sure what he'd do, but she'd already started it. "You heard me. You say I've changed. Well, I've got one up on you. I'm not sure I ever knew you. Your whole past was a lie. Your present is a lie. And more than that, I don't know who I am. I've always been Ben Ferguson's wife or girl or something. But Ben Ferguson is an old man I've never met!"

He tried to grab her hands again. "Honey, you're blowing this all out of proportion. You know why I lied about my past. I thought you of all people would understand."

"That's another thing: how you can be cold and mean one minute, and then be the nicest, warmest person in the world the next? How you can change your feelings like a dimmer switch. What's real?"

"I'm real, and we're real."

"How can you say that? You've kept me in this marriage by manipulating me with guilt. While you've been out forging friendships, I've been stuck home alone in the woods. Those people at the fair were saying I was a terrible person. Maybe I am. I feel terrible and selfish. But I want out, Ben. Out of my life, out of our marriage, a marriage that isn't even legal. I can't do this anymore."

All that warmth seeped right out of his expression then. "Everyone's been telling me for years that you don't deserve me. I kept saying it wasn't true, that they just didn't know you like I did. But they were right. You're trash. I should have left you at the trailer park where the rest of the trash lives. You could have lived underneath one of the trailers like an abandoned dog. Someone might have thrown you scraps, and you would have bitten them the first chance you got. Now I know why the Emersons didn't want you. Why your mom left you. I couldn't see what everyone else saw because I was blinded by love. But you've ripped away my blinders, sweetheart." He swept her with a derisive look, but she kept her chin up. "I know trash when I see it."

When he turned to leave, they were both stunned to see their previous client standing in the doorway. Mrs. Pullman looked just as stunned.

"I'd decided to get that flea treatment you suggested. I . . . guess I'll get it later." She left.

Ben looked even more infuriated. "Now you've humiliated me in front of someone else. Just grind me farther into the dirt with your heel. That's what you're good at."

He slammed the door behind him and took off in the van.

It seemed like a long time before Katie felt herself breathe, really breathe. Fifteen minutes later she stared at the door and ran the unbelievable conversation through her mind again. It was over. Everything she felt had a sharper edge to it: fear, joy, hope. No matter that she had no place to go, freedom sent a rush of exhilaration through her. For the first time in years, life held possibilities beyond Flatlands, beyond being Ben's wife, beyond paying for every kindness. Asking him for a divorce was the first time she'd taken something for herself . . . besides making love with Silas. The first time she'd made a choice.

She didn't want to think about where Silas would fit into this new life of hers. If he would at all. The only shadow was that she'd have to face Ben again. He wouldn't give up that easily. How far would he go to keep her with him? The phone finally shook her out of her trance.

Silas's voice sounded so welcome, she slid into the chair. "You okay?" he asked. She could hear his radio in the background and the sounds of the vehicle's engine.

What had he felt from her just then? "I'm"—she smiled—"all right. For the first time in a long, long time, I'm all right. I just took my life back, and I can't tell you how good it feels. Then again, I don't have to, do I?"

"You don't sound too upset about that."

"Maybe I'm getting used to it. What did you feel?"

He paused, as though absorbing her acceptance. "A whole bunch of feelings. Not all of them were good."

"I just lost a husband. That's the good part. Having nowhere to go, no way to support myself, that would qualify as the bad part. What about you, Silas? You lost your dog. Are you all right?"

"I'm trying to tell myself how old The Boss was, how it was his time to go. He was in pain. What do you mean by losing a husband and taking your life back?"

"I asked—no, told—Ben I wanted a divorce. He stormed out of here."

For a moment, he just contemplated that. "I'm proud of you, Katie."

"I'd be prouder if I'd done it a long time ago." She considered telling him that The Boss may not have died a natural death, but decided to wait on that. "Where are you?"

"I'm investigating some ghosts."

"Want some company?"

"No, I've got to do this myself." He paused, giving her hope that he'd change his mind. "Katie, I want you to come back to Atlanta with me."

The statement stunned her. "Really?"

"I want you out of this place. I want you safe and away from all these people. I want you to be happy. Look, I've got to go. We'll talk about it later."

She curled her fingers around the phone. "Okay." The other line rang in. "I'd better get that."

"These fires are moving in pretty fast. Keep your ear to the radio. I'll be back for you soon. Stay there, okay?"

That call was the first of three canceling appointments because of the fires. Two were readying their spreads and one was gathering people to help those closest to the fires. She didn't even bother to volunteer to help.

Silas wanted to take her to Atlanta with him. The offer scared and excited her at the same time. There was nothing in Flatlands to keep her there now. If she could pack up her squirrels, life would be perfect.

Or would it be? What was Silas offering her exactly? He wanted to take care of her, to make her safe. Like he had with Celine. Not that she feared disappearing. What she feared most was not being with Silas in the real sense of the word. If he continued to pursue his dark career and push away her love, where would she be?

Luckily, they weren't boarding any animals at the time, so she didn't have to worry about evacuating them. However, she did have herself to think of. A few weeks ago, she would have seen the fire as the force that might have ended her life just as her mother's life was ended at twenty-seven. But like her mother, she had too much to live for now.

She unplugged the computer that held all their records and set it near the door for easy evacuation. She took a long look at the place that had once been a refuge, where she'd visited Gus and where the kind Ben made her earn the kitten's keep. It had never occurred to her before that he never made other people pay for his benevolent services. He often gave them away without expecting a thing in return.

Because he'd wanted her for himself. Now that she'd stepped out of her old life, it was as clear as air. He'd kept her isolated at home and at his side at work.

She stepped outside to assess the situation. Roiling dark smoke obliterated the northern sky. Once in a while the smoke would thin enough to let a stream of sunshine through, and then it would thicken again. It was hard to believe that behind all that ugliness lay the pure, bright sun. Just like her life.

Black ashes drifted through the air. The smoke muted the sun into soft, diffused light and cast everything in shades of orange. It wasn't real anymore. Her world, her life, everything had taken on a surreal cast.

Two helicopters toted buckets of water, and a small plane flew overhead to douse the flames. Her chest tightened when she realized just how close the flames were. This wasn't one of those fires that happen out in the scrublands or in some other town. This fire was heading toward Flatlands. How close would it get? People's lives would be ruined, their hopes and dreams and homes. She didn't care about the house she'd never considered a home, but what about her dreams and her life?

She pulled out the piece of paper and paged Silas. She put 911 at the end of it as he'd told her to. She waited. Waited some more. Sent another page. Checked the phone lines to make sure they were still operating. Silas was her protector; why wasn't he returning her page?

She wondered if he could feel the fear growing inside her. She walked to the cemetery, taking in the gravestones in case she never saw them again. She glanced toward the far reaches, where the mound had caught her eye before. She'd forgotten all about it.

She walked toward it, moving farther away from the hospital. Something crunched beneath her shoe. Bones were scattered on the ground. Not a bird, but another hapless creature. She jerked away, her old superstition rearing its head. Dread tightened her chest and added to the smoky dryness of her throat.

In the distance, camouflaged by the smoke, it almost looked as though a fresh grave had been dug. That couldn't be. Who would have been here lately? Surely not the Ghost, who disposed of his victims so thoroughly.

Despite the omen that tightened her chest, she walked farther into the recesses of the woods. There it was, a fresh grave surrounded by orange dirt. And a few yards beyond that, the mound that had caught her eye in the first place. That one wasn't as obvious. In fact, there wasn't anything wrong with it; a layer of old leaves covered it the same way it covered some of the other unmarked graves way back here. But the leaves looked different. Arranged.

She dropped to her knees before the fresh grave and started digging with her hands.

Silas hung up with Katie and focused on the road ahead. Ashes stuck to his windshield, and the world had an eerie orange glow to it. A helicopter flew overhead carrying an orange bucket of water to the fires. A wall of smoke billowed into the sky in the distance. At the juncture of the highway heading north, the police turned back everyone but residents. Silas turned around and headed back, sure he'd probably missed the road.

He found it on the way back. The road was overgrown by weeds, and wild blackberry bushes camouflaged the red gate. The gate was locked with an old padlock that wasn't old enough to have been put there by his father. He left his vehicle parked by the gate and walked into the woods.

The feel of death permeated the place, just as it had years before. The old, red barn was set a good distance from the road. The only thing left of the house that had once been here was a stone chimney. It was still blackened by the fire that had claimed the place years before Silas and his father had moved there.

Some of the weeds were crushed, evidence of a recent visitor. The distant sound of a fire-engine alarm whined. His eyes burned from the smoke. Maybe the fire would eat this place up. He should have burned it long ago.

It wasn't Flatlands that made him keep this land for so long. It was Katie. Now she would return to Atlanta with him and his life would be complete. She'd be his at last, something he'd been wanting for longer than he'd admit. But if she belonged to him, wouldn't that mean that he belonged to her?

He slid his hand in his pocket and pulled out the crystal she'd given him. He ran his finger along the smooth edge. He was the selfish one. He wanted her, but didn't—couldn't—give himself back. He slid the crystal back in his pocket and approached the barn. The windows had been boarded up, something he knew his father hadn't done.

The door was padlocked, too, but the old wood gave way after several sharp pushes on the door. It was dark and musty inside. He left the door open so some light could get in, but between the woods and the smoke, it was still dark. As soon as he stepped inside, he felt the other darkness. It was the darkness that lived in the souls of the men he studied.

The kind that lived in his soul.

He didn't remember there being a bed here, and that bed gave him the willies. He realized why with the force of terror. The flashes he'd seen from the killer's eyes. This was where he tied the girls up.

Silas stumbled backward. At first he thought the clang and the stunning pain in his head were part of the terror. He tried to turn around to see who had hit him, but his legs gave way. His vision blurred and his thoughts rattled around in his head.

Everything went black.

                          ⤳ CHAPTER 21

KATIE HAD BURST into tears at the sight of The Boss's
ear poking through the dirt she'd clawed through. This was
where Silas had buried him, in her cemetery. She pushed
the dirt back now, feeling silly for her dread.

Her tearstained gaze alighted on the mound farther back.
She wished she could take one fresh breath of air. Her
mouth tasted like an ashtray. She glanced back toward the
hospital building, now in the smoky distance. She should
wait there for Silas. He would be here anytime now.

She pushed herself to her feet and walked farther back.
This was probably going to be nothing but her overactive
imagination, but she was compelled to push away the layer
of leaves. Beneath that the dirt was loose. She should go
back and wait, go back . . .

Her hands, already covered in orange dirt, started digging again. She didn't have to go far when she spotted the
swath of denim. She tugged on it, and eventually it came
free of the dirt. It was a faded pair of overalls. Tucked in
the pocket was a gold ring and cheap watch. Her chest
squeezed tight as she continued digging. Beneath one
sneaker lay a pink uniform—it still bore the tag that read
"Geraldine."

She stumbled backward, making unintelligible noises.
She bolted through the cemetery toward the intersection
leading to town. A flashing light and cluster of trucks in-
jected her with hope. People. Safety.

She could hardly breathe when she reached the road
where Sheriff Tate was setting up a roadblock to keep people from taking the road that went past her and Silas's

house. Harold was parked nearby, his truck loaded with what must be the most valuable items from his junk barn. His pit bull stared at her from the passenger seat. Two other men were setting out barricades.

"The grave," she gasped, leaning against Tate's car.

The men continued with what they were doing as though she were invisible. Tate's radio crackled with one of the deputy's voices. "Mrs. Thorne's barricaded herself in her house," Tate told Harold.

She tugged on Tate's sleeve. "I found Geraldine's clothing."

He finally looked her way. "Where's Ben?"

"I . . . don't know." Her chest hurt so badly, she could hardly talk.

"As you can see, we're a little tied up at the moment trying to save property and life. If you'd treated your husband better, maybe he'd be around to help you. I suggest you get on over to the diner where some of the families are gathering and see if you can catch a ride out of town. This thing"—he nodded toward the wall of smoke—"it's coming and you don't want to be here when it does."

"I'll see what she wants," Harold told Tate. "Then I'll head over to the Thorne place and see what I can do."

"Appreciate it, Harold. I've got too much on my plate to be dealing with hysterical women." Tate tipped his hat at Harold and got into his car.

Was he talking about her or Mrs. Thorne? Or both? Katie yelled, "Check out the old cemetery! The grave in the back!"

He pulled away without a backward glance.

"Now, what the devil are you talking about?" Harold said, moving in closer. The tic throbbed by his eye.

She glanced over to the shopping strip plaza that held the diner. No way was she throwing herself into that viper pit, especially not after her outburst at the fair. And no way was she showing Harold the grave. "I . . . I must have been mistaken." She ran back through the cemetery feeling Harold's gaze on her back the entire way.

By the time she pulled herself up the steps to her house, she could barely breathe for the exertion and smoke. It stung her eyes and burned her throat. She had to blink several times to clear the tears from her eyes.

She pushed her way into the house and ran through the broken living room to the bedroom. Adrenaline coursed through her, putting her on automatic pilot. She pulled one of Ben's suitcases out of the closet and threw in the outfits Bertrice had given her along with a few other clothes. She tucked the pictures of her mother into a side pocket.

When she walked into the office, she had to stop for a moment. Drawers were open, papers were scattered everywhere. Similar to the destruction in the rest of the house, except this was more purposeful. Ben had been here and he'd cleared out his personal papers—along with her own, she soon realized.

She climbed onto the kitchen counter and dumped out the change in the tin over the cupboards. All of their money was tied up in their household account and the veterinary hospital's business account. All those *Cosmo* articles warning her to have her own money echoed in her mind. But that Katie of the last few years had been afraid to bring up the possibility of having her own money. Ben would have talked her out of it with the simple reasoning that he was the main provider. She'd never even asked that he add her name to the deed on the house. At least she had a few dollars.

She took one last look around the house. There was nothing here for her. There never had been. She tucked her suitcase just inside the door and ran through the woods to Silas's house.

The sight of the empty driveway sent more chills down her body, despite the heat enveloping her. Smoke drifted through the trees like ghosts. Everything was dark, and it was getting harder to breathe. Though she knew it was fruitless, she screamed Silas's name anyway. She waited a few minutes, listening to the sounds around her. No birds chirped, not a breeze anywhere to ruffle a leaf. Everything waited in deadly anticipation. Fear welled inside her, for herself and for Silas. Where was he? Why hadn't he come back for her?

The house stood alone and abandoned. It didn't matter that Silas had put on the homey touches of the door and the rocking chair on the porch; he was leaving this behind. When they got through this—and they would get through it—he would do the same thing to her. He might set her up in a new life, but he'd back off once she was settled in. He'd take off to chase the shadows of the latest murderer . . . and leave her behind, too. Oh, he'd always be her protector, stealing into her heart whenever she was distressed. The distance between them kept her out of the shadows and him out of the light. But it didn't keep her from loving him.

She turned and ran back through the woods to her house. Branches clawed at her and smoke burned down into her lungs. When her body wanted nothing more than to collapse, the image of fire sweeping through the woods kept her running.

Running where?

She'd never felt this alone and abandoned before, not even right after her mama died. There was nowhere to go, no one to trust or depend on. Something had happened to Silas. It was the only explanation. He was out there somewhere, maybe hurt. And she was here, trapped.

When she reached the porch, she had to drop to the steps and try to breathe. Her mama hadn't given up, hadn't given in to the world's bleak circumstances. For the first time in a long time she drew strength from her mama's memory. Something terrible had happened to her, either before or soon after Katie had been born. Ellie had forged on, even though she'd lived in fear of men. She'd back down from a fight, but she'd protected her daughter and given her a good life. Katie closed teary eyes and prayed, just like she and her mother used to.

I know I haven't been the best person, especially lately. I want another chance to make my life right. Remember when I used to pray for the lost souls, for the girls who were hurt and scared. Right now I'm praying for myself. And I'm praying for Silas. He's been lost for a long time, and now he's really lost. Please bring him back to me. And get us both out of here.

She opened her eyes. Time to get moving. But they closed again as she added one more prayer. *And tell Mama I love her and I always will. Tell her I'm sorry for being mad at her all these years.*

The smoke was getting thicker. She coughed long and hard as she pulled herself to her feet and went inside. Hot pain seared her chest. She tried once more to call Silas's beeper. As she started to hang up the phone, someone grabbed her arm.

For a second, she felt relief—Silas was here, lurking inside the house as he'd done before. But it was Gary's face she took in when she turned around.

"I'm glad I stopped by here," he said. "Come on, we've got to get you out of here. If the winds shift, this place is toast."

"Let me go!" She jerked away from him, though she couldn't loose herself from his grip. "I don't want your help."

Frustration laced his features. "I understand why you don't trust me. I don't want to hurt you. I never wanted to hurt you or scare you. I've been going about this the wrong way, but it's the only way I know how." His hands tightened around her wrist. "I'm not sure if Ben's coming back. Last time I saw him he was giving Bertrice a ride home after her car broke down. But I'm not sure you should trust him anyway."

Something in her expression prompted him to go on. "Ben's playing games with you, Katie. Do you know why the folks in town don't like you? First of all, you're a snob. You never come into town much, you don't socialize. People don't think you deserve the doc, who's painted himself as a saint. You won't give him a baby, even though he wants one. You think the town fair is silly, which is why Ben had to force you to volunteer. And you have separate bedrooms now because you're in love with Silas."

She was shaking her head all through his speech. "That's not true. Well, except for the last part. But why would they think those things? How did they know about the separate bedrooms?"

Gary let go of her arm and took a step back. "Because that's what Ben's been telling them. He's been playing everyone against you."

She was shaking her head in disbelief even as the pieces fell together. Maybel's snide comment about giving him babies, the hostility she'd encountered lately, and their refusal of her help despite the poster begging for help still being in the window. Knowing the cross came from Silas. She didn't want to believe Gary. He was the enemy.

He glanced at his watch. "Katie, there's more. He's the one who wrecked this place. Having gone on a destructive rage before, I recognized the senselessness of the vandalism. Let me get you out of here."

She could barely get her mind around what he'd just told her, even though it rang with truth. "I have to wait for Silas."

"If the wind changes direction, or increases, that fire's going to sweep through here like the Tasmanian devil. You can't outrun it."

She moved farther away from him.

"Katie, trust me." Desperation intensified his features.

If he was the killer . . . "I can't."

"Yes you can. I could never hurt you." He moved closer. "I came back to Flatlands for you. Because I needed to connect with you." She backed up to the wall. "Because you're my sister. My half sister."

All the breath had left her lungs, and all she could do was stare dumbly at him. He gave her those few minutes to absorb his words. Her first instinct was to deny them just as she'd denied his words about Ben. Instead, she looked at him for the first time. Brown hair like hers. Brown, almond-shaped eyes like hers, wide-set like hers. And in those eyes the desperate need for her to believe. In those eyes, the truth.

"My father"—Gary looked away for a moment before continuing—"raped your mother. I saw it happen."

"No," she said, though once again the pieces clicked together: her mother's fear of men, her father's obscurity, and those warnings about staying away from Sam Savino. It also explained the eerie way he looked at her whenever she did run into him.

"I was just a little kid. I didn't even realize what I was seeing. Your mom used to clean for us. My mother always went to a friend's house to play bridge while your mom was cleaning. I usually had to go with her, but I wasn't feeling well so she let me stay in bed. I guess my father didn't know I was in the house. He came home for lunch and started talking to Ellie. I don't remember what he said. I was at the top of the stairs about to come down for a drink when I heard her crying. I thought he was just pushing her around, like he pushed everyone around. I figured that's the way it was. But he did other things, and I watched, too scared to come downstairs and too frozen to leave. I knew it was wrong, what he was doing. I couldn't believe he was doing it, so I buried it in my subconscious."

She could see the pain in his eyes as he remembered details she didn't want to hear.

"That was inside me when I saw you with that stray kitten. I didn't understand why I associated strays with you, or why it made me so angry. I didn't understand until years later—until I had to take a rage-management course. It came back to me then." He lowered his head. "I'm sorry for the pain I caused you. Maybe for the pain I'm causing you right now. But I feel a need to reconnect with my family again. My father's still a bastard, and my mother's a dishrag. That leaves you as my only real family."

He jerked her against him so fast, she didn't have time to respond. "Katie, forgive me for what I did all those years ago," he whispered. "Be my family."

Family. The word left her feeling warm and mushy in-

side, though she was still disoriented at being held so tenderly by Gary. Could she trust him? She'd trusted Ben all
these years, and he'd been sabotaging her. She sorted
through the facts she could get her mind around. The way
Ben had played intermediary between her and the Emersons. He'd told her they were only using her, that they
didn't really want her in their family. What had he told
them? And Bertrice! Maybe he'd been listening when she'd
told Katie about the belly ring.

Gary finally stepped back. "I know I've dumped a lot
on you. I've been trying to tell you this for weeks now."

Before Katie even had time to respond, a metal pipe
swung from around the corner and knocked Gary to the
floor. He groaned, and his arm twitched once, but he was
out. Ben stepped around the corner. She'd seen that cold
look on his face before, and it scared her no less now than
it had then.

"Did he hurt you?" he asked, not even looking down at
Gary. His gray eyes were locked on her.

"My God, what have you done?" She dropped down to
check Gary's pulse. It was there, though a tenuous pulse
of life. The cut on his head was welling up, and blood
seeped out to stain his hair.

Ben pulled her to her feet. "I thought you were afraid
of him. Now you're acting as if he's your best friend. Or
even your brother."

How much had he heard? Enough apparently. "He was
going to get me out of here. I thought you'd left."

His eyes glinted like a sharp-edged knife, but it was his
soft voice that sent a shiver of dread down her spine. Why
hadn't she seen this cold, unemotional core before? Only
when he'd poisoned The Boss, and before that, just
glimpses. "I wouldn't be much of a hero if I left my wife
to be ravaged by a fire, now would I?"

He smelled like smoke and sweat, and his hair and clothing were disheveled. Blood was splattered on his forearms.
He followed her gaze. "Gary's blood." He held out his
other hand to her. "Let's go, before the fire moves in."

She could only stare at that hand, also stained with blood. "That's not Gary's blood." Dread and fear coiled inside her. "Whose blood is it?"

He turned his hand as though admiring the pattern. "Silas's. Katie, he's a killer, just like I've been telling you. I caught him red-handed. He'd been keeping a woman hostage at an old barn on the south end of his property. She was handcuffed to a bed, arms and legs spread. Naked. Silas had the knife in his hands when I walked in on him." Ben's eyes were glassy as he put himself back in the scene. Agony and regret strained his voice when he said, "I tried to stop him, but he shoved me away. Before I could get to my feet, he'd sliced her from the butterfly tattoo on her shoulder down to her pelvis. I attacked him, we fought. He tried to kill me, too. But I won. You're safe now, Katie. No one will hurt you now." He focused in on her at last. "You believe that, don't you?"

No, no, no! Her brain was overloaded with information. *The tattoo. Bertrice had told her that Geraldine had a tattoo on her shoulder.* Her blood was rapidly crystallizing into ice. *Ben had seen the tattoo.*

"We need to get out of here, Katie."

"I'd better pack some things first." She held herself together and walked to their bedroom. The gun was still in the nightstand. She tried to keep her voice modulated and her pace easy. He followed her, but she blocked his view of the nightstand drawer when she pulled out the gun and tucked it into a canvas bag.

"Katie, you don't seem very upset about Silas being a killer."

She felt stiff and shaky, but she turned to Ben with a calm expression. "Is he dead?"

"That's all you care about, isn't it, that Silas is okay. What about me? What about Geraldine? You are one selfish girl, aren't you? But you always have been. You took and took and took from me, and never gave me what I wanted most: your love. Yet, you always wanted more than I could give you. Is that what you liked about Silas? Did he give you what *you* wanted most?"

She once thought she'd hated Gary, but it was nothing compared to the way she felt about the man she'd called her husband for nine years. A man she didn't know at all. She wasn't going to be intimidated anymore.

He moved closer. Her fingers tightened around the gun inside the bag. She searched his face and saw only disappointment.

"You love him, don't you, Katie? Why couldn't you love me like that?"

"Ben, please leave. I know you've got a lot of things to take care of, and you don't need to worry about me. You don't have to be my hero." She thought of Gary lying in the kitchen. She had to call for help. And she had to find Silas.

He took hold of her arms. "You're afraid of me, Katie. Why?" She wasn't sure if he was smiling or grimacing.

She held back all those words about his manipulation and sabotage and said in a calm voice, "I don't feel like I know you anymore."

He touched her face, bringing the blood into her line of vision. "Oh, but you do know me, Katie. You do know, don't you? I can see it in your eyes. Something gave it away. It might have worked if you weren't so in love with Silas that you wouldn't believe me about his killing a woman. I should have figured love would be blind. And you don't love me, never have, so you're not blind where I'm concerned."

It felt as though ashes coated her throat, filled her lungs and the arteries to her heart. Oh, God, what had he just admitted to? *Be calm, play along.* "I did . . . love you, Ben."

"I used to think that, but now I'm not so sure. But you're right: you never knew me. No one did. That was the best part."

Dread mounted with each word he spoke so casually. "It was you, wasn't it?" she asked.

"Ah, Katie girl, you used to be so quiet and meek, and

you believed everything I said. Then you started acting up, seeing Silas on the sly, wearing those ridiculous clothes . . . So you're asking me, straight-out, if I'm a killer? As a matter of fact, I am." He smiled as horror dawned on her face. "I love this part. It's even better than the sex."

Even though Ben held her hands, she still had the trigger in her grip. She couldn't have moved at that moment, though, as the truth seeped into her brain and chilled her through. "Why?" was all she could ask.

His smile was even more chilling than his answer: "Because I like it."

She knew that Silas was dead, knew that if Gary were still alive, he wouldn't be for long. And she knew she was dead, too.

"How could you live with me and do . . . that to those women?"

"If you mean the killing part, it's because I truly enjoy killing. It's my secret pleasure. Having power over someone's life is intoxicating. Even better when they beg for their lives and you let them believe, just for a while, that you're going to let them go. If you mean the sex part, it's the control that gets me off." He shook his head in exaggerated movements. "It killed me that the one woman I loved, I couldn't get excited with. When we married, I tried to go straight, I really did. But it's addicting. I tried fantasizing for a while to stay hard while we had sex, but even that stopped working. The injury was a stroke of luck, even though it put me out of commission for a while."

Her whole body was trembling in waves now. "Why didn't you kill me?"

"Those women weren't really women to me; they were objects. You were a woman, a person. My wife."

He'd been fantasizing about murder while having sex with her. It made her stomach ache with disgust. She forced out the words, "And the shoes?"

"To keep me going between my guilty pleasures. I love having something as innocuous as a shoe on the side of the road symbolize sex and violence."

Silas had been inside his head. It had been Ben's thoughts and desires that had haunted him. Ben's darkness hidden under the light he showed the world.

"Why did I start killing women, is that what you're wondering?" he asked, mistaking the expression on her face. "You're looking for that one incident, that one reason, aren't you? Makes it simple that way; easier to digest. Maybe it started with the rejection I experienced as a child, being dumped on the church steps, tied to the door. Or maybe that's *why* I was tied to the door. All I know is I never liked fluffy baby chicks—I wanted to kill them. I never wanted to kiss girls—I wanted to hurt them. But I learned early on that taking what I wanted, or hurting things I didn't like, wasn't acceptable. So I got sneaky about it."

She felt weak and ravaged inside. Outside, smoke drifted past the window like phantoms. "Did the real Ben Ferguson molest you?"

"That's when I knew I'd lost you, when you didn't buy my story hook, line, and sinker like you used to. No, he never touched me. I'd hit a dog with my bike, and he drove by and thought I was trying to save it. I went with him to the clinic and helped him. He taught me a lot about respecting animals. After that, I never hurt an animal intentionally."

"Except for Silas's dog. And the raccoon."

"I wanted to hurt Silas the way he'd hurt me. I didn't like killing his dog. Just like I didn't enjoy killing Ben. He was a nice man who gave me a second chance. And I tried to take it, I really did. Just like with you. But he caught me at a few lies, and he wouldn't tolerate it. He was real funny about that. I told him the kid who mowed the lawn was stealing the lawn equipment. I wanted to be the only kid in his world so he wouldn't be tempted to replace me. I don't think he believed me. I could feel it, that he was moving away from me. He didn't believe what I said." His face had transformed from the cold-steel expression to the scared kid. "I was going to lose my home and the only man who was ever like a father to me," he whispered.

"So you killed him before he could reject you."

He only nodded. "It was the first time I'd ever killed someone. It gave me no pleasure. It was a necessary killing." He blinked in surprise when she pulled the gun out of her bag.

"Take me to Silas. Now."

Once he was over the surprise, he took on a casual pose. "Katie, you're not going to shoot me."

She cocked the hammer. "I will." All those times Silas had warned her to be ready to shoot someone she knew . . . how right he'd been. She touched the gold cross he'd given her when he'd warned her about the killer: *It's someone you know.*

Ben moved forward to take the gun. She could do this. Squeeze the trigger, hit the wall behind him in warning. Instead, the gun merely clicked. Oh, God, she'd taken the bullets out. He grabbed the gun and tossed it on the bed.

"Katie, I loved you, I really did. You are the only person I ever loved besides the doc."

She realized something Gary had said. "Where's Bertrice? You gave her a ride this afternoon."

"And a good thing, too. That's how I spotted Silas's vehicle near the barn. Even though I leave no evidence behind, I couldn't take the chance that he would figure it out. You know, every time I'm around him, he gives me the creeps."

Because he's in your head, she wanted to say, but kept it to herself. She tried hard not to think about Silas. "Where's Bertrice?"

"The fire's moving in, and it's time to move on anyway." He surveyed her. "If I let you go, would you tell on me?"

"No one would believe me, not since you've turned everyone against me," she said, angry that he was giving her hope.

He smiled at her. "All because I loved you, Katie. You can't blame a man for wanting his wife to himself."

"As a matter of fact, I can."

"Everything I've done, I've done for you. Except the killings. Those were just for me. I'm taking the van and heading on down the road." He tenderly touched her face, but she flinched away from him. "As I was saying, not that anyone will believe you, but you have a choice. See, I'm giving you that choice you say you never had, because I'm such a nice guy." He waited for her to negate that, but she wasn't fool enough to incite him. "You could get to town and try to convince someone that I'm the terrible bogeyman. They might track me down, they might not. Or you could go to the barn and try to save Silas."

She sucked in a gasp of air. "He's alive?"

"If he hasn't bled to death." He chuckled softly. "But he's not going anywhere fast. And the fire's moving in from that direction. So, that's your choice: Try to stop a killer or save your boyfriend." He pinched her chin hard. "How selfish are you going to be, Katie girl?"

She was frozen as he casually walked to the door. He turned around, looked at her. "I would never hurt you. You believe me, don't you?"

He *had* hurt her, and no, she didn't believe him. She wanted to play along with him, nod her head. But she couldn't move. He was pleased by her response—or lack of it—anyway. He smiled and walked out the door.

She ran to the dresser drawer to find the bullets she'd removed. They weren't there. She would have shot him, she was sure of it. Because she remembered something from Silas's books: Serial killers don't stop killing unless they're caught or they die.

She ran to the front room in time to see Ben pulling out of the driveway in their van. She ran back to the kitchen and checked on Gary. He was alive, but still unconscious. She grabbed for the phone, but somehow expected only silence. He'd probably cut the lines when he'd returned. Ben wasn't a fool. Which meant . . .

She ran outside to find Gary's Explorer. Gary had parked on the side of the house so she wouldn't see it when she returned from Silas's. The hood was up, and inside, wires were dangling loose. The radio was smashed. She tried to start the vehicle anyway, but knew it wouldn't start.

She glanced down the driveway. Ben was right; she might be able to run to town and find someone to alert, but they'd never believe her. Tate and Harold had virtually ignored her earlier. She glanced behind the house, where smoke drifted through the woods. Silas was there; she was pretty sure she could remember how to reach the barn, though it could take more than an hour to get there. She probably had only a couple more hours of daylight left.

Ben could be lying about him being alive. It was a possibility she couldn't ignore.

She already knew she'd have to take that chance.

CHAPTER 22

THE SMOKE WAS disorienting, but Katie managed to find the barn. She heard sirens in the distance and the whir of a helicopter over the trees' canopy. Help was right there, and yet so far away.

And Ben, where was he? Long gone or waiting somewhere for her? Playing his games?

Her heart hurt from fear, and her chest hurt from breathing smoke. She had prayed the entire way, and now she'd find out if those prayers had paid off. The door was padlocked. She called Silas's name, hoping he was well enough to respond. No answer. She walked around the barn, telling herself she was looking for other ways inside and not for Ben. When she came around to the door again, she noticed it was only repositioned to look as though it were still intact. It had already been broken in.

She shoved the door open and peered into the gloominess. The first thing she saw once her eyes adjusted was the bed Ben had mentioned. Silas wasn't lying on it cuffed to the railing. She searched the back corners of the barn, and then turned toward the front portion. What she saw shattered her heart . . . and caved in her insides.

Silas was nailed to the wall.

A guttural sound escaped her mouth. She fought the urge to turn away. There was a spike driven through the palm of each hand, just like Jesus Christ's crucifixion. Blood oozed from a gash on the side of his head, another eerie resemblance. He was lying on the floor, his head leaning against the wall. She rushed forward and dropped to her knees at his side.

"Silas, please don't be dead. You can't die yet, we've got too much unfinished business between us." His pulse was a lot thinner than Gary's had been. Ben had probably hit Silas with the pipe, too, and then nailed him to the wall after he was unconscious. Thank God for that last part anyway.

After a desperate search, she found an old hunting knife tucked beneath the springs on the bed frame. "Oh, God, oh, God," she said, standing in front of him contemplating her next task. There wasn't time to be squeamish or gentle about it, though. She knelt before him and pried the stake out of one hand, then the other. Blood had dripped down his arms. Having them nailed at head level may have saved him from bleeding to death. She kept talking through the whole ordeal. She took off her white blouse and ripped the sleeves off with help from the dull edge of the knife. She wrapped each hand in one sleeve and put her blouse back on.

"Silas, hang in there. You were right, so right, and I was such an idiot. With all your charts, you must have figured out where he put the women he'd taken. I know everything now. I was married to a killer. And now I'm letting him get away, but I had no choice."

Her voice got louder and louder as she worked, and when he finally slumped over, she sounded nearly hysterical. There wasn't time for hysterics, though. She gently tapped his face and called his name.

Slowly his eyes opened, though they weren't focused at all. His pupils were dilated. No way was she getting him to walk back to her house. Wait! His vehicle had to be there somewhere. Unless Ben sabotaged it as he had Gary's Explorer.

"You think about coming around while I find your car. I'll be right back."

She stopped at the door. What if Ben was waiting until she left Silas for a minute? He liked letting them think he was going to let them go. She couldn't forget that, not ever.

She turned back and found him out cold again. "Silas!

No time to sleep now! Dammit, come back to me!" She kissed his slack lips hard. "We've got to go, and no way can I carry you out of here."

She waited some of the longest moments in her life until his eyes slowly opened again. They still weren't focused. He started to lift his hands to see them, but she held his wrists down. Blood seeped through the white cotton bandages. "It's not pretty, believe me. Keep your hands pressed together. We've got to get you and Gary to a hospital. Silas, please get up. I need you, more than I've ever needed you. Help me get you out of here."

He was sitting up against the wall where he'd been nailed. She wrapped her arms around him and tried to stand up. He put his hands on her back, but jerked away in pain.

"Let me try this without your help," she said, then grunted with exertion. He braced his shoulder against the wall and shakily got to his feet. She kept her arms around him for a moment, relishing the feel of him alive and warm next to her. But a moment was all she could afford. "Let's go," she said and guided him toward the door.

The smoke rolled through the trees now, obliterating the forest in the distance. She swore she could hear the crackle of flames, though she couldn't see any through the smoke. He coughed with the first inhalation of smoke. Her lungs were almost used to the burning feeling, but each breath she took was getting shallower, more painful. His balance was off, too, making them sway as they headed toward the red gate. It was closed, and just beyond it sat the Navigator.

When they reached the car, she helped him lean his forearms against the hood and yanked open the door. Only it didn't open because it was locked. At least the hood was still closed and the tires were intact. Ben hadn't bothered to tamper with the car because he hadn't expected Silas to get out of that barn. The thought shivered through her as sinister as the smoke around her.

"Stay here for a second. I'll be right back."

She could barely see the woods on the other side of the road for the smoke. She ventured to the highway to see if

another car was anywhere nearby to help her. She doubted
the road was even open with the smoke cutting down the
visibility. Returning to Silas, she hoped against hope the
keys were somewhere in his pockets. Finding them sent a
rush of relief through her. She helped him into the passenger seat and reclined it before closing him in. He looked
the color of concrete.

She started the car and backed out onto the highway. At
least they were heading away from the fires as they returned
to her house. No sign of Ben there, either. She told Silas
to stay put and ran inside to get Gary. He was groggily
trying to get to his feet.

"What happened?" he asked in a slurred voice, rubbing
the back of his head. His fingers came away sticky with
blood.

"Ben hit you with a pipe. Come on, I've got to get you
and Silas to the hospital."

"Ben? Silas?" he said, letting her lead him to the Navigator.

"It's a long story."

She helped Gary into the back seat and headed toward
Gray, the nearest major hospital. Silas was looking at her
in a glassy kind of way as she drove. She reached over and
touched his arm before returning to the task of driving like
hell.

Katie had, of course, been questioned when she brought in
two victims with concussions and the injuries Silas had
sustained. Sheriff Tate had been contacted and had asked
that Katie remain at the hospital until he could break free
and find out what—his words—in tarnation was going on.
She'd tried to tell the Gray police officer about Ben, but
whatever Tate had told him had the man giving her ques-
tionable looks.

The adrenaline had long since drained away to leave her
as limp as wet toilet paper by the time she had been looked
at. All she wanted to do was collapse in the waiting area.
Instead, she hauled herself to the pay phone and called Ber-

trice. Katie's first prayer was that Bertrice was there, safe and sound. The next prayer was that her mother wouldn't answer.

It rang several times, long enough for Katie to think about whether she wanted to leave a message if a machine answered. Finally, it was Bertrice's breathless voice that said, "Hello?"

Katie slumped against the phone booth partition. "Thank God you're okay!" Tears of relief slipped into her voice. "I'd heard that Ben gave you a ride home, and Ben's a— I don't want to get into that right now. I just wanted to make sure you were all right."

"Katie, is that you?"

"Yes, it's me. I know you don't like me—"

"Katie, I like you. I was just pissed about you telling Mom about my belly-button ring. I'm sorry I got so mad and quit."

"I didn't tell your mom about that ring; Ben did. Ask your mom. He probably told her I asked him to call, but I never even mentioned it to him. He must have overheard us. Anyway, that's not why I'm calling. I wanted to make sure you were all right."

"I'm fine. We're getting the house ready in case the fires move in. Did you hear, they're tracking a big storm system that's heading this way. They're holding off on the evacuations for now. Do you and Ben need help getting your place ready, just in case? We're almost done here."

"Don't go near Ben! No matter what, if you see him, don't go near him." Katie couldn't keep the fear from her voice.

"Katie, you're scaring me. I mean, Ben was acting weird. He was taking me home, right, and he saw Silas's truck parked on the side of the road and he went, like, nuts. He got stopped at the intersection because of the fire, and he told me to get out of the car, that the cops would get me home. Then he took off."

"All you need to know right now is he can't be trusted."

"Oh, my God, Katie, you're calling from the hospital in Gray. What's going on? Are you all right?"

She must have caller ID. "Silas and Gary are both here. I think they'll be all right, though Silas was hurt pretty bad. I"—she turned to the orderly who had just called her name—"I gotta go. I'll talk to you later."

They let her in to see Silas. He was still in the emergency area. Her knees went weak at the sight of him lying in bed. A gauze bandage was wrapped around his head, and his hands were bandaged. But his eyes were a little more focused now and they followed her into the room.

"You all right?" he asked in a slightly slurred voice.

"You've got to be kidding. You're the one in the emergency room and you're asking me if I'm all right?" She leaned against the side of the bed and pushed back a strand of his hair. "Can't you tell I'm all right now?"

He shook his head, then closed his eyes. "Still dizzy when I do that." He opened his eyes again. "I can't feel anything. It's gone. Maybe the blow to my head dislodged something. Tell me what happened. I was in that barn and everything went dark. I vaguely remember you getting me out of there."

He looked even paler after she was finished telling him everything. "I should have figured it out before it was too late," he said.

"You were doing everything you could."

"You were living with a serial killer, for God's sake! You could have been killed."

"Not while we were living together. Those women were only objects to him. He saw me as a person."

He closed his eyes for a few minutes. Just when she thought he was asleep, he mumbled, "You let him get away."

"What did you say?"

His voice was so faint, she had to lean closer to hear him. "You should have left me and called someone to catch him. Now he'll keep killing. And if I can't feel him anymore, I won't be able to find him again."

Her fingers tightened on the edge of the bed. "If you'll recall, I let him go to save your life. You're saying that was wrong?"

He lifted his hand toward her, but let it drop on the bed. "I'm just one life. He's going to keep killing . . . innocent women . . . no way to stop him now."

"Ben said I was selfish. Maybe I am. Maybe I saved you because I love you. Because I had some insane idea that I could get you to accept that love. But I see that's impossible." The tears she'd been holding back all this time started filling her eyes, and she swiped them away. "You can't even accept the gift of your life! How could you ever accept love?"

"Katie," he said in a slurred voice, lifting his bandaged hand again.

She stood. "No, don't say anything. Let me talk. If you want to live your life in the shadows, I can't stop you. But I'm not going to let you be my protector or my caretaker unless you learn to accept protection and care-taking, too. It's a two-way street. You can't keep being some guardian angel from a distance. I've given years of my life to a man I don't think I ever really loved, because I felt I owed him. You have my heart, maybe you always have, and I want to give it to you. I can't be in a one-sided relationship anymore. I want it all. I've tasted what's been missing my whole life: passion, real love, emotion. That's your fault, fella. I expect nothing less from you. If you can't give me that, and accept it from me, then you're going to Atlanta without me."

She could see the pain in his eyes, but she had to stay strong.

"Katie, I . . . I've been doing it from a distance so long, I don't know how to do it up close."

"Do what?" She wanted to hear the words.

He met her eyes for a moment. *Say it, dammit.*

"Love you," he said finally in a pained voice. "I'm not sure I can be the person you need me to be. That doesn't mean I don't want you in my life."

"You can't have it both ways anymore, Silas." She glanced down at the bandaged hand that rested next to hers. "I'm sorry to lay this on you right now. Almost losing you made me evaluate a lot of things. I've been a fool for a long time. I'm taking charge of my life. I have to, for my own sanity. I'm going to find Ben. Unfortunately, I'll have to use your car since I don't have one. Another mark on the fool chart for me." She started to take a step away.

"Katie, wait."

"What?"

"Don't go looking for him without me. He'll kill you this time." He started to get up, but she put her hand on his chest. It didn't take much to get him to lie back again.

"You're not going anywhere for at least two days according to your doctor. And all I'm going to do is find out where he is and contact the authorities. Not Tate, but someone who isn't ensnared in Ben's web of deceit. I have your beeper number. I'll let you know where I am."

And with that, she left. She heard him call her back, but she ignored it. If she'd thought for a second he was calling her to say he would try to accept her love, she'd run back. But all he wanted to do was change her mind about finding Ben on her own. Silas was right; Ben would kill her. But he had to catch her first.

She nearly collided with a nurse. "Oh, sorry about that!" the nurse said. Nodding toward Silas's curtained booth where he was still calling for her, she asked, "Are you with Mr. Koole?"

"In more ways than I'd like. Why?"

She lifted her eyebrows in question, but thankfully didn't ask what she'd meant. "I have his things, wallet and the like, that we found in his pockets. Would you like to keep them for him?"

She took the plastic bag. "I'll keep them safe." She removed the beeper from the bag. "But please see that he gets this."

She'd briefly seen Gary earlier, though he was pretty groggy. He was sleeping now, so she left him a note about getting in touch later. She'd have to sort out how she felt about that whole situation later.

And Silas, too, she thought, as she glanced up at the hospital on her way out. But first, she was going to find the man who'd stolen her life, and a lot of other lives, too.

Katie didn't get far as she neared Flatlands. The authorities had set up roadblocks and were sending people back. Barricades and police lights flashed into the sooty night air.

The officer leaned toward her open window as she pulled up to the barricades. "Ma'am, if you're going to Macon, you'll have to turn back to Gray, go southeast on Highway Eleven and take Forty-nine down."

She had planned to return to the house to get her suitcase, but the mention of Macon shivered down her spine. Why?

"Ma'am, you all right?"

She blinked. "Yes, I'm fine. Macon. Thank you."

She turned around and headed back toward Gray. Had Ben mentioned Macon recently? The town was stuck in her subconscious like a well-aimed dart. Macon. She paged back through the last few days of her memory, of the times when she hadn't known the terrible truth about her husband. But she didn't have to go that far—only as far as that morning. Mrs. Turner had spoken about her brother in Macon, the veterinarian who was dying of cancer.

And wouldn't Ben need a new identity? He couldn't chance using his current name and qualifications in case Katie did convince someone of the truth. She tried to remember what Mrs. Turner's brother's name was. It was Scottish . . . and started with a B. She had plenty of time to remember before she'd reach Macon.

It was late by the time Katie reached Macon, and even later by the time she found a hotel with a vacancy. She'd had to get on the Interstate and go up four exits before finding a hotel that wasn't booked for Macon's annual festival. She was almost positive she was going to cry if this clerk said they were booked for the night.

She nearly cried anyway when he said they had two rooms left. She obviously looked like hell from the expression on his face.

"Lot of people coming over from your way 'cause of the fires," the young man said. "Hope they get it under control soon. Hope those storms brewing over the area let some of that rain loose. They've already lost six thousand acres and fourteen homes. Must be tough going."

"You don't know the half of it," she said in a smoke-ravaged voice, signing the credit card receipt. She was glad the clerk hadn't noticed that she looked nothing like a Silas Koole, the name on the credit card.

One look in her room's mirror validated the clerk's impression of her. Forget the frazzled hair, bloodshot eyes, and smoky smell that permeated her—she also wore some of Silas's blood on her modified shirt.

The thought of that blood, and of him, made her drop down on the side of the bed. *Don't think about him now. Stay focused.*

She had her purse, but hadn't thought to get her small suitcase when she'd helped Gary out to the car. The thought of her house burning didn't bother her in the least, other than what would happen to her squirrel and bird friends. But the thought of losing those few pictures of her mother broke her heart.

She stretched across the bed and pulled out the phone book from the nightstand drawer. The name hadn't come to her during the drive, but she was sure it would ring a bell in the phone book. Her finger traveled down the list of veterinarians, and didn't have far to go when it stopped on Dr. Ken Buchanan.

Though her pulse raced, her body absolutely would not budge now that it was in a prone position. Several nights of bad sleep, combined with the horrors of the day, were too much.

Okay, she'd take a shower and eat before heading out.

She was going to have to get a change of clothes, too. Maybe she could find an all-night discount store. She'd do that right after she ate, right after she took a shower, right after she closed her eyes for just a few minutes . . .

She jerked awake the next morning and felt panic settle into her belly along with acute hunger. The first thing she did, after using the bathroom, was call the Buchanan Veterinarian Clinic. When the receptionist picked up, Katie asked, "Is Dr. Buchanan in?"

"No, afraid not. He's not workin' much these days. Dr. Kane's takin' his patients," she said in a thick, Southern voice. "We're actually closed on account of the festival and all, but I'm in for a couple of hours doing some billing. Is this an emergency?"

"Yes, but not the animal kind. I'm looking for Dr. Buchanan particularly. Do you know if his sister is here with him?"

"Oh, you mean Mrs. Turner? She's a sweet lady, ain't she?"

"Yes, she is. I'm a friend of hers, and I'm . . . watching her cat, Tubby. Fuzzy, I mean. I've got some bad news for her, and it's something I should tell her in person."

"Oh, dear," the girl said in a genuinely sad voice. "I thought she brought Fuzzy with her. Especially with the fires out thatta way and all."

"Fuzzy wasn't feeling well, so she asked me to take care of her. You know how she is about her cat."

"Oh, my, I sure do. Well, I ain't seen her this trip, but I know she usually comes over for the festival."

"Can you give me Dr. Buchanan's home number and address? She left it with me, but in the all the confusion, I've misplaced it."

The girl recited the information. "But they probably won't be there. They'll be at the festival, I'm sure. Everybody'll be there, includin' me in about thirty minutes."

"I'll look for them there, too. Thanks."

The girl was right; no one answered at home. Katie took a shower, then headed to the nearest department store and bought a new outfit, sunglasses, and a sunflower-adorned straw hat from the sale rack with her cache of change. All she had to do was make sure Ben was there, and then find a police officer to tell her story to. He could at least be detained for assault. With all of Silas's notes in the back of the Navigator, they'd probably be interested in checking further into the case—and hopefully detaining Ben until they had some kind of evidence.

Evidence. There would be no evidence, not unless she could prove that Ben was in the area when each abduction occurred. The jewelry and clothing might not be of help if he hadn't left any evidence. She glanced at the pay phone outside the department store. She should let Silas know where she was and what she was doing anyway.

She dialed his beeper number and left a voice message. "Hi, it's Katie. I'm in Macon. I think Ben is here trying to get another identity with a Dr. Ken Buchanan. They're probably at the big festival that's going on this weekend. Don't worry, I'm just going to find him and alert the police. And try to convince them he's a killer. Hah, that'll be easy. Anyway, I know you're kind of tied up, and I don't know what's going on with the fires, but I need your help. I need you to get the computer out of the hospital so we can compare those dates to when Ben was out of town. It's just inside the door. It's not locked, though I'm sure you can get in anyway. If you could get my suitcase out of my house—it's by the front door, too—I'd appreciate it. I'll check back with you in a while and see how you're doing. Right now, I need to find Ben. Oh, and I'm sorry, but I had to use your credit card for my hotel last night. Okay, bye."

Just leaving him a message ripped her heart apart. What a damn fool she was about men. Well, she was going to rectify one of those mistakes. She got back into the Navigator and headed to the address the girl had given her. The big white van was nowhere in sight. Mrs. Turner's sedan was there, however. Had Ben ridden over with her? He'd probably want to ditch his van, if he thought there was a chance of the police were looking for him. He hadn't gotten away with murder all these years by being careless.

The curtain in the front window of the small house shifted slightly. She watched it for a few minutes, but saw no sign of a face peering out. Could be Fuzzy, she supposed.

Speaking of easy-to-spot vehicles . . . Silas's beast of a car wasn't likely to blend in, either. She headed over to where the festival was being held. The streets were closed off and parking areas had been created for the event. The place was already busy. She found a spot at the far end of a row and turned off the engine. When she reached for her new sunglasses, her fingers brushed the plastic bag the nurse had given her.

Katie had been so tired when she'd finally found a hotel and realized she'd need money for the room, she'd only taken out the wallet. Now she picked up the bag and remembered how scared she'd been that she was going to lose him.

"You never had him, not really. He only had you."

She crushed the empty bag in her hands—no, not empty. She'd almost missed it. At the bottom of the bag was . . . the crystal she'd given him. Her heart stopped beating for a moment. He'd had it on him, maybe in his pocket. He'd been carrying that crystal, the gift she'd given him and that he'd taken. Did it mean there was hope?

She couldn't let herself think about it. The flow of people into the festival area was picking up. A scan of the immediate area showed no sign of Ben. She was on her guard nonetheless as she stepped out of the vehicle. She tucked the crystal into the pocket of her white shorts and headed toward the entrance. Admission was two bucks, a donation to those who had suffered from the fires. She spent her remaining money on orange juice and a breakfast sandwich.

A Dixie band was jamming in the far right corner. Even at ten in the morning, kids were already running around with cotton candy and ice-cream cones. It reminded her of a larger, more sophisticated version of Flatland's fair.

She reminded herself to put on her sunglasses, at least some disguise. She wasn't used to wearing them. All she had to do was cruise around the festival until she spotted Ben. If he was trying to finagle Dr. Buchanan's identity, he was no doubt using all that phony charm on both him and his sister. If he wasn't there, she'd stake out the house.

It was already warm by eleven-thirty. An up-and-coming country band was now commanding the main stage. When she spotted Mrs. Turner at last, her heart went into triple time. The man walking at her side looked pale and fragile, though he laughed at something his sister said. Ben wasn't with them.

She watched them for twenty minutes, waiting for Ben to join them. Though Mrs. Turner occasionally glanced around as though looking for someone, Ben never showed. Back to the car, then, to cruise by the doctor's house. Maybe she'd been wrong about this. Maybe Ben was long gone in some other direction.

The door handle on the Navigator was burning hot, and she pulled back her hand with a hiss. When she reached for it again, a hand came from behind her and covered hers. Before she could even take that in, an arm went around her and covered her mouth, and a voice whispered in her ear, "You're smarter than I gave you credit for. But it ends here, Katie girl."

Silas checked himself out of the hospital—against doctor's orders—as soon as he got Katie's message. He would have done it last night, but when he'd tried to get up, he'd passed out. He was still dizzy, still had a hundred pile drivers inside his head, but nothing was stopping him now. He narrowly missed Gary who looked as though he'd been heading toward Silas's room. He'd been dressed in a hospital gown.

Bertrice was waiting by the doors, fidgeting. "Are you sure you should be out of the hospital yet?" she asked when he joined her.

"I don't have a choice. Thanks for coming."

"If my mom found out . . ." She shook her head, but her expression grew dark. "Silas, I still can't believe what you told me . . . about Ben."

He couldn't believe she'd come to the hospital to see him that morning. After getting Katie's message, he'd asked her to stick around. "It's hard to believe that someone you think is nice is really evil inside. It's easier to think someone like me is a murderer."

And he had thought that once. He felt relief, even though deep inside he'd known he couldn't kill anyone. But the connection was too eerie. And now the connection seemed gone, both with Ben and with Katie. With everyone. He wasn't sure if the concussion had knocked something loose or if, because of the painkillers, his empathic feelings were subdued. For the first time in his life, his brain was free of other people's feelings.

That left his own feelings banging around inside him. They were more unsettling than anything he'd ever felt.

"Do you know where I can get a car? I'd rent one, but I don't have my wallet." He followed her to an old truck.

"My brother's working on my car now, getting it ready for the big exodus if they can't keep holding the fires at bay. This is his truck." She looked at him. "Katie's in trouble, isn't she?"

"More than she knows, probably. I need to get to Macon right away."

"Ben killed Geraldine and Dana, didn't he?" Her voice sounded tight, but that was the only indication Silas had as to her inner feelings.

"Yes."

"Take the truck. Do whatever you have to do to catch him. And to keep Katie safe. Drop me off at home. I'll get a ride to the hospital and get that computer for you."

"Thanks," he said.

Bertrice's lower lip trembled. "Kill the bastard, okay? Do it for Geraldine and Dana."

Killing Ben would be harder without his gun. Ben had probably taken it after conking Silas on the head. He'd been coaching Katie to shoot someone if it came down to it; now he had to think about the possibility of taking a life, too. If Ben hurt her . . . Silas didn't want to think about it.

The sky behind him was a dark mass of storm clouds. The truck rattled and shook as he neared eighty. He couldn't afford to go too fast, not while driving someone else's truck and without his driver's license. Going the speed limit wasn't an option, either. Gripping the wheel was a painful proposition, though, even with the bulky bandages. He eyed the bottle of painkillers on the seat, but he didn't want to waste time opening the bottle.

He still hadn't tuned into Katie's feelings. That may or may not be a good thing. All his life he'd viewed his empathy with mixed feelings. Mostly they ran to disdain. Celine had convinced him that his was a gift from God, given to him for a reason he would understand someday. Then she'd been taken, and his gift hadn't helped one bit. When he'd started seeing through the killer's eyes—through Ben's eyes—he'd once again been grateful for this gift. He thought it would save Katie's life, at least, even if she hated that he could see into her soul. Now his wish had come true, and his "gift" had disappeared when he needed it the most.

He started to tighten his fingers on the wheel as another realization hit him. The action and realization both hurt as much. Katie's love had been the same kind of gift, given to him even though he'd never asked for it. He'd rejected that gift, too. Celine had offered him her love, too, but he'd turned her down. Then he'd lost her forever.

Katie's love was even more precious. He patted his shirt pocket—no crystal. No talisman against the darkness that lived inside him. But he didn't need a crystal. He'd known that all along. He needed Katie to keep away the shadows, to pull him into the light.

And now that he was willing to try to accept the gift she'd offered him, he might lose her forever, too.

The needle bobbed just over ninety miles per hour. Macon was thirty minutes away.

CHAPTER 23

"I'M PROUD OF you. You made the selfish decision in trying to save Silas. It's nice to see some human faults in you.
For the longest time, I thought you were perfect. Everyone
has evil inside them, but I couldn't find any in you. But all
you needed was a little temptation, and you slid right down
into the gully."

Katie's terror mounted with each passing minute. Ben
drove them in Silas's car to the outskirts of Macon. It was
a rural area, like the stretches between Flatlands and the
other towns. She was handcuffed to what people called the
Jesus strap. If anyone needed Jesus just then, it was she.
She leaned her cheek against the tethered wrist and closed
her eyes. Her prayer had worked last time—Silas had been
alive. Now she was being selfish and praying for herself.

Ben hadn't looked at her since they'd headed out of
Macon. He'd checked on her peripherally, but he hadn't
met her eyes once. "Did you tell Silas where you were
going?"

She wanted to say yes, that he was probably on his way
now. But that wasn't going to save her now. The only thing
that would do was guarantee that Ben would speed things
up. "He's in the hospital," she said in a dull tone. "He was
unconscious when I left him."

The only thing that could save her, if Silas was indeed
heading to Macon, was that spooky empathy. His words
about not having the feelings dampened that hope.

He smiled when he saw a road leading off to the left.
He turned onto it. In the distance, an old farmhouse sat
surrounded by abandoned fields. The fence was broken in

places and overgrown with weeds. The road leading to the house was gutted out in spots. The cuffs bit into her wrist every time they hit a pothole. She hated Ben driving Silas's car, though she thought it was odd that of all things that should bother her.

He drove through one of the broken spots in the fence and pulled up to the house. The front porch was nearly collapsed; glittery eyes peered out from the darkness beneath it.

"Home sweet home," he said in a chipper voice. He held the gun against her side as he unlocked the cuffs. He clamped the other cuff around his wrist.

"Ben, what are you going to do with me?"

"Don't call me that." His voice had changed to a clipped one on those words. He pulled out the large duffel bag he'd taken from his van. She heard metal chinking inside and shivered.

"You want me to call you Larry now?"

"I don't want you to call me anything."

He was depersonalizing her, making her an object. He jerked her out from his side of the vehicle and pulled her toward the house.

"You can't kill me," she said, hating the desperation in her voice. "You said you couldn't because I'm your wife."

"You're not legally my wife, as you pointed out," he said, testing the first tilted step before stepping onto it. She was forced to follow each tenuous step. "I don't know you anymore. Your hair . . ." He tugged on a hank of her hair. "Those clothes . . . you're just like the rest of them."

"I'm not, Ben. I'm that little girl you wanted to possess. You've seen me grow up, you've seen me every day for years. I gave you foot rubs."

The windows were broken out. The wooden door was warped, but he managed to shove it open. Dust and cobwebs covered everything. Critters scurried across the floors as a shaft of daylight shot across the old floorboards. They were thrust back into the dimness when he pushed the door closed again. A disintegrated wicker chair sat in the middle of the room, the only piece of furniture left. Something, or many somethings, had been eating away at the wicker strands and gnawing on the wood. The cabinets in the kitchen were left open, two of them on the verge of detaching from the ceiling.

He was looking around fondly, remembering another time, another woman. Another victim. "I used this place years ago. I was afraid the sleeping pills I slipped you would wear off by the time I got home, so I had to find someplace closer. The barn worked out wonderfully."

No wonder she'd been groggy sometimes in the morning. "Are you going to kill Dr. Buchanan like you killed Ben Ferguson?"

He pulled her down a dark hallway. "No, I just want his documentation. Mrs. Turner was kind enough to let me stay with her and Ken. I pretended to be sick this morning, so I could look for his birth certificate, diplomas. I was supposed to meet them at the fair later. Luckily I saw you drive by. One last loose end to tie up, and then I'll find another place to settle into."

"And you'll kill more women."

He smiled, though he still hadn't looked at her. "It's what I do."

The back room wasn't as dusty as the rest of the house, though he obviously hadn't used it in a few years. There was no bed, only a naked frame that had no head rail like the one in the barn. Fear was now pulsing through her as she thought of those other women and her own fate. Especially when she saw the rusty steel rings secured to ceiling rafters exposed by the rotting wood. She involuntarily jerked away, but couldn't go far.

"Ben, please don't do this. It's me, Katie. You can't just pretend you don't know me."

He tugged on the rings, testing them. Not even looking her way in response.

Silas, if you're there, if you're with me at all, please, please come. She had to believe he would at least look for her, even though she'd left him the way she had. But if he couldn't feel her anymore, all he'd have to go on was the festival. She and his car would be gone. He'd never think of coming way out there. And, she realized with hope dimming, he had no transportation or way to get a car.

Ben pulled the bed frame beneath the rings, dragging her along with him.

She was keeping her eye on the gun he'd set on the windowsill. "Ben, do you hate women?"

"Ben's dead."

"Do you hate women?"

"There you go, trying to psychoanalyze me again. No, I don't hate women. I love women. They're wonderful and soft and their bodies can do such marvelous things."

She was sorry she asked, especially from the awed expression on his face. More sorry for the images that crowded into her mind. Silas had experienced Ben's heinous crimes through the victims' eyes. Would he experience her own? She looked deep inside her, but couldn't feel him.

Oh, God, I'm on my own.

Ben had set the duffel bag on the floor nearby. He unzipped it and pulled out two more sets of handcuffs. She'd tried to remain calm, looking for an opportunity to escape. That calm was eroding away. He would put the other cuff around her wrist and hang her from those rings. What else did he have in his bag of tricks? She realized she'd seen that bag in the back of the van a few times. Not once had she thought to open it.

But Ben surprised her. He clamped the cuffs around her ankle. She jerked out of his grasp when he grabbed the second pair.

"No! You can't do this!"

He was far more experienced at securing women than she was in escaping a madman. He simply pulled her off balance. She landed on the floor with a hard thud. Her hip took the brunt of the fall, and it was no comfort to know that pain would be the least of what she'd go through. She still fought him, kicking and trying to pull her knee up into his groin. He pinned her down so she was immobilized, then clamped a cuff on her other ankle.

She put up a fight again when he stepped onto the bed frame. They both crashed to the floor. This time he took the brunt of the fall. She was still cuffed to him by her wrist, but the gun was within reach. As her free hand neared the handle, something hard slammed into her head.

Everything came and went for a few seconds. She couldn't think straight, couldn't think past the stark fear. He tossed the black bag back to the floor. He'd hit her with it. She felt him unlock the cuff that linked them. As she tried to collect her senses, he hoisted her over his shoulder and stepped onto the frame again. *Get it together, girl. Once you're hanging, it's all over!*

He grabbed her ankle and raised it toward the ceiling. Metal clanked against metal. She summoned her strength and bit him in the side. He jerked back, and just as she was about to push him away, he grabbed her other ankle. She tried to twist around, but she heard the metal cuff hitting the ring on the ceiling. He moved out of her reach—and left her hanging from the rafters by her cuffed ankles.

He was rubbing his side, looking not at her but at the rings. She thrashed her arms around, but he stood just out of her reach. The metal bit into her bare ankles. When he pushed the bed frame away, what she saw stopped her tears—two more rings with chains attached to the floor. To secure her wrists with. The blood rushing to her head made her eyes feel like they were bulging out.

"Don't worry, it'll be over before your brain explodes," he said in a flat voice. "The last girl I brought here lasted for about a day. Her mind went first, though there wasn't much left of her anyway. I could have brought some drain opener and let you die the same way your mother died. You were so afraid of poisons since your last birthday, thinking you'd go like she did. As it turns out, you are, sort of."

He may as well have slammed her with the bag again.

"You killed her?" she asked in a hoarse voice. "My God, why?"

"I wanted you," he said so simply, it almost made sense. At least to her blood-gutted brain. "She didn't want you anywhere near me. Necessary killing."

He waited for her reaction with relish. She wouldn't give him the satisfaction. She turned her anger and shock inward. It wasn't fair what Ellie had gone through in her young life. Being raped by a respected man in town, being poor, and then being murdered in a horrible way.

Ellie had kept her anyway. No matter that she was a product of rape, Katie had known pure, motherly love. Though Ben could take her life, he couldn't take that away from her.

That was *if* she let him take her life. She swung toward the window, though she was nowhere near the gun. He saw what she was trying to do and stuffed the gun in the back waistband of his pants. He stood just out of reach of her clawing hands. "I can see that I'm not going to enjoy this," he said in a rather disappointed tone.

Enjoy it? He was sick, and again it stunned her that she'd been married to him all these years and never saw it.

"Then just kill me," she said, trying to sound as strong as she could. "I'd hate to be unenjoyable." She was out of luck and out of chances. She felt the edges of the cross against the bottom of her chin.

"I'll have to think of Silas. His reaction when he finds you here a few weeks from now." That thought seemed to up his enjoyment factor. "I'll make sure to let him know where you are."

Oh, geez, don't think about it. But the grotesque image sprang forth, making her close her eyes at the churning of her stomach. The gnawed chair, the glittery eyes, all hungry, all waiting. When she opened her eyes, Ben was watching her.

"You're not mad at me for killing your mama? Or are you so perfect and wonderful that you forgive me? You seemed to forgive Gary for hurting your cat."

She remembered Silas saying the killer wondered if she'd forgive him if she knew. "You don't deserve forgiveness, now or ever. You'll go to hell without my forgiveness."

"But you'll get there first."

"I'm not going to hell."

He smiled then, the chilliest smile she'd ever seen. "You won't know the difference before long."

She closed her eyes again to shut out the image of him. She saw her life. It didn't flash before her eyes like she imagined when she heard the expression. She skimmed over it, dipping briefly into recent memories of Silas. She'd at least experienced passion in her life. Silas had loved her without expecting anything in return. Her real regret was not being able to accept that love on his terms. He was the only one who had given her something without obligation, besides her mother and God. She had to believe that by accepting God's love, she'd be at least saved in eternity if not in life.

"Do you remember when Harold asked if you'd rather be killed by someone you knew or a stranger?" he asked. "You never did answer."

"You were a stranger the whole time I knew you."

That seemed to amuse him. He turned to get the duffel bag he'd thrown to the floor. It was now beneath the corner of the bed frame. More metal clinked inside the bag. He threw out the other set of cuffs, a knife, and the pipe.

That's when she noticed the gun sticking out from his waistband. He reached around inside the bag. She swung forward and clawed at the handle. She was inches short of reaching it. Adding force to her swing, she grunted with exertion and grabbed for it again. The grunt made Ben start to turn around. He jerked back as her fingers locked around the handle. Her hands were sweaty, but she gripped it with everything she had in her.

"Damn you!" he said, lunging for it.

She cocked the handle, just like he'd taught her. Once

the initial shock passed, his expression wasn't afraid, but curious.

"What now?" he asked, his arms crossed in front of him.

She didn't know. "Just stay right there."

This time he wasn't going to taunt her about not being able to shoot him. And this time, she was more than willing to shoot him. But she had to look at her options first. If she demanded he get her down, he'd have to get close to her, close enough to grab the gun back. Or he could grab it when she tumbled to the floor.

"If you shoot me, you'll just die here anyway, with my rotting corpse to keep you company." His face almost looked boyish. "We could cut a deal, and you . . . you get to make another choice. I'll leave you the key to the cuffs right here." He took out the silver key and set it on the floor just out of her reach. "You live, I go free. I know you're too selfish to die for a cause."

She started to reach for the key, but he said, "Uh-uh," and kicked it farther away. "That's your choice. Let me walk out of here, and I give you your life."

"You asked if I was mad that you'd killed my mama." Her voice quivered when she said, "I am mad. This mad."

She pulled the trigger. The bullet exploded through his chest. He staggered backward, a shocked expression on his face. That moment of surprise he loved so much. Then he reached toward her. She shot him again. And again. *Justice for Mama, for Gus, for the Boss, and for Silas.* Justice was a cause worth dying for. Anger and rage fueled her finger. It wasn't pleasure she felt at killing him. Only pure, selfish hatred. His gaze never left hers until he fell against the wall and slid to the floor. His chin rested on his chest. He lifted one shaking hand and touched the blood on his torn chest. When he looked up at her, his hand dropped. His eyes went glassy.

She couldn't breathe. She watched him, watched his chest remain still as death. Even when she took her first halting breath, she didn't trust that he was dead. She waited until she was sure. Another jerky breath became a sob. She dropped the gun and covered her mouth.

She pushed the horror of having killed another human being into a box inside her. That's where she'd shoved the realization that Ben had killed her mother, that Sam Savino was her father by force of rape, of finding Silas nailed to that barn wall . . . it was all in there, about to explode. She couldn't explode yet.

She grabbed the gun that was still warm and aimed at the base of the ring on the ceiling. The shot hit the corner of the metal and ended up inside the attic. Dust and debris floated down over her. She squinted and aimed again. The gun clicked.

"No, no, no." She checked the chamber. It was empty.

A sound from Ben's direction sent her twisting around to face him. He'd slumped over. She dropped the gun and tried for the key. It was under the corner of the bed frame. She tried stretching, reaching, even sucking in air to bring it closer. The bed frame was also out of her reach. She tried using the gun, but was still five inches too short. She pulled herself up and held onto the rafters. The blood pressure eased. After a few moments, her eyes felt normal enough to search for a way out. It was dark and musty in the attic. Two bats flew erratically, probably frightened by the gunfire.

She tugged at the base of one of the rings. It was still hot from being shot at. She shook the ring with her foot and tugged on it with her hand. Ben had picked the thickest, sturdiest beam to attach the hooks to. Her ankles were bleeding from her frantic movements. After a while, her arms were beginning to shake. She tried different positions, different ways to hold on to the beam. Eventually, she had to let go and hang again.

It was over. Ben would no longer kill. Maybe she'd be hailed as a hero when or if they found her body. Big deal. She didn't want to be a hero. She wanted to live, to love . . . to love Silas.

She heard something drop to the floor. Her heart tripped

when she saw the crystal lying in the dust. She stretched and reached it. Her fingers wrapped around it and she pressed it to her mouth.

If you're out there, Silas... if you're tuning in... I want you inside me. I want you to read my feelings, to be there when I need you. I'll take your love anyway I can get it. I just want another chance.

Silas had Dr. Buchanan summoned to the band shell during the festival. It was clear that this was an emergency by Silas's desperation. The man and his sister approached hesitantly. Silas realized he looked a bit mad, with his disheveled hair and bloodstains on his shirt, not to mention the bandages on his head and hands.

"Is Ben Ferguson with you?" he asked.

Mrs. Turner shook her head, question in her eyes. "No. He wasn't feeling well this morning, but we just walked back to the house to check on him and he wasn't there either. What's wrong?"

"Did you see Ben's wife, Katie?"

"No, why should we?" she answered. "She left him, you know. After all these years—"

"Are there any abandoned buildings, barns, anything like that around here?" He seemed to like using old buildings to house his victims. *Don't let Katie be a victim.*

"What's this about?" Buchanan asked, putting his arm protectively around his sister's shoulders even though he looked the weaker of the two.

"I can't explain it now. A woman's life is in danger. Please tell me, are there any abandoned buildings around here?"

"Not that I know of," he said.

Silas was already weaving through the crowd to the truck. The pounding in his head was so severe, he nearly passed out on the bench seat. His hands were throbbing with pain. The bottle of painkillers was lying beside his head. He blinked away the haze and took the bottle in his awkward hands.

He has her.

The knowledge went bone deep. Silas struggled to sit up. He'd thought he could keep his empathy at bay now that it was gone. If he could keep it away by taking the painkillers, maybe it would go away forever. Even when Katie had stormed out of the hospital, he'd held onto the hope that he'd be normal. Maybe he wouldn't spook her anymore. That was before he'd known she was going to do something stupid like track down Ben. It was his fault; he'd accept that much responsibility. He tossed the painkillers on the floorboard. They rattled inside the bottle.

And so he closed his eyes and tried to summon it back. For the first time since he'd given up on Celine being alive, he prayed.

Hey, God. It's me. Silas. I know it's been a while, a long while. I don't expect you to give me all the answers, or even to tell me where Katie is, but that would sure help. All I'm asking is that you give it back to me. I know I haven't been real happy about having it. Maybe I'm not using it the way you wanted. But you gave it to me for a reason, and I have to believe that reason is Katie. I know I've been real ungrateful. I want to make it right. Please help me.

He started feeling it a few minutes later. It came slowly, as though out of a fog. Not fear, but hopelessness. She'd given up. He tried to focus harder. He was tired, so damned tired. Fatigue pulled him down. He reached deeper inside himself.

The brief flash confused him. He saw an old room, a gun and a bed frame . . . *on the ceiling*? It was upside down. No, *she* was upside down.

He pounded on the steering wheel before pulling back with a hiss of pain. He focused again, trying to see more of the room. How was he ever going to find her?

He got a brief feeling of apprehension. Odd given Katie's previous hopelessness. A knock on the window startled him.

Dr. Buchanan and his sister stood outside the truck. Silas rolled down the window.

"Took us a few minutes to track down where you'd gone to," he said. "There are a couple of places out toward Flatlands. Just out of Macon. A couple of farms went under years ago. They've been out there so long, I don't even think about them anymore. I used to take care of their livestock and I was sorry to see them go."

"Where?"

Buchanan gave him directions as best as he could remember. Silas thanked the man and tore out of the parking lot. He'd probably passed those roads when he'd come into Macon. Why couldn't he have felt her then?

Because he wasn't ready to reaccept his gift. But Katie wasn't giving him much to go on. *Hang in there, Katie. Please, do it for me.* He tried not to think about what she'd gone through and why she was upside down as he searched for the landmarks the doctor had given him.

He had two choices. When he came upon the first road, he stopped and took it in. The dirt road was rutted and obviously hadn't been used much in recent years. But it had been used recently. The weeds were flattened. He could feel his chest tighten as he stared at the faded street sign. He turned down the road and looked for the outer reaches of the old farm.

His chest got tighter when he spotted the old place set far from the road. Another road snaked through the waist-high weeds—someone had recently taken this road, too. He swerved onto an even more rutted road.

When he saw his Navigator, he slammed on the gas pedal. The truck barreled through the opening in the barbed-wire fence and across old cotton fields. His headache increased tenfold with the truck banging over the ruts, but he didn't slow down. Weeds whipped across the windshield. He pounded on the brakes and jumped out, only realizing then that he hadn't put the truck into park. It rolled forward and bumped into his Navigator.

As soon as he jumped onto the porch, he yelled, "Katie!"

The boards creaked and groaned beneath his weight, but he didn't stay on them long enough for them to give way. His gaze swept the living and kitchen area. God, he couldn't breathe. His whole body hurt at the prospect of finding her injured. Or dead.

"Katie!"

"Silas?"

He'd stepped into the back bedroom as she said his name. She was upside down, and her face was red from the blood going to her head. But she wasn't bloody. She was alive, alive enough to make a sobbing noise at the sight of him.

"Is that really you?" she asked in a raspy voice as he rushed toward her. "Or am I hallucinating?"

"It's me. Are you all right?"

He couldn't help running his hands over her, making sure she was in one piece, not believing that she was there and alive.

"I'm all right now. How did you find me?"

"Later. Let's get you down from there."

"The key's right there."

His gaze went past the little key to the man lying in a pool of blood. Ben. He tore his eyes away and lifted Katie to relieve the blood pressure. His fingers tried to fit the key into the lock. He fumbled once, cursed, and then got it right. He was only dimly aware that his hands ached, that they'd started bleeding again through the bandage.

And then she was in his arms, and he didn't care if his hands fell off. She wrapped her arms around him and started bawling. He carried her out of that god-awful room and down the precarious steps. His legs couldn't hold him any farther. He sank to the ground with her in his arms.

"Are you sure you're all right?" he asked, touching her because he still couldn't believe it. Her ankles were bleeding and bruised, but they were only superficial injuries. He touched the gold cross she was wearing. He'd never reject a gift from God again.

She nodded, holding on even tighter. "I'm dizzy."

"Give your blood time to redistribute. You'll be okay."

"I k-killed him."

"I know you did. I'm proud of you." He wasn't going to tell her how afraid he'd been that she wouldn't be able to do that when the time came. When she rubbed her nose, the other end of the handcuff flopped around. He unlocked that one and threw it.

"He killed my mama."

He didn't know what to say to that. He'd suspected, but it was so ugly, even he couldn't have faced that possibility head-on. He just held her and whispered her name against her head. He'd never let her go again. That was a possibility he *could* face head-on.

She finally cried herself out. He offered her his shirt to wipe her face on. "Silas, he said we all have evil inside us. It's true, you know."

"I know." He brushed her hair back from her damp face.

"But it's okay." She reached up to him.

He took her hand and pressed it against his mouth. "It's okay," he repeated.

Her eyes widened. "The crystal! It's still in there."

"I don't need the crystal to chase away the shadows. I've got you now."

"You had the crystal with you." He heard the question in her voice, saw it in her eyes.

"Yeah, I had it with me. But it doesn't matter, because I've always had you in here." He gestured to his heart.

"Silas . . ." She drew out his name.

"What?"

"No, the question is, what now? After we call the police and try to explain all this, what then?"

He knew what she was asking, what she needed to hear. "I was thinking about writing mystery novels. What do you think?"

She blinked. "I think . . . that's a good idea."

"Maybe with a veterinarian as the protagonist."

"Frank Martorana already writes a best-selling mystery series with a veterinarian sleuth."

"Okay, how about a veterinarian's assistant? You could help me do the research."

"Okay," she said, again drawing out the word.

"A sexy, but cute, assistant." He squeezed her tighter against him.

Her mouth quirked in a near-smile. "And does this sexy-but-cute assistant have a love interest?"

This wasn't easy, but she was going to push him to the wall anyway. He looked up at the blue sky, considering. "Definitely. Not just a love interest, but a husband who adores her. And she's always giving him gifts and stuff."

"I see." She nodded, considering. "And does he accept them?"

"He works on it."

"Hmm, I guess that's acceptable. But the big question is, does it have a happy ending?"

He couldn't wait a second longer. He kissed her, God, how he'd been wanting to do that for so long. When he came up for air, he said, "Yes, I believe it does."

⟶ EPILOGUE

ONE WEEK LATER ...

KATIE HAULED OUT the last of the boxes and loaded them into the Navigator. "That's the last of the usable items. We can drop these off at Goodwill on our way out of town."

Silas nodded toward the one lone box she was keeping. "Are you sure that's all you want?"

"There was never much of me in that house. I just hope I can get the legalities untangled so I can sell the place to Rebecca." Her childhood friend, now married with three children, still lived in Possum Holler. Katie wanted to give them a chance at a good, secure life. Silas had agreed to sell his land to the town if they promised to fix up Possum Holler and give it some respectability.

Once in a while she could still smell the smoke from the charred areas just a few miles north. That horrible day she'd spent with Ben at the farm near Macon had been a blessed day for Flatlands—the rains had come at last to drench the fires.

Goldie jumped into the back seat and settled onto the sheepskin bed. The Cartwrights had dropped by with their payment for Goldie's care. When they'd seen how happy Goldie was with Katie, they'd offered the dog to her. The fact that Goldie was pregnant may have played into their generosity, but Katie accepted anyway. She'd already decided one of the pups would be called Bruce, in honor of The Boss.

The crime-scene tape had just that morning been lifted by Sheriff Tate. He and Gary were giving the house and grounds a once-over for anything they might have missed.

"That seems to be everything," Tate said as he and Gary approached the Navigator. "He covered his tracks well."

"Except for the grave Katie found," Gary added.

Tate gave her a sheepish grin. "I'm sorry I didn't believe you. You gotta understand, Ben—or whoever he was—had us boondoggled but good. When Gary told us what he'd been doing . . . well, we all felt pretty bad about it."

Katie could only nod. That particular wound was still a bit raw.

Tate nodded toward the packed vehicle. "We wouldn't mind if you stayed around. This is your hometown, after all."

She closed the rear door. "I appreciate that, but I'd just as soon leave it all behind me. I'm sure you understand."

Tate nodded. "Thanks for your cooperation, both of you. The copies of your notes, Silas, will help us put everything together. Help some of these girls' families go on as best they can." He smoothed his collar. "Well, I guess I'll let you get on your way, then. Gary, see you back at the station."

When Tate was gone, Gary walked closer. He shook hands with Silas first. "Drive carefully, hear? You take good care of my sister." Katie loved the way he said that word, with affection and warmth. Both shone in his eyes when he turned his gaze to her. "I talked to my former captain on the Atlanta police force. He's seeing what he can do about getting me back again."

"After you finish the anger-management course?" she reminded.

"Absolutely. Hell, there isn't much to be angry about anymore." He chucked her gently on the chin. "I've got a lot to be happy about, though. A sister . . ." He turned to Silas. "And a brother-in-law to boot."

Silas hadn't gotten used to Gary being her brother yet, but she admired him for giving Gary a genuine smile.

"You be good," Gary said, giving her a hug. "And good